DESTINED TO BE LOVERS

As Dirk held Lamorna close, the feel of her against him, the scent of the sweet moorland in her hair, caused his pulses to throb madly. A searing hunger blazed in him as his lips took possession of hers. He had imagined kissing her for so long, and now his body cried out with joy, wonder, and triumph.

She drew back, touching his face, exploring the planes and hollows, threading her fingers through his dark mane while he trembled. He kissed her eyelids, her temples, the fluttering at the base of her throat, murmuring her name, before he covered her mouth with his once again.

But soon he regained some measure of sanity. This was no place or time for lovemaking; she could not stay—her presence endangered them all should anyone come looking for her.

"You must go, my love," he said hoarsely.

"I don't want to leave you," she whispered.

He kissed her again, his heart turning over. "I love you, Lamorna." He had never thought to say it and his voice quivered.

"And I love you, Dirk Killigrew," she said. "And I feel no shame for it."

"We will meet again soon, my dearest one. Until then I'll dream of this."

He kissed her once more, swiftly, and then they moved together to the stone tunnel.

IF ROMANCE BE THE FRUIT OF LIFE—
READ ON—
BREATH-QUICKENING HISTORICALS FROM PINNACLE

WILDCAT (722, $4.99)
by Rochelle Wayne
No man alive could break Diana Preston's fiery spirit... until seductive Vince Gannon galloped onto Diana's sprawling family ranch. Vince, a man with dark secrets, would sweep her into his world of danger and desire. And Diana couldn't deny the powerful yearnings that branded her as his own, for all time!

THE HIGHWAY MAN (765, $4.50)
by Nadine Crenshaw
When a trumped-up murder charge forced beautiful Jane Fitzpatrick to flee her home, she was found and sheltered by the highwayman—a man as dark and dangerous as the secrets that haunted him. As their hiding place became a place of shared dreams—and soaring desires—Jane knew she'd found the love she'd been yearning for!

SILKEN SPURS (756, $4.99)
by Jane Archer
Beautiful Harmony Harper, leader of a notorious outlaw gang, rode the desert plains of New Mexico in search of justice and vengeance. Now she has captured powerful and privileged Thor Clarke-Jargon, who is everything Harmony has ever hated—and all she will ever want. And after Harmony has taken the handsome adventurer hostage, she herself has become a captive—of her own desires!

WYOMING ECSTASY (740, $4.50)
by Gina Robins
Feisty criminal investigator, July MacKenzie, solicits the partnership of the legendary half-breed gunslinger-detective Nacona Blue. After being turned down, July—never one to accept the meaning of the word no—finds a way to convince Nacona to be her partner... first in business—then in passion. Across the wilds of Wyoming, and always one step ahead of trouble, July surrenders to passion's searing demands!

Available wherever paperbacks are sold, or order direct from the Publisher. Send cover price plus 50¢ per copy for mailing and handling to Penguin USA, P.O. Box 999, c/o Dept. 17109, Bergenfield, NJ 07621. Residents of New York and Tennessee must include sales tax. DO NOT SEND CASH.

ECHOES OF THE HEART

MICHELE YOUNT THOMAS

P

**PINNACLE BOOKS
KENSINGTON PUBLISHING CORP.**

PINNACLE BOOKS are published by

Kensington Publishing Corp.
850 Third Avenue
New York, NY 10022

Copyright © 1996 by Michele Yount Thomas

All rights reserved. No part of this book may be reproduced in any form or by any means without the prior written consent of the Publisher, excepting brief quotes used in reviews.

If you purchased this book without a cover, you should be aware that this book is stolen property. It was reported as "unsold and destroyed" to the Publisher and neither the Author nor the Publisher has received any payment for this "stripped book."

Pinnacle and the P logo Reg. U.S. Pat. & TM Off.

First Pinnacle Books Printing: March, 1996

Printed in the United States of America
10 9 8 7 6 5 4 3 2 1

for Caroline

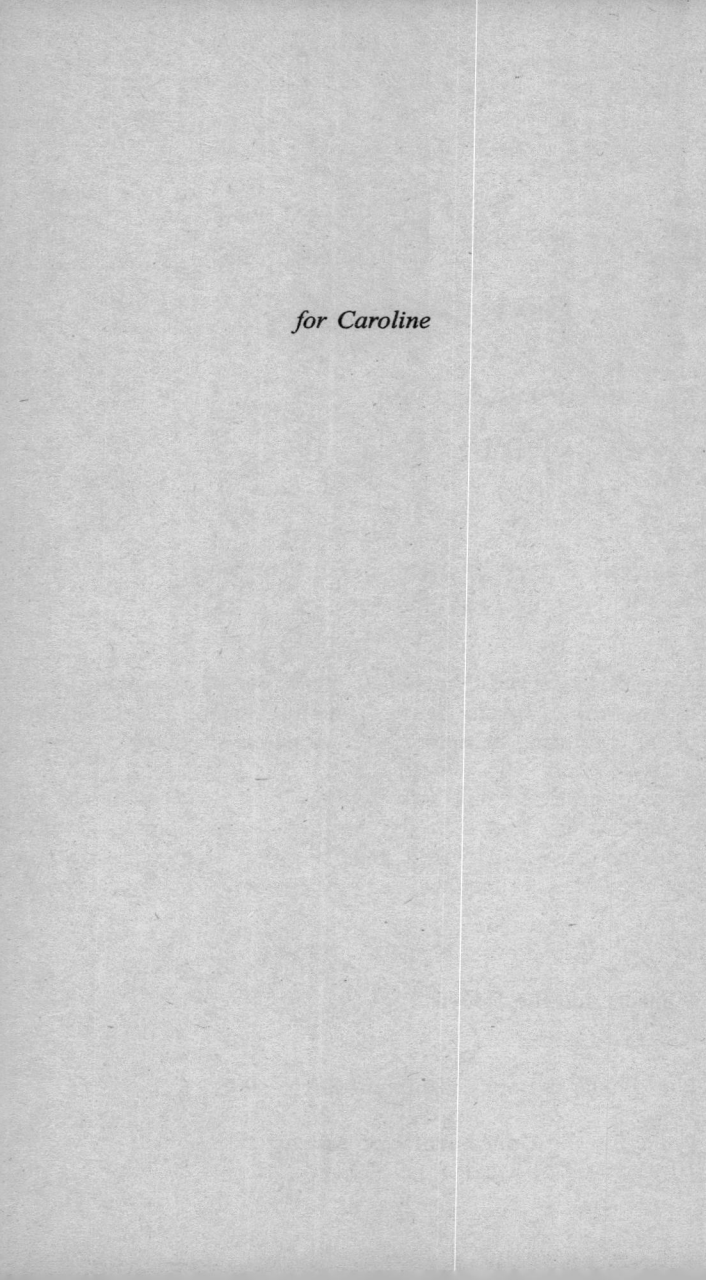

Part One

1902

One

Outside the gracious New York townhouse, it was snowing. In the dim, blurred light of the gas streetlamps, Fifth Avenue was grooved and pocked from the passing horses and carriages, their sounds muffled. Across the avenue, snow fell thickly in Central Park, padding the stark bushes into roundish bulks, cushioning the graceful branches of the evergreens and secreting the carefully laid paths.

Tonight, as on other nights, the park reminded Laurel of Brambles, her family's estate on the Hudson River fifty miles north. The snow would be shrouding the whimsical Dutch gables and massing about the grounds in a dense silence that was comforting.

If only her mother had agreed to her tentative request that she go up there to stay. But Mrs. Willard had been appalled at the mere suggestion. Leave New York for the country in February? Laurel did have odd notions, she remarked balefully, at times distressingly so. Just imagine if she had full rein to give in to them, her mother had added, assuming it was up to her to see that her daughter did not. At this, of all times, her younger sister Flora's engagement ball—so far the most significant event of the season in the Willards' social calendar. What on earth could Laurel be thinking of? Didn't she realize what people would say?

Yes, Laurel *did* realize. And they would say it whether Laurel was in New York City at her proper place by Flora's side or whether she was skulking, as her mother would say, up at Brambles. As the speculating would go on regardless, Laurel would have much preferred being far removed from the glittering ball, enjoying the undemanding stillness and solace of the country.

They—the ubiquitous "They"—the all-powerful New York Society—would say that yet another of Laurel's younger sisters was either married or spoken for, while she was not. Wasn't it a pity, they would say, that the wealthy, illustrious Willards could not seem to find a husband for their daughter who was now twenty-two years old—or was it twenty-three?

Maude, the eldest, had been married five years before and was now the mother of three children. Celeste, two years younger than Laurel, and her new husband, Lionel, had returned just before Christmas from their wedding trip to Italy and Switzerland. And now eighteen-year-old Flora was engaged to Harry Granville, that delightful scamp. All very predictable and as it should be. True, Laurel's one brother, Tyler, had not yet set his sights on a particular young lady, but that, too, was as it should be; he was only twenty-five. It was different with young men.

Turning away from the window with a heavy heart, Laurel looked dejectedly at the gown laid out on the bed. Pink taffeta, naturally. They were always pink or pale blue or lavender or white. Her mother did not acknowledge the existence of any other wardrobe colors. And why should she? Those colors had always served her well and were just as becoming to Laurel's sisters. The Willards were a tall, willowy, fair-haired family with pale, delicate skin and blue eyes. Handsomeness tempered with restraint. Even the blue of their eyes was soft and misty. No one had ever thought to call it *chilly*. And it would have been sacrilege to refer to their complexions as *washed out*.

No, it was Laurel who fared poorly by comparison. Short, barely more than five feet tall, her hair dark, her skin tending toward the sallow. Her eyes, large with thick, dark lashes, were an unusual shade of violet-blue that those paying homage to Mrs. Willard and her three blond daughters generally overlooked.

And, unhappily, the difference was not only skin-deep. Everyone agreed that Linette Willard was one of New York's most elegant and brilliant hostesses, and stately Maude was following her lead with the young married set. Celeste had grace and charm, and Flora, with her infectious frivolity, was a darling. But Laurel Willard was, quite frankly, a disappointment, an aberration in this family of tall, blond charmers. Nature had played a poor trick on Linette and Charles Willard, placing Laurel between the two eldest, Maude and Tyler, and the two youngest, Celeste and Flora. The girl—scarcely a girl any longer—was tongue-tied and ill at ease with none of the natural Willard assets. The fault certainly didn't lie with the head of the household; Charles Willard was a capital fellow with an easy manner and booming laugh. It was almost as though . . . but no one dared even to entertain such a shocking notion because Linette Willard was so highly placed and well thought of. To give credence to foolish ruminations was to threaten the whole fabric of New York Society, and those that upheld it would have gladly cut off their right arms rather than make one tiny tear in that fabric.

Laurel was obviously a throwback to some past generation of Willards or Tylers, Linette's family name, or their kin, and it did not do to probe too closely into one's antecedents of the previous two centuries. Not every family solidly entrenched in New York Society had aristocratic Dutch or English forbears. If the truth were known, many ancestors were of quite humble origins, though most attempted to disguise that fact.

Laurel reached for the dress just as the maid came into the room. "Mrs. Willard said I'm to help you now, Miss Laurel. There's not much time."

"Is Flora ready?" asked Laurel resignedly.

"Yes, and lovely, too, all in white with gardenias and pearls.

And Miss Maude is downstairs with Mr. Jack. Oh, the hall is a sight with ivy coiling up the columns and white roses and the lamps in the ballroom smelling so sweet with the oil—"

"Yes, Mandy, I'm certain it all looks splendid, but you had better help me with my gown and hair before Mother becomes impatient." She turned her back on the maid.

What is the matter with the silly fool, thought Mandy, jutting out her lower lip as she lowered the gown over Laurel's head and deftly did up the back buttons. Sulking up here when such a grand occasion was about to begin. Why, if I had a gown like this and lived in this house with little to do but go to parties—no ironing, mending, polishing, dusting . . . Ungrateful wretch, Miss Laurel was. Didn't know her good fortune.

Laurel's eyes met hers in the mirror, serious, contemplative. She knew precisely what Mandy was thinking. If she could take my place I'd step aside gladly, Laurel mused. Perhaps Mandy, with her cheerfulness and bright auburn hair, would fit in better than I do. Yet she was not so naive that she believed she wanted to take Mandy's place. The maid was as much a part of the New York social world as Laurel was, but on the other side—the invisible side. The side that was far more populated and made occasions such as Flora's ball tonight so successful. Mrs. Willard could not have hosted a ball for over one hundred people had she not twenty-three servants to carry out her instructions.

If only Mother had agreed to the rose taffeta rather than the pink, Laurel thought as she pinched her cheeks to make them rosier. The deeper shade would have brought out the warm color in her face. As the ivory would have. But, as Flora was to wear pure white, ivory for Laurel would have been out of the question.

"I'll wear my garnets from Grandmother," said Laurel.

"But your mother told me the pearls," countered Mandy, frowning.

"The garnets."

Mandy opened her mouth to protest, then shrugged. If Miss Laurel insisted on going against her mother's wishes and wearing the garnet necklace, rather common jewels—even the housekeeper had a large garnet brooch—she, Mandy, could not be blamed. As she clasped the necklace about Laurel's small neck she had to admit that they looked good. The wine-red color brought a pretty flush to her throat.

Laurel fastened on the matching earrings and stood still while Mandy brushed her hair and wound it into a fashionable knot. On impulse, Laurel reached out and took a red rose from the vase on the dressing table. She clipped it short with her gold scissors and handed it to Mandy.

"Please pin this in my hair," she said.

Mandy looked doubtfully at the red rose, just beginning to open. "What about the white roses your mother sent up?"

"I'd rather wear the red. It will go well with the garnets." Why shouldn't she have her way in this trivial thing?

Without another word, Mandy took the rose, pinning it alongside the topknot. "I think it needs another," she said, stepping back. When the second one had been secured, Laurel said, "Thank you, Mandy."

The two young women smiled at one another. "Enjoy yourself tonight, Miss Laurel." There was wistfulness in her tone but for once no veiled reproach.

There was a knock on the door; it was another of the Willard upstairs maids. "Mrs. Willard says Miss Laurel is to come down—the guests will be arriving very soon."

Laurel nodded wearily and moved down the corridor to the great marble staircase.

Linette Willard stood in the hall below, ready to greet her guests as they arrived. Not all hostesses conducted their balls this way but Mrs. Willard preferred it to randomly welcoming friends and acquaintances in the midst of the dancing and eating. Tonight, Linette was stunning in a blue velvet gown. She was as statuesque and slender as the day she was married, and proud of it, just as she was proud that the years had put only a very few fine lines about her eyes and mouth. She knew she looked her best in the pearly gaslight rather than the new harsh electric light one or two of her friends had installed in their homes. At her side was Harry Granville, the next young man she would welcome into her family. Beside Harry was Flora, her face alive with excitement and triumph. It was her night. She had chosen—and most importantly, been chosen by—one of New York's most dashing bachelors. Next to her was her father, the affable Charles Willard, patting the hand of his youngest and favorite daughter as she chattered and fluttered. Maude, the eldest and most serious of the four Willard daughters, stood by her rather rotund husband, Jack, who was speaking to Tyler Willard.

Laurel's hand moistly clasped the banister as she surveyed her family. Look at them, she thought. They all seem so *right*. Whereas I . . . I don't fit. Oh, if only . . .

"Oh Mamma! How delightful everything looks!" cried Celeste, who had just handed her sable wrap to a footman. "And just look what Lionel has given me!" At her throat was a necklace of diamond teardrops.

"Beautiful, my dearest," said Linette. She smiled at Lionel approvingly.

"There you are, Laurel," said Maude. "One more minute and you'd have upset Mother."

"Celeste just got here," said Laurel stiffly.

"Yes, but with Lionel. That is quite another matter."

Because I am an unmarried daughter living under my parents' roof, thought Laurel. Because my place is always at their side, forever and amen. Linette looked across at her dark-haired daughter. Gracious, the child was wearing garnets, of all things! How could she when I specifically said. . . . However, it was too late to do anything about it now.

"Laurel," said her mother, "please make an effort tonight. Not for my sake but for Flora's and your own." Her voice was coolly deliberate.

For the next half-hour, the Willards graciously greeted their guests, introducing Harry to each of them. He was already well-known to most everyone, of course, but it was understood that Mr. and Mrs. Willard were presenting him as their future son-in-law.

"You'll be losing your last little one," said Mrs. Stokes, an enormous old dowager in purple. "I well remember when both my girls flew the nest."

She's not the last, protested Laurel inwardly. *I'll* still be here. But she was not surprised when her mother did not remind the old lady of that fact.

"Celeste, did you hear?" said a young lady. "Marjorie has left Edward!"

"Left your brother?" Celeste's eyes widened.

"Yes, and Mother says she won't receive her any longer. She's disgraced us all. She'll have to leave New York, of course, because if Mother won't receive her, neither will anyone else. Last night she was seen at the opera with that Bohemian, Mrs. Lascoe. She told Mother she wants to *write books* and Mother answered that people in our family do not do such things and being Edward's wife was quite enough." The young lady moved on.

"Old Phillips has lost his money, I hear," said a young man to Tyler Willard. "Stupid fool, putting most of it into that odd invention. He's had to resign from all his clubs. Hello, Laurel. How are you this evening?"

"Well, thank you."

"How does it feel, Laurel, to have your chit of a sister getting ready to walk to the altar? You had better hurry!" said Mrs. Whitley.

Laurel smiled weakly, her face flushing. Tyler glanced down at her and said, "Never mind that old battle-ax, Laurel. You and I have plenty of time. I don't know when I'll be ready to think of marriage. By the way, you don't look bad tonight."

Laurel grinned, a dimple appearing in her cheek. "Thank you, Tyler. That's very gallant of you."

"No, I mean it. You look quite nice, pretty." She did. Her cheeks were rosy and those intense violet-blue eyes bright. Probably from Mrs. Whitley's well-chosen warning, he thought irritably. Old cow. "Come on—we've stood here long enough. Let's dance."

"Oh, I don't want to, Tyler. You dance with Sally Cochran or—"

"First I'm dancing with my shrimp of a sister. Come on, be a sport." He did not have to add, *You'll just make Mother angry if you slink off somewhere.*

Laurel allowed her brother to lead her into the ballroom with its long mirrors and ceiling of blue and white clouds. The orchestra was playing, as usual, a Strauss waltz. She knew that her mother always reminded Tyler to partner her sister several times in the course of the evening so she would be seen on the dance floor. But Tyler was easy-going and kind; he did not treat Laurel with the disapproval or impatience so characteristic of her mother and sisters. Her sisters' husbands, Jack and Lionel, would also be requested to dance with her. It was all so stupid and humiliating. If only she could escape—and not just for one evening. She hated all of it: the gossip, the rules, the customs, even the mild scandals which structured and titillated the New York social scene. She felt a sudden burst of empathy for Marjorie Graham, who had left her husband and was trying to pursue a life of her own. *She has more courage than I do,* thought Laurel. *And she knows exactly what she wants to do. I never liked Edward Graham; he has a wet mouth and mean, small eyes. I won't marry someone like that. I won't marry anyone. When I'm older, I'll retire from this life and live at Brambles. Mother will probably be relieved by then to see me go.*

Tyler's friend, Christopher, asked Laurel for the next dance. When it was over, he thanked her, escorted her to a chair, and went off in search of the sort of young lady to whom he could easily talk. Laurel Willard, well, one was polite to her because of Tyler but she was not his type. Flora Willard, now—but she was engaged to Harry Granville, the lucky dog.

"A handsome young man, Christopher Sinclair," announced the old lady beside Laurel.

Laurel nodded. I'm supposed to be making an effort, she told herself glumly. What does that mean? Flirt with a man, flatter him, say clever things? *I can't.* She clenched her hands, repressing a sudden image of herself sitting in the drawing room at Brambles reading a book in peace.

"Laurel, would you be so good as to get me a glass of punch? I don't see a maid," said Mrs. Fortescue.

Obediently, Laurel rose. A young lady whose time was not taken up with dancing often had to fetch and carry for the elderly women. Perhaps her mother would consider that *making an effort.* Perhaps not.

"Not a bad-looking girl, not at all," said Mrs. Fortescue to Mrs. Whitley. "But there's no spark there."

"The others got it all, I daresay. Look at Flora—she's gay tonight. And lovely."

"It will be a June wedding. Four months off. Just before the Newport season," said Mrs. Fortescue with satisfaction. "I understand that The Elms, owned by that coal baron from Philadelphia, will be finished in time for the season. In the grand French style, so I hear."

"Speaking of Newport, have you heard that Tessie Oelrich's husband will be living in San Francisco from now on? She, of course, will stay on the East Coast. Nothing official or anything—but what do you make of that?" The two ladies bent their heads together for a comfortable chat.

Jack, Maude's husband, stopped Laurel on her way to the dining room where the elaborate food and drinks were set out on the enormous mahogany table and sideboards.

"I think the next dance is ours, Laurel," he said shyly.

Laurel smiled. She liked Jack. He was quiet and at times seemed overwhelmed by her stern goddess of a sister. There was no question as to who ruled the roost.

"Thank you, Jack, but I've promised to get Mrs. Fortescue some punch. In a little while, all right?"

Now that the ball could be said to be in full swing, she wanted to get away. She doubted her mother would notice. And if she did, she would later regard her recalcitrant daughter with the baffled exasperation Laurel knew well. *If you could only think of someone other than yourself,* her mother would say.

Laurel caught sight of Flora dancing. She was chattering all the while, glancing up at her partner through her lashes. He was a tall, dark-haired man she did not recognize—not that she could be sure, though, when she couldn't get a clear look at his face. Flora wouldn't mind if I left now, thought Laurel. It's what she would expect.

"The last of the Willard girls, eh?" said someone close by in the crowd.

"Well, no, there's still the short, dark one."

"Oh, yes . . . Well, if nothing else, she'll look after her parents in their old age . . ."

Laurel bit her lip. She grasped a cup of punch and, her hand trembling, splashed it on herself, making deep pink splotches down the front of her gown. It was the last straw. She set down the cup, her eyes pricking, her face scarlet. She would leave right now. Even Mother could not insist she remain at the ball in a stained gown.

She hurried from the dining room out into the spacious hallway, not wanting to go back through the ballroom. Mrs. Fortescue would have to find another errand-girl.

Standing in the hall beneath the ivy-twined, Italian marble columns was her brother Tyler and Timothy Stanton. With them was another man. Laurel tried to walk nonchalantly past them, holding the skirt of the gown to conceal the stain.

But Tyler forestalled her. "There you are, Laurel. I was just telling Derek he'd met every one of us except you. Not that she looks like a Willard, does she? When she was a child, people would say we'd picked her up somewhere."

Laurel's face was hot. How could he? And in front of a stranger, too.

"How are you, Laurel?" said Timothy.

"Fine," said Laurel abruptly, her voice shaking a trifle. "If you'll excuse me, I must go—"

"Laurel, this is Derek Tregarth. From England. He's cousin to the Tregarths we know in Pittsburgh. You remember them. Derek, my sister, Miss Willard."

Laurel shot her brother an angry, mortified look. Didn't he see she wanted to get away? Didn't he see the splotches on her gown? No, he just wanted to introduce her to yet another man she'd feel uncomfortable with. Her mother had probably requested this as well.

Swallowing hard, she turned her disconcerted, over-bright gaze on the stranger and started to say, "Good evening."

But the words never came out. Laurel's heart began to pound. Not furiously, but slowly, dully. Her hands dropped the sides of her gown and clenched into fists, the nails digging into her palms.

"No . . ." The negation, the refusal, the denial filled her mind. There was nothing else.

"What on earth is the matter with you, Laurel?" said Tyler. "You're white as a sheet." He, who was never self-conscious, laughed self-consciously, suddenly aware of something odd in the atmosphere. Timothy stirred uneasily, shifting from one foot to the other.

Derek spoke first. "Good evening, Miss Willard." His voice was cool, controlled, but his gaze was as unwavering as her own and as full of dismay.

Dismay? thought Laurel. Recognition then. *Recognition?* Her head spun. She could say nothing.

"Are you feeling unwell, Laurel? I'll—I'll take you upstairs," said Tyler. He grasped her arm and could feel her trembling. Maybe she was coming down with something. First her face was red as though she were angry or feverish and now this. This *blighted* look. And she was ashen.

"Will you honor me with a dance, Miss Willard?" said the Englishman.

Tyler glanced at him in some irritation. Couldn't he see the girl was unwell? Dancing? She could scarcely stand. He started to say something but to his surprise, Laurel took a step forward and put her hand on the arm Derek proffered. Without a word the two walked out of the hall into the ballroom.

Tyler frowned. "I don't think she should be dancing. She looked . . . Oh, well, I suppose she's all right. But . . ." Confused, he asked, "What do you know about him, Tim?"

"He's from the main branch of the Tregarths, those that didn't come to America. He's been staying with his relations for a month or two, I believe. I met him when I was in Pittsburgh at New Year. Quite legitimate, certainly. Owns tin mines or something. Nice enough, but quiet, serious. The ladies liked him, I recall. I hope you don't mind my bringing him tonight."

"What? Oh, Lord, no! I could see Mother was favorably impressed with him, and Flora, of course, said he was 'devilishly handsome.' But I still think Laurel looked ill and, well, Tim, you know Laurel. You know how shy she is with everyone she's known all her life. But she went off with him as though . . ."

"As though what?"

As though in a trance. Tyler shook his head, smiling sheepishly. "Forget it. Let's get something to eat."

In the ballroom, Derek was waltzing with a dazed Laurel. Ordinarily she worried that she might make a misstep or wondered what on earth to say to her partner. But her mind was empty of those trivial thoughts. There was only a compulsion to look up into his dark eyes. And then it came again—the bewildering clutch of dismay.

When the dance ended, with neither of them having spoken, he let her go. Laurel was on edge, her nerve endings jangled, the strange numbness dissolving. Had she actually been staring at him all through the dance? Her mother would be horrified. A lady never did that. A lady only occasionally stole glances at her partner.

Laurel's pallor had gone and the trembling had passed. "Well, thank you. I—I hope you enjoy New York, Mr.—er . . ." What was his name again? How embarrassing! And her gown—the stains . . .

"Don't go." He took her arm again.

"Laurel! What on earth have you done to your gown? Mother will be furious!"

It was Flora, standing next to them with Harry. Flora was indignant. Laurel standing there with red, blotchy stains on her dress at *her* ball. Flora did not admit to herself that it was the sight of the handsome Englishman holding Laurel's arm which annoyed her.

Laurel's face went hot with embarrassment.

"I'm afraid I must take the blame for that, Miss Willard," said Derek easily. "I spilled some punch on your sister a little while ago. She wanted to go up and change but I asked that she honor me with a dance."

"How naughty of you, Mr. Tregarth. Poor Laurel. Not that you liked that gown, did you, Laurel?"

"Not the color, no." Tregarth, that was his name.

"Well, it's a different color now—or parts of it are. I'm relieved I wasn't in your way, Mr. Tregarth, although I did enjoy our waltz," she said archly, confidently waiting for him to ask her again.

"As I did, Miss Willard. However, I shouldn't like to take you from your fiancé. And your sister has agreed to partner me again."

Flora made a sound like an infuriated kitten after Derek and Laurel had begun their second waltz. "I don't like him, Harry," she said. "Who is he, anyway?"

Laurel was asking Derek, "What part of England do you come from, Mr. Tregarth?"

"Cornwall."

"Cornwall. Where is that? Two years ago we went to France

and Italy. We stopped for a week in London. Mother, Celeste, and Flora went shopping and I went to the British Museum."

He grinned. "And what sort of place is that for an American heiress?"

"Don't call me that. I'm not . . . like that." She spoke almost fiercely.

"Like what?"

"Like . . . the rest of them here. My sisters, all of them."

His eyes rested on her thoughtfully. "To answer your question, Cornwall is in the southwest of England. And until the middle of the last century, it was isolated from the rest of the country . . . purely Celtic, not Anglo-Saxon."

"You sound as though you regret the change."

He shrugged. "I regret many recent changes. But they are inevitable."

"Thank you for what you said to Flora about my gown . . . the stain, I mean."

"I would have said anything to keep you by my side," he said in so low a voice she wondered if she had heard him correctly.

When the dance finished he suggested another.

"Oh no, that—that isn't wise. People will begin to talk." She flushed. "Not, of course, that there's anything to talk about. I only meant . . . well, people are so foolish."

"I've never cared what people say. But if you've no wish to dance then by all means let's have some champagne." He took her elbow and threaded their way through the crowd.

"What does that Englishman see in Laurel Willard, of all people?" asked a disgruntled debutante.

Her friend raised one eyebrow. "Perhaps he's lost all his money and is after a rich American heiress to rebuild his crumbling castle."

"But *Laurel?*"

Others at the ball had noticed the tall, broad-shouldered stranger. "So that's what happened to my punch," said Mrs. Fortescue ironically. "Well, good for Laurel."

"Mother," said Maude to Mrs. Willard, "do you realize that for the last half-hour Timothy Stanton's English friend hasn't left Laurel's side? Several dances and now they've gone into the dining room together."

Her mother, eyes and ears focussed on a dozen details at once, took a moment to comprehend matters. "Laurel? Why, the last time I saw him he was dancing with Flora. Where is she, by the way? I want to make certain she speaks to—"

"He danced with Flora some time ago, Mother. Then Tyler introduced him to Laurel and he appears to be taken with her. I just thought you ought to know," said Maude, with a pucker in a brow.

Mrs. Willard clasped her daughter's long fingers. "Oh, Maude, you don't mean it! Taken with Laurel? Wouldn't it be wonderful? Not that we know much about him, though. I can write to Olivia Tregarth in Pittsburgh."

"It's a bit early for that, Mother."

"Yes, of course you're right, dear. It's just I'm so amazed."

"For goodness sake, Mother, she's not ill-favored. And she *is* a Willard. Has Father met him?"

"Oh, yes. He considered him quite well-spoken, as I did. Maude dearest, do you think . . . ?"

"Your eyes," Derek was saying to Laurel in the corner of the dining room where they had found seats. "They are . . . extraordinary. When your brother introduced us . . ." His black brows drew together, then he looked away. He was conscious of an inexplicable feeling of dread.

Laurel's color rose. Gentlemen were not supposed to make personal remarks on such short notice; certainly none had ever been made to her. But this was different. The initial shocked exchange of . . . of what? . . . in their gazes, the apprehension, the compulsion pulling them together. Yet they had said little.

"I almost didn't come tonight," said Derek. "How strange that seems now."

Strange and unimaginable, thought Laurel.

"Tell me about your home, about Cornwall," she said.

"The house is Elizabethan, built of granite. It's been in the family always, since the first Tregarth—Conan—made a fortune out of tin."

"Tin?"

He grinned, his face lightening. "Not romantic enough? I daresay you'd prefer diamond mines, or gold. For centuries, Cornwall supplied most of the world's copper and tin. That day, however, is ending—has been ending for the last few decades. New, larger deposits found in Malaya, Chile, and Australia have led to the closure of many Cornish mines. Thousands of miners have already emigrated. My father closed one of ours years ago. Mine is still open, still running, but it's a dying trade."

"Do you mind?"

He shrugged. "The world is vastly different from the way it was two hundred, even one hundred years ago. My ancestors added to their fortunes over the centuries, but the change had begun when my father was young. He invested wisely in engineering firms, among other things. That's why I was visiting in Pittsburgh. My grandfather's younger brother established an iron foundry there. I don't really need the mine."

This was true; his inheritance was secure. But the poor bastards who work for me need it, he thought. The day will come when I have to close the mine and let the men go. But not yet, not yet. Derek did not understand why he felt unduly responsible for his miners, why he had such an affinity with them. His father hadn't. It was the way of business, he had said. When he had closed Wheel Faith, hundreds had been thrown out of work. Most of them had been forced to leave Cornwall for South America or Australia where new, richer ore deposits had been discovered. For a Cornishman to be forced to emigrate was a terrible thing. The Celtic strain was strong; they were a conservative, insular people, profoundly ignorant of the world outside. It was the coming of the railway in 1859 that had opened up Cornwall to the rest of England.

And now they were losing their distinctive heritage, their proud isolation. Now the engine houses stood crumbling above the crashing sea, as obsolete as the ancient standing stones on the brooding moors.

Still, there was less money than there had been in Derek's father's day. And, with the mine running at a marginal profit, there would be less to leave as a legacy to *his* children. Diana Cardew obliquely reminded him of that from time to time.

Diana. He'd scarcely thought of her at all these last months. With an effort he tried to call her face to mind. But he could see nothing except Laurel's arresting violet-blue eyes, her warm, flushed face and slender throat. He wondered what she would look like with her dark hair falling over her shoulders . . .

"Do you miss it? Cornwall?" She had watched the changing expressions on his face with fascination.

His eyes narrowed. "Very much." He hadn't enjoyed this trip as much as he had anticipated; he had been ready to return home for weeks now. But something had held him off, prevented him from booking passage on an ocean liner. He had decided to accept Timothy Stanton's offhand invitation to visit him in New York and planned to leave shortly for England.

"They say the Cornish are not happy away from Cornwall," he said lightly. "Fish out of water."

"I understand what you mean, I think. I've always felt like a fish out of water here. It's different at Brambles."

"Brambles?"

"Our country house, in the Hudson Highlands. It's rather deep in the woods and overlooks the river. I love it. I read and take long walks . . . but Mother doesn't like to stay there for long. It's rather isolated, you see, and that's precisely what appeals to me and what she finds tedious. I would have been up there now if Mother hadn't insisted I be here for Flora's ball." And if I were at Brambles, I wouldn't have met you, she said to herself. The realization was appalling; she experienced an almost physical pain.

"I'm grateful to your mother, Laurel," he said softly and her heart began to thud again.

He was very good-looking. His hair was thick, black, and wavy; his face was chiselled, well-defined, with a square jaw. But it was his dark, brooding gaze which enthralled her.

"I'd like to see Brambles. And I'd like you to see Cornwall."

"I would like to, Derek." She used his Christian name as easily as he had used hers. It was not until much later when the ball had ended and the guests had taken their leave that Laurel questioned the startling intimacy of their limited conversation; there had been none of the customary hedging, the pretense, the coyness which characterized most meetings between unattached men and women.

She also had not noticed the interest and speculation she and Derek had aroused.

"Laurel!" cried Celeste, clutching her arm. "Whatever were you talking about all the time? You've quite stolen the attention away from Flora, you know. Her nose is a bit out of joint. She expected people to talk about *her* all night."

"What do you mean?"

"I mean, little innocent, that everyone is talking about you and that handsome Englishman. Surely you must have noticed the attention you were attracting."

"Why no . . . I—oh, I hope they won't say anything foolish. We were just talking. He—he misses his home. He told me about it." Laurel, dismayed, was desperately trying to make light of the whole evening.

"Oh, Laurel, I'm so happy for you!"

"Don't, Celeste, don't say that." She spoke urgently; she had gone pale and cold.

"Why not? He's plainly very taken with you." Her voice was frankly surprised but delighted.

"Because you mustn't . . ." She could not tell her sister that she felt confused—and afraid. "I'm very tired. I'm going up to bed."

Celeste was disappointed. Wasn't this the most exciting

thing to have happened in Laurel's life? And now she refused to talk about it; she wanted to go to bed. But she kissed her sister on the cheek and went into the smaller sitting room where the rest of the family was talking over the evening's events.

Flora did not want to talk about Laurel. She wanted to be told again how radiant she had looked, how gracefully she had danced, how splendid the ball had been. Maude shared her reluctance but for different reasons. What did they know about this man? And he had behaved badly, spending all his time with Laurel and causing talk to arise about them. That was not how gentlemen were supposed to behave.

"Well, after all this, his attentions had best be honorable," said Tyler, grinning.

"Oh, Tyler, hush. He may be a fortune hunter—or worse. He may have been making a fool of Laurel." Maude's tone was severe.

"You saw them, Maude. They were *absorbed* in one another. If he was making a fool of her, he was making one of himself as well."

"I've always wanted one of my girls to marry an Englishman," said Linette.

"That's the first I've heard of it, Mother. Isn't Harry good enough for you?" Flora asked peevishly.

"Don't be such a goose, Flora. You've had your triumph," said Tyler. "You may have to step aside and let Laurel have hers."

But as the days passed that looked far from likely. Laurel waited in vain on the day after the ball for a note or even a call from Derek. That afternoon she went for a walk in Central Park, desperately hoping she might meet him. Timothy Stanton's townhouse overlooked the park as well, and perhaps they were out for a stroll or ride. But the only people she saw were

Cornelia and Abigail Thurston-Brown. Cornelia asked her where her romantic Englishman was.

"He's not *my* Englishman," Laurel said indignantly and went home, her boots soaked and muddy from the melting snow. Her frustration was so great she felt she would burst.

Flora was still sulking. Early that evening she asked Laurel if she had heard from her new beau, knowing full well she had not. Linette Willard was nearly as frustrated as Laurel.

"He's not my beau, Flora." Laurel spoke dully, her chest constricted.

"I suppose he'll be going back to England soon," said Flora in a smug tone.

Laurel nodded. The sight of her stricken face pierced Flora's brittle envy. "Oh, Laurel, forgive me. I am a beast. I hope he calls very soon. I'm—I'm certain he will."

Laurel said nothing.

The following day she was in bed with a fever and no one spoke to her of the handsome Cornishman. Flora brought her a box of chocolates and sat beside her on the bed, chattering frantically, until Laurel told her she would like to sleep. Flora was as relieved to go as Laurel was to be alone.

Mrs. Willard had sent for the doctor who, noting Laurel's flushed face and rapid pulse, ordered several days in bed. Strangely there were no other symptoms: no chest congestion or sore throat or aches in her limbs. The fever had flared up suddenly and would doubtless leave her in the same way; there was no need for alarm.

Linette was not alarmed, not this time. Laurel had come down with these mysterious fevers before. The first time was when she was eight or nine. She had not only been in a high fever, but delirious as well, and her skin had been covered with angry-looking red blotches. The family was up at Brambles and the local doctor had not known what to make of her condition. He had ordered a fire built in her room though it was early May, well into spring. Laurel had been fretfully dozing, but when the fire was lit she sat up in bed and became hysterical, screaming that she didn't want a fire, that it was hot, burning, horrible!

Flora had begun to cry at seeing her sister; Maude and Celeste had stood in the doorway, appalled. Linette had ushered them all from the room and ordered the fire put out. Gradually Laurel's shrieks and sobs had become whimpers; later she fell asleep. She had slept for the remainder of that day, through the night until late the next morning. When she awoke the fever was gone and the red marks on her skin had disappeared. She seemed not to recall her terror of the fire or her outbursts. Linette did not wish to remind her.

A similar occurrence had happened several years later, though this time no fire was lit as it was August and the Willards were in Newport. A doctor said that the fever and red blemishes were not actual physical illness but a form of nerves. Mrs. Willard accepted this and the next time the symptoms appeared she was not worried.

Naturally, Laurel was reacting to Mr. Tregarth's evident loss of interest; it was unfortunate, very unfortunate, but these things happened. Linette had had high hopes but she was also a practical woman. It was doubtless all for the best. And it wasn't as though the man had a title; he might also be virtually penniless although Tyler believed that was not the case. Thank heaven she had put off writing to Olivia Tregarth.

At least Laurel had outgrown that childish fear of fire; there had been none of that wild-eyed maniacal behavior in years. Yet she had always been careful to stand back from the flames, had never reached out cold hands to be warmed . . . Linette felt a burst of unaccustomed tenderness for the daughter she barely understood. Perhaps when Laurel was recovered they could go up to Brambles as she had requested some days before. It might be just the thing before the frantic preparations of the wedding began. Flora might not want to leave New York and Harry, but it would only be for a week or so. I had better not say anything to Laurel though, she thought, since I might change my mind.

As it turned out, Mrs. Willard did change her mind once Laurel was on her feet again. She had decided that the best thing would be for Laurel to go out in society with her head held high. None of this running up to Brambles. That wouldn't do at all. She told Laurel briskly that they were to attend the Astors' ball that night.

"Please, Mother, please don't make me go. Everyone knows I've been ill. You can tell them I still am. I won't go anywhere—not even for a walk in the park." The violet-blue of her eyes was darkened, murky. There were shadows under them.

"Nonsense. You are quite well. People will say you are avoiding parties, that you have let that—that man throw you over, that you are hiding, that your heart is broken. You must show them it is not."

"Oh, Mother, won't you ever understand? I don't care about those people. I don't care what they say. I only want to be left alone. I want to go to Brambles. Tyler can take me."

Linette's mouth tightened. "You and Tyler are not going anywhere. I happen to care what people think of the members of this family. We never do anything to disgrace ourselves; neither do we wear our hearts on our sleeves. There will be many people at the ball. Why, you most likely won't even see that man. But you are going."

Laurel bit her lip, her face lowered so her mother would not see the tears welling up.

Linette closed the door behind her. Yes, the girl's heart was bruised but she would get over it. The fellow was worthless—a rake or a fortune hunter. Flora had told her he had shown interest in several other young ladies in the past week, yet not in the single-minded way he had with Laurel. He was obviously making it clear that he enjoyed the company of more than one debutante. Flora now considered him vulgar and not to be trusted. Maude agreed. Tyler, though, had said "I've nothing against him. He's good company. But I don't think he's right for Laurel, anyway. There was something strange about the way they both acted."

"What do you mean? He—he didn't take any liberties?" Linette had asked sharply.

"In our dining room with people on all sides?" Tyler was scornful. "Of course not. I can barely recall it now, just that for a moment or so I thought Laurel was going to faint. And he was so—possessive, I suppose. Oh, well, the whole thing's blown over now and I'm sick of discussing it."

When her mother left the room Laurel buried her head in the pillow. I don't want to go. I can't. I can't see him. If only he's not there. Dear God, please don't let him come.

Flora burst in with her usual vivacity. "What are you going to wear, Laurel? I'll help you decide."

Laurel mumbled something into the pillow.

Flora sighed. "I know how you feel, Laurel." That was not exactly true. She tried again. "At least, I know how *I'd* feel. But you must go to the ball. I promise I won't leave your side all night. Harry and I will stay with you."

Laurel smiled weakly. "That's very kind of you, Flora." She did not place much reliance on her flighty sister keeping her promise, but it was well meant.

"Remember, Laurel, there'll be hundreds of people there. You probably won't see him at all, even if he goes. And if you do see him, act as if he's not there. That's what I've been doing. In fact, I snubbed him good last night," Flora said proudly.

Laurel groaned.

"Oh, Flora, don't you see that makes it worse? He'll know it's because—because I'm hurt and you feel sorry for me . . . Oh, damn him!"

Flora giggled. "Laurel! I've never heard you say that! But that's the spirit. We Willards don't care two pins about Derek Tregarth. He's nobody. You know what Mother says: we must only show the world our brightest faces."

How easy that is for each of you, thought Laurel, when

everything always goes your way. But she merely said, "What should I wear?"

"Why don't you wear the ivory gown you wanted to wear to my ball?" suggested Flora eagerly. This was more her domain—clothes and appearances. She hadn't much experience with consoling people. "It suits you—and you can wear my emerald earrings and choker."

"Thank you, Flora," said Laurel, touched. "That's sweet of you. I—I promise I won't disgrace you tonight."

"Of course you won't. It will be as if we'd never met that man. I've an idea. I'll go get some of my rice powder. It will smooth out your complexion." And tone down the smudges under your eyes, thought Flora.

"All right, Flora. I'll try it."

Two and a half hours later Laurel came down the stairs with Flora. Linette studied her approvingly. The girl would do. Somehow Flora must have rallied her. She was looking quite her best in the ivory satin gown with leg-o'-mutton sleeves and a swath of lace at the bodice. Her dark hair gleamed and her face had lost its yellowish tinge and looked translucent.

"What will I do with all these beautiful ladies?" said Charles Willard teasingly.

"You will escort us, of course," said Linette smoothly. "Shall we go?"

The night air was bitterly cold and dry. The two girls shivered and huddled together in the carriage. Linette Willard always seemed impervious to hot or cold, neither extreme able to affect her composure.

"Harry is coming later with Tyler," said Flora. "So I'll sit with you for a while, Laurel."

"Now, Laurel, I forbid you to hide in a corner all night. Flora, you keep Laurel with you and your friends."

"I'm going to dance with each of my daughters tonight," said Charles. "The cardroom will just have to do without me."

Oh, Father, thought Laurel, not you, too. If only everyone

would leave her alone. She hated pity. And she did not want to hover on the outside of Flora's circle.

But she danced twice with her father, spoke politely to Flora's friends, danced a few more times, and finally sat down with Maude, greatly relieved. This isn't bad at all, she thought. I haven't even seen him, whether he's here or not. The evening is almost half over, and I haven't been conscious of people taking any notice of me. Just another couple of hours and then we can go. But her brittle composure did not last.

Laurel glanced about the room and froze. There was Tyler, with Timothy Stanton and Derek. Her hands began to tremble; she clasped them tightly in her lap. Her face flushed. "I—I think I'll go and—" She was rising from her seat.

Maude touched her arm. "Just stay right here, Laurel. You may get up in a little while and I'll go with you. But not yet. Now let me tell you the clever thing that Johnny said this morning. He was having his oatmeal and . . ."

Laurel smiled and pretended to listen. Her face felt stiff, unnatural. All the while she was conscious of Derek dancing with Cornelia Thurston-Brown across the room. "I'll come over and see the children soon, shall I?" she said brightly.

"Jack wants to go to Florida soon, Laurel. Perhaps you'd like to come with us."

Laurel detested Florida—the heat, the insects, the overwhelming flatness. "Thank you, Maude. I'd like that."

Maude patted her hand. Laurel seemed to be holding up well. Maude remembered a time, years before, when she too had been fond of someone who had not returned her interest. But she put that thought hastily aside. It did not do to recall such things. One might begin to question the course one's life had taken.

"I've just spotted Letty Covell. I must speak to her about something. Do you want to come with me?"

Laurel shook her head. "No, I'm fine. I'll sit here. You go on."

Now Derek was dancing with Abigail Thurston-Brown. She

could see his dark head above many of the others. He was smiling that odd smile of his, only one corner of his mouth turning up. Laurel bit her lip. Yet she did not look away. She regarded him somberly, without hurt, without embarrassment, a profound, knowing look. He turned his head slightly and their eyes met.

My God, thought Derek. His sharp intake of breath was audible. The dance was over. He left Abigail Thurston-Brown on the dance floor without a word and began to move through the crowd toward Laurel. Abigail watched him go, her mouth agape.

No! Something snapped in Laurel's head. *No, not again. I must leave.* Rising, she made her way along the perimeter of the room as quickly as she could. In the hallway she asked the maid for her wrap and stood frantically waiting. In the next room she saw Derek glancing about keenly and forgot all about her wrap. Rushing across the hall to the door, she startled the two footmen. "Open the door, please. I'm leaving."

She dashed out the door, down the front steps, and along the sidewalk, not conscious of the cold. Her heart was pounding, heat and adrenaline coursing through her veins. The streetlights shone on icy patches here and there but she took no precautions, hell-bent on the ages-old flight for self-preservation.

"Laurel!" she heard his voice calling her. "Laurel!" Footsteps behind her, running. She had to get away, away. Suddenly she was gripped from behind and wrenched to face him.

"Are you mad? Do you know how cold it is?"

"Let me go. I'll be home soon enough."

"You'll be frozen soon enough," he said roughly, wrapping the cloak about her. "I assume this is yours. The maid came out with it—that's how I knew you'd left the ball."

"Thank you." Now that he had caught and stopped her she felt the biting cold. "It's only a few more blocks. I'll be quite all right now. Good night, Mr. Tregarth."

"I'll see you home." He seemed to say it against his will and this did not escape her.

"I don't want you to see me home. Just leave me alone." She whirled away, hastening down the street.

Now the tears were spilling down her cheeks; the dread, the anger was gone, leaving only despair. If only he hadn't followed her, touched her . . . I'll go up to Brambles tomorrow, she thought. I won't ask Mother; I'll just go. I'll send them a telegram when I arrive. I won't come back. It will be bliss to be away from him.

Again rough arms reached out and gripped her, spinning her around. Struggling, she slipped on the ice, losing her balance. He caught her, his arms going round her, crushing her to him, his warm breath on her icy tears.

"Laurel, it's no use. You can't leave me. I tried . . . I tried not to see you. But you belong to me. We belong together. I know it now."

Curiously she felt no wonder at his abrupt admission. "But . . . I don't understand. I thought that first night there was something between us," she said slowly. "But then afterwards you—"

"I know, I know," he answered impatiently. "I don't understand it myself, any of it. I barely know you. And yet—I know I want you."

She caught her breath. His mouth came down, uncertainly at first, then forcefully, bruising her lips. At the initial touch her body gave a violent shudder. She went limp, clinging to him. A tiny sound escaped her, whether of protest or acquiescence she did not know.

He held her in the dimly-lit street, his face against her soft hair. He did not tell her that after their first meeting he'd been both afraid and angry. That he'd wanted to hurt her, even punish her. And now this . . .

It was all madness, this fierce compulsion. But one he could no longer fight.

Two

The fashionable New York world was astonished by the announcement of Laurel Willard's engagement to Derek Tregarth of Cornwall, England. Some, like old Mrs. Fortescue, were touched, and wished them well. Others peevishly wondered how it was possible that a little mouse like Laurel had snared such a catch as the handsome Englishman. There were plenty of other willing heiresses; why he should choose Laurel was anybody's guess. In the comfort and intimacy of their sitting-rooms, they asked one another whether the couple would actually get to the altar. Men had been known to turn skittish when nearing the paddock. Derek Tregarth would not be concerned with public opinion. Look at the way he had pursued Laurel in that bold way at her sister's engagement ball, only to have his interest wane immediately thereafter. And now this sudden announcement! Ladies, young and old, wondered what to make of it.

When it became plain that the engagement was not adhering to the prescribed routine, there was more speculation. Engaged couples yielded to society's dictates: the announcement in the newspapers reinforced by congratulatory parties, the families on both sides visiting back and forth, months of leisurely planning, the couple appearing together in public, scrutinized, benevolently or not.

Yet even in this, Laurel Willard had to be different. Linette and Charles informed their friends that the wedding was to be in a few weeks' time, months before Flora's. No, there would not be a double wedding. Laurel's was to be a small affair. Very small.

This was not Linette's wish. To marry off two daughters so well was quite a feat. Why shouldn't she be allowed to relish it to the fullest? She longed to give Laurel the lavish wedding she was organizing for Flora. For once in her life, Laurel was the envy of many of her acquaintances. Why, then, this hole-in-a-corner affair? It didn't look right. Surely Laurel knew that she owed herself—not to mention her mother—the opportunity to flaunt her good fortune.

But Derek was adamant. He had been away from his home and business long enough; there were matters he had to attend to. He refused to put off the wedding. When he had approached Charles Willard with his wish to marry Laurel, he had stated that the wedding would have to be held within the month. Charles did not try to dissuade him.

"Fellow needs to set his affairs in order," he told a stunned Linette. "Perfectly understandable. And you know Laurel is eager to see her new home. No reason for delay. You'll have plenty to do planning Flora's affair, you know. Afterwards we'll take a trip. Visit Laurel in England, eh, my dear?"

Linette was scarcely mollified. But there was nothing she could do; her protests were in vain. It was a new experience for her and one she did not like. She was used to having the upper hand, directing things and people as she pleased. And she was accustomed to her family putting aside their own desires in favor of hers. But Laurel had ever been an uncooperative daughter. Now she was moonstruck, thought Linette with irritation. Here she was, allowing Derek to dictate the terms of this unexpected event.

"Really, Laurel, if you give in to him even in the planning for the wedding, you are setting a poor precedent," warned her mother. "You want him to consider your wishes in the future, don't you? If you are not careful, you'll wind up being bullied."

The irony of this admonition was not lost on Laurel, but

all she said was, "Please, Mother, try to understand. I want to marry Derek as soon as possible. He's not forcing me to do anything I don't want to do. We both want the whole thing over and done with."

Linette gave up.

Laurel was firm on her choice of honeymoon destination as well. After the wedding they would take the train up to Brambles for a week before sailing to England. She wanted to share her special place with Derek. After an initial reluctance, he agreed.

The reactions of her brother and sisters to the engagement were mixed. Celeste and Tyler were delighted; Maude was wary, Flora vexed. The eldest and youngest of the Willard siblings felt varying degrees of mistrust for Derek. In fact, it was Maude's spoken concerns which caused Linette to discard her own doubts.

"Goodness, Maude, I'm surprised at you. He is perfectly eligible. Your father is well satisfied on that account. Do you think we would permit Laurel to marry someone who was not? It's an excellent match. Never in my wildest dreams did I think that Laurel would be so fortunate. He is impatient to marry her and take her back to England. It's really quite romantic. You ought to be pleased for Laurel's sake."

Laurel was happy, Maude had to admit. But she was dazed, besotted. When Derek was present, her eyes were openly adoring; when he was not with her, she was distracted, lost in a dreamstate. Maude thought of herself and Jack. He was a good husband—kind, loyal, dependable, generous. She had never adored him. Yet she would not have wished to be in Laurel's place. But not wanting to exasperate her mother further, Maude kept her last concern to herself. Derek's abrupt decisions, the swiftness of the arrangements, suggested to Maude that he was afraid he would change his mind.

"You have only to glance at them to see how much in love they are," declared Linette.

Laurel was in love, no doubt about that. But Maude wasn't

so sure about Derek. He was difficult to fathom. Yet what possible ulterior motive could he have? Charles was assured that he didn't need her money. It was extremely doubtful that he merely wished for an American wife. And if he did, there were others. So he must care for her. It must be love. But not the comfortable, placid love with which Maude was familiar.

Flora was happy for Laurel; she had told her so several times. But she longed to ask how Laurel could have agreed so readily to marry a man who had been cruel to her. He had avoided her most pointedly. Flora did not like it. Her Harry would never have behaved in such a fashion, even had her own sense of pride permitted it.

When Laurel had first told her she had gasped, "But Laurel, do you believe him to be truly sincere? Why, only last week we had decided he was a cad!"

Laurel's face stiffened. "You don't understand, Flora. It was all wrong, the way he acted. He knows that now. We were meant to be together."

Flora stared at her older sister. Laurel's steady, serious gaze nettled her. "Honestly, Laurel, you talk as if you've both been waiting for each other all your lives." She did not believe in love at first sight. How could one possibly fall in love with someone before one knew whether he was eligible or not?

"That's exactly what I do mean," said Laurel gravely.

"Do you actually believe—?" Flora bit her lip. She had been going to say, *that you are the only woman he's ever loved?* Derek was ten years older than Laurel. He must have known lots of women. Yet, seeing her sister's radiant face, she could not finish.

To do her justice, Flora was only a little put out that Derek and Laurel were the focus of so much attention. "You'd think she was the debutante and not I," she grumbled to her mother, only to have Linette turn on her sharply.

"The gossips have enough to talk about without thinking you jealous of Laurel, Flora!"

Flora went red. She was not used to her mother snapping at her. And jealous . . . of Laurel? She was speechless.

Linette softened instantly, adding, "When the time is near for your own wedding, Laurel will be long gone. And I am determined to give you the wedding of the season." Derek's insistence on a small family affair still rankled. And all in their own home, too—no procession of carriages from the church. There was something furtive about it. However, the Pittsburgh Tregarths were coming. That was something.

Laurel and Derek had little time to be alone. In the afternoons they walked through Central Park, often in the company of one of Laurel's sisters. In the evenings they attended the theatre or opera or parties together with society avidly looking on.

Despite what she had told her mother, Laurel had been as startled as anyone by Derek's impatience to be wed. She had assumed that, as her engagement had followed Flora's, so would her wedding. Yet it was reasonable of Derek to wish to return to Cornwall; he did not want to remain in New York for months.

"Would you rather I went back to Cornwall now and returned for a summer wedding?" he had asked her.

She had gone pale at his words, her stomach lurching uncomfortably. She could not bear the idea of him leaving. Why, what if he did not—but she refused to finish the thought.

"Of course not," she had said faintly.

His arm encircled her shoulders. "Can I be blamed for wishing to have my wife all to myself?" His voice was low, caressing. "And for longing to show her her new home?"

She shook her head, leaning against him, taking strength.

"There is so much I want to show you, Laurel. You will love Cornwall, I hope."

"I know I will, Derek."

Sometimes he spoke to her of Cornwall, of its history. He was knowledgeable and she listened to him with interest. She learned it had been settled thousands of years before by people from the Mediterranean and the Aegean who mined for copper and tin to make bronze, who buried their dead in tombs of granite slabs and traded with Egypt and Crete. These people had worshipped the Great Mother, the fertile earth goddess, erecting stone circles and menhirs in her honor, practicing their weird rites with torches at night to the sound of the sea.

Later the Celts had conquered Cornwall, bringing a more advanced culture and trade with the Irish, Bretons, and Welsh. The Celts had worshipped the sun with fire festivals. Their priests, the Druids, used the stone monuments erected in the distant past by the former race. They sent tin across the channel to Brittany, over the Pyrenees, down the coast to the port of Marseilles. This ancient tin route of the Mediterranean brought prosperity and cultural exchange to Cornwall. But all that changed when Julius Caesar and his Roman legions conquered France and most of England, halting the trade between Brittany and Cornwall.

"For the next fifteen hundred years, Cornwall was completely isolated from the rest of European civilization," Derek told Laurel. "The Romans never conquered Cornwall—you won't see remains of paved roads or aqueducts. The Saxon invaders did not even reach Cornwall for three hundred years. They were stopped at a great battle by, it is said, the real Arthur in the year 500. Not a king, but a great Roman-British warrior."

Irish monks had sailed to Cornwall in the sixth and seventh centuries, converting the Celts. These monks shrewdly gave Christian interpretations to pagan superstitions rather than trying to abolish them. The Cornish could continue to do what they had always done, such as paying tribute to the wells which were now used for baptismal purposes. Sacred sites and crossroads were marked with wheel-headed crosses, reminiscent of prehistoric standing stones.

Eventually the Saxons, no longer barbarians but Christians as well, took over Cornwall, though they could not protect the people from the Viking raiders who burned villages, murdering or making slaves of the citizens. The Normans organized Cornwall into the feudal system, considering the country bleak and primitive. Gradually the smaller landowners became more powerful and, by the Tudor period, were involved in the tin trade which had been revived at the time of the Crusades.

"Conan Tregarth found huge resources of tin on his land and prospered, building Tregartha," said Derek. "For centuries the family owned two mines—Wheel Faith and Wheel Charity. My father shut down Wheel Faith some years ago, but Wheel Charity is still operating."

Conquered by the Saxons and then the Normans, but always left to itself, even as recently as the eighteenth century Cornwall was removed from the rest of England, its people pursuing their own way of life, their own customs. "It was a foreign country, really, with its unique culture, folklore, even language. Today there are reminders of the olden days, but they are swiftly vanishing."

Laurel loved to hear him talk of his home; she listened eagerly to all he told her. She began to be as anxious to leave for Cornwall as he. But not before they had spent a week at Brambles.

There was not enough time to send to Worth for Laurel's wedding gown. Linette had to content herself with a New York dressmaker. The girl seemed to care little what she wore. They finally decided on candlelight taffeta and lace. Nor was there time to provide an adequate trousseau. Relieved, Laurel assured her mother she would order new things when they stopped in London. From now on, she thought, she would select her own wardrobe.

Laurel and Derek were married on a wet, dreary day in early March. The air was raw and the rain came down hard. It was just as well they did not have to go to the church, thought Linette. She was not troubled by the thought that such weather boded ill for the marriage. Linette was not a superstitious woman.

But a few of her acquaintances took tea by their fires and

discussed the peculiar courtship and the hastily-made wedding plans, capped by this unlucky weather.

"It's what one would expect," said Cornelia Thurston-Brown to her sister. "The whole affair has been so odd and rushed. Vulgar, really." Abigail nodded. They were not invited to the wedding.

"Never mind, Laurel," said Flora, who did not doubt that the sun would shine brilliantly on her own wedding day in June. "It always rains in March."

Laurel did not mind. She scarcely noticed the weather. The previous night she had been unable to sleep, and in less than twenty-four hours she would be married to Derek. She had paid little attention when Linette had ordered new nightgowns trimmed with lace and tied with narrow satin ribbons. They had not seemed real somehow, or was it that the nights they were meant for seemed unreal? But now, very soon in fact, she and Derek would be alone as husband and wife. That her husband was a passionate man she had no doubt, although their hours together in the last weeks had been quite decorous. What would he expect of her? Would she disappoint him? And what of their life together—what sort of husband would he be? She realized with a sickening jolt that she knew very little about him.

Celeste had come to Laurel's room on the morning of the wedding. She had noticed Laurel's pallor, her reluctance to respond to Flora's prattle. Celeste drew her own conclusions.

When Flora left the room, Celeste spoke quietly. "Laurel, if there is anything you'd care to ask me—about, about being married and so forth . . . that is, about tonight . . ."

Laurel did not look at her. "Tonight?" she echoed and was dismayed to hear her voice jittery and shrill.

"Yes. When you get to Brambles. When you are both alone. I—I wasn't sure what would happen myself, not precisely." Celeste moved over to the window and pretended to look out. "There's nothing to be afraid of. It is—well, it can be quite pleasant. You get accustomed to it, at any rate. Derek loves you, as Lionel loves me, so . . ." Celeste frowned. Somehow she could not compare Derek with her own indulgent husband. But Derek must love Laurel. He certainly devoured her with his eyes, not caring who noticed it. Celeste admitted to herself that she found Derek's intense, brooding gaze unsettling. There seemed to be so much in it—what, one couldn't know. In their own circle, people's lives were practically an open book. But they knew so little about Derek Tregarth. His mother and father were dead; he had no brothers or sisters. But what kind of person was he? Celeste now appreciated the reasons behind marrying someone in your own set, someone you had known for years. There were fewer surprises that way.

Celeste's intuition told her that nothing she could say to Laurel would prepare her for a life with Derek Tregarth. He was not a man easily known or understood. He was not like Lionel—easy-going, tolerant of her wishes. As Harry would be with Flora. As Jack was with Maude. As their father was with their mother. These men gave way to their ladies in most things, without, of course, realizing they were doing so. Celeste was not used to feeling intimidated by any man. But that was precisely how she did feel with Derek Tregarth.

"Everything will be all right, you'll see, Laurel," she said somewhat lamely, coming away from the window and giving her sister a quick hug. "Just think, you'll be sailing for England next week! Lionel has promised we shall visit you within the year. I daresay your house is going to need some attention?"

Laurel smiled. "Derek's father had running water and other improvements installed some years ago. It's not a medieval castle, you know."

"Well, thank goodness for that," giggled Celeste, relieved that much of the tension had left Laurel's face. "Oh, just look at the time! I'll send for Mandy—you must begin to get ready, Laurel!"

After that Laurel had no time to be apprehensive. The ceremony was to be held at three o'clock with a champagne reception following. At a quarter past six, their train would pull out of Grand Central Station.

She took a long, hot bath while Mandy laid out her things. Her bags were already packed. As a wedding present Derek had given Laurel a single strand of graduated pearls. She would wear those today.

"When we get to Tregartha, you'll receive all the family jewels," he had said. He derived a particular satisfaction from the thought of giving her the rings, brooches, tiaras, and necklaces studded with precious jewels. It would please him enormously to see her wearing his family's finery. He had never wished to see another woman adorned in them. She was the one. That she seemed to be uncomfortable with elaborate jewelry did not concern him. Not then. He did not know that the engagement ring of diamonds and sapphires felt heavy on her finger, that she would have much preferred a simpler setting.

Linette came in while Mandy was seeing to the last of Laurel's toilette. The dressmaker had done very well; Laurel looked radiant. The candlelight color warmed her complexion. There were glossy lights in her pearl-studded dark hair. On her small feet were satin slippers, dipped in tea to match her gown.

"Oh, my dearest," said Linette, "you look lovely. What a happy day this is! You are very fortunate."

Laurel smiled faintly. She understood her mother very well. Laurel had finally achieved something of which the family could be proud. Her vagueries, her contrary nature which had so maddened her mother, were all forgiven in this hour of triumph. Yet Laurel felt no bitterness toward Linette. Laurel herself did not understand what lay at the root of her dislike of society, so how on earth could her mother understand?

"Is Flora ready?" she asked. Flora was to be her only attendant.

"I'll go and see." With a swish of her rose skirts she left the room.

"Thank you for everything, Mandy. You've made me look wonderful," said Laurel.

Mandy shook her head. "It ain't me, Miss Laurel. It's happiness. I—I hope he'll be good to you," she added, blushing.

"My whole life has completely changed," said Laurel. "And it's all because of Derek. Sometimes I've thought what would happen if I had never met him. It—it frightens me. I can't imagine life without him now."

"It will be different over there in England," said Mandy. "But you'll take to it, I'm sure." *As you've never taken to things here,* she added to herself.

Linette was in the doorway, Flora behind her in a more subdued shade of rose. "It's time, Laurel."

When Laurel began her descent of the marble staircase, the haze which had often overtaken her in these last weeks again blunted her senses. She barely noticed the guests in the drawing room, the lavish displays of hothouse flowers, the scent of gardenia, or the sounds of the harp and piano. Derek, standing somberly by her brother Tyler, was the only reality. She drifted to him as though walking in water, their gazes locked. He slipped the wedding ring on her slender finger and a deep vibration, like a tolling bell, throbbed within her. Derek did not kiss her.

And then there were toasts and champagne and plates of delicacies which neither she nor Derek tasted, and laughter and jokes from Tyler, and congratulatory wishes from the guests. Derek responded with easy charm, but Laurel was quiet and grave, detached from the lighthearted celebration. Flora had to remind her twice when it was time to go upstairs and change.

Celeste and Flora accompanied Laurel to her room. Linette was busy with the Pittsburgh Tregarths. Maude was busy with her three children; it was their first wedding—and their first wedding cake!

"I shouldn't care to go up to Brambles at this time of year," said Flora. "Only think how dreary it will be. It may rain the entire week."

"Oh, hush, Flora," said Celeste. "Laurel won't mind the weather. You will write to us, Laurel, won't you? From Cornwall, I mean?"

"Oh, yes, Laurel, you must," Flora added. "I'm simply agog to hear about your ancient manor house. Will you go to London often?"

"I shouldn't think so, Flora. Derek is tired of travelling; he wants to return to Cornwall and stay there."

"Well, you've always longed to stay buried in the country, though it wouldn't do at all for me. Still, there must be other people you'll meet, friends of Derek's. Has he spoken of any?" Flora added.

Laurel shook her head. "I'm sorry I'll miss your wedding, Flora. I know it will be splendid. You must write me all about it."

"Your wedding was perfect, Laurel," said Celeste. "Just right for you." I only hope *he* is right for you, she thought.

"I'm thankful it was small and relatively private. I'd have hated hordes of people looking on."

Flora smiled "You didn't notice anyone but Derek, it seemed to me. You barely said two words to anyone."

"Well, why not? He is, after all, the reason for the ceremony and reception," said Celeste, frowning at her younger sister. "It just proves how much in love they are."

Flora sniffed. If that was love, she wanted nothing to do with it. The way Laurel and Derek appeared to be so absorbed in one another was incomprehensible to her. There was something indelicate, even unseemly about it. Laurel worshipped him with her eyes. I'll never get that way over Harry, she thought with relief.

Laurel was looking at her reflection in the tall mirror. She wore a dark blue travelling costume with leg-o'-mutton sleeves, white ruffled blouse, and dark blue hat with a sheen of feathers. "Well, I suppose I'm ready," she said. She was conscious of a flutter of dismay at the pit of her stomach. Her lower lip trembled slightly.

Celeste linked her arm in Laurel's. This was not the time to express uncertainty or second thoughts; it was much too late for that. "We will all visit you before long, Laurel," she said bracingly. "And, of course, we'll see you next week, before you sail."

Laurel nodded. She had yearned for nothing more than to belong to Derek; she should not be getting cold feet now.

"Derek will be waiting impatiently," said Flora. "Not that there is anything wrong with that. Promise not to let him bully you, Laurel."

Celeste uttered a stifled exclamation. "The only unmarried girl in the family giving marital advice! For goodness sake, let's go downstairs before Mother comes up."

They went below. In the hall there were hugs and kisses. Linette's eyes were moist; Tyler put his hand on Derek's shoulder, saying he looked forward to riding and hunting on the moors. Derek took Laurel's arm and they went out into the March twilight. The rain had stopped, blown away by a piercing wind.

In the carriage Derek took her face in his hands. She quivered, the violet-blue of her eyes darkening. Her soft lips opened beneath his. When he finally lifted his head, his pulses throbbed violently and his breathing was quick and ragged.

He had known lust before, but this was not lust. His feelings went far beyond desire and the need for satiation. *She's mine,* he thought. *Mine to treasure.* A sense of awe came over him, and a deep gratification. He was also conscious of an unaccustomed tenderness, an urge to protect her. He had promised to cherish her, and he would.

Weeks later, these emotions would be as alien to him as the corroding anger would have been now.

A carriage was waiting for them at the small Gothic style station. Its driver was Michael Bond. He and his wife and son were the caretakers at Brambles. Linette had offered to send up one or two of the help, but Laurel had assured her mother there was no need. She did not want to be observed by curious maids who would report their every move to the staff of the New York townhouse.

Rebecca Bond had laid out a late supper in the dining room: corn chowder, slices of rare roast beef, potatoes in their jackets, and a green salad. For dessert there was an apple pie with sharp cheddar cheese. They drank red wine, and Laurel's cheeks grew rosy and warm with nervousness.

She began to babble. "You haven't seen the house yet. Tomorrow you'll be able to see the Hudson out those windows. My room overlooks it as well . . ." Her voice trailed off; she gazed down at the rings on her finger. Her heart began to thud.

He reached across and took her hand, caressing it with the ball of his thumb. "I love you, Laurel. From the first I—just knew. Let's go upstairs."

No one was about; the Bonds had tactfully withdrawn to their part of the house. Derek's hand was at the small of Laurel's back. On the landing was a huge window. In daylight it framed the back lawn, woods, and river. Nothing showed now but a velvety blackness.

When they reached Laurel's room, she glanced about her, disconcerted. It was a young girl's room with nosegays strewn across the wallpaper, demure organdy curtains at the windows. Derek's presence was incongruous, overwhelming.

A silver tray held a decanter of brandy, two glasses, and a bottle of champagne. "Would you like some champagne?" Derek asked.

"N-no, thank you." She had suddenly become chilled.

"Brandy, then?"

"I—" She had never tasted brandy. It was considered a man's drink.

"Come, it'll warm you. You've gone rather pale. I'll have one as well."

"All right." She turned away from him, unfastening the frog buttons of her jacket with shaking fingers. When she faced him, she saw he had done the same. Under his crisp white shirt his chest and shoulders looked very broad.

"Here." He handed her a glass.

She sniffed it cautiously. Her face was still and solemn, her eyes dark pools.

"Try it."

The liquid burned her mouth and throat. She sputtered inelegantly and set the glass down. "I don't want it." Her voice was tremulous.

He gazed at her steadily. "There is nothing to be frightened of, Laurel. We belong together. You know that, don't you?"

She moved her head slightly, still not looking at him. He set his own glass down and went across to where she stood rigidly. "Look at me, Laurel."

Slowly she lifted her eyes to meet his. He took her in his arms and held her tenderly against him. Her head rested on his chest; she could hear the beating of his heart.

His fingers moved to her hair; he began to pull out the pins. When it fell luxuriant and soft over her shoulders and down her back, he drew her face close to his. She was trembling violently. The violet-blue eyes closed, the thick sweep of her lashes was under his lips. With his mouth he began to explore the curve of her cheek, the creamy hollow at the base of her throat. Letting out her breath in a long sigh, she put her arms about him. She had a powerful feeling of being protected, cherished. Leaning against him, she reached up to kiss his jaw, his cheek. And then his mouth was hungrily possessing hers, and he was the one to shudder.

She was life itself to him, though he did not say it. He could not. Lifting her in his arms, he gave an inarticulate groan. His last coherent thought was that never before had it been like this . . .

The next day was bright though still cold. After a late breakfast they wandered about the grounds. Yellow and purple crocuses poked up from the damp ground; the masses of forsythia were sprouting tiny buds. Far below them the river flowed, blue and calm. Once Laurel thought she heard the crashing of waves. Puzzled, she peered through the bare trees down to the water.

"Laurel, what is it?"

She shook her head, smiling. The sounds were gone. "Derek, promise me something. Promise me we'll always be this happy." Her voice was low, urgent; the vivid color of her eyes had deepened to a dusky plum.

Derek put his hands on her shoulders. "We will be. Otherwise there would be no point to—all of this."

But she was frightened, her face pinched and white.

"You're cold," he said. "Let's go indoors." She said nothing, allowing him to lead her to the house. He asked Rebecca to make them some tea, and they drank it in the library where a fire burned and crackled.

Watching her, Derek longed to make love to her again. The need to protect her had diminished, overshadowed by his aching desire to possess, to know again that wild, clamoring ecstasy as their bodies joined. She belonged to him. For some peculiar reason he had difficulty believing it. He could not imagine what would have happened had he left for England directly after his visit in Pittsburgh. He could not bear to think that he might never have met her.

Going over to her chair, he drew her to her feet. She had lost that look of bewildered vulnerability. Lifting her face to his, she kissed him. His need for her grew fierce. It was all he could do to stop himself from taking her right there and then. They went upstairs and the bedroom door closed behind them.

Later, much later, the hunger would remain, the all-consuming craving to claim her slim body again and again, but the joyous abandon which he knew at Brambles would be gone.

* * *

A few afternoons that week they took a carriage ride upriver, Derek driving them himself. The Hudson Highlands were still starkly gray-brown except for the green upswept branches of the towering spruces. At times the river was a rich cobalt; at others a sluggish bayberry; once, leaden and tossing. Villas and castles crested the mountains. They drove by ash-yellow fields, red barns, and white farmhouses. Twice they stopped for luncheon at an inn, drinking hot buttered rum and eating braised lamb or capon with stuffing.

Laurel asked Derek questions about himself which he answered a bit self-consciously. He told her about his old nurse who still lived at Tregartha; she had looked after him until he went away to school. He did not remember his mother, who had died of pneumonia when he was two. At night Laurel lay beside her husband, her body and mind overflowing with contentment, with the *rightness* of it all. She had lost her initial shyness and now gave herself up freely to her husband's embrace.

Later, much later, she was to recall those nights of unrestrained rapture, of a singing happiness, and wonder whether she would ever know them again.

At the end of the week, Michael drove them to the station and they took the train back to New York. In two days they would sail for England. Laurel's family welcomed them, her sisters remarking on her new confidence and serenity. Derek was relaxed, with only a touch of his arrogance. Linette, well-pleased, told her husband that Laurel seemed to have found her niche at last—and it was little short of a miracle. At the pier, the Willards renewed their promises to visit the couple later that year, or early in the next. And then Laurel and Derek were alone in their stateroom.

Panelled in mahogany, it was quite luxurious. The furniture was upholstered in apricot damask. There was a large bathroom with marble tub and painted cherubs on the blue and white ceiling. Charles Willard had ordered flowers for the newlyweds; the stateroom smelled sweetly of the peach roses.

They went up on deck for a while, watching the harbor dwindle and recede until Laurel said, "I'm cold. Let's go and have some tea."

The ocean liner, catering to many English people as it did, furnished a proper tea in its parlors. There were watercress sandwiches, cucumber sandwiches, chicken sandwiches with chutney, currant scones with butter and jam, cakes, pastries, and chocolate candies, all served on gold-rimmed crockery printed with the ship's name.

After tea they left the cream-colored parlor and searched out the library, selecting a few books for the voyage. That night they drank champagne with their lobster dinner and then danced in the ballroom. Later, alone, they lay naked in each other's arms, watching the stars twinkle through the porthole.

And so the journey passed. The sea was relatively calm for March. Laurel had feared being seasick but she had only an occasional queasiness. Derek, she learned, had never been troubled on that account, not even in storms. "I've an iron stomach," he said with the lopsided grin she loved so well.

One incident served to mar the trip slightly. One night Derek had sat up in a chair reading and smoking a cigar. Eventually he dozed off, the cigar slipping from his fingers onto a table beside a pair of Laurel's gloves. The fabric smouldered and then caught fire, suffusing the stateroom with an acrid stench.

Laurel stirred in her sleep, uttering little mews and moans. Then she was awake and staring across the room at the burning gloves. Her chest began to heave; great, sobbing gasps rose from her throat.

Derek woke and very quickly put out the flames, opening the porthole to clear the air. When he looked over at Laurel, his stomach churned.

She was on her knees on the bed, her hands and arms shielding her face, batting at the air. Her agonized cries appalled him, the whites of her eyes caused him to shudder. Rushing over to the bed, he took her in his arms and tried to speak calmly through her terror.

"It's all right, darling. It was only a small fire, and it's out. You're perfectly safe. I'm sorry I was so careless—it was the cigar."

She seemed not to hear him, not even to see him. He tried to control her flailing arms, feeling a sickening wave of primeval fear. He forced her to look at him. "Laurel, stop it! Take a deep breath. Laurel, it's all right. The fire is out. You are safe. I'm sorry I frightened you. Hush, hush. There is nothing to fear." He went on in this vein for some time before she began to respond. Her cries ceased, her eyes lost their manic stare, and she stopped struggling, allowing herself to be soothed.

When he sensed it was all right to release her, Derek got up and poured her a glass of brandy. Then he remembered the other time he had given her brandy, on their wedding night, and again the overwhelming tenderness, the urge to protect her filled him. He would keep her with him always and never allow anything evil or frightening to touch her. He would keep her safe from all harm.

His brows drew together in confusion. Harm? Evil? What possible evil could threaten her? His head swam. He took a deep breath of the cold, salt-laced air and then shut the porthole. She sipped the brandy from the glass he held to her lips.

"Better?" he asked.

She nodded.

"Have a bit more."

She did, and the last of the strain left her face and slight frame. Derek covered her with the bedclothes and lay down beside her.

After a time he said softly, "I never knew you were so afraid of fire."

She did not reply at first. She had turned on her side, away from him. "I—I thought I was over it. Just a foolish childhood fear. It's been years since I . . ."

"Were you ever in a fire, as a child, or did you know someone . . . ?"

"No, never. I told you it was foolish. Let's not talk about it any longer. I'm sorry I alarmed you." He face was hot. She had made an exhibition of herself. A few wisps of smoke, some flickering and charring, and she had lost her senses. What must he think of her? Why had she reacted so violently?

Apprehension was creeping over Derek, displacing the tenderness. He reached over and put out the light. She fell asleep and he lay listening to her quiet, even breathing. Unable to shake off the vague sensation of dread, he slept uneasily.

They did not refer to the incident the next day. Laurel was determined to behave as if it had never happened, and Derek was relieved she was acting normally. He did not see the crimson marks on her arms and chest which she hid under a blouse. When it came time to dress for dinner, they had faded.

The ship docked on a dismal gray morning and they took a train to London. They stayed there a few days, sightseeing, and Laurel ordered a large trousseau to be shipped to her.

The third week in March they left for Cornwall.

Three

At Saltash they crossed the Tamar, the river which divided Devon and Cornwall. Again Derek experienced the almost spiritual thrill that he had always known when returning to his native land from school, and later, from business trips.

"You're entering an enchanted land now, Laurel," he said jokingly to cover his emotion. "To cross this bridge is to journey back in time."

Laurel was gazing out the window of the train, conscious of her own rising excitement. She had enjoyed the trip through the southwest of England. The fields were already green and lush, dappled with grazing sheep and cows. She glimpsed soaring church spires and thatched-roof cottages. It was lovely and peaceful.

There were few stretches of level ground during the first few miles in Cornwall. The train clattered on stone and timber viaducts which transversed the steep, golden-brown valleys. The landscape was very different from the cultivated green tranquility through which they had ridden earlier in the day. Now they crossed desolate high ground which dropped to wet bogs. Silver-gray clouds billowed across the sky, swallowing the sun, then separating, releasing it only to engulf it again. The resulting play of light and shadow on the moors was beautiful and eerie.

In the distance were great high tors, topped with granite boulders and pillars. Laurel saw a wild pony galloping, but when she pointed it out to Derek it had disappeared between the desolate hills into the stony valley below. A strong wind blew over the stunted bracken, flattening the yellow gorse and diffusing the trail of black smoke from the train.

A little later they passed a number of squarish granite buildings, each with a conical tower on one side. They were abandoned, crumbling.

"Closed mines," said Derek. "Engine houses. The tall things are the chimneys. Useless now."

"Except yours . . . and there must be others still."

"A few." His voice was curt. "But hundreds have closed since my father's day. And thousands of miners have been forced to emigrate."

"Where did they go?"

"To the copper mines of Michigan, the gold fields of Australia and California. Just before the decline, the investors were making more than four hundred percent profit annually—my grandfather, for one. Not that the miners themselves were ever paid more than a pittance. They often worked nearly eighty hours a week when cutting a rich lode. They had to climb down two thousand feet of ladders in those days where the temperature would often be fifty degrees warmer than on the surface. The conditions were very poor, dangerous; there was little or no thought for the miners' safety. And all that only to keep starvation at bay . . ." His face had hardened, his deep-set eyes narrowing.

She had not heard him talk this way before. "It upsets you to think of the injustice."

He shrugged, annoyed with himself for rambling on. He had nearly forgotten her presence. "Conditions are better now. We have gigs to replace the rickety ladders, and we use mechanical drills in place of the old tools. And I pay good wages that provide not merely the bare necessities but comforts as well." He would continue to do so until the mine gave out and he had to close Wheel Charity once and for all. But not yet.

Derek had other plans which Laurel's dowry would help to

realize. He was going to invest in what Arthur Quiller Couch viewed as the saving of the Cornish economy. Something was desperately needed to replace the dying industries of farming, fishing, and mining, industries which had sustained Cornwall since prehistoric times. This was the development of Cornwall as a holiday resort.

On one level Derek deplored the idea of tourists flocking down from London, labelling the natives "quaint," with accommodations of all sorts to cater to them. But the times called for drastic measures if Cornwall and what remained of its culture were to be preserved. The climate was temperate, its summers the longest in England. Other charms were the miles of spectacular jagged coastline, beaches, ancient ruins, opportunities for long ambles on the moors and headlands, and sailing when the sea permitted. Along the south coast grew profusions of palm trees, camellias, rhododendrons, and hydrangeas which added to the wild beauty of the place. Derek thought wryly that he was fortunate that Tregartha was in the bleak, windswept northwest—little chance of a tourist invasion there.

But just now Derek had no desire to contemplate the future. He wanted to show Laurel Cornwall—his Cornwall—while it was still the same.

"We'll explore the countryside on horseback," he told her.

"Is Tregartha in a town or village?"

"Hardly. It's out on the moors, quite isolated, with just a few acres of cultivated land around it. Pendreath is the nearest village."

"Is it near the sea?" She wondered if the house overlooked it, as did her family's cottage in Newport.

"Not far—about two miles. When Tregartha was built, it wasn't the thing to erect manor houses above the sea, at least not on the northern coast. It wasn't practical or comfortable, the wind being too cold and damp."

The mist was rising, the massive clouds lowering, obscuring

the tops of the moorland tors. They had tea in the dining car and then returned to their carriage.

Derek was thinking about the mine and all the matters which would demand his immediate attention. From this his thoughts drifted to people he had not seen in long months—his servants, employees, friends. And Diana Cardew. He was well aware that Diana had considered him her property. Yet he had never intentionally given her the impression that they had a future together. He wondered how she would take the news of his marriage.

He knew she was often bored and lonely at Kilworthy, especially when her brother Lyle had taken it into his head to rush off and fight the Boers in South Africa. With only her invalid aunt for company, she had often invited Derek to Kilworthy for rides, picnics, and dinners. She invited other neighbors as well, but only for propriety's sake; it was Derek she cared about. If not for him, she would have gone to London long ago, in pursuit of constant amusement. Not that Derek realized all of this. And the thought of marrying her had never appealed to him, despite the fact that she was considered beautiful and clever and managed Kilworthy, its lands and tenants, very well. Such duties bored Lyle. Doubtless that boredom had led to his impulse to join the army. He had returned wounded, but alive. Many others had not.

By the time the train halted at Bodmin, it was dark. Laurel shook off her sleepiness in the bracing breeze. A carriage awaited them with its driver, a beefy man in overcoat and hat.

Removing his hat, he said, " 'Tis good to see 'ee, sir."

"It's good to see you as well, Mark. Mrs. Tregarth and I long to be home."

"How do 'ee do, ma'am? Ever since the telegram came, we been ready for 'ee, sir, and the missus. A bride from New York—that set the place on its ear, I can tell 'ee. Mrs. Lanyon and they girls been workin' from top to bottom. We be that glad for 'ee, Mr. Derek, and proud. Tregartha's been needin' a mistress for a long time."

"You're right, Mark."

" 'Ee's been away too long, Mr. Derek, and thas a fact."

"I know it."

Mark's voice had a clear ring to it; his pronunciation was unusual to Laurel. She was startled by the easy familiarity with which he addressed Derek, almost as a fond uncle. The Willard servants would never have spoken in such a vein.

They climbed into the carriage. "How far to Tregartha?" asked Laurel.

"About an hour," Derek replied. "We have to go northwest over the moors, toward the sea."

"An hour? Oh . . ." She was dismayed; it had been a long day of travelling and she looked forward to a hot bath and a change of clothing.

"Never mind. We'll be there soon enough."

"Oh, I really don't mind. The air feels wonderful and smells so fresh and sweet, now that we're away from the station. I'm just eager to see my new home, that's all. I didn't realize it was so far."

"A hundred or so years ago it would have taken much longer and been far more uncomfortable. There were few roads then—just rough tracks full of stones, dirt, and puddles. Much of Cornwall was impassable by carriage. Cargo was transported on the backs of mules and the Goonhilly ponies. The villages were remote from one another and the villagers rarely travelled, if at all. Each village had its own customs and fair days."

"Fair days?" she echoed.

"Yes. At Helston there was the Furry Day on May 8."

"What was that?"

"A day to welcome in the summer. First, with a procession, the Hal-an-Tow, through the streets, followed by the Furry Dance at noon. It's still held every year, but Dr. Polgreen says it's deteriorated a great deal from what it once was. Very pagan, of course—its roots go back possibly thousands of years."

"Dr. Polgreen?"

"A friend of mine. He's writing a book on the fast-fading Cornish customs."

"Tell me another."

"Well, there's the Hobby Horse on May 1 at Padstow. Same idea, really. There is also a procession, this one led by the 'dancer'—a man dressed in female attire—and the horse."

"A real horse?"

"No. It's worked by a man inside the head—all black, with a ferocious face and oaken jaws with nails for teeth. It's rather hideous. On its journey through the streets, the horse purposely bumps against women, 'for luck.' Again there are all sorts of pagan overtones—fertility, fruitfulness, the glories of summer. At the end of the parade, the horse is ducked in the water. A symbolic sacrifice to preserve the cattle from disease and death. In ancient times it doubtless would have been a real sacrifice, a drowning."

"Heavens! What about the villages near Tregartha? Any unusual customs in our neck of the woods?"

He frowned. "I do seem to recall Henry Polgreen saying something once about a Green Lady—I suppose, like the Green Man, another symbol of vegetation, a good crop."

"Listen to that wind. I suppose you're going to say it's a banshee."

"A banshee!" he cried in mock outrage. "You are in Cornwall, Mrs. Tregarth, not in Ireland! And those are the wish-hounds baying."

"The what?"

"Wish-hounds, or whist-hounds. 'Whist' is Cornish for something both strange and sad. A stretch of Whistmoor is part of Tregartha land."

"What do hounds have to do with it?"

"They are the headless, howling dogs which race across the moor in pursuit of the doomed spirit, Tregeagle."

"Poor Tregeagle! Does he deserve that?"

"Most certainly. It's said he committed every diabolical

crime known to man. At his deathbed he left his vast wealth to the church in hopes that the monks could save his soul. But his deeds were too ghastly. All they could do to save him from the fires of hell was to appoint him endless impossible tasks such as emptying Dozmary Pool with a leaking limpet shell. The devil, cheated of Tregeagle's soul, sends his hell hounds to chase him round the pool and across the moor between dusk and dawn. Their frenzied yelping and his cries, moans, and gasps for breath can be heard at night all over Cornwall."

Laurel giggled. "And to think I always felt sorry for Ichabod Crane! It's a wonder anyone ever goes out at night in this place!"

He laughed with her. "The Cornish have explanations for everything. A whimpering in the heather stalks? That's the Spriggans who live in the barrows and cromlechs—stone formations out on the moors. They're said to blight crops, steal children, drive away cattle—very unsociable fellows."

"You're joking!"

"Not at all. We also have the Small People—the spirits of those who inhabited Cornwall thousands of years ago before the Celtic invaders. They've been getting smaller in size since the birth of Christ and one day will dwindle away altogether. Many people swear they've seen them. The Piskies will lead you astray into bogs with their fairy lights. The Buccas, or Knockers, live far down in the mines and woe to the miner who does not leave a bit of his lunch for the little creatures. Good household spirits are called Browneys, and there are mermaids who will sing to lure men to their deaths. And the witches ride through the air on stalks of ragwort, casting the evil eye on their enemies."

"Stop, stop," she begged, hiccuping with laughter.

"I told you you were entering an enchanted land."

"I'm beginning to see what you meant. Surely people nowadays don't believe all that?"

"Not the way they used to, no. We've had the Age of Science and, before that, in the mid-eighteenth century, John Wesley's conversion of Cornwall to Methodism. He had an enormous influence on the Cornish, and gradually, their superstitions and folklore diminished in importance. Rather a shame in some ways, though he brought about the civilizing of Cornwall."

"What do you mean?"

"Before John Wesley and his friends began to speak in Gwennap Pit, the Cornish were a lawless lot. The English considered them little better than savages and heathens because of the smuggling and wrecking that went on continually."

"Wrecking?"

"Yes. When a ship foundered close to land and broke apart, the people would come from miles around to comb the shore for cargo, parts of the ship, anything. You have to understand that they were desperately poor and malnourished. They regarded shipwrecks as acts of God sent for their benefit. To drag pieces of timber away for firewood was better than nothing. They would go armed with sharp axes and hatchets . . . there were drunken brawls, even drownings. But these wrecks were often the only way people got tea or coffee and other things they couldn't afford. They either kept parts of the cargo or sold them. Most of the time no malice was directed toward the ship or its crew. But they were determined to take the spoils, sometimes fighting to the death over them."

"I suppose they can't be faulted, especially if they were hungry."

"Wrecking was one of the Cornish practices John Wesley strongly disapproved of. He preached and wrote reproachful letters on it again and again. He also disapproved of excessive drinking, though not drinking altogether. Wesley himself drank wine and brandy. It was gin he abhorred, claiming it destroyed the lives of miners and their families. They were a Godless lot, those early Cornish, and many were reformed by Methodism. The hellfire and brimstone images, the lugubrious hymns about sin and death, appealed to the Cornish nature the same way the stories about fairies, ghosts, demons, and giants did. One gradually began to replace the other."

"I had no idea . . . what a fascinating place," Laurel said.

"I hope you will be happy here, Laurel," Derek said, taking her hand. "We're nearly there."

She put her face close to the window. "Really?"

They were approaching a large house. Lights illuminated long leaded windows.

"Tregartha was built in 1572 in the shape of an E, for Queen Elizabeth. The long ends of the E project from the body of the house as does the shorter central bay. There's a scalloped gable above each section. You'll be able to see far better tomorrow."

It wasn't quite as large as she had expected. Not like the enormous sham Tudors along Newport's Cliff Walk. Tregartha was small in comparison, but the real thing, a perfect jewel of a house.

The carriage stopped and the front door opened. Derek helped Laurel down from the carriage, then introduced her to Mrs. Lanyon, the housekeeper, a plump figure in a black gown.

"You be most welcome, Mrs. Tregarth," she said. "This be a wonderful day for we at Tregartha."

"Thank you, Mrs. Lanyon. I'm very happy to be here."

The servants were lined up in the front hall, the men on one side, the women on the other. "This be Dolly and Coral and Daisy and Tansy. They do help in the house. And here be Jem, my nephew, and Reeve and Luke and ol' Tom."

Laurel smiled at them shyly, saying how glad she was to know all of them. Derek spoke behind her. "I've missed all of you," he said, "and this place as well. I know you will serve Mrs. Tregarth as you have always served me."

"Aye, sir," they answered, the women bobbing curtseys, the men nodding. To Laurel's relief none of their faces was unfriendly.

"Tregartha'll be the talk of the duchy now that us have an American mistress," said one of the men.

Derek laughed; again Laurel was surprised by the intimacy expressed between master and servants. It was obvious that Derek was well-liked by his staff. She hoped they would come to like her also.

At the end of the line stood an old woman. Her gray hair was covered by a starched lace cap; she was bent over. That she was a person of importance in the household was readily apparent.

"Laurel, this is Martha," said Derek. He bent and kissed the withered cheek.

His nurse. Of course. "How do you do, Martha?" Laurel said warmly, holding out her hand.

The old lady's grip was surprisingly strong. "I've prayed often for this day. Welcome to Tregartha, Mrs. Tregarth. I hope 'ee'll be very happy here."

Mrs. Lanyon said, "There be a fire in the Hall, sir, and in the drawing room. But Mrs. Tregarth may be wishin' to see her room."

"Yes, Mrs. Lanyon, I would indeed," said Laurel.

"You go with Mrs. Lanyon, Laurel," said Derek. "I'll be up in a bit."

"Martha don't often leave her rooms," said Mrs. Lanyon as they went up the stairs. "The pains in her back be bad. But nothin' would keep her from payin' her respects to 'ee, ma'am."

"That was very gracious of her," said Laurel.

"Keeps to her room, she do, but there be not much she misses. Her came to Tregartha afore any o' we, but for ol' Tom who tends the gardens."

The walls of the stairway and landing were panelled in a crisscross pattern of dark wood. There was an oil painting of a man with cold, narrow eyes, dressed in clothing of the eighteenth century. Laurel did not like it. "Who is that?"

"Oh, one of they ol' Tregarths, I reckon," said the housekeeper.

They walked down the corridor, which was carpeted in wine-red, stopping at a doorway near the end of the hall. Laurel entered the room. There was a magnificent four-poster, heavily carved, hung with blue silk curtains. The same fabric draped the diamond-paned windows. An old chest, nearly black with age, stood at the foot of the bed, and two large wardrobes graced opposite sides of the wall. The room smelled faintly of furniture polish and the flowers filling two Chinese vases.

"It's splendid, Mrs. Lanyon."

" 'Twas the mistress's room, her that was Mr. Derek's mother. The dower chest belonged to her family. Through there 'ee'll find the bathroom and dressing room. I saw to it myself that everything were laid out proper for 'ee. Didn't want to leave it to they feckless girls to do—not the first time 'ee were to see it."

"Thank you. I know I'll be very comfortable here. It's a lovely room."

"Mr. Derek ordered all new fabric for 'ee from London. It were yellow afore."

"Do I have time to take a bath before dinner?" asked Laurel. She had no wish to upset household routine on her first night there.

"Aye, ma'am. And if 'ee needs help, pull that cord. Tansy or one of the others'll be along."

Mrs. Lanyon departed and Derek came in soon after. "Well?"

She turned to him. "Oh, Derek, need you ask? I love it! Mrs. Lanyon told me you'd ordered new curtains and things. Such a lovely shade."

"Violet-blue. To match your eyes," he said. "My room is through there. These are the largest bedrooms. If there is anything you don't like, or wish to add, simply say so."

He went to take his own bath and dress for dinner. Laurel

relaxed in the huge tub before sending for Tansy to help her dress. She decided to wear her new purple velvet gown with heart-shaped neckline. She showed Tansy how to arrange her hair and then dismissed the girl.

Derek knocked at the door and then entered. He was wearing black and white, carrying a crushed velvet bag. He went over to Laurel and kissed the nape of her neck.

"I have something for you," he said softly. He had looked forward to this moment for weeks, imagining it, savoring the satisfaction it would bring him. He held out the drawstring bag.

Laurel pulled open the string and drew out a necklace of glittering sapphires and diamonds. They winked and sparkled in the candlelight. There were drop earrings to match.

"I suppose I should have asked you what you were wearing," said Derek. "I had these in mind when I chose your engagement ring. They've been in my family for three hundred years."

Laurel stared at the large, heavy stones with their ornate gold clasp. They felt cold in her hand. "They are magnificent, Derek," she murmured. "Would you like me to wear them?"

He could not mistake the lack of enthusiasm in her voice. Dashed, hurt, he heard himself saying, "You don't like them."

"It's not that, Derek. It's just that they are a bit too much for me. You know I don't like ostentatious jewelry."

"Ostentatious!" he repeated, astounded. How could his family's jewels be considered ostentatious? What on earth was the matter with her? Didn't she understand how much this meant to him?

"I was thinking . . . my pearls would go very well with this gown."

"As you like." She had not realized his eyes could look so cold. They cut off her smile. He took the necklace and slipped it inside the bag.

Too late she realized her mistake. "I'll wear them another time, Derek. Tomorrow."

"It doesn't matter." He turned away.

But it did. For some reason it mattered very much. She saw that now. She was suddenly afraid. She had failed him. She had not reacted in the way he had expected. Why hadn't she asked him to fasten the necklace on her? Couldn't she have worn it for a few hours?

"Please, Derek, I'd like to wear them," she said.

"I said it doesn't matter!"

She flinched as though she had been struck. Her eyes grew dark; she bit her lip.

"Shall we go down to dinner?" His voice was cool, distant. There was a rift between them; it was unmistakable. Gone was the open intimacy they had shared.

The dinner was delicious but Laurel had lost her appetite. Her throat felt choked with unshed tears. Not wanting to offend Mrs. Lanyon, she tried to eat a few bites of every course.

The Hall was a long, spacious room with a coffered ceiling and one wall made up of rows of small-paned windows. There was a huge fireplace with a carved limestone mantel. High up at one end of the room was a minstrel's gallery. The floor was slate, the walls painted white, the furniture dark and gleaming from years of polishing. Doors with Gothic arches led the way out.

After dinner they sat in the drawing room with its ornate fireplace and mouldings and Empire furniture. Laurel was wretched, struggling to make conversation, desperate for the inscrutable look to leave Derek's face. She wanted him smiling and light-hearted again.

But he did not respond. Finally he said, "You must be tired, Laurel. I suggest we retire."

She nodded mutely, almost relieved to abandon the charade of an enjoyable evening. She longed for bed and oblivion. Surely tomorrow Derek's good humor would be restored.

They went upstairs together, Derek to his room and her to hers. Tansy came to help her out of her gown. "Thank you, Tansy. You may go to bed now."

"Thank 'ee, ma'am. Good night."

Laurel sat at the dressing table, brushing her hair. She felt weary and depressed, bewildered by the turn of events. She found herself wishing she was back in New York. At least there she knew what to expect.

Derek came in. She stole a glance at him in the mirror. She tried a joke. "You look as grim as Tregeagle."

His gaze sharpened; he frowned. There was a brooding tenseness in him. She set down the hairbrush, drooping and forlorn. Then she got up and went toward the bed.

He had been watching her. Her hair fell in shiny waves over her shoulders. She wore a nightdress with full sleeves, ruffled at the cuffs and at the v-neck bodice. It outlined her small breasts and slim thighs. He reached for her and pulled her roughly against him.

"Derek, I'm sorry—about the necklace—I'm so sorry," she mumbled into his shoulder.

"Hush," he said and his mouth took hers with a fiery intensity. There was a new and different quality to his lovemaking. The tenderness that had heretofore tempered his passion was gone. She was pliant and yielding in his arms, but still he took her angrily, crushing her down on the bed, his ardor fierce and furious. He claimed her, bruising her skin with savage kisses.

As though he were proving something to me, thought Laurel later as she lay awake. As though he were telling me I am his, and not to forget it, convincing me and himself. His arm lay heavy across her sore breasts. She pushed it aside, hoping he would not wake up. He didn't. Finally, she, too, fell asleep.

The next morning Derek woke her with soft kisses. She was naked; her nightgown lay in a torn bundle on the floor where he had tossed it. He saw with a shock the bruises on her throat and breasts. Had he made those? He was appalled.

"Forgive me, Laurel," he whispered, nuzzling his face

against her cheek. He barely recalled his violent lovemaking. He had been resentful that she had not appreciated his gift of the sapphire necklace, but that seemed trivial now, absurd. Her tastes were very simple; he should have realized that weeks ago. He *had* realized it, in fact, but overshadowing his realization was the near-obsession to lavish his family's jewels on her. "With my worldly goods I thee endow," he had said, and meant it. No matter that she was an heiress and possessed her own supply of worldly goods. It had been bestowing *his* on her that had seemed of great significance. Now he wanted to forget the whole distasteful business.

Laurel, too, was relieved that last night's constraint was behind them. Derek had many business matters to see to, so she amused herself by exploring the house. She went into the kitchen to meet the cook, who pressed her to take a piece of her freshly-baked "fuggan," or raisin cake. Later she wandered in and out of the bedchambers and sitting rooms before going up to the top floor of the house to see the nursery and schoolroom.

My children will be up here one day, she thought happily. As she stood looking about the schoolroom, she heard a shuffling sound behind her. Turning, she saw Martha standing in the doorway.

" 'Tis nigh upon twenty-five year since this room be used," she said. "Not since Master Derek went away to school. But 'tis been kept clean and painted. I knew 'twould be needed again."

Laurel smiled self-consciously. "I hope so."

"Would 'ee care to come to my room for a cup of tea, ma'am?"

She was touched. "Very much, Martha. Thank you." She followed the old lady down the hall. Martha leaned heavily on her cane. They entered a suite of two rooms, a cozy sitting room and bedroom. Martha gestured for Laurel to sit down in a large stuffed armchair before she filled the kettle with water. She continued to make her own tea as she had always done, though her meals were brought to her.

"Mrs. Lanyon tells me you have lived at Tregartha a long time."

"Aye, nigh upon thirty year. I came after the former missus died, she who were Master Derek's mother. He were just a young 'un then. We each had need o' the other. His mother were gone and my man and son, too."

"Oh, I'm so sorry."

"A minin' accident," Martha said briefly.

"So you and Derek had one another."

Martha nodded. "Aye. Mind 'ee, there were the bad times, too."

"Bad times?" Laurel echoed.

"He were a rare boy, the master. Could get up to tricks. And then he'd say, 'I didn't do it, Martha. It was *him.*' "

"Him? Did he play with another boy?"

"Him he called Dirk. Not a real 'un. Someone he made up. Dirk did things Master Derek couldn't own up to. His father didn't like it at all. He were a hard, strict man."

"An imaginary playmate . . ."

Martha poured the boiling water into her brown teapot. " 'Ee do love the master?" she said.

Laurel was slightly taken aback. "Well, yes, of course I do."

Martha nodded. "He were never one to show his feelings, but I can see he do love 'ee, too. 'Ee must hold onto that, even . . ."

"Even?" prompted Laurel. She was beginning to feel uneasy.

Martha handed her a cup of tea. Her hand was gnarled, the joints swollen. "At times the moods come upon him and he be as dark as a storm cloud. 'Twas always that way. When his father said it were time to send him to school, he didn't want to go. He ran off. Then, when he were found, he wouldn't eat for days. He didn't want to go to school, he told his father. He wanted to go to sea."

"To sea!" Laurel was startled.

Martha nodded. "He were only a boy o' ten, but tes what he wanted. He were sent to school and ran off again. He were found by a constable down at the docks in Plymouth, tryin' to get work on a ship."

"What happened?"

"He were brought back to school and punished summat cruel, I reckon. After that he didn't run off. And he stopped his talk o' goin' to sea. I wondered when he were older if he'd be wantin' to join the navy, but by then he seemed to forget what he wanted so as a boy."

Laurel didn't know what to say. It wasn't that the story itself was that unusual—many children refused to fall in easily with the wishes of their parents. Perhaps she felt such dismay because the boy was Derek. But it looked as though his father had been right. Derek had apparently lost his earlier infatuation with the sea; certainly he had never mentioned it to her. Laurel was slightly troubled by the story. Again it struck her how little she knew about her new husband.

"I can tell 'ee be a true lass," Martha said. "And tes all God's will. Even my man and boy dyin' like that. Better to die quick than to cough with rotted lungs like some. And then I come to Tregartha."

"How terrible it must have been for you," Laurel said inadequately.

"Tes all long past now. But I knew . . . that day. I were cleaning pilchards in the fish cellar. And sudden-like, I knew."

Laurel felt a prickling at the back of her neck. She set down her cup of tea. This was all more than she had expected when she accepted Martha's invitation.

"When the moods come on the master, 'ee must be strong, and do what your heart tells 'ee. And don't 'ee forget he do love 'ee. Master Derek never before wanted to marry, though he could always have his pick."

"Thank you, Martha, I'll remember," said Laurel. She rose shakily. "And thank you for the tea."

The old lady nodded. She seemed weary. Rocking back in her chair, she closed her eyes. Laurel left her rooms and went back downstairs, pondering what Martha had told her. She had witnessed one of Derek's "moods" herself—last night, when she had been reluctant to wear the sapphire necklace. And what of the time in New York, following Flora's ball? The way he had avoided her . . . And then the night he had pursued her down the icy street, astonishing her with his unexpected proposal of marriage. Were these more examples of his 'moods'? Unhappily she recalled his stormy possession of her last night. But these thoughts were foolish. How did they possibly relate to a boy of ten who had wanted to go to sea? And Martha's mention of an imaginary playmate . . . that wasn't so odd. Her own sister had had one for a few weeks. Flora had wanted someone younger than she in the family, Laurel remembered. It had not lasted long.

Just before sunset, the rain stopped. Derek and Laurel walked in the wet garden. The air was cool and delightful; it blew away the lingering traces of uneasiness Martha had aroused in her. For the first time Laurel saw the house clearly, and considered it even more beautiful than she had the previous night. She was enchanted with the curved gables, the crenellated chimneys, the mullioned windows and the soft grays and ambers of the granite walls. Beyond the house lay the high, brackeny hills and tumbled valleys of Whistmoor.

"In a few months the moors will be purple with heather," Derek told her.

Laurel breathed in the sweet air scented with spring rain, growing things, and woodsmoke. "I'd like to go riding tomorrow, see something of the countryside. Unless you have too much work to do," she added.

"Poor Laurel. I've neglected you today. We'll make a day of it tomorrow, I promise."

"Oh, I enjoyed myself. I explored the house. I—I even had tea with Martha."

"Did you now? And was it hideously dark and strong?"

She gurgled with laughter. "Yes. I couldn't drink more than one cup."

"She's always made it that way, in the same brown pot."

"She told me something about you as a boy."

"And what on earth would that have been?" He was smiling, so she went on.

"That you had an imaginary playmate named Dirk," she said lightly.

He stiffened. "That? Childish nonsense."

"Flora had one too—Eliza, I think her name was. Or Edith." She was watching him closely.

A muscle jerked in his cheek. "Ridiculous."

"Not at all. You were an only child."

"How in the world did this come up in conversation?" he asked irritably.

"Well, we had been in the schoolroom and I suppose Martha was remembering . . ." She had no intention of telling him that Martha's words had been a kind of warning.

"Martha talks too much." His voice was cold.

Laurel bit her lip. She shouldn't have mentioned it. She should have anticipated his reaction. She took his hand. He glanced down at her, his face softening. But his eyes were wary and a trifle remote.

The next day was clear and bright with a keen wind blowing across the moors. Derek and Laurel set out at midmorning with a picnic lunch packed by the cook. Laurel wore a new riding habit of lapis blue.

"We must stick to the tracks today," said Derek. "After yesterday's rain the ground will be especially boggy. Always remember that when you go riding alone."

Overhead a few ravens circled and dipped as Laurel and

Derek cantered, enjoying the sun and wind on their faces. Before long they reached Pendreath, a peaceful but isolated village of stone cottages. They crossed a little bridge over a stream, stopping at a church with a Norman tower. The arched windows reflected the stately sycamores growing alongside the stream. Securing their horses, they went inside the granite church. Its interior was simple, like most Cornish churches, and filled with a cool, bottle-green light. Derek pointed out the fifteenth-century benches with their carved ends—a jester, sword-dancer, fiddler, bagpiper, and a number of male and female saints.

"I would expect the saints, but the other figures seem strange in a church," Laurel observed.

"The Cornish often carved secular images on their bench ends," said Derek. "At Rowenstow, a good way up the coast, there's one of a mermaid holding a looking glass and comb." He did not tell her that, as a youth home from school, he had been fascinated with the carving and had often ridden up to the old church at Rowenstow to see it. But he had not thought of it in years. Curiously, the memory now filled him with displeasure. As had Laurel's reminder of his imaginary playmate. It was unsavory somehow. He banished it from his mind.

They rode through the village where a few men were seen working in their gardens. Derek called out greetings, and a woman, who had stepped out to sweep her porch, bobbed a curtsey.

Beyond the village they passed a number of cottages scattered over the moor. These were empty, crumbling, the fields gone to waste, bracken covering the stone walkways. The small windowpanes were dull, glazed from years of harsh weather and neglect.

"The owners have all had to emigrate," explained Derek. "You'll see many like this."

Laurel was subdued; to her the abandoned cottages seemed unbearably melancholy. She had emigrated herself, but because she had chosen to, not because she could not make ends meet. She had not been forced to leave her home—she had left it willingly. Just as she had married willingly, for love, unlike others she knew in New York whose parents had forced them into joyless unions.

They rode on, growing close to Rough Tor, an enormous russet-colored hill whose slopes were pocked with granite boulders. The horses slowed to a walk as they climbed to the top. A circle of nine standing stones, each over eight feet high, crowned the hill.

"The Virgin Sisters," said Derek. "Prehistoric, about four thousand years old, erected for who knows what reason. Henry Polgreen says the people then had come from Iberia—what is now Spain and Portugal—and worshipped the Earth Mother. These monoliths probably marked the place where fertility rites were held. Much later, the Christian Church claimed they were sinful women whom God had turned to stone."

"Why the name, then?"

"Virgin Sisters? Oh, another story says nine nuns were buried here and the stones erected for them. Take your pick."

"Shall we have our lunch here?" asked Laurel. "The view is glorious."

"You don't mind the wind? It's stronger up here."

"No, I don't mind." She took off her hat; her hair had begun to escape its pins but she did nothing to remedy that. They spread out a blanket.

"Let's see what Peggy has for us. Some real Cornish food, I hope," said Derek. "Good—pasties. And some cider. Just the thing."

They ate and drank hungrily, the food tasting especially delicious out in the sweet, bracing wind. Laurel gazed pensively at the tall stone pillars; they looked secretive, mysterious. She imagined them on a bleak day swathed in mist—that would be an eerie sight. Inside the baked dough of her pasty were beef, carrots, and potatoes. The cider was potent; a relaxing warmth crept into Laurel's limbs.

"New York seems so far away—unreal, somehow," she said dreamily.

Derek reached over and kissed her hand. "Do you like Cornwall so far?"

"Very much, Derek." She gestured about her. "There's a strange quality about it—it's different from any place I've ever been. And yet there's something very appealing—stirring, really."

Later they mounted the horses and followed the old track down the opposite side of Rough Tor. For a time there was nothing in sight but the desolate moorland of Whistmoor—the time-battered ridges and valleys jagged with rock formations. Its very wildness struck a chord deep within Laurel. She felt exhilarated, intensely alive.

Derek showed her one of the massive "shuddering stones"— a boulder balanced on a pivot atop a granite foundation. "Touch it," he said.

Gingerly she reached out and pressed the boulder, only to jump back when it shifted. Derek grinned. "It won't roll off its pivot. It's been this way for thousands of years, but opinions differ about whether it was formed naturally or by man. Terrible things are said to happen to the person who attempts to overturn a shuddering stone. People used to fortell their futures by the way the stone moved. Touching the rock nine times at midnight was supposed to ensure that a man never had bad luck. But if a woman did the same thing, she would become a witch."

"Hah! Grossly unfair!" cried Laurel.

"It's been a sacred place down through the ages, revered by the Iberians, Celts, and Christians. Each culture imbued it with supernatural powers, handed down in a sort of folk memory."

They rode through a stretch of woods, the track becoming wider beyond the trees. They passed horse-drawn carts and a woman driving a flock of sheep. Ahead was a tiny picturesque structure with a pointed roof, its entrance low and narrow. Ivy and brambles matted the stone walls, hiding much of their dilapidated condition.

"One of the holy wells," said Derek. Bending low, they stepped inside into a grotto with an arched roof. Ivy clung to the inner walls. On the floor was a stone basin filled to its moulded brim with gurgling water.

"There's a spring nearby that feeds into the well," said Derek. "The water is always fresh in here because of the hole in the basin. People would bring their children to wash here, to make them strong and healthy. Like the shuddering stones, the water in these wells was supposed to have magical powers. Girls would try to divine whom they would marry, that sort of thing. Different wells were believed to cure different illnesses. St. Nun's Well was said to cure madness. Lunatics would be brought there and ducked. Some wells were said to cure epilepsy, rheumatism, scrofula. People would leave votive offerings—thin strips of cloth or pieces of string tied to greenery near the well. Henry believes the practice dates back to Neolithic times. Again, the folk memory."

"How old is this building? Surely not thousands of years?"

"No. The Celtic Christian monks built these baptistries around the wells. They lived in them, and used the water to baptize their flock. The people already believed the well to be magical, so the monks took advantage of that. But the baptistries are old—fifth or sixth century."

"Are we near the sea?"

He nodded, grinning. "I've taken you on a roundabout journey. We'll ride to the water now."

As they rode, the amber brackeny heath gave way to wind-flattened, grassy headlands. Laurel could smell the sea. At the cliff's edge they reined in, looking down on the surf below as it slammed against the jagged promontories. The wind was strong and salty. They had to shout to be heard. Walking the horses along the headland, Laurel spied some stone ruins and cried, "What's that?"

"Only a hill fort."

"I'd like to see it."

"What?"

She gestured toward the ruins. He shook his head. "I need to get back now, Laurel. There is work I must do."

"Just a couple of minutes, all right?" she called.

He watched her ride over to the hill fort. Why was she interested in that place? He was suddenly impatient. But he stifled his reluctance and followed her.

"What is it?" she asked again.

"A Bronze or Iron Age fort, built to defend the coast from sea invaders. The tribe would gather inside with their animals and tools. Well, you've seen it. Let's go."

She did not heed the constrained note in his voice. "Look, there's something down there."

"Laurel, it's a jumble of rocks, that's all."

"No, there's an opening," she said excitedly. Swiftly she dismounted, drawn by a growing compulsion. She hurried over to a section of the granite wall where a dark hollow yawned. Stooping, she cried, "It's a tunnel!"

His voice was testy. "It's only a fougou. Laurel, stop, don't go in there!"

She was past hearing. Inside the tunnel, she reached out to touch the roughly-hewn sides. It was damp and musty-smelling, and there were puddles near the entrance. The stone floor was slippery, but Laurel stepped in further. She did not mind the growing darkness. A powerful impulse drove her deeper into the fougou.

"Laurel!" shouted Derek furiously. "Laurel!" Why on earth had she gone into the bloody place? Grimly he got down from his horse and followed her, his jaw clenched tight.

He went through the dark passage, stooping. It opened up into a large, round room. He blinked his eyes, trying to accustom them to the semi-darkness. The room was paved, the sides corbelled. The sound of the sea was very faint.

"Laurel, for God's sake! What the hell do you think you're doing? Come on—the place stinks, it's unhealthy!"

"Oh, Dirk, I'm afraid for you. They're coming . . . it's a trap!" Her voice was a whisper, strangely unfamiliar. Her pale face swam before him.

Without a word he savagely gripped her arm, pulling her out of the room and along the passage. In the sunlight, she shielded her eyes which had darkened to almost black. She was trembling.

Why in God's name had she called him *Dirk?* And that singular uncanny whisper . . . His face was thunderous. He thrust her onto her mount, conscious of an inexplicable revulsion.

It was all her fault. She had betrayed him. He had been a fool to believe she loved him, that she would throw in her lot with his and go away with him. She . . . Dazed, he shook his head.

"I'm sorry, Derek. I thought it looked interesting," Laurel said, frightened by the expression on his face. "Is it dangerous?"

"How the hell should I know? I don't make a practice of investigating those places! I should think it likely it could cave in at any moment."

But he had not been concerned with that sort of danger. It had not even occurred to him, despite what he told her. The place itself repelled him, especially when she had displayed what seemed to him an unholy fascination. She had been enthralled . . . What was that line from Keats? "La Belle Dame Sans Merci hath me in thrall . . ." He was the one who'd been enthralled, convinced of her love. Then why hadn't she come? What a fool he had been! At the last she had not been able to give up her security, her position . . .

"Derek, what is it? Derek, you look so odd," cried Laurel anxiously. "Are you all right?" She shook his arm.

His head cleared; he felt the sharp wind in his face. In his ears the raging surf was audible. "Let's go home," he said. She nodded, anxious to leave the hill fort as well.

Neither of them realized that they had reached a turning point. They would not be able to recapture the earlier untroubled days of their marriage. There was no going back.

Four

Again that night when Derek made love to her, he did so with barely-concealed anger and resentment. He did not hurt her, but, though there was undeniable desire, there was little joy in the act. Afterwards he fell asleep and she sat up in an armchair, wrapped in a blanket. What was wrong? It seemed she was always displeasing her husband. Something was happening to them that she did not understand. It had begun on their arrival at Tregartha. She frowned. No, that wasn't precisely true. There had been that fire in their stateroom on board ship. Had that been an omen of things to come?

But Derek loved her. She knew he did, and Martha had said so. Martha had told her to be strong.

Her unhappy brooding was abruptly cut off by an anguished cry. In the wavering candlelight she saw Derek's hands clawing about his neck, an unbearable terror in his wide-open gaze. He began to gasp for breath.

Crawling in beside him, she gently shook his shoulder. "Derek, wake up. You're having a nightmare. That's all. Wake up."

His eyes stared wildly at the ceiling; his fingers gripped his throat. She tugged at them.

"Derek, listen to me. You're having a bad dream. A nightmare. You must wake up!" Pulling the tangled sheets from his rigid form, she pressed her body close to his.

"Wake up, Derek!"

His eyes closed; she was able to bring his arms down to

his sides. Holding both hands tightly, she said soothingly, "It's all right, Derek. It was just a nightmare. There was nothing real about whatever it was. And it's all over now."

When he opened his eyes she saw with relief that the hideous look of torment was gone. But his skin was clammy and hot; he took ragged breaths, shuddering.

"What was it, darling? What frightened you so?"

He shook his head. "S-stupid dream. Sorry to wake you."

She did not tell him that she hadn't been to sleep. "What was the dream?"

"I—I was choking . . . couldn't breathe."

Reaching for the covers, she drew them up. They lay side by side for a while, not speaking. Then he said, "That dream. I've had it before. Not in years, though."

"How awful for you. I'm glad I was here."

"Laurel," he said hoarsely. "Don't—don't ever leave me. Promise you'll never . . . leave."

"I promise."

Laurel was alone in bed when she awoke the next morning. To her surprise it was after eleven o'clock. When Tansy came in with her tea tray she asked rather breathlessly, "Have you—have you seen Mr. Tregarth?"

"The master be out, ma'am. Went to the mine hours ago. He told Mrs. Lanyon and we not to wake 'ee."

"But—" Derek had promised to take her to the mine the next time he went. Why had he not awakened her? Well, she could ask the way to Wheel Charity and meet him there.

She ate her breakfast and put on her riding habit. Then she went down to the stables. "Has Mr. Tregarth returned from the mine?"

"Not yet, missus," said Luke.

She got directions from him and he saddled a horse for her. " 'Ee oughtn't to go now, missus—the sky be lookin' worse and worse."

She nodded impatiently. "I'll be careful."

The clouds were low and heavy in the sky. Whistmoor unfolded before her, starkly desolate. Its mood was ominous today, almost sinister. But she was determined to locate the mine—and Derek.

As it turned out, she never got to the mine. She met Derek about halfway there on his way back. He looked surprised to see her, and none too pleased. "What are you doing out here? It's going to storm."

"I was riding to find you. They told me you'd gone to the mine. I wanted to see it."

"Well, another time, Laurel," he said. There were lines about his mouth and shadows under his eyes. "I thought you needed your sleep this morning."

"The same could be said for you," Laurel said. "Derek, about your dream—"

"—Let's get back to the house, shall we? Before the sky opens up." He did not look at her.

So he was not going to discuss his nightmare, or allow her to. Another forbidden topic between them, like his imaginary playmate, like the fougou. Not that she remembered much more than his anger.

That night she again surrendered her body to him, but her spirit felt drained and battered. She had fallen asleep when the sounds woke her. Derek was gasping, striking out at the air. The bed shook with his violent movements.

"Derek, Derek!" This time she was not gentle. He must stop these horrible dreams. Why did they continue to plague him?

He sat up, raking his fingers through his thick, dark hair. His voice was surprisingly firm. "Go back to sleep, Laurel. It's nothing."

"Nothing! Derek, you can't say that, you can't believe it!"

"I said it was nothing. A bad dream. Everyone has them."

"But night after night, the same dream? And so horrible that you . . ."

"That I what?"

"Well, moan and cry out. It—it frightens me."

"There is only one cure for that," he said, reaching for his dressing gown.

"Wh-where are you going?" she asked in dismay.

"To my own room. That way you won't be disturbed."

"Derek, no! I didn't mean . . . please don't go. I don't want to be alone. Please, Derek." She gripped his arm. Her dark hair spilled over her breasts, her body was slim and marble-like in the moonlight. Yet he felt only distaste.

"It's better this way, Laurel. At least while I'm having these foolish dreams."

"Derek, that is not the answer, don't you see that? Something is terribly wrong and the dreams are only a part of it."

"I don't know what you mean," he said curtly. "We'll both sleep better apart."

"I don't care about sleep, Derek. I'm talking about *us*. We're not the same. *You're* not the same." But it was no use. He refused to acknowledge what she was saying, he refused to listen. Her frantic desperation had merely caused him to retreat further into hardened indifference.

Oh, God, what is happening? she wailed inwardly. What on earth am I to do? She buried her face in her hands and began to cry. The door shut quietly behind him.

In the days that followed, they met at meals, but on few other occasions. Derek spent most of his time at the mine. He did not suggest that she accompany him, nor did she ask. He was civil, but distant. And he did not touch her.

"It do wring my heart so to see her poor face red with weepin'," said Mrs. Lanyon to Peggy, the cook.

"Do 'ee know what to make of it?" asked Peggy.

"Married a few weeks and behavin' like this. What be the master thinkin' of, I ask 'ee?" Mrs. Lanyon shook her head sadly.

"He's takin' to sleepin' in his room, I hear," said Peggy. "Ought to be ashamed of himself, bringing her all the way here where she don't know a soul, and then treatin' her so ill. I wonder what Martha makes of it."

Laurel got up one morning and decided to ride out to the ancient ruined hill fort. She had nearly forgotten about it. Derek would disapprove, of course, which made her even more determined to go there. Her defiance slightly eased the tight knots inside her.

This time she was prepared; she had brought a candle. She would be able to investigate the fougou. As she drew near, her excitement grew, and the sense of urgency. She forgot about Derek and what he might think. She thought only about the fougou. She must go in—she *must!*

Once inside the tunnel, away from the sea breeze, she lit the candle. Ahead of her the passage sloped downward. Picking her way along it, she reached the large, round chamber. Laurel held out the candle and gazed about her.

It was constructed of large blocks of granite in beehive fashion, corbelled inwardly, rising to a domed roof several feet above her head. The air was musty and cold; she shivered. There was nothing much to see—Derek had been right. So why the undeniable impulse to come here again? She was about to turn and go back when she noticed another passageway leading out of the room.

It was lower than the first—she was forced to bend low to walk through it. Yet she did not notice the discomfort in her back nor the stiffness in her shoulders. The dank air no longer bothered her.

He must be here. An enormous yearning welled up within her; she ached with it. She stood in another domed room, this one smaller. Looking wildly about, she saw it was empty. Her shadow loomed on the stone wall. She sobbed forlornly and rushed back into the passage, striking her head on the roof.

She swayed, her head throbbing viciously. The dank air nauseated her. Stumbling in haste along the tunnel, she did not notice that she had dropped the candle. She was crying now, though not from the pain in her head. When she was outside she stood gaping about her. The horse was gone; she had neglected to secure him. It was pouring rain. But neither of these realizations accounted for the hopeless despair which overwhelmed her. Sinking to her knees, she continued to sob.

Derek had returned home from the mine and was working on some accounts when one of the men knocked at the library door.

"Well?" he said curtly.

"It be the missus, Mr. Derek."

"What about her?" His voice had taken on an ugly note.

Reeve twisted his hat in his hands. He was well aware that things were not as they should have been between master and mistress; the entire household knew they were not sharing the same bed. "Beggin' your pardon, sir, but Mrs. Tregarth's horse—it came back without she."

"What?" Reeve had got the reaction he wanted; Derek had bolted up from his chair.

"Aye, sir. Mrs. Tregarth went out ridin' nigh on two hour ago. The horse came back alone."

As Reeve told it later to the rest of the staff, the master was across the room and had pushed past him before he could move. He had rushed out to the stables, Reeve chasing after him. He told each man to ride in a different direction; they would all look for her. The rain was coming down in torrents. Derek was already soaked to the skin just from the run to the stables. Leaping on his own horse without saddling it, he galloped off toward the sea.

Where in God's name was she? He held one of his hands in front of his eyes to block the rain. The ground was wet, boggy. His horse stumbled once, lost its footing. Would Laurel remember to stick to the track? Could she? Or was she lying somewhere hurt, bones broken—or worse? He was frantic. He did not remember that lately he had wished to avoid the sight of her. He began to shout her name, but he could barely hear himself above the din of wind and rain.

His eyes widened, then narrowed. No, he wasn't seeing things. There was a drooping, stumbling figure in the distance. He urged his horse on faster. It was Laurel; he saw the dark blue of her riding habit. Enormous relief surged through him.

But when he reached her, the relief had changed to a cold fury. Her hat had come off and her hair was flattened down her back and shoulders. There was mud on her skirt and on her boots. For some reason he took a perverse pleasure in her bedraggled state. She didn't look the grand lady now, did she?

"Where the hell have you been, Laurel? The entire household is in an uproar! Your horse came home alone."

She looked up into his blazing eyes and said dully, "I'm sorry. The horse ran off." She put her hand to her head. "I feel sick." Her face was white as a sheet in the grayness that engulfed them.

"The mist will be rising. Come on." He set her on the horse and climbed up behind her. "Where were you?"

"I went to the fougou."

Derek uttered an angry exclamation. Again, that damned fougou! "I forbid you to go there again, do you understand?" he snarled.

"It wasn't any good anyway," she said listlessly. "It was empty."

He felt a prickling between his shoulders. Empty? Of course it was empty. What had she expected? Dread began to seep through him.

Back at Tregartha he carried her limp, drenched form upstairs. Mrs. Lanyon had prepared hot water bottles for the bed. Derek sent Daisy for some brandy before stripping off Laurel's wet, filthy clothes. He found a nightgown and slipped it over her, then toweled her hair. She took a few sips of the brandy and then sank against the pillows. Derek drew the covers about her shoulders.

Soon she was asleep. Derek sat beside her, his face inscrutable, his thoughts muddled. She had set the household on its ear. Now she would likely take a chill and become ill. Gazing at her, the crescents of dark lashes against her pale face, he again felt the need to protect her. But she had made a fool of him, riding off like that, telling no one where she was going. And to that damned fougou! Bitterness rose in him like bile.

When Laurel awakened, it was Martha who sat beside her.

Laurel did not take a chill, but she spent the next couple of days resting in bed. It was as though there was a veil between her and the world. It was far less painful that way. When she was up and about again, she and Derek were like polite strangers, both withdrawn, fortressed. At night Laurel would lie awake, longing for something she could not identify. She could not know that Derek did the same.

One afternoon they had their first visitors. Laurel was resting in her room; she had become weary and lethargic of late. Mrs. Lanyon woke her. "I hate to disturb 'ee, ma'am, but there be callers below."

Laurel sat up groggily. "Callers?"

"Aye. Miss Cardew and Mr. Cardew, from over Kilworthy. They be downstairs with the master." She seemed agitated.

Laurel tried to clear her mind. She noticed Mrs. Lanyon's odd manner and her nervous, jittery movements as she drew aside the curtains. Her voice was tremulous and her eyes refused to meet Laurel's. And she knew that there was something about these visitors. Or one of them . . .

"Very well, Mrs. Lanyon. Send one of the girls to me and I will get ready."

She saw the relief in Mrs. Lanyon's face. "I'll tell the master 'ee'll be down shortly."

Laurel went across to the wardrobe where her new gowns from London had recently been put away. Who were these people and why had they come? She was so tired, so listless. She did not feel up to seeing anyone. Indifferently she took out the first gown she saw, a pearl-gray with cherry-colored ribbons and trim. Daisy came in and helped her into it. She brushed Laurel's tumbled hair and arranged it deftly in a loose topknot. Daisy seemed as agitated as Mrs. Lanyon had. Or perhaps "agitated" was not the right word. Excited, perhaps, agog. But why?

"Who are these people who have so graciously descended on us?" she asked the maid.

"Miss Diana Cardew and Mr. Lyle Cardew, ma'am."

"Married?" She had not noticed the "miss."

"No, Mrs. Tregarth. They be brother and sister." Daisy was searching Laurel's face for a sign of something. Her gaze was speculative. It unnerved Laurel.

"I trust my appearance is all that it should be, Daisy?" she asked sardonically.

Daisy had the grace to look abashed. "Aye, ma'am. 'Ee looks very well." But privately she wished her mistress's eyes shone brighter and her cheeks weren't so pale. And there were violet shadows beneath her eyes. Daisy's heart went out to her. She looked so miserable—but if only she wouldn't reveal any of that misery this afternoon . . .

"Well," said Laurel, "on to the slaughter." Now, why had that phrase come to her? Slaughter, indeed. That was the kind of remark which had so infuriated her mother. She squared her shoulders, took a last glance at her reflection in the mirror, and went along to the staircase. Relieved that her mistress seemed to have overcome her blue devils, at least for the present, Daisy hurried down the back stairway to tell the others.

Diana Cardew sat in the drawing room, concealing her true feelings. There was no trace of the tumult inside her in her coolly smiling manner or in her lovely face. She had teased Derek good-naturedly about bringing home an American heiress, as had the Duke of Marlborough some years earlier. She was looking her best in a severe black riding habit which set off her golden-red hair and long-lidded green eyes. Her cheeks glowed from the ride across the moors; she had refused to go by carriage. She would not meet Derek's bride with anything but high color and high spirits. Her pride was her strongest possession, that and her love for Derek Tregarth. For years those two sentiments had motivated most of her actions. That they sometimes conflicted was inevitable, but never more than now.

Diana had learned the terrible news of his marriage just before Derek's return to Cornwall. She had overheard two of her maids gossiping—one had a cousin who worked at Tregartha. Quietly going into her room and shutting the door behind her, she had stared into her mirror and begun to laugh. She had laughed until the tears rolled down her cheeks, until her hysteria became choked convulsions. Then she had smashed the mirror. Years of deliberation, of prudent maneuvers to secure the only man she would ever love, who held her tantalizingly at arm's length, but whom she was certain would some day belong to her—they were all for nothing. After a period of time—a very long one, to Diana—when he was apparently in no hurry to take a wife, he had suddenly and unaccountably chosen another. *I should have gone to America myself,* she thought in anguish. *Oh, why didn't I go?*

But now she sat in the drawing room she had always assumed would be hers, listening to Derek talk about his trip, entertaining him with the latest social gossip. From time to time her brother Lyle glanced at her in admiration. This visit had been her idea; he would not have suggested it, knowing how she felt about Derek.

She had come down to breakfast that morning and said, "I believe it's time we paid a call to Tregartha. The newlyweds have had sufficient time to themselves, and Derek will consider it remiss if we do not visit. What do you say, Lyle?"

He had agreed readily; the ride there and back, the visit, would serve to fill the long afternoon. And he jumped at the chance to escape Kilworthy for a few hours.

Laurel entered the drawing room. Not waiting to be introduced, she smiled at the two fair-haired guests. With her hand outstretched, she said, "Miss Cardew, how do you do? And Mr. Cardew. It's good of you to call. I'm sorry to have kept you waiting. Please, sit down."

"I've asked Mrs. Lanyon to bring tea, Laurel," said Derek.

She nodded, sitting beside him on the Empire sofa with its scrolled arms. "Do you live nearby, Miss Cardew?"

So Derek had never even mentioned her to his new bride. Diana forced herself to smile charmingly. "At Kilworthy—it's not far. Do call me Diana. Laurel is a lovely name. What do you think of Tregartha, and Cornwall?"

"I've fallen in love with both," Laurel said evenly.

"Cornwall must seem vastly different from New York. I sincerely hope you won't find it too dull here."

"I can assure you I won't," said Laurel. "Oh, thank you, Mrs. Lanyon," she said as the housekeeper set down the tea tray.

"You must tell us how you and Derek met, Laurel," said Diana. "I won't conceal from you the fact that all of Derek's friends and acquaintances were surprised, to say the least, by the news of his marriage. And to an American." She smiled broadly, revealing straight, white teeth.

She's beautiful, thought Laurel. Graceful and elegant—voluptuous, too, with her wide red mouth and generous curves. With her practically on his doorstep, why on earth did Derek choose me? "Derek came to my sister's engagement ball in February."

Diana nearly caught her breath. "I understand you were just married in early March! I had no idea Derek could be so impetuous." Her long, green eyes teased him while inside she was fuming bitterly. They had met and married in a matter of weeks! How on earth had such a thing been possible?

Laurel stole a glance at Derek. He was saying something to Lyle about the estate. He seemed quite at ease. She felt her own brittle control grow tenuous. How long would these two stay? She knew instinctively that she and Diana could never be friends.

Diana set down her teacup and said, "Well, Lyle and I haven't just come to call, although we have been most anxious to make your acquaintance, Laurel. We have also come with an invitation."

Lyle started. An invitation? It was the first he'd heard of it; she'd mentioned nothing to him. What was going on behind those green eyes of hers? The last thing he wanted was to have people at Kilworthy. Not that he disliked Derek, nor did he bear him any grudge for not marrying Diana. His wife seemed all right. She had nice eyes of an unusual color—blue with a tint of purple. Her face was rather ordinary and she hadn't much figure . . . not that her figure or lack of it was of any consequence to him.

Laurel realized that Derek had deftly veered the conversation onto another topic before Diana could issue her invitation. She didn't think it would do much good. Diana seemed a strong-minded woman; if she was determined to invite them to Kilworthy, she would not leave until she had obtained an answer. Just then Derek turned to speak to Laurel, and Laurel, rather than looking at her husband, glanced across at Diana. She caught the stark hunger in the woman's gaze before it was swiftly suppressed.

So that's the way it is, she thought. That explained Mrs. Lanyon's dithering and Daisy's excitement. Diana must have been in love with Derek for years. Perhaps people had assumed they would marry one day. Why hadn't they? Why, for that matter, had Derek married *her?* Laurel saw a future of hollow misery stretching ahead of them. Her head throbbed; the bleakness of her thoughts showed in her pinched face.

Watching her, Diana felt a sudden surge of hope. Something was amiss. Husband and wife were behaving just as they ought, yet the atmosphere between them was strained. A slight lovers' spat? No, Diana's intuition told her, it was something more. The conviction grew as she observed them. The girl's composure was wearing thin; her eyes had a haunted look. Were both of them regretting the hasty marriage? Time would tell. And she was determined that they should come to Kilworthy. She would lure Derek away from this American chit if it was the last thing she did. And the victory would be that much sweeter after the desolation of the last month.

Now she didn't have to fight her instincts. Diana had longed many times for Derek to make love to her, but she had repressed her desires. They had exchanged a few kisses over the years, that was all. And they had been more at Diana's instigation than at Derek's. Yet he had responded, and she was certain that he would again. This time she would not allow pride or false modesty to hold her back.

Diana smiled at Laurel. "I must tell you what I have in mind. It's in the way of a celebration: your marriage, Lyle's recovery from the wound in his leg. A house party at Kilworthy. It's been ages since we had one." That was only partly because of Lyle. The main reason was Derek's absence. Diana had had no desire to plan social events which Derek could not attend.

"I thought it would be amusing to have a Beltane Festival as they used to do in Cornwall. You know, Beltane, the wicked Walpurgis Night when witches were supposed to flit about, the eve of May first. I'll invite Dr. Polgreen so he can tell us all the old customs. What do you say, Laurel, to a real Cornish festival?"

"It sounds . . . very interesting," said Laurel lamely. Actually, she had no idea what Diana was talking about. She only knew she did not wish to go to Kilworthy.

But Diana had turned jubilantly to Derek. "See, Derek? Laurel needs to get out and meet people. You can't keep her

ECHOES OF THE HEART 95

buried at Tregartha forever. We've all left you to yourselves for weeks now, but the honeymoon is over." She tilted her head to one side.

It certainly is, thought Laurel, and she knows it. But there is something she does not know. I may have a surprise for her. And for Derek.

"It's good of you, Diana," said Derek smoothly. "Well, Laurel?"

They were all looking at her. She tried to read her husband's expression. Did he wish to go? She heard herself saying, "I've heard a great deal about Dr. Polgreen from Derek."

"And you must meet him. The house party will be the ideal opportunity. It will begin on April 29. Perhaps even our resident ghost will make an appearance!" Diana said gaily.

"Ghost?" Laurel echoed. "Do you really have one?" She blinked at Lyle and saw he had stiffened. Hot color flooded his face, yet his thin nostrils were white.

"Lyle insists we have, though I must say I've never noticed anything out of the ordinary. It seems to have just taken up residence at Kilworthy since Lyle's return from the war. Perhaps someone besides Lyle will sense its presence!"

Lyle was furious with his sister. It was all he could do not to get up and limp from the room. She was making a fool of him in an attempt to claim Derek's attention. But the awkward moment seemed to have passed; Derek was saying something about a play they had attended in London. At least Diana had not told them that he'd changed rooms, moving his things out of the six-sided room in the old part of the house which had always been his. Not that that had helped. Whatever it was was not confined to that room. Whatever it was had pursued him. The beastly cold, the feeling of loathing levelled at him, his own helplessness—it was worse than anything he had experienced in the war. And so at night he drank brandy, a lot of it. Usually it helped. If he could drink himself into a stupor before going upstairs, if he could fall, insensible, into bed . . .

* * *

"Do you want to go?" asked Laurel when they had gone.
"Hmmm?"
"To Kilworthy, Derek. Do you want to go?"
His voice was cool. "Not especially."
"Well, she took our acceptance for granted. I couldn't think of an excuse. You neither, evidently. But one has occurred to me now. Let's go away, Derek."
"Go away?" His black brows drew together. He regarded her in pained surprise. "Why on earth should we leave Tregartha? We've only just come. Or do you think that Tregartha is haunted, too?" She saw a trace of his old lopsided smile.
Perhaps it is, thought Laurel. It's as good an explanation as any. "We could go to the south of France, or to Switzerland. Just for a few weeks." She took a deep breath. "Derek, I love you. And you've said you love me. But something has gone wrong. We've lost something. Perhaps if we were to go away for a time . . ."
"You think we'd find it?" He shrugged. "Perhaps you're right. But I'm not leaving Tregartha. You may, naturally, do whatever you wish. If you'll excuse me, I have some work to do."
When they met that evening, their polite masks were once again in place, all the more secure for having slipped down hours before. Laurel had retreated behind a protective haze once more, her emotions numbed.

One afternoon there was a knock at her sitting room door. It was Martha. Laurel had not seen the old woman in weeks. She asked her to sit down and rang for some tea. Through the haze she saw Martha's eyes regarding her with pity and concern.
"I've come about 'ee and Master Derek," she said. "Does he know?"

"Know what?" asked Laurel dully. She did not want to talk about Derek.

"That 'ee be goin' to have a baby?"

Laurel winced. Her vagueness dwindled; grief penetrated her mask. "How—how did you know?"

"It's a look 'ee have," was all Martha said.

Laurel regarded her in dismay. "No, I haven't told him. How can I? We don't talk any more. He thinks we should never have married."

"It were meant for 'ee two to meet and marry. But tes brought 'ee and the master closer to the pain, the fear . . . to what ails him."

"What should I do?" She brought up her hands in a helpless gesture.

"Don't give up. Fight for what belongs to 'ee. The day 'ee came to my room I felt it. 'Twas a darkness, and tes grown since. 'Ee must face what be comin', 'ee and the master. And take care when 'ee goes to Kilworthy."

Even Martha was warning her about Diana Cardew. She would provide a diversion, perhaps a temptation, to Derek. Laurel said nothing.

"There be bad times ahead, missus. But the master do love 'ee. If 'ee minds that, it will come right in the end. Don't 'ee forget that the master be sufferin' as well. The baby may be the savin' of 'ee."

They rode to Kilworthy on a beautiful, clear day. A gentle wind blew over the rugged hills which were bright with splashes of pink and orange anemones. The carriage took them through Pendreath, over the stream where the sycamores stood guard. Gradually the moors gave way to lush green downs.

"Are Diana's parents still alive?" she asked Derek, rousing herself from her vagueness.

"No. An aunt lives with them at Kilworthy. But she's been

bedridden since she was in her twenties, I believe. She fell from her horse a long time ago, before I was born."

"Do you know her well?"

He shook his head. "I've had very little contact with her over the years. Once in a while she would be brought down to dinner when there were guests."

They were clattering through the streets of Landrawna, a pretty village with stone cottages nudging one another in stair-step fashion. It was set high on a half-moon shaped cliff, and there was a sheltered harbor below dotted with fishing boats.

"Kilworthy is not much farther," said Derek.

Out of the carriage window Laurel saw rich, cultivated fields; they were climbing up and away from the sea. A short while later the house came into view. It was vast and sprawling with towers sprouting haphazardly from the roof.

"Rather hideous, isn't it?" said Derek. "The basic house was Jacobean, but Diana's grandfather remodelled it."

Laurel did not answer. She was staring at the house. Derek heard her swift intake of breath and turned to look at her. Her hand was pressed against her stomach in an instinctively protective gesture that he did not understand. Her heart had begun to hammer and there was moisture beading on her upper lip. She felt hot and stifled. Holding her handkerchief to her mouth, she tried to fight off the rising queasiness.

Derek was still watching her. "Are you all right?" he asked, his voice neither cool nor distant.

Through the nausea she managed to nod. She took several deep breaths. This was not the time to tell him, not as they were arriving at Kilworthy.

The carriage went around the circular drive and turned to pass under the stone gatehouse. The darkness closed in; Laurel gripped the seat, willing herself not to cry out. There was a drumming in her ears. She felt trapped, imprisoned . . . she had to escape.

And then they were beyond the gatehouse, back in the warm sunlight, passing the tall, clipped yews which fronted the house. Laurel swallowed with difficulty, but the nausea was subsiding along with the unreasoned panic.

I have nothing to fear from Diana Cardew or her house, Laurel told herself firmly. Because I am carrying Derek's child.

Five

Diana greeted the Tregarths with great animation, brushing her cheek against Laurel's and leading her across the black and white tiled floor to the curving staircase. Derek followed a few steps behind. On the floor above, she stopped.

"Here are your rooms. I hope you'll be quite comfortable."

Rooms. So Diana had allotted them separate bedchambers. She was providing yet another barrier to add to those already between them. Wilting from her inexplicable recoil at the sight of Kilworthy, Laurel could not summon enough energy to feel angry.

"If there is anything you need, you have only to ring. Luncheon will be served in about half an hour. I'll leave you both to get settled." Her sea-green eyes moved from Laurel to Derek, resting deliberately on his face. She looked lovely in her turquoise gown.

When she had gone, Derek went into his room and shut the door between them. With a sigh, Laurel opened one of her bags and began to dress for luncheon. They had just arrived, and she was already longing for the ordeal to be over.

They met the others in the drawing room over glasses of sherry. The furniture was upholstered in gold velvet. Long, heavy curtains draped with elaborate tassels framed the tall windows. On the floor was a magnificent Oriental carpet in shades of burgundy, gold, and blue.

Laurel took stock of the weekend guests. There was Cynthia Lantallick, a cold, haughty woman in her early thirties who did not warm to Laurel in the slightest, and her husband, Michael, stocky and affable. There were also Mrs. Roslyn, a widow, and her daughter Annabel, a demure girl of about nineteen. And there was Dr. Henry Polgreen, an older man with thick white hair and bright blue eyes. He had greeted Laurel warmly and she expressed appreciation for the thoughtful note of congratulations he had sent them some weeks earlier.

"We all thought Derek a confirmed bachelor," boomed Michael Lantallick. "Could have knocked us down with a feather when we heard he'd brought back a bride from America. That was the last thing we ever expected, eh, Doctor?"

Diana looked down the long dinner table at Michael. He had had plenty to drink already and it was barely past midday. Rumors were circulating about his business failures, but she had seen neither him nor Cynthia in several months. That he had always been jealous of Derek Tregarth she was well aware, having derived considerable amusement from it in the past. As for Derek, he had always seemed unconscious of the other man's thinly concealed envy.

Cynthia Lantallick's supercilious gaze surveyed Laurel as she conversed with Dr. Polgreen. She was beautifully dressed, of course; one would expect that of an American heiress, thought Cynthia. But Cynthia disliked Laurel's voice with its flat vowel pronunciations. And she was rather a nonentity. What on earth had possessed the arrogant Derek Tregarth to marry her? She had always assumed that he and Diana Cardew would make a match of it. I wonder what Diana's feeling now, she thought with a slight smirk. It might be interesting to observe the three of them. If only Michael would not drink too much and make a fool of himself—and her . . .

Not much of a figure, Michael was thinking about Derek's new bride. He liked more curves himself. She was a bit pale and unhealthy-looking, too. Not at all like Diana, who was radiant today; he had always thought Diana would make an ardent bedmate. But she had never had eyes for anyone but Derek. Years before at a Twelfth Night party, he had kissed her, but she had rebuffed him with her cool, mocking gaze and soft laughter. Wonder how she's taking the little American bride, thought Michael maliciously. Probably wishes she could claw her eyes out. Diana wasn't as young as she once was. She'd waited years for Derek Tregarth to make up his mind and now suddenly he was no longer available. Why had she organized this affair? Diana and Lyle hadn't attended any of the recent social events; the excuse was given that Lyle was recuperating from the wound to his leg. He seemed none too fit now, his face haggard and the limp obvious. Would he walk down the aisle soon with Miss Annabel Roslyn? Her mother must hope so. The Roslyn household was not as prosperous as it had once been. Whose was? Michael thought bitterly. Whose—except Derek Tregarth's. And now he has his wife's millions. Perhaps that explained his bizarre marriage. Perhaps Derek's finances weren't as sound as people believed. But even Michael had to admit that wasn't very likely.

Dr. Polgreen was telling Laurel that he had visited Canada some years before where two of his nephews were living.

"I daresay many of us have relatives who've settled across the Atlantic," said Mrs. Roslyn.

"That's right, Mrs. Tregarth," said Michael. "You've done it the wrong way round. Americans don't come here to live. It's the Cornish who emigrate. Cornwall's a dying land." His voice had a trace of sourness.

"Changing, certainly, but not dying, I hope," said Dr. Polgreen pleasantly. "We must look to different horizons. Cornwall can no longer live isolated as it once did—the world has become too small for that. And our heyday of mining for tin and copper is over and probably will not be revived. But hopefully those who have emigrated have gone on to better lives, better wages."

Michael scowled. The wages his family had paid their miners had always been adequate. Why, they had had roofs over their heads, hadn't they? If they couldn't manage on the money they made, it was their own fault. The mine had even employed a doctor who had seen to their health. Precious waste of money that had been, his father had often said so. And then when the mine began to run low, he and his father had been forced to let a number of them go. They had gone over to Wheel Charity, Derek Tregarth's remaining mine. Michael had been appalled when he heard how much he paid his miners. The man was a fool, Michael's father had snorted. He'd be ruined in a twelve-month. But he had not been. It was the Lantallicks' mine which had produced less and less tin and yet cost more and more to run. His father had died, leaving a mountain of debts which ate away his inheritance and Cynthia's portion. The mine was closed for good now and they were on the verge of ruin. And Derek Tregarth, as cool as you please, had brought home a millionaire's daughter! Michael's heavy face darkened. That damned fellow had the devil's own luck.

His wife Cynthia had not wanted to come to Kilworthy. She'd complained she had nothing to wear and she had no desire to sit at table with a vulgar American who would doubtless flaunt her wealth in all their faces. But Michael had got round her. He'd told her to order what she liked from the dressmaker. And how would they pay her? she'd asked witheringly, but was quick to oblige. Neither of them wanted to discuss the issue uppermost in both their minds. The house and lands were mortgaged; Michael still owed the bank a large sum. He had to do something soon, though. Those damned money-lenders would take everything unless he found a way to bring in some capital. He had heard talk about a new venture of Derek's and wanted to be in on it. The man had an uncanny knack for increasing his means.

"Derek tells me you are writing a book about Cornwall," Laurel was saying to Dr. Polgreen.

"Let's just say I'm collecting information on the old customs and superstitions," he said, smiling. "Most of them are fast disappearing, such as the ceremony of 'crying the neck.' "

"What is that?"

"A sort of ritual begun long before Christianity—no one knows how far back it goes. It was watered down over the years to the version which existed until this last century when machines put a stop to the work which once had been done by hand. 'Crying the neck' was a way of celebrating the harvest of corn or wheat. I witnessed it many times as a boy. The 'neck' was the top of the last stalks of corn to be cut. It represented the body of the corn spirit which had just been beheaded in the harvest. In a solemn ceremony, the reapers would mourn the death of the corn spirit and then the mood would change; there would follow much laughter and merrymaking, and the neck itself would be decorated with ribbons and flowers and hung in the farmhouse kitchen. In the remote past, a human being would have been sacrificed to prevent failure of the crops. But after the Irish monks Christianized Cornwall, that grisly practice was abandoned and a more benign one developed in its place. The significance of the 'neck' was lost; it became merely an enjoyable tradition that the harvesters looked forward to. There would be a great feast provided by the landowner as well."

"There are parallels in some of the myths of the ancient civilizations," said Derek. "In Egypt, Osiris was the god of the harvest. He died violently but was resurrected. The Romans observed the Egyptians performing similar acts when they were announcing the death of Osiris every year. The ancestors of the Iberians who settled in Cornwall were from Egypt, and must have brought the original custom with them in the New Stone Age. They're the ones who erected all our stone monuments—tombs, most of them."

"Even the way the Cornish people speak, their word-order, resembles Iberian syntax," said Dr. Polgreen. "The English—and Americans, of course—would say, 'Are you going to do it?' But the Cornish man or woman who has not been formally educated says—"

"—Going to do it, are 'ee?" broke in Diana, and they all laughed.

" 'Ee' being the provincialism of 'thee,' " added Dr. Polgreen.

"Tell us about the Beltane festivals, Doctor," said Diana.

"Well, those ceremonies held at the beginning of May, or May Eve, were to ward off bad luck. May was believed to be the month of witches and evil spirits. The Celts built enormous bonfires and executed their criminals by burning them; Julius Caesar wrote about it. In more recent times it became the custom to fashion the figure of a man or woman out of greenery and burn that. It would be tossed into the fire to keep evil away, and for healthy livestock and a good crop."

"I thought bonfires were lit on Midsummer Eve," said Annabel.

Dr. Polgreen nodded. "They were. The Midsummer bonfires were lit to pay homage to the sun on the summer solstice. The Beltane fires had a different purpose. The Celts depended on their herds for survival. The animals grazed all summer and then provided the people with food for the following winter. In May, for whatever reason, they believed their animals to be especially vulnerable to death and disease caused by witchcraft. Hence, the various ceremonies. Later, of course, they became harmless festivals which had lost their grimmer significance."

"I find all of this rather tasteless," said Cynthia Lantallick. "These boorish old customs are better off buried and forgotten, Dr. Polgreen. Let them die. This is the early twentieth century, after all. Surely you do not wish to go back to those barbaric times."

"Of course not, Mrs. Lantallick," said the doctor, not at all offended at her rebuke. "And, yes, many of the old ways do seem foolish, even outlandish, to the broadened minds of today. But I do believe it's most important that they be collected before they vanish altogether. Future scholars may wish to study and analyze these customs to better understand the human psyche. There is a growing interest in the cultures of prehistoric times. Sir James Frazer's comprehensive study, *The*

Golden Bough, is a prime example. In my own small way I wish to gather the myths and practices of the Cornish people. Cornwall is unique, or it was, because of those old ways. Studies on what makes Cornwall distinctive, even those in travel books, will draw visitors and, hopefully, boost our failing economy."

"So the Londoners can come down and gape at us?" asked Cynthia waspishly. "And talk about how backward and superstitious the common people are? I don't find that notion appealing in the least, Doctor."

Michael frowned at his wife. He should have spoken to her about what was on his mind. Now she could ruin everything. Derek and Henry Polgreen were agreed on the necessity of the conversion of the Cornish economy.

"Not at all, Cynthia," he said amiably. "The good doctor is right. Cornwall will be an ideal place for visitors. Its summers are the hottest in England; our moors are as good as any in Yorkshire for riding or hunting, flowers bloom on the southern coast most of the year, and there's the sea for sailing and fishing. If Dr. Polgreen's book makes 'em want to come, I say it's an excellent thing!"

"And do you expect us to take in paying guests, Doctor?" asked Diana, amused.

"I'm certain that won't be necessary, Miss Cardew," Henry Polgreen assured her, smiling.

"Rumor has it Derek here is thinking of building a hotel for visitors who'll come for a dose of clean sea air and a few of Dr. Polgreen's tales," said Michael.

There was a slight pause. "You, Derek, running a hotel?" asked Diana, her wide, red mouth parting in a provocative smile. "What a fascinating idea."

"I didn't say I would run it," said Derek shortly. His face showed no expression.

"No, indeed," said Michael heartily. "He could find a good man or two to do that for him. An investment, eh, Derek?"

And you can put your wife's money to good use, he added to himself.

Laurel was as startled as any of them. Diana was quick to note this and the realization pleased her. So he had not discussed his plans with her. It was another sign that their marriage, so new, so precipitant, was failing. What a good idea this house party had been!

"My family goes to Newport every summer," said Laurel. "That's in Rhode Island, on the ocean. It's beautiful, and I know the town has profited in many ways from the summer visitors. It was prosperous before the Revolution, but fell on hard times. The economy has been revived by the New Yorkers and others who come in the summer."

Cynthia suppressed a yawn. She found all this talk of economy very tedious. Not to mention *vulgar*. People weren't supposed to talk of such things, at least not on social occasions. For her part she hated the discussion of money. Even more she hated the discussion of no money. Deliberately she smoothed the sleeve of her new pale green gown.

"What about you, Mr. Cardew? What do you think of summer visitors descending on Cornwall?" asked Mrs. Roslyn. He had said little all through luncheon despite her efforts to draw him out. She was greatly frustrated and perplexed by his distant manner. Poor, dear Annabel—so sweet, so pretty—deserved far more attention than he was paying her. Before Lyle had left for South Africa, they seemed to have reached an understanding, although nothing formal had been said. But since his return he had not written or called. Annabel had written to him, welcoming him back, and asking him to call when he was able. They had heard nothing until Diana's invitation. *At last,* Mrs. Roslyn had thought. And Annabel's sagging spirits had been given a great lift. But now, here they were at Kilworthy, and Lyle was acting quite unlike his old self. He had always been cheery and playful.

"I can't see the harm in it, ma'am," Lyle answered. He didn't care whether Cornwall sprouted an army of hotels. Or whether the place died a total death. It meant nothing to him. His hand shook as he reached for his wineglass. He had slept fitfully the night before, jolting awake every so often in fear the cold had come. It never did, but his dread of it made it impossible for him to sleep soundly. If only Diana had not invited Annabel and her mother! She had sent the invitation without telling him.

"I thought you liked Annabel Roslyn," she had said in surprise to his protests. "The two of you were fond of one another before you left for South Africa. I thought you'd want to see her, now that you are feeling better. If you are worried she will think less of you because of your limp, I'm certain you're wrong."

He had wanted to shout that he never wanted to see Annabel again. There was no earthly reason why he should. But of course he couldn't say this to Diana. He had angrily limped from the room, his face set in lines which aged him far beyond his twenty-four years. The only reason he had gone along with her plan for the weekend house party was the desperate hope that with Kilworthy full of guests, he might get a brief respite from whatever it was that plagued him relentlessly.

After luncheon, Diana suggested a walk in the extensive formal gardens behind the house. They rose from the table, though not all of them elected to go outdoors.

Out in the garden, Laurel observed that Diana had maneuvered the situation to her own advantage. She made a pretense of asking Derek's advice concerning one of the sluices on the estate and swiftly spirited him away. Laurel was left with Dr. Polgreen, Annabel, Mrs. Roslyn, and Lyle.

"Your sister tells me you have taken an interest in your father's greenhouse," said Mrs. Roslyn brightly to Lyle.

Damn Diana! Couldn't his one haven belong to him alone? It was his sanctuary and he resented Diana mentioning it. "I'll show you, if you like," he said politely, and they walked down the gravelled path toward the glass structure.

It was warm and humid in the greenhouse. Laurel began

to feel queasy again. She took a few steps away from the others. Their voices flowed over her as she swallowed hard, trying to subdue the rising nausea. Perhaps she had better go outside—the cool breeze would restore her.

Turning, she saw Lyle reach out, cup one of the blooms in his hand, and stroke a petal with his fingertips. Laurel stared, mesmerized. Her stomach heaved violently. She uttered a strangled moan and stumbled toward the door.

The others looked over in surprise. Dr. Polgreen caught her arm and she swayed against him. He led her gently outside. Her face was a sickly greenish-white; she looked quite ill.

"Come, Mrs. Tregarth, we'll go and sit on that bench there. It was uncomfortably close in there, wasn't it? I'm not too fond of greenhouses myself. They remind me of the tropics—I spent a lot of time there sweating in my tent."

His voice seemed far away. "Dizzy . . ." Laurel whispered.

"Bend forward. That's it. Put your head down, further down, between your knees. Don't give a thought as to how it looks. It's the best cure for a dizzy spell. Now, breathe slowly and deeply."

"Those flowers," she murmured. "Like pale skin. His fingers . . ." She shuddered.

The doctor was puzzled. He had assumed the rich meal had not agreed with her. She doubtless wasn't used to heavy English fare, at least not in the middle of the day. Dr. Polgreen felt a spurt of irritation toward Derek. He ought to be here with his new wife, not leaving her among strangers. Whether it was nerves or the luncheon, the girl wasn't well.

"Do you think you could sit here for a few minutes alone? I want to get you a glass of cold water."

Laurel straightened. "No, please don't go. I'm feeling better. I don't know what came over me in there." She smiled wanly.

He studied her critically. Her color was improving and her voice sounded stronger. But her violet-blue eyes were dark, the pupils enlarged.

"How about a cup of tea? Or some brandy might be better." Why, he wondered, did she look like someone who had sustained a terrible shock?

"You mean, go back to the house?" she asked.

He nodded.

"All right," she said gratefully. "I'd like a cup of tea." She stood up and was relieved to see her balance was restored.

A possibility occurred to him. She could be expecting a child. That would explain everything, except the odd words she spoke just outside the greenhouse. He did not clearly recall what she had said—something about Lyle's flowers. Possibly they had reminded her of something painful, a funeral perhaps. That would also account for the stricken look in her eyes.

They walked back to the house, crossing the terrace and entering the hall. Inside a small sitting room done in purple and dark green, Laurel sat down and Dr. Polgreen rang for tea, a cloth, and a basin of cold water.

"I'm afraid I'm a bother," said Laurel.

"Not at all, my dear. I know you are feeling better; you look better. But a cold compress on your forehead and at the back of your neck will further restore you. Humor me, my dear. Your husband is a great friend of mine, despite the difference in our ages. Sometimes I feel he's like a son I never had. When he wrote me from New York about your upcoming wedding, I was overjoyed."

Laurel smiled. "I can scarcely be making a good impression. I'm not ordinarily sickly. It's just lately I've . . ." She broke off when the maid came with the tea tray.

Dr. Polgreen poured her a cup with plenty of milk and sugar. She took it, sipping slowly. He was tempted to delicately put forth the question about her possible condition. She might not have guessed herself. It was appalling how little upper-class young women knew about the workings of their own bodies. The lower classes were much more matter-of-fact in such matters. But Derek's bride was an American—surely they had more sense and less modesty.

Laurel pressed the cold cloth to her forehead. "You ought to rejoin the others in the gardens. I'm perfectly well now."

"I've seen those gardens many times, Mrs. Tregarth."

"Won't you call me Laurel? I've been looking forward to meeting you for weeks. Derek speaks very highly of you. I admit I've felt a bit ill at ease today. You all know each other so well and I didn't even meet Derek until recently."

"We're an insulated lot here, I'm afraid. The best thing Derek could have done was to bring back a wife from abroad. Cornwall, and the Cornish gentry, are in need of some new blood, if you'll forgive the expression."

"Things . . . happened very swiftly," said Laurel. But now time had slowed to a crawl and their future was a murky, sluggish river. She made an effort to change the subject. "I've been fascinated by what I've seen of Cornwall—the Virgin Sisters, the shuddering stones, the fougou . . ." The last came out inadvertently.

"Ah, yes, the fougou. Now that is interesting unless one is claustrophobic. That would have been the refuge of the people in Iron Age times or before. They could hide underneath the fort if they were threatened. Perhaps it also served as a cool storage area, or a sort of hospital where the sick were tended. Doubtless it was used in different ways by different people."

I *knew* it, she longed to say. I knew my way in, and Derek got so angry . . . But she couldn't tell him that; it sounded crazy.

Dr. Polgreen went on. "For instance, it's believed that the fougous were used by smugglers back in the eighteenth century."

"Smugglers?" She smiled. "Sounds like something out of a novel. Robert Louis Stevenson or someone like that."

He grinned. "Pure romance, isn't it? But I can assure you that smuggling played a great part in the history of Cornwall."

Just then Derek entered the room. "So here you are, Laurel. I've been looking for you."

"Have you?" she asked softly, something not quite a smile curving her lips.

"Lyle said you'd left the greenhouse with Henry. Are you all right?"

"Quite. Dr. Polgreen has looked after me very well." There was no mistaking the sharp glint in her gaze or the hostility in her tone. Derek flushed, glancing from her to the doctor. "Thank you, Henry."

Dr. Polgreen stood up. "Your wife and I have been enjoying a most pleasant talk. But she should go up to her room and rest. I place her in your capable hands, Derek."

Derek nodded stiffly, not meeting the doctor's eyes, which were mildly reproving. He and Laurel went upstairs. When they reached her room, she said, "There is no need for you to remain. I'm certain you can find some way to occupy your time." She went over to the dressing table and sat down. Derek stood in the center of the room, his black brows drawn together. He had not seen her like this before—aloof, even sarcastic. Lately she had been quiet, subdued, and that had made it easier for him to disregard her.

"What was wrong with you?" he asked after a pause.

"In the greenhouse? Oh, a touch of indigestion. The place was stifling, and after all that rich food . . ." She shrugged, her tone dismissive. She began to pull the pins from her hair.

"I'm relieved you're all right."

"Are you?" In the mirror she looked at him, again with that odd, mocking smile. "So—did you help Diana with her pressing estate business?"

He made a careless gesture with his hand. "A muddle over a drain. Nothing Lyle or one of the men couldn't have dealt with."

"But none of them would do for her, would they? Well, were you pleased?"

"Pleased about what?" he echoed.

"To be reunited with your old lover."

He gazed at her in shock. "I don't know what you mean, Laurel. Diana is not—and never was—my lover. I was gone a short while and then went back to the gardens to look for you. Lyle said you seemed unwell and Henry was with you. I searched the gardens and then came to the house." The sight of her, the tone in her voice, unnerved him. Her wealth of dark hair spilled over her shoulders. His pulses began to throb.

Laurel was unfastening the buttons of her gown. "Oh, yes, I disappeared, too. With the good doctor." She laughed shrilly. Lifting the gown over her head, she tossed it onto the floor.

Swallowing with difficulty, Derek took refuge in indignation. "I hope you are not attaching any significance to my leaving you after luncheon. I came back as soon as I could."

"Why, what sort of significance, Derek?" Laurel turned around to face him. "That Diana used a paltry excuse to be alone with you, and that you went with her willingly? What possible significance could I draw from that?" Her gaze was mocking, her voice low and sweet.

"How in hell should I know?" he cried furiously. Her face was tilted up to him. He could not stop looking at her bare throat and the tops of her breasts pushed high by her corset. With an effort he dragged his gaze back to her face. But that was impossible as well. Now he was drowning in her violet-blue eyes.

She stood up and came toward him. "You don't believe that I'm jealous, do you? That I resent you being alone with her? That I don't trust you? Surely you can't believe that. Not when we are so much in love, so happily married, so eager to be together like this . . ."

He could barely breathe; his senses were overflowing, his loins pounding.

She laughed again and wound her arms about his neck, pressing her body against his. She smelt faintly of violets, her skin soft and white. She lifted her mouth to his.

With something between a cry and a groan, he gripped her

fiercely. His body shuddering, he took her mouth hungrily, and then her throat, the gentle rise of her breasts. He held her tightly as though she might try to pull away. But she did not try. Her desire was as raging as his. She was beneath him on the bed, her petticoat pushed up about her waist. He did not even remove his clothes. His former abstinence, his iron control erupted in a white-hot union more explosive than any either had ever experienced. And she was saying over and over again, "Dirk, Dirk, Dirk . . ."

Diana was not at all happy. When she had asked Derek his advice about the drain, she had expected that he might be grateful for the ploy. That he would be glad of the opportunity to be alone with her. He used to enjoy her company, her energy, her quick wit. She had observed the way he and Laurel acted like strangers. They had barely looked at one another, much less spoken. Diana had been overjoyed; the American bride was not to his liking. Hope had stimulated her, made her radiant. Hadn't Michael Lantallick ogled her all through luncheon? She had felt intoxicated with expectancy.

Yet later, when they stood by the drain and she showed a pretty reliance on his opinion, he had answered her somewhat curtly and then suggested they join the others in the gardens. Diana had tried another pretext, this time putting her hand on his arm and standing close enough so he could smell the scent of carnations that she used.

But he had not responded. His expression was bland, his manner remote. It maddened her. How she wanted him! But she was not a fool. She had spent years waiting for him; she could wait a few more hours. This was not the time—that was obvious. With an offhand humorous remark she had led him back to the gardens. But Laurel was nowhere to be seen; she had gone off with Dr. Polgreen. The others thought she had felt faint. Derek's face had become grim as he strode away without a word or backward glance.

The rest of the party had returned in a desultory fashion to Kilworthy. Dr. Polgreen had met them with the news that Derek had taken Laurel upstairs to rest. She was feeling much better. Mrs. Roslyn suggested to Annabel that they take a rest as well, and Dr. Polgreen had gone with Lyle to play billiards. Diana was left standing alone in the hall. Oh, to hell with all of them, she thought.

One of the maids was speaking to her. "Miss Diana?"

"Yes, what is it?" she snapped.

"Miss Cardew be askin' for 'ee, miss. She wants to see 'ee summat fierce."

Diana uttered a stifled exclamation. What did her aunt want now? Why must she bother her when the house was full of guests and she herself full of frustration? She had no patience with Aunt Morva's whims, even less now. Why didn't she send for Lyle instead? They used to be close before he had gone off to fight the Boers. But since his return he had spent little time with his bedridden aunt, and she had stopped asking for him. The long chess games they had enjoyed together were a thing of the past. Once he had called their aunt an old witch. He'd looked shaken, frightened. Whatever it was that kept him awake at night, drinking brandy until all hours, Aunt Morva knew something about it. Lyle claimed it was a ghost. Well, she had a surprise for him.

"Very well, I'll go up and see her now," she told the maid.

Aunt Morva's bedroom was in the original section of the house. She sat up in bed, fully dressed, her silver hair coiled regally on top of her head. The room itself was crowded with furniture—tables, jostled chairs, bookshelves, bureaus, and chests. There was barely room to move about. But then Morva never left her bed, except when she was carried downstairs by two of the men. On the walls were photographs of a much younger Morva on horseback. Forty years earlier, she had been an outstanding rider, taking prizes at shows and hunts. Her father had left the running of the stables to her, even the procuring of the horses and their breaking in. To the grooms her word was law.

And then one day she had bought a magnificent black stallion. He did not take to Morva as other horses did. He did not take to anyone. The head groom advised Morva to sell him, but she had been determined to break him, to train him to become her new mount. What animal had opposed her for long? This horse would be no different.

She hadn't named him yet. She always waited until she had broken in a horse before she gave it a name. When they were wild and untrained, they seemed almost mythological. That was especially true of this horse.

Morva was good with animals—calm and soothing. But she had a ferocious temper. Once a maid had accidentally singed one of her riding habits. Morva had slapped the poor girl quite viciously. She couldn't abide incompetence or what she viewed as disloyalty.

Neither could she abide it in the black stallion. He was her horse and he would learn to follow her lead. Never had an animal defied her for so long. Then one morning he had seemed to submit. She was triumphant; she had earned his trust, his acceptance. No horse had proved her master yet, she had cried. The grooms were instructed to saddle him, to put the bit in his teeth.

When she was thrown, Morva had managed to extricate her feet so that she wouldn't be dragged. But she could not protect her back. And she had not stood on her legs since.

Diana had never had much to say to her aunt. As a child, she had been frightened by the prematurely lined face, the sharp tongue, and critical gaze which seemed to see right through her. She had dreaded the visits to her aunt's room that her father insisted she make every Sunday afternoon. Lyle, though, had not minded.

"So one of the chits finally gave you my message," said

Morva coldly. "Or did you just decide now to honor me with a visit?"

Diana sighed. "I came as soon as I heard you wanted me, Aunt. I've been busy entertaining my guests. What is it you need?"

"Who is here today?"

Was that all the old woman wanted? Surely one of the maids could have relayed the guest list. "Dr. Henry Polgreen, Mrs. Roslyn and Annabel."

Morva let out a harsh cackle. "Was that your notion or Lyle's?"

Diana stiffened. "I thought it would be good for Lyle to be with Annabel. I don't understand him at all since he got back from South Africa. He and Annabel seemed to have a sort of understanding before he left . . ."

"Like the understanding between you and Derek Tregarth?" said the old lady shrewdly.

Hot color rose in Diana's face but she kept her temper in check. In a verbal battle her aunt was always the victor.

"You won't do it, my girl," her aunt went on.

"What, Aunt?"

"Marry off that brother of yours."

"I am not trying to marry him off! I just thought he needed to be with people again."

Morva's gaze was mocking. "You had one reason and one reason only for this house party, Diana. Simply to see Derek Tregarth. But he's not alone, is he? He's brought his American bride with him."

"Is this why you sent for me?" asked Diana, bridling. "To remind me of Derek's marriage?"

Morva's bony arm shot out, gripping Diana's wrist. "I want to see her."

"What? See whom?"

"The new Mrs. Tregarth."

"Now why on earth—"

"Bring her to me."

Diana shook off her aunt's grasp and rubbed her wrist. The old lady was acting very strangely. She rarely agreed to see any visitors, had not done so in years. "She's resting now, Aunt Morva. She wasn't feeling well after luncheon."

"I'm not surprised. Not in this house. Not at Kilworthy. She must sense it as I do, as I have these last months. It's growing."

Diana stared at her aunt in puzzled exasperation. What on earth was she talking about? She sounded quite balmy. "Perhaps I should send for Dr. Polgreen, Aunt. You don't look well."

"Of course I don't look well, you foolish creature! I haven't looked well in forty years! What has that got to do with anything? I won't have that doctor up here. But I must see the girl!"

"In heaven's name, why? *Why* do you wish to see her?"

Morva leaned back against the pillows. She looked drained, exhausted. "It won't be to gloat, Diana, because he chose her over you. I simply want to talk to her."

Diana's hands balled into fists. "Derek was mine! He was mine!"

Morva wearily shook her head. "No, girl. He was never for you, though you tried hard to make him so. And now I know how betrayed you feel. But there is danger in feeling that way."

"Oh, what do you know of it?" cried Diana. "What do you know of anything, shut up in here the way you are? How can you possibly understand?"

Morva did not answer right away. She put out a trembling hand to draw her blanket over her legs. "I understand all too well. About you and Lyle—and myself. We are being judged, punished."

Diana frowned. "Punished! You sound like one of the chapel-going servants."

"Lyle knows. Or a part of him does."

Diana was becoming impatient. "I don't understand you,

Aunt Morva. What does Lyle know? The only thing concerning him is Kilworthy's ghost!"

"I would not jeer at him if I were you, Diana."

"Not you, too! Don't tell me you believe in his ghost as well! Do I have a surprise for the both of you! Another guest is on her way. We'll see what she has to say on the subject. She's a famous medium, and I've invited her to join the house party," said Diana defiantly.

Morva's eyes glittered darkly in her white face. For a few moments she did not speak. Then she said softly, "You are a fool, Diana."

Diana flushed. *"I'm* the fool? What about Lyle? He'll have to admit it's all nonsense. She's a fraud; these people always are. It will be amusing to catch her up to tricks. An interesting form of entertainment, you'll have to admit."

Morva turned her head to gaze out the window. "You have done something very stupid, very dangerous by sending for that person. And with the others here, the Tregarths . . ." Morva looked back at her niece. "If I were you, Diana, I would hope with all my heart that she is indeed a fraud."

Minerva Grey was used to people assuming she was a fraud. It did not worry her. She was a medium because she had no choice. She did not need the money; her family had left her well-provided for. Often she did not charge a fee. Her parents had died when she was entering her teens and she had gone to live with her maternal grandparents, respectable if unimaginative people.

The first demonstration of her peculiar ability came a year following her parents' death. She went to a schoolfriend's birthday party where they began to play a game of "Hide and Seek" about the large old house. Minerva opened a door on the second story which led to a small back stairway, now unused, the boards layered with dust. She climbed up two floors and found herself in a small area of the attic.

Delighted with her hiding-place, she was startled to see that someone else had discovered it before her—a little girl of about six or seven. She did not recognize her but that was hardly surprising in that army of children. The hostess believed that when one of her children had a birthday party, the others should be able to invite their friends as well. As a result, the parties at this house were chaotic, noisy, and very popular. One could be assured of many playmates, a splendid tea, and a good time.

"So you found this place, too," said Minerva. "You were quick. Well, we can share it."

"I was afraid when I heard you coming," said the little girl, her eyes wide.

"Why? Did you think I was 'it'? We won't be found for some time."

The child stared blankly at Minerva. Her face was very pale. "I was afraid you were my cousin Samuel. He—he sometimes looks for me."

"Oh, do you live here? Are you one of Emily's sisters?"

"I haven't any brothers or sisters. I'm an orphan. I live with Aunt Janice and Uncle Tony. And Samuel." She whispered the last name, giving a shudder.

"Are you cold?" Minerva asked. She glanced about the room. It was small, the walls dingy. There were damp patches on the ceiling. One window provided dim light, but there were no curtains and no furniture.

She studied the little girl, perplexed. What she had first taken to be a white party frock looked more like a nightdress. It was loose-fitting and came down to the child's feet.

"Where are your shoes?" asked Minerva. "Aren't your feet cold?"

The child shook her head, her fair hair long and wispy. "It's always warm up here in July."

"In July, perhaps, but certainly not in March," said Minerva. "You ought to be wearing shoes. It's cold out today—that's why the party is indoors and not in the garden."

ECHOES OF THE HEART

"Oh, is there a party today? I didn't know." For a brief moment she looked excited, but then her face resumed its drooping expression. "My aunt doesn't often give parties. But I'll stay here. I—I might see Samuel if I went down. If there is a party, he won't come looking for me."

Minerva frowned. "Who is this Samuel?"

"I told you. He's my cousin. Samuel Pringle."

"Samuel Pringle? I don't know him. This is the Eliotts' house, you know."

The little girl's huge eyes stared at Minerva. Slowly she shook her head. "I think you must be lost."

"What's your name?"

"Alice. Alice Pringle. What's yours?"

"Minerva Grey."

"Would you brush my hair, Minerva?"

"All right. But I haven't a brush."

"There's one on the dresser. It's Sally's. This is her room."

"Sally?"

"She's one of my aunt's maids. She lets me come in here to—to hide . . ."

Minerva's bewildered gaze swept the bare room. "A d-dresser?" she managed to ask.

"Yes, it's just there—oh!" The child gave a hollow gasp. "It's gone. And the bed, too. Where is it? Where is it?"

Minerva shook her head numbly.

"B-but if there is no bed, I can't hide under it! I can't hide from Samuel. Oh, please help me! Don't let Samuel near me—please!"

Waves of cold were rolling over Minerva. Speechless, she stared at the terrified child. She could not move. Every muscle, every joint was locked in place.

Then came the sound of footsteps on the stairs. The child's head jerked. She began to moan and plead with Minerva. "You must help me. It's him—it's Samuel. Don't let him . . . don't let him . . . t-touch me!"

Minerva was a statue of ice. She had never felt so cold, so

rigid. She could not even look behind her to see who was entering the little room. She could only watch Alice. And wish that she could not.

The child was shrinking back against the wall. On her face was a look of helplessness and hopelessness that Minerva was never to forget. Alice whimpered as she slid down the wall. Tucking her head and clasping her arms about her knees, she said, "No, no, nooo . . ."

Suddenly Minerva felt a violent tremor. Spinning around, she gazed at the doorway. There was no one there. Yet she had heard the footsteps herself. Pressing her hand to her mouth, she turned to look back at the child whose soft, pitiful cries had now ceased.

Minerva was alone in the room.

When, minutes later, she burst into the drawing room, white and shaken, a kind of order came over the happy confusion. The merry-makers stopped their shouting and playing, staring in silence at the distraught girl.

"A little girl . . . a little girl upstairs . . ."

Every woman with a daughter gasped and knew that first moment of horror when their worst fear materialized.

"What little girl?" asked Mrs. Eliott sharply. "Is she hurt?"

"I—I don't know. She—she's gone."

"Gone where?" shrieked one mother. "Who?"

Minerva's teeth were chattering. "She—she w-wasn't at the p-party. Her name is Alice Pringle. She was so afraid of her cousin Samuel. She—she wanted me to protect her. And now she's gone!" Minerva burst into wild sobs.

"Minerva Grey, what do you mean by this display? Polly, bring some cold water and a little brandy. I don't know what on earth has got into the girl. Now, Minerva, there is no child named Alice Pringle at this party. Nor is there a boy named Samuel. You have upset everyone with your hysterics. Calm down or I shall have to send for your grandmother."

Minerva sniffed and swallowed hard. Every mother, every child was staring at her. "But I *saw* her. I *talked* with her," she said. Her voice shook. "Alice Pringle. She was in the attic."

Mrs. Eliott surveyed her with increasing disfavor. "You are being wicked, Minerva. I don't allow lying in my house. Those attics have not been used in many years. There could not possibly be a little girl up there."

Minerva nodded, her eyes full of remembered shock and horror. "She was there. But . . . I think she's dead."

Six

Minerva was not invited back to the Eliotts' house. Emily Eliott was instructed not to play with her. So were all the other pupils at Miss Long's School for Girls. Miss Long saw no alternative but to dismiss Minerva. It was a pity, as the girl was remarkably bright and studious, but she had to consider the other students. Or, to be exact, their parents. Miss Long had received a number of letters from men whose wives had witnessed Minerva's scene in the Eliott drawing room. They had given their husbands no peace until the letters were composed and sent. Words such as "unbalanced" and "unstable" were used to describe Minerva. That Miss Long herself had never observed these qualities in the girl was beside the point. She had the well-being of her school to protect. But Miss Long, somewhat to her relief, was too late. Before she could post the letter concerning the dismissal, she had received one herself from Minerva's grandfather. He was removing her from the school.

The newspapers had got wind of the strange affair—how they did so was never explained. The ladies in the Eliott drawing room would never have related it to a common journalist, so perhaps one of the servants had passed on the story for a bit of spending money. The resulting articles ought to have vindicated Minerva. But, as is so often the case, they only served to turn what had been a distressing incident into a public sensation.

An old woman living in the town, after hearing of the Grey

girl's odd experience, recalled an old story she had heard in her youth. The reporter listened eagerly and then did some research of his own, coming on a tragedy which had occurred in July of 1798. The house had been built some years earlier for a Mr. Anthony Pringle and his bride. Mrs. Pringle had subsequently given birth to a boy named Samuel, and, when that boy was sixteen, an orphaned niece, Alice, had come to live with them. Less than a year later, the niece's small, broken body was discovered on the terrace at the back of the house. The inquest determined that she had fallen from one of the maids' rooms in the attic. The maid herself was not considered in any way responsible for the tragedy, but shortly afterward she left the Pringles' employ. It was not understood what Alice had been doing in a part of the house confined to the servants. There was one further piece of information that, at the time, was given no significance. Samuel Pringle had twice been expelled from school on grounds that were never revealed. Eventually the Pringles sold the house and left the district.

"The maid's name was Sally," said Minerva to the reporter who stopped her in the street. "She may have told Samuel's parents that he was . . . cruel to Alice, and they may have dismissed her. Or perhaps she could not stay in the house any longer and left of her own accord. She must have been too frightened to speak out. But she knew that Samuel was . . . evil. Poor little Alice—she may have jumped out to get away from him, or perhaps he pushed her because he was afraid she would tell his parents what he had been doing to her."

For days people crowded onto the sidewalk before the Eliott house and gaped. Mr. and Mrs. Eliott were furious. They and their friends, all affluent members of the town, denounced Minerva. They said she had heard the gist of the story somewhere and then had enacted the melodramatic scene to draw attention to herself. Others were kinder, stating that the loss of her parents had unhinged her mind so that she had imagined conversing with another orphan.

Minerva's grandparents reeled from the series of blows.

Nothing in their comfortable lives had prepared them for this event. Their granddaughter had become notorious, and not only in the Midland industrial town in which they lived. Minerva's overnight reputation as a "ghost hunter" was as bewildering to them as their own social ostracism.

In spiritualist circles Minerva was hailed as extraordinarily gifted. Letters came from all over England: she was entreated to contact dead loved ones; she was asked to visit houses their owners claimed were haunted. She was examined by a number of doctors who talked of changes in a girl's body at puberty and the arising hysteria which might ensue. Before long, the implications of their theory had branded Minerva "depraved" and "corrupt."

It was these last charges which brutally ousted Minerva's grandparents from their state of impotent shock. They bundled her off to Ireland to live with a distant relative. Surely in that remote place her notoriety would die a natural death.

But the imposed exile had anything but that effect. In that Celtic country, removed from the restrained, phlegmatic English, Minerva's abilities persisted, even blossomed. She visited a church where unaccounted-for lights and soft moans had been reported off and on for hundreds of years. Emerging from the building some time later, she did not cry nor was she frightened. In a voice weak from exhaustion and sorrow, she told the tale of a monk who took a village girl as his mistress. When she became pregnant, he had murdered her and buried her body under a section of the stone floor. Despite protests from the priest, the stones were dug up and the skeleton of a young woman found. The remains were given proper burial, and Minerva herself attended the service. That day she knew what her life's work was to be. There was no escaping it.

Minerva never again had an experience such as the one in the Eliotts' attic where she saw and spoke with a spirit. Perhaps the doctors had been right after all and the event was linked to her adolescence. When she was older, that particular ability had vanished. But she was still highly gifted, her senses tuned to emanations seldom noticed by others. The reasons behind the hauntings she investigated did not elude her for very long.

On her way to Cornwall that day in 1902, she was forty years old. She had never married. After her grandparents had died, never regaining their former status in the town, she moved to London and had lived there for most of the last nineteen years. She also travelled—to America, to Egypt and India. Friend to Oscar Wilde, to the later Pre-Raphaelite artists, to Alfred, Lord Tennyson, who himself was a strong believer in spiritualism, she spurned organizations such as Madame Blavatsky's Theosophical Society. She did, however, read the spiritualist's writings, considering seriously Madame Blavatsky's belief in astral projection and the idea of rebirth adopted from the Eastern religions.

Minerva Grey refused to hold seances. Ectoplasm never issued from her mouth; phantom faces never appeared on parts of her clothing. There were no rappings on tables or elevations of chairs. Those trappings of spiritualism did not interest her and were so often found to be worked by human hands. Her quiet, unassuming approach now kept her, for the most part, out of the public eye. She was no longer the subject of sensational news articles.

In the popular sense of the word she was not a medium. She considered herself an observer and recorder of past violent emotions. Often she was consumed with an overwhelming empathy and sadness which severely drained her spirits and energies. After one of these episodes, she would have to go to bed and rest, sometimes for weeks. Minerva had a devoted servant named Bridget who had accompanied her from Ireland. Bridget knew how to look after her beloved mistress. She had strongly objected to the proposed trip to Cornwall. Minerva had not recovered fully from her last endeavor in Lancaster where she had put to rest the emotional traces of a young woman who had been drowned as a witch well over two hundred years before.

Diana Cardew's letter was like many others Minerva received. Vague, it offered "something of interest" and was blatantly patronizing. Minerva generally refused these invitations. She was careful to preserve her gift and strength for the cases she instinctively sensed required her particular abilities. Despite the tone of the letter, Minerva was convinced that this was such a case. Diana Cardew might want a court jester at her house party, but she was merely the link. Bridget began to pack Minerva's things.

Minerva was often mistaken for a schoolmistress or governess. She was small in stature, and always tidily, even primly, dressed in grays, blues, and browns. Her hair, which was still a handsome honey-brown, was worn in a severe knot at the back of her head. She wore spectacles over eyes which were the color of sherry. She was the kind of person easily overlooked by those who did not come into contact with her peculiar talent. Neat in habits, she spoke only when it was necessary. Long ago she had submitted to her unusual lot in life and was at peace with herself. In most of the troubled situations she was asked to remedy, she was freeing the unhappy vestiges of women who had been wronged. Acknowledging their suffering, she assumed it, and in doing so, redeemed them. She understood well that sometimes betrayed women refused to move on, clinging to locales after death where they had been victimized in life. The horrors that had been imposed on them were relived over and over until the cycle could be broken. At times the spirits struck out in rage at the living, instilling a terror and turmoil that echoed their own.

Minerva Grey did not meet the guests at Kilworthy until dinner. She had changed her brown plaid travelling costume for a gown of midnight blue with white collar and cuffs. She had no inclination toward fashionable, elegant clothes.

Her bedroom was an inferior one. On an upper floor at the back of the house, she was set apart from the other guests.

This did not trouble her. There were things of far greater significance on her mind.

Purposely going down to dinner ten minutes early, she took a seat in the corner of the candle-lit drawing room where everyone was to gather. From this vantage point she could carefully observe the others without being noticed.

Diana herself started when she saw the small, still figure watching her from the shadows. "Miss Grey, I presume?" she said a bit testily. "I was informed that you had arrived. I hope you are comfortable?"

"Yes, Miss Cardew."

"Well, I daresay you'd like a few details. My brother—"

Minerva held up a hand. "Please, Miss Cardew. I would prefer to discover for myself. How many people do you have staying here?"

"Myself, my brother, and seven guests, not counting yourself."

Minerva did not answer immediately. Then she said, "And is there not one other, aside from the servants?"

Diana looked blank, then she nodded. "You must mean my aunt."

"An older lady."

Diana lifted one eyebrow. If the woman expected her to be impressed, she would be disappointed. She could have learned of Aunt Morva's existence from the maid who showed her her room. Diana refused to be taken in.

"She's afraid," said Minerva softly.

The look of contemptuous amusement was wiped from Diana's face. How on earth did Miss Grey know that? For Morva *was* afraid; Diana had witnessed that for herself that afternoon. And it was highly doubtful that her aunt would reveal her state of mind to one of the servants. She might show anger, but not fear.

Slightly shaken, Diana took stock of Minerva Grey. The woman was not at all what she had expected. She had envisioned a flamboyant character dressed in layers of gaudy folds with a painted face and strings of colored beads or stones. Someone to bring this party to life, someone to amaze, to entertain. But this poor slip of a creature in her plain gown and spectacles was all wrong for the part.

"Well . . . I have heard remarkable things about you, Miss Grey. I hope in the next couple of days you will bring something of interest to light." But she found it doubtful. This woman looked to be as dull as the party had been thus far, despite her mention of Aunt Morva.

Minerva knew that Diana was disappointed in her quiet manner and unprepossessing appearance. She had encountered that reaction many times before. The most theatrical mediums were the best known. Too often they were also frauds.

A fair-haired young man of medium build entered the room. His face was lined with discontent and something more. There were dark circles beneath his eyes. He tugged impatiently at his collar.

"Lyle, there you are. You must meet our surprise guest. Miss Grey, my brother, Mr. Cardew."

"Good evening, Mr. Cardew," said Minerva.

"How do you do, Miss Grey?" Lyle said in a polite but clearly puzzled tone. He glanced at his sister for clarification. Who on earth was this middle-aged woman sitting in their drawing room?

"Ah, I hear the others coming," said Diana. "Lyle, pour the madeira. And don't neglect Miss Grey."

Cynthia and Michael Lantallick came in. Just behind them was Dr. Polgreen. The men wore black and white evening dress; Cynthia was in claret satin which ill became her sallow coloring.

"Evening, all," said Michael cheerfully. "Newlyweds not down yet?"

No one answered him. Annabel entered with her mother. She wore a white organdy gown trimmed with lace. Lyle handed out glasses of madeira, Minerva taking hers with a word of thanks. So far she had gone unnoticed by the guests, which was just as well.

When the last two to arrive walked into the drawing room, Minerva scrutinized them with heightened interest. The dark-haired young woman wore a silk gown which alternated between blue and violet in the flickering candlelight. She smiled and nodded at the others, but Minerva could perceive an almost tangible sheath surrounding and insulating her. That she had created it herself for her own protection, Minerva was confident.

The man, evidently her husband, was tall with black hair and an uncompromising square jaw. He drank his wine in one swallow, watching his wife out of the corner of his eye. She did not look at him.

"Before we go in to dinner," Diana began, "there is someone I'd like you all to meet. An addition to our party, Miss Minerva Grey."

Minerva rose and came forward, startling a few of the others who still had not noticed her. She was introduced to each of the guests, who wondered how to place her. She was obviously not one of them, and yet here she was at Kilworthy ready to take her seat at table with them. Laurel and Derek Tregarth, immersed in their own thoughts, did not speculate about her at all.

"Miss Grey is a famous person," Diana said. "She often visits old houses such as this one, don't you, Miss Grey? You see, she is a spiritualist."

Mrs. Roslyn and Annabel wore identical expressions of amazement; Cynthia Lantallick surveyed Minerva with unconcealed distaste while her husband emitted a foolish guffaw. It was left to Dr. Polgreen to say, "Of course. I thought your name sounded familiar, Miss Grey. It is an honor to meet you. I have followed your work with great interest."

Minerva inclined her head. She was rather taken aback by the doctor's words. She had scant respect for the medical profession, and not just because those in the field scorned her occupation in blistering terms. She could not know then that it was his absorption in the strange beliefs of the Cornish people which had broadened his mind. He never dismissed or discounted what could not be explained rationally.

"Diana!" Lyle, red-faced, glared at his sister.

"I asked her here for you, Lyle. She can conduct a seance and draw out your ghost."

Lyle was furious; he jerkily poured himself another glass of wine and drank it.

"I do not conduct seances, Miss Cardew," said Minerva quietly.

Diana turned from her angry brother to Minerva, her brows raised. She was embarrassed by Lyle's reaction but refused to show it. "There must be some sort of a misunderstanding, Miss Grey. I thought it was a medium's business to hold seances."

"If I were a medium, I would doubtless do so," was the calm reply.

Diana glared at her. What sort of game was this woman playing? She ought to send her packing. The woman had come under false pretenses. How dare she refuse to conduct a seance? Did she actually believe she was here as an ordinary guest?

Minerva smiled slightly. "You have invited me and I have come, Miss Cardew. That is enough. You will not be disappointed." Minerva's gaze was steady and reassuring. Diana felt her displeasure evaporating. She turned away from Minerva and led the way to the dining room.

The dinner was lavish, but the atmosphere at the table was not a festive one. Lyle was hunched over in one of his sulks, and Derek refused to be drawn into bantering with Diana. Instead, his brooding gaze was focussed on his wife. Laurel was seated between Michael Lantallick and Henry Polgreen. Diana had expected Minerva to relate some of her experiences, but instead she and the doctor were talking about the Lake District. Cynthia and Michael were trying to draw Laurel out with little success. She was detached, offering no conversation of her own.

No breeding, thought Cynthia contemptuously. No notion of the proper way to behave. Did the Americans eat in silence? What was wrong with her? She threw Derek a withering look. Surely he could see that the new Mrs. Tregarth was impossible. Pale, sickly-looking, too, in spite of the ravishing silk gown. And where were the famous Tregarth jewels? Laurel wore nothing save her wedding and engagement rings. Even Cynthia herself had a few remaining pieces they had not been forced to sell, and she flaunted them proudly tonight.

What a grim, dull lot we are, thought Diana irritably. She gave up all efforts to charm Derek and sat glumly eating her dessert. Minerva Grey had to speak her name twice to get her attention.

"I should like to go over the house tonight with your permission, Miss Cardew."

"Why, certainly, Miss Grey." Perhaps the evening was not entirely lost. "Are we permitted to accompany you?"

"If you wish."

Lyle abruptly stood up and tossed his napkin onto his chair. "I'll leave the ghost-hunting to any of you who are interested," he said. "For my part I'll play cards with those who are not." He left the room, Annabel gazing after him in dismay.

"Your brother does not appreciate my being here," said Minerva.

Diana shrugged her shoulders. "He's the reason I asked you here. He swears the house is haunted."

Michael Lantallick laughed. "Lyle's gone off the deep end and no mistake, Di. He'll be seeing vampires next."

Diana would have made a sharp retort but Minerva spoke first. "You are amused, Mr. Lantallick. Many people are. But Mr. Cardew is right to feel something . . . unhealthy . . . in this house. Whether or not there is any harm intended remains to be seen."

Michael gaped at her. Derek rose. "I'll go and search out Lyle, if you will all excuse me."

"Annabel and I will have an early night," said Mrs. Roslyn stiffly. She disapproved of Minerva's presence and the proposed excursion.

"Very well," said Diana, her mouth tightening. "I hope you will sleep comfortably." It had never occurred to her that her houseguests would be anything but enthralled by Miss Grey, whether they took her seriously or not. She was distinctly put out.

"Don't worry, ladies. I shan't abandon you," said Michael. "The good doctor and I will see that you come to no harm, eh, Henry?"

Laurel said nothing, but she rose obediently and followed the others into the hall. As for Cynthia, she was bored. Any diversion would be better than nothing. Minerva seemed a colorless person, but she was prepared to give her the benefit of the doubt.

They each took a candle in a holder and began to wander about the rooms on the ground floor. Before long Minerva stopped and shook her head. "This is not the original part of the house."

"Well, no, it's not," said Diana. "My grandfather added this wing." *Probably one of the servants had told her, or even the man at the railway station. Or perhaps she knows something about architecture.*

"We must go to the original section," said Minerva.

"Very well. We don't use that part of the house any longer, except for the room belonging to my aunt. Lyle had a room there as well, but has since moved out."

They trooped down a long corridor to a heavy oak door at the end. "This particular door hasn't been used in some time," Diana explained. "It may be stiff. Michael, would you?"

"At your service, Di." He gave a few tugs before the door creaked open. A whiff of cold, musty air met them; the candles flickered.

"A drafty passageway," gloated Michael. "Just the thing for ghost-hunting, eh, Miss Grey?"

Minerva ignored him; Cynthia's glance was scornful. Laurel had trembled in the sudden breath of cold air. Her face in the dim, flickering light was white with deep shadows about her eyes and mouth. They went through the door and stood in a panelled hallway.

"Kilworthy originally belonged to the Roscarrock family," said Diana. "In the last century my great-grandfather bought it. His son, my grandfather, didn't care for the house and so he chose to enlarge it rather than restore it."

There was a Great Hall with minstrel's gallery, vast and cavernous. Their footsteps echoed loudly on the stone floor. In the drawing room were dim portraits and lumps of grimy, tattered furniture looming up in the shadows. Diana led the way up a long, wide staircase, the woodwork chipped and scratched. They filed into a large bedroom. The light of the candles revealed an ornately-carved bed, the hangings filthy and moth-eaten.

Minerva set down her candle on the chest of drawers. She stood quite still. The others watched her with varying degrees of anticipation. Did she sense something?

Yet it was Laurel, and not Minerva, who claimed their attention. She had flinched and slumped heavily against Doctor Polgreen.

"Mrs. Tregarth, are you unwell? Come, we'll go back into the hall. The air in here is rather bad."

Not just the air, thought Minerva. Something else. Something very wrong. But it eluded her. She retrieved her candle and followed Dr. Polgreen and Laurel from the room. Disappointed, the others went after her.

"This is damned dull," hissed Michael to his wife. "Wish I'd gone with the men to play cards."

Diana opened a few more doors to reveal gloomy rooms filled with furniture and hangings that had not been cleaned or aired in many years. The musty air was thick and fetid with mildew. They filed down the corridor, then went around a corner and up three steps to a closed door. Hesitating for a moment, Diana twisted the knob and pushed it open.

It was an unusual room, six-sided. Three of the adjoining sides were windows and projected, bay-style, from the outside wall. Beneath the windows was a built-in seat upholstered in velvet.

"Charming," said Cynthia.

"Dashed odd room," said Michael.

But this room was not damp like the others, and most of the furniture looked fairly new. "This was—" began Diana.

"—Your brother's room," finished Minerva.

"You seem to know a great deal, Miss Grey," said Diana. "Tell us then, what is wrong with this room, if anything. Is it haunted?"

Her voice challenged Minerva. Let's see what sort of a tale she'll concoct, thought Diana. Cynthia covered her mouth to conceal a yawn. So far, Miss Grey had proved deadly dull. But Diana had backed her into a corner; she had to answer.

Minerva tilted her face up slightly. She held her hands out, palms face up. She had felt the cold all along, but it was strongest in this room. She closed her eyes and opened her mind, stiffening her body against the shock of entry.

But then there came a great, choking cry. The others spun wildly about to see Laurel standing on the threshold. Her hands were pressed to her cheeks and she was shrieking uncontrollably. The others gazed at her in horrified stupefaction, chills running down their backs. Even Dr. Polgreen could only look at her, aghast.

Swiftly Minerva was beside Laurel, pushing her from the room, the two women lurching and stumbling together, Laurel still emitting those hideous sounds.

"My God, what's wrong with her?" Cynthia was the first to find her voice.

"We must get her to her room," said Minerva.

"I'll take her," said Dr. Polgreen grimly. "Mrs. Tregarth, Mrs. Tregarth, you are perfectly safe."

"Drag her, if you must—or carry her. But take her away from here!" cried Minerva.

Michael Lantallick took one of Laurel's arms while Dr. Polgreen supported her on the other side. She did not resist; indeed, she seemed scarcely conscious of those around her. Gradually her harsh screams quieted to pitiful cries as the men led her down the corridor. Cynthia followed behind them. She had got her diversion.

When Diana turned to Minerva, there was no scorn or patronage in her gaze. "What—what was in that room?" she whispered. "If she felt it, you must have, too. And Lyle refuses to sleep in there . . . but I noticed nothing at all out of the ordinary."

Minerva did not answer at first. She leaned against the wall, taking deep breaths. When she did speak her voice was infinitely weary.

"Be thankful, Miss Cardew, that you noticed nothing. For there is a great deal in that room, all of it terrible to endure." Straightening with an effort, she began to walk down the passageway. Diana, speechless, followed her.

In the morning Laurel seemed fully recovered. The others were surprised and somewhat embarrassed when she and Derek appeared in the dining room for breakfast. No one had yet referred to the appalling scene in the six-sided room, but it was on the mind of everyone who had witnessed it. Those who hadn't either knew nothing about it or assumed that she had merely felt unwell again. Minerva Grey did not come down for breakfast.

Laurel herself had only the haziest recollection of the previous day's events. She greeted the other houseguests courteously and consumed a rather large breakfast, wondering idly where the small woman who wore spectacles was.

Dr. Polgreen had given Laurel a sedative when he and Michael reached her room. He sent for Derek and told him that Laurel had become frightened in the old part of the house; he did not elaborate. By that time Michael had gone and Laurel was on the verge of sleep.

Derek had stood by his wife's bedside, looking down at her sleeping form. She lay on her side, one hand curled under her cheek. She looked very young and defenseless, not at all the temptress who had aroused his violent lust only hours before. A strand of dark hair spilled over one eye; he reached over to brush it aside, his fingers trembling as they touched her skin. Then he blew out the candles and went to his own room.

Sometime in the night he had another of his dreaded dreams. There was a savage grip about his neck; he writhed in bed, making strangling sounds. Then, with a howl, he bolted awake. Quivering with horror and confusion, he buried his face in his hands and wept. Laurel slept undisturbed in the next room.

The following morning Diana asked that Dr. Polgreen lead them on an expedition of local places of interest. The party agreed to meet at the stables one hour after breakfast to choose their mounts. Two of the servants were to join them later in the day with a picnic conveyed by pony trap.

"If there is anyone who doesn't feel up to coming, it's perfectly all right," said Diana. She looked at Laurel.

Laurel raised her brows. "Do you mean me? Of course I'm coming. Derek has told me there is no better guide than Dr. Polgreen." She smiled at the older man, who was relieved to observe no ill effects of the night before.

Diana's lips compressed. This morning she had convinced herself that Laurel's display last night was no more than ridiculous histrionics. However, she had hoped that Dr. Polgreen would advise the girl to have a quiet day. Then she would have been able to ride beside Derek as she often used to do, striking an excellent contrast with his sickly, nervous wife. It had not occurred to her that Derek might stay behind to keep Laurel company. She was impossible, not at all the right sort of wife for Derek. They couldn't possibly be happy together. It must be obvious to everyone that the American bride was unbalanced.

Cynthia, too, had come to the conclusion that Laurel was dotty. Why, even that spiritualist woman appeared saner than she did. The proud Derek Tregarth had married a loon. For her money, of course, why else? She could not be trusted out in public. Cynthia wondered how long it would be before Mrs. Tregarth retired permanently at Tregartha like that mad wife of Mr. Rochester. She could give Derek an heir, Cynthia supposed, but would his wits be addled as well?

Minerva Grey came down just as they were leaving the house for the stables. She, too, was dressed for riding.

"Oh, Miss Grey," said Diana. She had hoped to avoid Minerva for most of the day; the woman unnerved her.

"Thank you for sending up my breakfast, Miss Cardew," said MinervaI dryly. "I should like to accompany your party, if I may."

"Certainly. I—I didn't know whether you rode or not," Diana said lamely. Oh, why had she invited that woman here?

"By all means," said Michael Lantallick heartily. "Can't search for ghosts in the daylight hours, can you, Miss Grey? Or at least not without an audience," he added and laughed.

Minerva did not take offense; she had been insulted many times over the years by cleverer people than Michael Lantallick. She studied Laurel in the sunlight streaming into the hall. Unlike Dr. Polgreen, she was not reassured by what she saw. There was a murky darkness about her that he could not see. She's getting closer to the danger, thought Minerva. The protective gauze has been torn. And there is nothing I can do except stay near to her.

Derek viewed Minerva with dislike. He did not trust her. He did not want her near his wife. She looked up at him suddenly and their gazes locked. In her eyes he saw pity and understanding. Taken aback, he flushed and turned away.

"Well, now that we are all here, shall we go?" asked Diana brightly.

From her window Morva watched the party make their way to the stables. Her hand clutched the windowsill, her bony knuckles whitening. I told Diana I wanted to see that girl, she thought wrathfully. How dare she defy me? Message after message, all ignored. The American bride had not come.

Last night she had heard the terrible cries from the floor below. Over and over again she had pulled agitatedly on the bellrope.

"Miss Morva, 'ee'll break that rope one day," said the maid who had finally come. "I can only move so fast."

"You're a lazy slattern! I don't know why my niece keeps you on," she cried harshly. "Quick, girl. What were those sounds, those screams a while ago?"

The girl looked blank. "Screams?" Miss Morva was losing her reason.

"Yes, you fool! Screams, in this part of the house!" Morva was beside herself with frustration. Her blue-veined hands were twisted like claws and there was spittle on the side of her mouth.

"I don't know about any screams. I did hear the American lady was taken poorly."

"Where is she now?"

"Mrs. Tregarth? Her's gone to bed, I reckon. The doctor be lookin' after she."

Morva's heart was jumping wildly in her breast. She forced herself to breathe slowly and deeply, relaxing her fingers and arms. "Get out, girl," she said.

The maid was happy to oblige. "She fair frighted me," she told the other maid with whom she shared a room. "I reckon she wanted to hit me, and all because her couldn't see that Mrs. Tregarth tonight."

The other maid, exhausted from the extra work demanded by the presence of eight guests, merely gave a snort before falling fast asleep.

The day was an ideal one for the outing. Strips of fleecy clouds banded the blue sky. The breeze was mild and deliciously scented. They rode over fields flecked with pink and orange anemones. Yellow gorse bristled along the hedgerow and clumps of blue thrift patched the low stone walls which were built in the crisscrossed "Jack and Jill" pattern.

When the group drew close to the sea, they slowed their pace. Soon they were walking the horses in a single file along the path of the cliff. Far below, the surf rushed and foamed against the sharp, puckered rocks. The hedgerow on the landward side grew twisted and dense.

Dr. Polgreen dismounted and began to push aside the masses of brambles, gorse, and honeysuckle. The others got down, secured their horses, and followed the doctor through the tall hedgerow. On the other side was a tiny roofless building, the stone walls laced with ivy, red flowers, and lichen stains.

"It's St. Isaac's oratory," said the doctor. "Most people don't know it exists. One of the first chapels in Cornwall built by an early monk well over a thousand years ago." He drew their attention to a round-topped stone cross standing crookedly nearby. "The early monks taught the people to bow and pray before the cross of Jesus rather than before the standing stones as they had always done."

Who cares? thought Cynthia, who had torn her skirt on a thorn. She was not interested in history. There was nothing appealing about those barbarians, dressed in skins and drinking ox blood, likely as not. Revolting. Why Dr. Polgreen kept harping on the Cornwall of the past was beyond her. When a few of the others went inside the stone structure, she did not follow.

"Very picturesque," Diana was saying. "What do you think, Miss Grey?"

Minerva nodded absently; she was watching Laurel.

"The water makes a lovely sound, does it not?" asked Laurel. She bent down and dipped her fingers into the basin. "It's cold."

Diana and Minerva gazed down at the stone basin. Ringed with stains, it was perfectly dry. Here we go again, thought Diana. She's stark, staring mad.

Derek had entered behind them just then. He had not heard Laurel's words, but he saw her crouched on the floor of the oratory gently rubbing her hands.

"Laurel, what on earth are you doing?" he asked sharply. "Get up."

Lifting her head, she turned toward him and stood up. Her face was radiant. Her eyes shone, her lips curved in a welcoming smile. When she spoke, her voice had lost its American flatness and was pitched higher.

"Oh, my love, you've come. I knew you would. For it was here that I became your true wife before God."

Derek blanched. He had taken her arm, but he now dropped it as though it burned him.

"Are you angry with me, my love?" Laurel asked. "I know 'tis been a while since we have met, but you know I cannot easily get away." She reached for Derek, but he jerked away, backing out of the oratory. She watched him leave, her violet-blue eyes dark with pain and uncertainty. Minerva gently took Laurel's arm and led her outside. Diana followed behind.

Dr. Polgreen and the others were talking about something in the newspaper that morning. They did not notice Derek's rigid pallor or Diana's revulsion. When Laurel had spoken in that strange voice, a wave of bitter animosity had washed over Diana, far more intense than her earlier contempt. For an instant she had had an overwhelming urge to strike Laurel, to beat her and take pleasure in it. The compulsion vanished as swiftly as it had come, leaving Diana trembling. Goosebumps prickled her arms. God, what is *happening?* she wondered.

"I think we ought to steer clear of the cliff," said Minerva aside to Dr. Polgreen. "Mrs. Tregarth may become a bit unsteady in the saddle."

Dr. Polgreen nodded. He should have considered that before. He spoke aloud. "We'll now head inland to Boscivey Quoit, a place far more ancient than this oratory. Some of us may care to ride at a leisurely pace. You others that don't we will meet there in a while."

Derek took off at a gallop. He had not glanced at Laurel. Diana, pleased, spurred her horse to follow him over the moors.

It will do no good, thought Minerva; he has no interest in you in this time either.

Laurel appeared not to notice. She was talking to Annabel Roslyn and Lyle, having returned to herself. Cynthia observed the two on horseback fading into the distance with wry amusement. Perhaps Diana is the one Michael should look to for influence on Derek, she thought. Not Mrs. Tregarth.

Damn, thought Michael. He had been ready to go after Derek. He had to talk to him today, alone. But if he and Diana were going to conduct a flirtation, now was not the time.

Eventually Boscivey Quoit loomed up before them, huge, forbidding. Three granite pillars rose twelve feet above the heath, roofed by a massive capstone. Minerva was conscious of a strong tingling throughout her body. The place had enormous reserves of energy, as did all ancient monuments.

Derek and Diana were waiting for them. "We had nearly given up on you," she said carelessly. Her eyes were bright and her face flushed. Derek said nothing; he was looking out over the undulating, brackeny moors, his face inscrutable.

"Built by the Druids, eh, Doctor?" said Michael.

"No, much earlier than that," said Henry Polgreen. "It's

over three thousand years old, from the Neolithic—the New Stone Age."

"Thought the Druids built all these old places," said Lyle.

"Well, they certainly *used* them," answered the doctor. "Because they were already considered sacred and mystical. However, archaeologists believe that quoits were originally constructed as tombs for important warriors. Food, drink, weapons, and tools would have been laid beside the body."

"That huge tomb for just one chap?" asked Michael.

"No, members of his family would have been laid to rest inside as well. Eventually, when the tomb would hold no more bodies, the stones would have been heaped over with earth to form a gigantic mound or barrow."

"Well, fancy that," said Mrs. Roslyn. She was not used to riding for so long. I'm getting too old for it, she thought. I should have stayed behind at Kilworthy. It might have been better for Annabel if I had. Perhaps Lyle would have been more forthcoming. So far he had treated her quite impersonally. Mrs. Roslyn sighed.

Minerva walked over and laid her palms on one of the enormous pillars. Closing her eyes, she sensed sacrifice, death, healing, invocation, renewal, and more. She drew strength from the energy flowing from the stones into her body.

Diana was seething with fresh humiliation. She had carefully planned what she would say to Derek when they reached the quoit ahead of the others. She had begun to speak with concern about Laurel. Was she happy in Cornwall? Did she miss New York? Was she often unwell? Had he spoken to Dr. Polgreen about her? The poor girl—and so on.

Derek had barely answered her, his eyes narrowed and peering into the distance. When she laid her hand on his arm, he still did not look at her.

"Derek," she had said softly. "Don't you see? There is something, well, wrong with Laurel. Everyone has noticed it. Her moods are strange . . . Derek, look at me."

Frowning, he turned to her. "It's none of your business, Di."

Encouraged by his use of her pet name, she went on. "It is a little my business. You and I are very old friends. I care very much about what happens to you." Her fingers tightened on his arm. "Oh, Derek, why not admit you made a mistake? She can't be a normal wife to you. Send her back to New York."

Impatiently he shook her off. "Don't be a fool, Diana." His voice was cold.

She had not expected so brusque and unmistakable a rejection. Two bright spots of color appeared in her cheeks. She glared at him. "Oh, go ahead then! Stew in your own juices! Your marriage is of your own making. She's as mad as a hatter—anyone can see that! You'll both be the talk of Cornwall—Derek Tregarth and his lunatic wife!"

He whirled around to face her, his eyes blazing in his white face. She knew she had gone too far. Recoiling, she stepped back a few paces. Pure animal fear replaced her anger. I've felt this before, she thought, terrified. Her head reeled.

And then she had seen the others riding towards them.

The last place on the tour before luncheon was the Holed Stone. It was Dr. Polgreen's particular favorite, a large round boulder with a perfectly round opening hollowed out of its center. He explained that it was originally a doorway to another burial place which had long since vanished.

"The body of the fallen warrior would have been passed through the large hole before being placed in the tomb," he said. "It had some sort of a magical or spiritual significance, perhaps symbolizing the afterlife of the warrior."

" 'Tis a healing stone," said Laurel.

Dr. Polgreen looked at her in surprise. "That is precisely what it came to be, Mrs. Tregarth. Sick children were brought here and passed through the hole nine times against the sun.

Even stricken adults would crawl through. The notion of a person making the journey through the hole was passed down over thousands of years. Even today some superstitious mothers bring their children here."

That's not what she meant, thought Minerva. She knows this place, just as she did the old chapel. From another time . . .

"Hey, I've got this trick knee that bothers me now and again," said Michael. "Think I ought to crawl through myself? And you, Lyle. Perhaps the stone hole will cure your limp." He laughed good-naturedly.

Lyle gave him a twisted smile. Michael Lantallick could go to hell. His leg was the least of his worries. He had not slept at all the night before. He looked terrible and knew it. They all assumed his leg was giving him pain, but in truth he scarcely felt it. Last night had been beyond imagining. If he had been able to move, he would have taken a pistol to his head and shot himself.

Seven

When Laurel returned to her room later that afternoon, there was a letter waiting for her. The sealed envelope was addressed to Mrs. Tregarth, the handwriting shaky and spidery. Her senses had gradually atrophied again; she was numb and listless. Feeling no curiosity, she nevertheless opened the envelope and drew out the folded parchment within.

Mrs. Tregarth,

I would very much like to speak with you. Please come to my room as soon as possible. One of the maids will show you the way. It is most urgent.

Morva Cardew

Laurel frowned. Who was this? Then she recalled the mention of a bedridden aunt at Kilworthy. It must be she. Laurel was bone-tired, drained. If only she were back in her own room at Tregartha. Taking off her dusty riding habit, she lay down on the bed. Her small breasts felt heavy and swollen; she loosened her corset.

A knock sounded on the door. "Who is it?" she called wearily.

"Emma, ma'am. One o' the maids."

"Come in."

"I be that sorry to disturb 'ee, ma'am, but Miss Cardew be askin' for 'ee."

"Yes, I got her letter," said Laurel, sitting up in bed. "But I'm very tired just now. I'll try to see her later."

The maid bit her lip. "Beggin' your pardon, Mrs. Tregarth, but her be wild to see 'ee. In a fair takin', she be. If 'ee don't come now . . . please, ma'am." Morva had already thrown a hairbrush at her.

Laurel was too tired to argue. "Oh, very well, but you'll have to help me dress. Please fetch the lilac gown from the wardrobe. And the matching shoes."

When she was ready, Laurel followed the maid up a flight of stairs and down a long corridor to a heavy, studded door. Passing through, they entered the old part of the house and Laurel again gave a shudder. Emma stopped outside a door and knocked.

"Come in," said a breathless voice.

" 'Tis Mrs. Tregarth," said Emma, opening the door. Now I'll finally have some peace, she thought, scurrying hastily away.

Laurel entered the room, looking past the jumble of furniture to the bed where a thin figure was propped against a mound of pillows. "How do you do, Miss Cardew?"

Morva stared at her. "They did not shoot the horse," she said.

"The—the horse?" echoed Laurel, puzzled. The closeness of the room made her instantly nauseous. Her head felt dazed, woolly.

"I would not let them. It was not the beast's fault, you see. Not really. Always I had to be the victor, the powerful one. Ironic now, is it not? For I am helpless, and have been that way for more than forty years. I have lived my life in the confines of this room. I have tried to accept . . . all of it."

Laurel did not know what to say. The old woman's voice was matter-of-fact, devoid of self-pity.

Morva gave a warbly laugh. "But I can still sometimes frighten the maids."

ECHOES OF THE HEART

I don't doubt it, thought Laurel. What on earth did this woman want of her?

"I have had many years to reflect, to accept," went on Morva. She peered at Laurel. "You do not look well, Mrs. Tregarth."

"I don't feel well. I was almost asleep when the maid came."

"You were reluctant to come to my room. Yet I would not have asked were it not of the greatest importance."

"What exactly did you wish to see me about?"

"Are you enjoying my niece's party, Mrs. Tregarth?"

"No." Why should she dissemble?

"I thought not. I told my niece I wished to speak with you, but she ignored my requests. Mrs. Tregarth, you must leave Kilworthy today. Now."

Laurel was startled briefly out of her dazed and queasy state. "Leave here . . . today? But—"

"Do not give a thought as to what Diana will think. Just go. This house . . . is no place for you."

"You are telling me that Diana is in love with Derek," said Laurel.

"Her feelings are inevitable, I'm afraid, but they do not concern me. You must leave here for your well-being, Mrs. Tregarth, and that of your child." And for my own, she added to herself, for I am afraid that if you do not leave, something horrible will happen to all of us.

"How did you know about—about—?" Stunned, Laurel did not finish.

"About the child you are carrying?"

"I've told no one. No one at all." Only Martha had guessed.

"Not even your husband?"

Laurel shook her head.

"Then, Mrs. Tregarth, tell him now! Tell him to take you back to Tregartha!" Morva's voice quivered, her brow was deeply furrowed. When Laurel did not answer, she went on, "This house is dangerous for you and your unborn child. Your husband as well. My niece and nephew are also in danger, as am I. But perhaps, if you leave . . . you see, you are the catalyst. If you leave, we may all be spared. At least for the present."

Laurel stared at the old lady. Her head was throbbing. The room receded; the woman in the bed seemed far away.

"Do you know anything of the Eastern religions, Mrs. Tregarth?" asked Morva.

"The . . . Eastern religions?" Laurel repeated stupidly.

"The concepts of Hinduism. Karma. Retribution for one's past."

Laurel shook her head. A tight band was boring into her skull. Her nausea was growing stronger. She had barely taken in Morva's words. She was dizzy. "I must go back to my room," she murmured. "I—I feel ill."

"Wait. I'll ring for the girl. She'll take you."

"N-no. I must go now." Laurel pressed her handkerchief to her mouth and moved toward the door.

"You must leave Kilworthy. Tell your husband to take you home. Tell him . . . about your child. There may have been another unborn child whose father did not know . . ."

But Laurel was already stumbling down the corridor. Morva slowly unclenched her claw-like hands. Her heart was again pumping wildly. There was nothing more she could do. She had warned the girl. Whether or not she heeded the warning was out of Morva's hands. The wheel of fate continued to spin no matter what. Events would proceed as they had been designed. Morva knew that she was foolish to hope that if Laurel and Derek left Kilworthy, disaster would be avoided. They were all trapped in a twisted pattern of their own making, doomed either to repeat or repair the mistakes of the past. Morva was powerless to stop the course. In this life that was her lot—to helplessly await the outcome, rather than to determine it.

* * *

Derek found Laurel in the bathroom, vomiting wretchedly. Her face had a greenish tint and was wet with perspiration. He bathed her face and neck with cold water and carried her to the bed. "I'll get Henry," he said.

She shook her head. "I just need to rest," she whispered.

"Let's leave Kilworthy, Laurel," he said.

But she was already asleep.

When the gong sounded for dinner, Laurel was still asleep. Derek had decided not to wake her. We'll leave first thing in the morning, he thought. What a hideous weekend it's been. Laurel was ill; that explained her strange behavior, her lapses into delirium. He had been a fool to feel those tremors of fear and dread today at the oratory.

The last straw had been the recent altercation with Michael Lantallick. Stupid clod—as if I'd ever take him on as a partner! That would be the sure road to ruin. The man couldn't add two and two.

Minerva Grey was relieved that Laurel had not come down to dinner. Sleep was the best thing for her at present. It was the protector, the strengthener. She would need all the strength and protection she could muster. There was no way to avoid the forces gathering in this house. What was coming, would come. Certain events would repeat themselves, had already been repeating themselves. And Laurel herself was at the very center of the whirling miasma.

Minerva was not feeling well, either. The emanations in the house were too strong, too thick and stifling. She glanced at Lyle. There was a sheen on his face in the candlelight. He sensed the vibrations as she did. There was a new tic at the side of his mouth. He made no attempt to converse with Annabel, who sat, crestfallen, beside him.

Michael Lantallick was obviously angry and disappointed about something. As for Diana, she was determined to salvage what was left of the weekend. Her pride demanded it; she would not willingly let the house party fail, though her private hopes for it had fizzled. She refused to admit that she had lost Derek for good—rather she cast about for a scapegoat for her frustration. And found one in Minerva Grey.

The woman was nothing but a fraud. She had accepted Diana's invitation under false pretenses, refusing even to hold a seance. The woman was no more a psychic than she was! Diana did not believe that one could communicate with the dead, but at least a seance would have afforded them some amusement. Diana conveniently forgot how eerie and alarming had been the experience in Lyle's old bedroom. And that had been due to Derek's peculiar wife. Even in there Minerva had failed them.

There was one final entertainment tonight. Then tomorrow they would all be gone. What a relief that would be! But first she would have a few things to say to Minerva Grey.

She assumed her bright, hostessy voice over the meal of roast duckling, peas, potatoes, and leeks. "I have a surprise planned for tonight. It's Beltane, remember. The eve of May Day."

"Have you erected a Maypole?" asked Mrs. Roslyn, matching her hostess's mood with an effort. She, too, had been vastly disappointed in this weekend, for it was obvious that Lyle was not going to propose to Annabel. She would take the girl away somewhere. There was nothing like new surroundings to mend a broken heart. She would get over Lyle, away from Kilworthy and Cornwall.

"No, I haven't," said Diana. "That is for May Day, not Beltane. Am I right, Doctor? Beltane was celebrated by the lighting of great bonfires, so I thought we'd have one here, at Kilworthy. Tonight."

"No—" breathed Minerva Grey, but no one heard her.

"Beltane as a festival has died out completely," said the doctor. "In isolated parts of Scotland, though, there are lingering celebrations. The children in some villages have a custom. A large piece of cake or unrisen dough is baked and burned carefully in one spot. Then it is broken up into small pieces, enough for all the children, and the pieces put in a sack. The children sit round a bonfire and pass the sack, each taking a piece. The one who draws out the blackened bit is 'it,' or the chosen one. That child is teased, chased about, and made as if he or she will be thrown into the bonfire. All perfectly innocent fun, but the connotations are clear."

"What do you mean, Doctor?" asked Mrs. Roslyn.

"Well, in pagan times, the ceremony would have been performed in earnest. There would have been no pretense. Men would have passed the sack about, and the chosen one would then have been sacrificed in a ritual execution."

"Primitive ghouls," said Cynthia. "As bad as Africans. Disgusting."

"Well, I can't promise you anything nearly so exciting tonight, but we will have a bonfire along with music and the traditional Cornish food and drink which was served on Beltane," said Diana.

"You should not do this," said Minerva Grey. "Especially not tonight."

Diana scowled. "I beg your pardon, Miss Grey?"

"I said that you should—you must not have this bonfire." She spoke so softly that only Diana heard her.

"Don't be absurd. It's already built. In a few hours it will be set ablaze."

"Don't do it, Miss Cardew."

This time everyone heard her. There was silence at the table as they all looked at Minerva in the wavering half-light.

"Kindly refrain from advising me how to entertain my guests," said Diana in clipped tones.

She has felt this before, thought Minerva. The frustration, the anger, the failure to win a man's love. And the consequences were most severe. The roots of recent events lay far back in the past, she was certain of that now. These desperate souls were not bound to one place, as the spirit of little Alice

Pringle had been. They had moved on, but none was purged of the bygone tragedy and blunders.

After dinner Dr. Polgreen accompanied Derek to Laurel's room. He looked down at the sleeping girl, her hair a dark cloud about her pale face.

"Her pulse is rather fast, though she appears to be resting peacefully," he said. "I see no signs of infection."

"She was quite ill this afternoon," said Derek. "Vomiting. Then she went to sleep."

"She's certainly sleeping deeply, but I see no cause for concern. In the morning we'll see how she is after her long rest. Doubtless it's the best thing for her."

Dr. Polgreen suppressed his strong impulse to disclose to Derek his suspicion that his wife was with child. It would explain the nausea, the mood changes, the weariness. The hours in the saddle today had exhausted her. In the early stages of pregnancy, women were often ill and lethargic. Yet his qualms were not altogether allayed. Mrs. Tregarth seemed highly suggestible and nervous. Dr. Polgreen could not forget her unreasoned terror the night before. True, some women experienced odd flights of fancy when they were carrying a child. Melancholia sometimes followed a birth, in rare instances lasting for months. There was no accounting for these things. Tomorrow he was determined to confront Laurel about her condition. But in the meantime he would say nothing of it to Derek; it was a wife's privilege to confide the happy news to her husband.

He looked across at Derek, whose intent gaze was fixed on his wife. There was something in his expression that the doctor could not identify. Minerva would have recognized the conflicting emotions of love and hate, yearning and distrust, but the doctor merely concluded that Derek was worried.

"She'll be fine," he said with more confidence than he felt.

"But we must let her sleep. She doesn't need to be involved in this bonfire scheme."

"Pretentious nonsense," said Derek. "Why on earth Diana should wish to reconstruct the past—why, even you have never advocated that, Henry!"

Dr. Polgreen smiled. "It can't do any harm. Although . . ." Pausing, he recalled Miss Grey's warning at the dinner table. He was open-minded enough not to disregard it. The woman had special gifts, he acknowledged. Yet what could happen? Surely with all of them at the bonfire any disaster could be prevented. And Mrs. Tregarth was fast asleep.

"It's ten o'clock—two more hours until the bonfire. Let's have a game of billiards," said the doctor to Derek.

Derek hesitated, gave Laurel one last look, and followed the older man from the room. Anything to get through this night so they could return to Tregartha tomorrow. Beyond that he did not think.

Minerva had gone to her room after dinner. Diana's rebuke had not disturbed her. She was used to people with limited perceptions. They could not be blamed. She had not expected Diana to call off the bonfire; it would doubtless have done no good anyway. Old loves, old hatreds, old fears, old evils— they were all converging, drawing to a head.

Long ago Minerva had accepted that interest in spiritualism was fueled more by titillation and morbid curiosity than by earnest searching for answers to the mysteries of life and death. She knew that she was a disappointment to her hostess and considered it ironic. All the murky, threatening forces swirling about them, and Diana was oblivious. Minerva's presence had not been required to raise them. It was Laurel and Derek and their unborn child who were at the center of the maelstrom. How can I help them? she wondered. I have never before worked to resolve a past life in a person now living. Indeed, it was little more than a theory to me before now.

Heretofore my experience has been with tormented souls already dead. Yet I believe that these souls have somehow transfigured into their present incarnations without cleansing themselves of the old. How or why, I do not understand.

She knew that in the law of Karma every act was sooner or later followed by a punishment or reward. The Christians believed that "what ye shall sow shall ye also reap," but that the judgment lay in heaven or hell. Minerva was convinced that it often lay back on earth, in another life and another time.

There were too many so-called haunted houses in Britain for the supernatural to be ignored. But despite the work of the Society for Psychical Research, few people were tolerant of the concept of reincarnation. No Christian wanted to believe that a soul might have to return to earth when there was the promise of eternal bliss, and of reconciliation with loved ones and the divine, after death. But perhaps this eternal bliss had to be earned . . .

At least some of the people in this house party had known one another in a previous lifetime. Perhaps even I, thought Minerva. Perhaps that above all other reasons is why I was summoned. All along I sensed something extraordinary taking shape here. A pattern of events had been woven in the past that was once again set in motion. They were being given the opportunity to set things right this time, but with such limited understanding that they were in danger of perpetuating the wrongs due to the tumult of past emotions. A chain of evil events had gone unpunished. Would this same evil destroy again, or itself be destroyed?

Minerva decided to return to the six-sided room in the old section of the house. This time, alone, without distractions, she might be able to fathom the welter of emotions which had left their trace. That the vestiges of the unhappy spirit was female, she had no doubt. She always knew.

* * *

Michael Lantallick was drinking brandy in his room.

"Any more of that and you'll miss the midnight revels," said Cynthia.

Her husband ignored her. "He asked me what experience I had in running a hotel! As though he has any himself!"

"I know. You've told me three times," said Cynthia irritably.

"Damned insolence. As if my name—my family—wasn't enough! The Lantallicks have for years been involved in financial dealings in Cornwall—mining, engineering, even the railways." Michael's heavy face was red. "That bastard—he wouldn't even take time to consider. 'I have to employ someone with experience, Michael, if this venture is to work.' We'd learn together, I told him. He actually laughed!"

Cynthia turned on her heel and walked briskly across the room. She was sick to death of hearing it again and again.

"You realize what this means, don't you?" When she did not answer, did not even look up from the needlework in her lap, his voice took on a high, strangled pitch. "Don't you?"

"Pray keep your voice down. I don't believe I want to know."

"It means we're ruined, bloody ruined! We've got nothing. No pot to piss in! The mine's gone, the house will have to be sold to pay the debts. We'll have to emigrate."

"Emigrate!" She gazed at him, appalled, while her embroidery fell to the floor.

He was pleased to see a reaction. "We'll have no choice, Cynthia."

"Emigrate!" she repeated hoarsely. "Are you mad? Give up everything we own, leave Cornwall?"

"Don't blame me, blame Derek Tregarth. Damn his eyes."

Cynthia gazed at her husband, his bloated, weak face, his bloodshot eyes, his shirt collar turned round and opened, his body heavy from overindulgence. Humiliation and disgust rose in her. It would always be like this, him blaming others for his ineptitudes, his failings. She saw him now as though for the first time.

Her lip curled. "No, Michael, it's not Derek Tregarth's fault that we are ruined. You cannot lay the blame on his shoulders just because he refused to employ you." Overwhelmed with bitterness, she left the room.

Annabel was playing the piano in the drawing room. She knew she was pretty in her pink silk gown and her garnet drop earrings and necklace. She had attempted over the last two days to show Lyle that she possessed all the requirements necessary for a country gentleman's wife. Not that any of it was needed; she and Lyle had known one another since childhood and he had to be well aware of her accomplishments. Yet it was all to no avail. She knew that Lyle was not going to ask for her hand. Anyone could see that he was unwell. The man who had returned from South Africa was not the amusing, cheerful companion of her youth. When he had not answered her many letters to him in the hospital, her pain and agitation had been great. Greater, she had to admit, than it was now. She had realized tonight that she did not wish to spend her life with this new Lyle who was jittery and withdrawn, whose eyes at times had a wild look. The last months of torturing herself, wondering whether or not he loved her, were over. She did not want him to love her.

Lyle was not listening to Annabel playing Chopin. He was not aware of Cynthia Lantallick entering the room and sitting beside Mrs. Roslyn. Nor did he notice when one of the maids set down a tea tray before the two ladies. Despite his reluctance to see Annabel and her mother and to play the amenable host, he had looked forward to the respite he hoped the weekend would bring. He had longed to be released from the aimless anxiety which, in the night hours, intensified into black, merciless terror.

Yet whatever it was which persecuted him had gained a

ECHOES OF THE HEART 159

new strength. The room where he lay had again turned bitterly cold. Unable to move a muscle, he was certain he was not alone. The air was thick with a vicious hatred, a pitiless condemnation. A foul, rotten smell assaulted his nostrils.

Abomination. He was an abomination. He could hear the words inside his head.

His wits had nearly left him for good last night. But at dawn a gradual lessening of the vile stench and the icy cold had begun. He could shift his limbs. Then came the tremors and he lay, shaking and sobbing, until the stream of warm sunlight shot across the room. An enormous sense of relief and comfort overwhelmed him, and he made up his mind. Never again would he spend a night at Kilworthy. Diana could have the cursed place. He would go somewhere warm and dry where the dampness would not seep into his stiff leg, where he would not shiver with cold. Somewhere peaceful, where he could sleep untroubled, night after night. After the bonfire, he would break the news to Diana and then go to an inn. She could have his trunks packed and sent there tomorrow. He would go to Italy, or Greece. Or Madeira. Or all of them.

But he was determined never to spend a night at Kilworthy again.

Morva had been ringing for one of the maids.

"You go," said Emma to Dot. "I been up and back all day. What can her be wantin' now?"

The other maid bit her lip. "I'll tend to her all day tomorrow, Em, I promise 'ee. But will 'ee go to her now?" she pleaded.

"Why?"

"I be afeared to go to the old part o' the house tonight. There be summat there, I feel it." She flushed.

"There be summat there, I reckon, tes the old bag herself," snorted Emma. "I'll go. But just 'ee mind 'ee keeps your word. I ain't to go up at all tomorrow."

"Aye, Emma. Goin' to the bonfire later, are 'ee?"

"Oh, aye—tes been years since I've seen a good bonfire. Folk don't built 'em like they used to when my mother were a girl."

Emma trudged up the stairs to Morva's room, hoping that whatever the old lady wanted would not interfere with the bonfire festival.

Morva sat up in bed, her fingers twitching at the bedsheets, her eyes ringed with violet shadows. "Mrs. Tregarth," she cried, "has she left yet?"

"What's that 'ee say, Miss Morva?"

"The Tregarths. Have they left Kilworthy?"

Emma stared at her in surprise. "No, Miss Morva. Stayin' one more night, they all be. The bonfire be tonight."

"The *what*, girl?" Morva put a hand to her breast.

"The bonfire Miss Diana asked the men to build out in one o' the fields. For some old holiday. Boltoon or summat."

"Beltane," whispered Morva. The word came to her instantly although she had never before heard it.

"Aye, tes so. With music and dancin' and lots to eat. Like in the old days, Miss Diana said."

"Like in the old days," echoed Morva. And knew this night would be her last.

Laurel stirred, alone in the room at Kilworthy. She had been having odd, baffling dreams. In one she had said, "Abomination. You are an abomination." But she could not see to whom she spoke. Somewhere someone was crying. She wanted to help, but it was too late. The only thing left to do was to flee. She would slip down to the ship, his ship. But then somehow she could not get there; they had stopped her, and now she was being dragged along the heath like a sack of potatoes, her screams bursting inside her head but making no sounds . . .

With a jolt she awoke, her heart hammering, her breath coming in gasps. At first she did not recognize the room.

Then she remembered they had come to Kilworthy for the weekend. She had been ill and Derek had looked after her. Had she been asleep since then? Where was Derek now?

"Derek?" she called.

There was no response. Gingerly she got out of bed and reached for her dressing gown. To her relief the room did not tilt, nor was there a return of nausea.

"Derek?" Opening the door to his room, she saw it was empty. His bed had not been turned down. She had to find him; they must leave Tregartha, just as the old woman had advised. At the thought of Morva, a chill ran over her. She hates me, thought Laurel. But that was ridiculous. Morva had asked to see her, had spoken to her with concern. She had known about the baby . . .

Laurel drew a swift intake of breath; her blood ran thick and slow in her veins. The older woman knew about the child. And she herself had discovered the vile secret well-hidden at Kilworthy. Monstrous . . . I must get away, she thought. I must leave Kilworthy right now. He is waiting for me.

She crept downstairs, still in her night attire. No one was about. The fire was dying in the drawing room hearth. There were no voices or muffled sounds to be heard.

Of course. They were all at the bonfire, she remembered. I'd forgotten tonight was Beltane. This time last year I saw him again. After I was wed. No, not wed in truth. He was never my husband . . . We will go away together and never return to Cornwall. We'll live in France and I'll bear him lots of children.

She rested her hand against her belly. It was slightly swollen now. She couldn't wait until it grew larger and rounder. And it would, once they were safely away. She would no longer need to conceal its surge beneath her skirts.

Laurel dazedly shook her head. Morva was right; she should tell Derek about the baby. She would tell him and then ask that he take her away from Kilworthy. Morva had warned her there was danger here for her and the child. Morva knew.

Hurrying down the central hallway, she flung open the French doors and went out into the night. Then she was running in her bare feet through the damp grass, veering across the wide expanse of lawn away from the gardens to the sprawling fields beyond.

She saw the orange mound of flames rising against the purple sky. Last year she had sung and danced and watched them burn the Green Lady. And they had gazed at one another in the dazzling glow of the fire . . . she had thought she would never see him again.

She could hear music. Fiddles, thin reedy whistles, and drums. It was cheerful, rollicking music. She recognized the tune. It was the song to welcome in the May.

> Unite, and unite, let us all unite,
> For summer is acumen in today;
> And whither we are going we all will unite,
> In the merry morning of May.

The villagers enjoyed this celebration of summer. The food was plentiful, the metheglin and ale potent, the tunes gay, the reels lively. The women had worked all day fashioning the Green Lady out of greenery, though this year she had not watched.

Laurel was nearing the huge round blaze. The dark sky above was flecked with burning embers and white ash. She gazed into the golden-red flames where the blue streaks flickered and writhed. She heard the ferocious roar, felt the blast of heat.

And she began to scream.

The others had not noticed her approach, but now they turned to stare, dumbfounded.

Derek was at her side. "Laurel—Laurel!"

She could not hear him. Her eyes were wild, the whites standing out in the firelight. She was flailing her arms, striking Derek as he fought to steady her.

ECHOES OF THE HEART

"What's wrong with her?" shrieked Cynthia. "Stop her, for God's sake!"

"She's mad!" Diana exclaimed. "Mad! She should be put away. You must see that for yourself, Doctor."

"Shut up, Diana!" snarled Derek.

"Take her to the house, Derek. Take her away from here. I'll give her another sedative once I've got my bag."

Derek swung Laurel into his arms and carried her across the field. Minerva was beside him, though he was scarcely aware of her presence. The others stared after them, aghast, hearing Laurel's terrified, high-pitched screams.

"What on earth can be wrong with that poor girl?" Mrs. Roslyn shook her head sadly.

"I thought she was asleep," said Annabel. She began to cry.

The servants had stopped dancing; the music had ceased. Yet the enormous bonfire raged on, crackling fiercely.

"I knew she was quite mad last night. You remember the way she carried on in Lyle's old room," said Diana. "Derek was a fool to marry her."

Lyle had spun around. *"What* did you say, Diana?"

"That Derek's bride is as mad as a hatter!"

"No! About *my old room!"*

"Gracious, Lyle, calm down. Last night when we were hunting for ghosts, we went in your old room. Mrs. Tregarth got very upset, just as she did now. You recall I mentioned your 'ghost' to them at Tregartha. Mrs. Tregarth, mad as she is, then imagined it."

"I suppose you think that's what I've done! Imagined it!" Lyle was shouting now, his face white, the tic by his mouth twitching uncontrollably.

"Lyle—control yourself! Of course you imagined it. What other explanation is there?" With a forced, embarrassed laugh, she glanced at the others.

"Damn you, Diana!" Lyle raged. "I tell you there is something there in that house! Call it what you like—but it's real . . . and it hates me."

"Hates you? Now Lyle, that's absurd. You—"

He shook off her arm. "I'm going to see Morva. She feels it, too. And then I'm leaving Kilworthy. For good."

Speechless, Diana stared after him. The others were as stunned as she. No one spoke. Exchanging dazed glances, they began to slowly make their way to the house.

In Laurel's room Dr. Polgreen was administering a sedative. It worked swiftly; she ceased to struggle, her cries became whimpers. Her eyes closed.

"This young woman is frightened out of her wits," he said. "But of what? Derek says that it's just since coming to Kilworthy that she—" He broke off, frowning. "Where is Derek?"

"He's gone," said Minerva Grey. "It has all been too much for him."

"Too much for him? Come, he's not a child, Miss Grey. He's made of stronger stuff than that. This is his wife!"

She shook her head. "He is not himself now. How long have they been married, Doctor?"

"About two months, I believe."

She glanced down at Laurel. "And since that first day, everything has been leading up to this."

"Miss Grey, I don't understand you. What—"

"—Doctor, look at Mrs. Tregarth!"

He jerked his head at the sudden urgency in her voice. But he was not prepared for what he saw. Laurel's face had turned bright red; there were angry welts on her throat and arms. To their horror, they watched as ugly white blisters appeared on her skin. She had begun to breathe erratically.

Dr. Polgreen took his stethoscope and pressed it to her chest. "Her heart's beating too quickly. I can't believe it—that sedative was very strong."

"It may have saved her life, Doctor. She was reliving something . . . horrible which happened to her a long time ago.

ECHOES OF THE HEART

When you gave her the sedative, you stopped her from reliving her own death, alone and unguided."

"Her own death!" Henry Polgreen stared at Minerva Grey, who stood so calmly before him. A slight figure, insignificant, really, until one looked through her spectacles at the amber eyes . . .

"Yes, Doctor. Not as Laurel Tregarth, though in that one, too, she was deeply bound to her present husband. And in that former life she was also with child."

"Did she confide her condition to you?" His mind could not take in what she was telling him except for the only thing which made sense.

She shook her head. "She didn't have to. Dr. Polgreen, I have opened my mind to this house. It holds secrets, terrible secrets. Mrs. Tregarth senses them and her fear is aroused. She cannot understand because she does not recall her past existence when she lived in this house. She feels only the fear, the pain. Lyle Cardew and his sister are entangled in this as well. There was evil done, and betrayal."

"Miss Grey," said the doctor impatiently, "I have no idea what you are talking about. Mrs. Tregarth is seriously ill. She needs to be placed in a special type of hospital."

"Are you saying you believe her mind is unhinged?"

"No, of course not. I only know that I am not equipped to look after someone with her . . . worries. As for the welts on her skin, I can rub some ointment on them but . . . God dammit, where is Derek?"

"We don't need him just now, Dr. Polgreen."

He laid his hand across Laurel's brow. "She is very hot."

"It is not a normal fever, Doctor."

He sighed. "Perhaps not. I'll admit I've never before seen anything remotely like this. All we can do is sit with her tonight and bathe her face and neck, trying to keep the fever down. The redness of her skin must be some sort of hysterical reaction."

"You admit you are baffled; you cannot diagnose her condition."

"That's what I say." His voice was irritable.

"Then please, Doctor, give me a chance. Let me try to help her."

"How?" he asked suspiciously. "What can you do?"

Minerva pressed her lips together; she must go about this cautiously. She could not afford to antagonize him—she had to inspire confidence.

"The trouble is not in her body, but in her mind, her spirit. I would like to sit with her for a few hours. I think I can help her come to terms with the . . . chaos . . . in her mind. She cannot face it alone. If she does, she may die or go permanently insane. I can help her, guide her in confronting what torments her. Then she will be able to put it all behind her once and for all, as will her husband, I hope."

The doctor regarded Miss Grey from under shaggy white brows. Again he perceived something in her eyes which held him. He did not comprehend the rigmarole, but, to his astonishment, he felt strength and assurance radiating from her. His own helpless frustration diminished. "How—how do you know she won't get worse?" he asked quietly.

"I am very much afraid she *will* get worse unless I am able to help her. I ask for your faith and patience, Dr. Polgreen. If, in the morning, she is not any better, you may send her to a hospital. But please allow me to do what I can for Mrs. Tregarth tonight."

Still he hesitated, the folds in his face sagging.

"Trust me, Doctor. It was no coincidence that I accepted Miss Cardew's invitation. I knew I would be needed in some way. I haven't always been able to discern this. You are open to many things, Doctor, despite your being a man of science. You realize that there is not always a rational explanation for everything that happens."

His mouth tightened. "What choice have I? Yet I'm

afraid . . . I'm responsible for her." He looked at Minerva, who said again, "Trust me, Dr. Polgreen."

"Very well, Miss Grey. You have until dawn. God be with you."

"Thank you, Doctor." When he had gone, she moved across the room and opened the casement window. The cool, scented breeze was on her face. It had been difficult to persuade the doctor; a portion of her strength was already gone. She took deep breaths of the night air, letting them out slowly, willing herself to relax. Refreshed, she went over to the bed and sat down by the unconscious girl. She laid her palm on Laurel's forehead.

Minerva closed her eyes. For a few moments she sensed nothing at all. There was no change in the atmosphere. She fought down the surge of panic. She could do this, she told herself sternly. It was the reason she had been sent here. Opening her eyes, she placed her hand in the basin of cool water. Then she again pressed it to Laurel's brow.

Laurel stirred, shuddering at the cold wetness. Then she suddenly went limp, and a slight smile formed on her face.

Minerva was no longer a part of the elegant bedchamber. She heard the sea pounding below the cliff, and the howl of the wind as it whirled round the house. But in the snug parlor of the vicarage, the three people sat in contented quiet.

Part Two

1705-1709

Eight

Heavy rain pelted the slate roof, plunging headlong down the moorstone granite walls of the simple vicarage at Rowenstow. It was a dwelling which resembled a farmhouse more than a home of the gentry. Like many others in Cornwall, Rowenstow was a poor parish, and the home of its vicar reflected this.

The best furniture was in the parlor: the highly polished ladder-back chairs with their needlepoint cushions sewn by the vicar's sister, the corner buffet displaying the good china on its lower shelves and, above, the tumblers and wineglasses standing upside down behind the thirteen-paned glass door. Beside the china bowls on the mantel were two tall candlesticks, very old, the brass worn to a smooth, warm patina. Silver spoons hung in the small cupboard, glinting in the firelight, and on the long table against one wall were a fine silver plate and punchbowl.

If the Reverend Samuel Hall had had his way, these pieces of silver would have been sold years ago to contribute to the parochial relief fund which was always sadly lacking. But Marya Hall, usually so amenable to her brother's wishes, had insisted that the few good things handed down through many generations should not leave the family. Someday they would comprise Lamorna's meagre dowry. The vicar loved his niece very much, and hastened to agree.

When Samuel Hall had been given the living at Rowenstow

over twenty years earlier, Marya had moved into the vicarage with him to keep house. She was now in her forties, a tall, thin woman with bony, stooping shoulders and a long, plain face. In the winters she was plagued with chills and severe coughs which made her weak and light-headed, though none, as she often told Lamorna, had got the better of her yet.

Lamorna was their younger brother's only child. He and his wife had succumbed to an epidemic which had swiftly ravaged the town of Launceston, where they lived.

Marya and Samuel had not seen the child since her christening; few people travelled any distances then. Launceston lay to the south and east of Rowenstow, which was situated on the northernmost reaches of the Cornish shore.

Lamorna had been taken in by a neighbor; she was two years old and a sweet, affectionate child. After one look at the little girl with her tumbled brown curls and vivid violet-blue eyes, what had been regarded as a duty became a godsend. The child had no other family. Lamorna was their responsibility and very quickly became their joy as well.

From an early age she enjoyed helping her aunt in the house. They had only one servant, Deborah, the childless widow of a sailor, and there was plenty of work to go round. The gentle vicar saw to his niece's education. She was an enthusiastic student. At age seventeen, she was better educated than most girls of her station, though far poorer.

The parish at Rowenstow was a wild, lonely place of headlands hundreds of feet high, deep gorges, and pitiless seas which raged against cruel, jagged rocks. In the summer the rugged heath was softened by golden gorse and purple heather, but even these were stunted and windblown. Bright carpets of wildflowers and tall headland grasses were not to be seen in this bleak northern corner of Cornwall. The breezes were rarely mild, the waves rarely placid. It was one of the most dangerous sections of the Cornish coast.

The local people lived in cottages strung out along the cliffs or moors where they eked out a meagre living by tilling the poor rocky soil and by fishing.

The whistling sound in the air had warned all day of bad weather to come. The month was October, the worst for storms at sea. In the afternoon the sky had turned iron-gray, and swells of black water began lashing against the jagged cliffs. From the church tower came the sound of the bellropes flapping wildly in the fierce wind.

By the time dinner was served in the parlor, it was pitch dark outside and the storm was raging full force. The Reverend Hall had expressed the concern they all felt in his prayer following dinner: "Have mercy on all men who sail Your seas tonight."

The wind whined down the chimney and rattled the windowpanes, but in the stone hearth the fire blazed comfortably. As on every stormy night, Lamorna was grateful to be safe and secure inside the vicarage. The walls were thick and sturdy, and she knew the storm could not touch the three inside.

In this she could not have been more wrong. The storm on that October night would herald a course of events which would determine the rest of her life.

Lamorna and Marya were each embroidering a pillowcase to be given as a wedding present to a couple in the parish whose banns had been read the Sunday before. Years ago, Marya had begun this tradition, making and embroidering linen cases for Rowenstow newlyweds. Theirs would be lives of grinding poverty; Marya believed they ought to start out with something fine. In most cottages the linen cases were treated with care, given far more washings than the family's clothes or, for that matter, the family members themselves.

It was close to ten o'clock, the hour they retired. The Reverend Hall had been reading aloud to his sister and niece as they sewed, though every now and again his mild voice was lost in the fury of the storm. Marya was just about to set aside her embroidery and light the candles to be taken upstairs when there came a pounding at the door.

Lamorna started. Who could it be, so late and in the midst of a storm? Perhaps someone had been taken ill. Marya's help was often sought in nursing. Lamorna hoped that neither of them would have to leave the vicarage tonight.

Deborah came out of the kitchen and went down the hall, grumbling to herself as she often did. They heard her slide the bolt back and open the door. There was the sound of voices, and then into the parlor came Will Pender, one of the local men. He wore no hat; his wet hair was plastered to his scalp, his coat, shirt, and breeches soaked and streaked with mud.

"Beg pardon, sir, miss, but tes a shipwreck!"

"Poor souls," said Marya, drawing in a long breath.

"I fear so, miss."

"Where, Will?" asked the vicar, standing up.

"In the cove below. There be dead men on the vicarage rocks."

"What about survivors? I pray God there are a few."

The man looked grim. "Aye, sir, but I'll not answer for them lasting the night down there."

"You mean the wreckers—" Marya broke off, biting her lip.

"There be scores of 'em down there already and many more to come, I reckon."

"Thank you for coming to me, Will. I'll go down with you."

"Wrap up well, Samuel, and take care. Are they—are they drunk, Will?" asked Marya.

"Well on their way. The cargo be all Cousin Jack."

"Don't worry, Marya. I shall return as soon as I can," said the vicar.

After the heavy wooden door had shut behind them, Lamorna's anxious eyes met those of her aunt. They had lived through similar experiences before, waiting apprehensively for

Samuel to return from the cove. "Cousin Jack" was the term for the cognac smuggled into Cornwall from Brittany. Shipwrecks were often followed by violence on shore as the wreckers fought for the spoils carried in by the rough waves. When they forced open kegs of brandy and drank freely, the white-heat excitement of a wreck was intensified, the people turning savage with greed. Old wrongs between villagers flared up once again under a black sky, and the simple farmers and fishermen, and their wives, often became an ugly mob. Yet both Marya and Lamorna understood the misery and poverty that drove the Cornish people to rejoice when a wreck was sighted, and to seize any cargo they could.

"Uncle won't be harmed," said Lamorna. "You know how the people depend on him."

Marya nodded, smiling faintly, but there was a pucker in her brow. There had been times in the past when innocent people *had* got hurt in the confusion and uproar following a wreck.

It was now past ten o'clock, but there was no question of retiring. They would wait for Samuel's return.

Outside, the men, heads bent, went down the long, steep path of the cliff. They were lashed by wind and rain, one hand shielding their eyes so they could make their way to the beach. Stumbling, the vicar gripped a boulder and righted himself. He had climbed down the cliff many times in all sorts of weather and knew the torturous route well. Still, the ground was slippery, the rocks and pebbles loose underfoot, and Will's lantern did little to reduce the blackness around them.

On the beach was a crowd of men and women. Shouts, cries, and raucous laughter blended with the roars of wind and crashing waves. Parts of the doomed ship's cargo littered the shore. Brandy streamed from kegs cut open with hatchets, filling the tankards brought from the cottages for that very purpose. One man held a keg above his head, tipping the liquid into his mouth and onto his face.

Samuel noticed a few scuffles and blows between men,

doubtless disputes over the booty, but these did not concern him. His eyes searched the black, boiling waves for the ship.

When his eyes grew more adjusted to the night and he spied the wreck, he felt the same shock he always did at times like these. For it was no longer recognizable as a sailing vessel. Battered and ripped by the sea and the cruel rocks, it was now under blows from the wreckers. What had once been a fine, sleek ship had become awkward chunks of timber, torn sails, and dragging cable.

A number of people stood knee-deep in the water, chopping and hacking at the hull. Casks floated about, quickly claimed by villagers who could never have afforded the tea and coffee stored inside. One woman gave an anguished cry as another reached a cask ahead of her. Another woman was busy pulling rings from lifeless hands as the drowned seamen washed ashore.

Samuel had witnessed scores of wrecks. He did not interfere with the wreckers, nor did he remonstrate with them. But what he did most forcibly condemn was the taking of life. English law declared that a vessel was not legally a wreck if man or beast escaped. In some areas of Cornwall it was not uncommon for shipwrecked sailors, coming ashore, to be brutally drowned by wreckers who sought to seize their cargo.

The Reverend Hall had forbidden this heinous practice when he had come to Rowenstow, and he believed he was obeyed. Yet he always went down to a wreck to supervise the bringing ashore of survivors.

"Jem!" he called to a man chopping timber. "Are there any left alive?"

"Eh?" The man looked up, squinting in the rain.

"The crew—any survivors?" shouted Samuel.

"Naught I know," said Jem, and continued his task. He would not commit murder, but he was not about to give up his booty to help the vicar search for half-drowned men. A man's leg washed against him; with scarcely a glance he thrust it away.

"There be 'un floatin' out there, but whether he be dead or alive there's no tellin'," said Will Pender.

Samuel peered at the pounding waves and could just make out a form floating on a large piece of timber.

"Help me, Will, and you, Bob. We must get him to shore."

Will and Bob took a moment to assess the situation. They had high respect for their vicar. But the body he was asking them to save might already be dead, and they would have wasted valuable time which could be spent gathering remains of the cargo for themselves. Then it occurred to both of them that they could divide the huge piece of the deck which supported the body. At least they would have firewood for their families—that was better than nothing.

Securing ropes around their waists that bound them to one another, they waited for Samuel to fasten the end to a boulder. Then they entered the raging surf. Many men had drowned while clearing a wreck, the returning backwater shifting the sand under their feet and throwing them off balance. The water was icily cold and the current strong.

"Don't go out too far," called Samuel to the younger men.

They could not hear him. As they waited for the waves to carry in the floating timber, other bodies washed by, the faces white and staring.

When the raft-like chunk of wood finally reached them, they saw it held two men. One sailor's eyes were open; he was clinging to the boards with one arm and holding onto his companion with the other. Samuel waded in and helped Will and Bob drag the piece of timber ashore with its human cargo.

"Be they dead or alive?" shouted Bob.

The men lay prone on the sand. Both were unconscious; the vicar felt each for a pulse. "Alive. But we must get them out of the storm. You take one and I'll find someone to help me carry the other. These two are, I fear, the only survivors."

Bob and Will lifted one of the men, skirted the rocks on the beach, and began the steep climb to the vicarage high above.

Samuel gripped a burly man by the shoulder. "We must get this man to my house. Help me, Isaac."

The man frowned and hesitated.

"Come on, man! Have some pity!" cried the usually mild vicar.

Reluctantly Isaac set down his pickax. To his neighbor he growled, "Lope off wi' any o' this and I'll slit your throat."

"Not I, Isaac," said the man. " 'Ee knows 'ee can trust I."

Isaac grunted. He stepped across a body that had washed ashore. All the clothes had been torn off and one arm was missing. The corpse was eerily like a marble statue in the darkness, except for the dreadful look on his face.

"Be he alive?" asked Isaac, pointing to the man whose legs the vicar was struggling to lift. He was not about to waste time hauling a corpse. That came later, once the wreck was picked clean. The vicar paid a few men to bury the bodies.

"He is now, but we must get him to shelter and warmth."

Grudgingly Isaac bent over and lifted the man's shoulders. "Ugh, he be a heavy 'un."

The vicar nodded; he was a little breathless. They carried the man over the sand and rocks and up the cliff path. Samuel was forced to stop several times during their ascent, but eventually they reached the house. The rain was slackening, but the gales were still frenzied. They would blow all night long.

"Be he the only 'un, then?" asked Isaac.

"No, there was another. Will and Bob took him up. All the others are dead, poor souls."

"Only nine or ten o' them, sir. Small crew. A smuggler's craft, I reckon."

The vicar nodded. "I believe you're right."

Marya and Lamorna were standing in the doorway. They moved aside so the two men could bring in their burden.

"Into the kitchen," said Marya. "There's a good fire lit. Deborah is seeing to the other sailor now."

Once in the kitchen, Samuel and Isaac gratefully set down

the tall man beside the companion he had saved from drowning.

"Thank you, men," said their vicar, trying to catch his breath. "We'll look after them now."

Will, Bob, and Isaac exchanged glances. It was Will who spoke.

"Beggin' your pardon, sir, but when they come to, 'ee ought to send 'em on their way. 'Ee knows what they say: 'Save a stranger from the sea and he'll turn your enemy.' "

The vicar had heard this superstition many times before. He knew it for what it was, a rationale for the callous disregard of sailors in distress. "Now, Will, I find it impossible to believe these wretched men could do me or my family any harm."

Will shrugged. He had given the warning; he couldn't force the vicar to heed it. The old clergyman did not know what was good for him. Will had no objection to saving a man's life, but he would never have taken an unknown sailor into his hovel.

"Aye, sir," he said, touching his forelock. "Good night to 'ee. Good night, Miss Marya, Miss Lamorna." He and the other men trooped out of the vicarage, eager to return to the beach. They had done their good deed.

"This has cost us, lads," said Isaac grumpily.

"The vicar be a good 'un. Don't he allus see we don't starve? We can do a mite for 'un," said Bob.

"Parson or no, he be a fool to take they two into his house. But there be no reasonin' with 'un."

They all agreed on that.

The two men lay on a spread on the flagstone floor of the kitchen. Samuel had gone for some brandy and Deborah for more blankets. Marya knelt beside them, wiping their faces and bodies dry. The surf had torn their clothes; coils of seaweed clung to them.

Lamorna stood at the kitchen door, gazing down at the two sailors. She was careful not to draw attention to her presence because she knew her aunt would send her to bed now that Samuel had returned.

The faces of the two men were tanned. The smaller of the two was lean and wiry. His trousers were in tatters. Marya dabbed at a long cut on his cheek with a clean cloth.

The other man was large-boned, a head taller than his companion. His trunk was bare and muscular. Long black hair fell over his shoulders; his closed eyes were deep-set. Lamorna studied his broad forehead, the slanted hollows in his cheekbones and about the square jaw. His hand and arm were streaked with blood from gripping the floating timber.

"Miss Lamorna, 'ee ought to be abed, not gawkin' at they," said Deborah sharply as she pushed past with a pile of woolen blankets.

Lamorna's cheeks flamed and she hastily looked away as Marya and Deborah spread the blankets over the men.

"Will they live, Aunt?" she asked. It would be terrible if they were to die after all. That had happened once before: an old man had been carried up the cliff to the vicarage some years ago, only to succumb to the effects of the shipwreck the next day.

"Both their pulses seem strong," said Samuel, coming into the kitchen. "I'll just give them a few sips of this, if they can bestir themselves."

He knelt beside the dark man. "Lamorna, come and lift his head."

She came forward and knelt down. Gingerly she touched the man's head, placing her hands underneath it. Samuel helped her to raise his neck and shoulders.

Lamorna caught her breath. On the man's back were long, ugly welts. Some were scars, others were still fresh and red. "He's been beaten, Uncle," she said.

"Aye. Cruel savages sailors be," said Deborah grimly. "I'll use some mixsher—'twill mend 'em quick."

ECHOES OF THE HEART

Lamorna stared down at the man's face which now rested in her lap. Her uncle bent over, supporting his neck. The stranger's eyes flickered.

"Drink a little of this, my boy," said Samuel, and held the tumbler to his lips. Some of the amber liquid spilled down his chin, but a little found its way into his mouth. He swallowed automatically, coughed, and opened his eyes.

He was looking up at Lamorna's face. She gazed down at him, her heart beginning to thud. He was the most handsome man she had ever seen. His eyes were nearly as dark as his hair, his teeth white and even.

"You're safe, my boy," said Samuel. "Safe at Rowenstow. Come, drink a little more."

The man's gaze shifted to Samuel. He drank another sip of brandy. "Zachy—Zachy—" he mumbled.

"Right here beside you. You saved him," said the vicar. "Don't worry. You are both in good hands. Rest now."

The sailor's eyes focused on Lamorna once again. Then he sighed, closing them. His head turned to one side.

"His hand and arm must be cleaned and bandaged," said Marya.

"I'll help," offered Lamorna. She felt strangely light-headed.

"There's no need for that, child. You must go to bed now. We'll look after them."

Reluctantly Lamorna lifted the man's head from her lap, setting it gently on the spread covering the hard stone floor. She stood up.

Deborah turned the man over and began to spread ointment on his wounds. He did not waken, though he moaned softly. Marya took a strip of cloth and began to bind it round his hand.

"If 'ee knows what's right 'ee'll send they off as soon as they can walk," said Deborah firmly.

"Oh, Deborah, how can you?" asked Lamorna. "You don't really believe that old superstition."

"They be part of a smuggler's crew, I reckon," said Deborah. "Don't want no excise officers nosin' their way into the vicarage."

"They rarely come up this way," said Samuel. "Rowenstow is too isolated. Even the smugglers themselves don't usually favor our cove with their landings. The ship these lads were on was very likely blown off course."

"Smugglers or not, I won't have their deaths on my conscience," declared Marya. "They will stay until they are fully recovered. Bank up the fire, Deborah, so it will burn through the night."

The kitchen fireplace was a large open hearth, high and deep. Great slabs of granite formed the foundation which stood a foot higher than the flagstone floor. To the left of the hearth was a high-backed settle. To the right was the wood corner, piled neatly with the daily supply of furze and bog turf Deborah gathered on the moors.

Deborah took an apronful of furze, brush, and several handfuls of stubbins, tough roots which burned slowly. Over these she laid a covering of turf. The fire would burn with a slow, dull heat. The black iron kettle over the hearth would also stay hot, the water boiling for their morning tea.

"There b'ain't nothin' more us can do tonight," she said. "I will look to they come early morn."

Lamorna, with a long backward glance at the dark, sleeping sailor, followed her aunt upstairs. But sleep eluded her. She lay listening to the surf raging against the cliffs. How terrifying it would be to be at the mercy of those black, relentless waves! It was a miracle that the two sailors had survived and now lay below in the kitchen. The dark one had saved his friend's life, her uncle had said. She wondered about him, seeing his strong, beautiful face and broad, muscular torso. She was aware that smugglers were often dangerous men, but he looked neither cruel nor savage.

By the next morning, the sky was clearing; white mounds of clouds shifted across the blue sky. But the sea still boiled beneath Lamorna's window, lunging and foaming at the slate cliff. Fortunately she could not see the beach from her room, though she could well imagine the bodies and remains of the crew wedged between the rocks and thrown up on the sand.

Splashing her face with water from the pewter basin, Lamorna dressed swiftly in a blue and white striped gown which laced up the front. She tucked a white fichu into the bodice and brushed her rich brown curls. Then she went downstairs and into the parlor where Deborah was setting the table for breakfast.

"Good morning, Deborah. How—how are our guests this morning?"

"Guests, es et?" Deborah snorted. "If 'ee means they two drowned rats asleep on the floor, they be on the mend, I reckon. They took some milky broth an hour ago."

Lamorna noticed that she had only set two places. "Where is Uncle Samuel?"

"Gone to the village with a few shillings to coax one or two men to bury the bodies afore the dogs be at 'em. He be wantin' 'em prayed over and put to rest today."

Lamorna shuddered. She looked down at her plate of fish and mashed potatoes, her appetite gone. Pouring a cup of strong, black tea, she liberally added milk and sugar and sipped it slowly.

Marya came in and sat down across from her. "You look pale, dearest. Not enough sleep, I daresay. The two sailors are going to recover, though. Now eat your breakfast."

Lamorna took a forkful of potatoes. "I'm not very hungry. I was thinking of those who—who didn't survive."

Marya sighed, her long face worn and sorrowful. "Your uncle is planning a service for them later today."

Lamorna nodded. Samuel refused to conform to the common practice of burying shipwrecked sailors without any sort of church rites. By law the drowned men were forbidden churchyard burial. A large pit was dug above the high-water mark and all the bodies dropped inside. Samuel was forced to fall in with this custom, but he did so only after having read the Burial of the Dead. He was determined that they should be interred with as much dignity and promise of the hereafter as was possible.

"Deborah said the two men had some breakfast."

"Nothing solid, but they each drank some broth. They are still quite weak," said Marya.

"Did they speak?"

"Barely a word. Enough for us to tell they are Cornish, however." This was not always the case. On other occasions the survivors of wrecks had been from Scotland, France, even Denmark. "Try to eat a bit, Lamorna. I need you to take some of Deborah's mixture of rugwort and treacle to the Martins' cottage. The youngest has a bad cold."

Lamorna felt sharp disappointment. She was to be sent away on errands rather than be allowed to see the two sailors.

"Later," said her aunt, noting her downcast face and slightly protruding lower lip, "later you may speak to our guests, when they have rested longer."

Lamorna looked across at her aunt, smiling gratefully. She began to eat her breakfast. Marya's thoughtful gaze remained on the girl's face as she drank her second cup of tea.

Lamorna was becoming a beauty. In the past couple of years she had lost the gawkishness of early youth. She had grown several inches in height, her waist narrowing, her small bosom swelling. She was seventeen, in some ways still a child and yet in some ways not. Her eyes were large and an unusual purplish-blue. Her mouth was full and rosy, her teeth small and straight. She had creamy skin with a light dusting of freckles across her nose. Two or three times a week she washed her hair, which curled naturally, despite comments from Deborah about vanity. Indoors it was a warm brown; out of doors it gleamed with copper lights.

Marya's heart contracted. Her love for the girl was strong, even painful. So young, so dear—and so soon to leave me, thought Marya. For before long she would be old enough to marry and have a home of her own.

Yet Marya also wanted to see Lamorna suitably wed. Sadly, her choices—not that a woman had much choice in the finding of a husband—were limited, despite her undeniable beauty, grace, and capabilities. She couldn't possibly marry one of the Rowenstow men—fishermen or laborers—and yet there were few opportunities to mix with the gentry of northern Cornwall. There were the Roscarrocks at Kilworthy, the Tregarths, the Trevanions, the St. Aubyns, the Pendykes, but to these families Lamorna would scarcely seem a fitting bride. The niece of an obscure parson with no connections and no dowry to speak of, the best she could likely hope for was to wed a prosperous farmer who owned his own land. She would be above him in class and education, but he could provide her with a good home. Yet Marya wanted more for her precious niece; she longed to see her happily wed to the scion of some great family.

Deborah came in to collect the breakfast dishes. She handed Lamorna a crock of her "mixsher," made by pouring boiling water over rugwort, grinding the herb, and adding treacle to sweeten it. There were no doctors within miles of Rowenstow, and the people would not have patronized them had there been. They put their faith in the ages-old remedies made from plants. "There be a doctor in every hedge," Deborah was fond of saying.

Lamorna went out the front door of the vicarage. It was a glorious day, the wind strong and invigorating. She felt her blood stirring. The stone path leading away from the vicarage connected with the narrow pony track which crossed the moor to the humble, straggling cottages—hovels, really—that made up the parish of Rowenstow. Behind her was the small church with its short west tower and three-gabled roof.

The track was rough and filled with puddles. With one hand, Lamorna tried to keep her skirts up so they would not trail in the wet and mud. The fury of the storm had flattened the gorse, but it glowed golden in the sunlight. All about her were the colors of autumn: the bright blue sky, the patches of dying heather that had faded to a pinkish-brown, the burnished gorse, the russet bracken. Across the moor rose a long barrow, said to be a burial ground for ancient Cornishmen. The villagers believed that on certain nights it was a gathering place for witches, so they stayed away. Lamorna passed a well and a wheel-headed cross which marked the crossroads. Murmuring a quick prayer for the suicides interred there, she hurried on until she reached the first cottage.

A baby was crying inside. Two older children were playing on the front patch of ground.

"Prudie, are you looking after your baby brother today?" she asked.

The little girl, her face smudged with dirt, nodded. "Ais, miss."

Some parents had no choice but to leave the children home alone while they worked miles away in the fields of a nearby landowner. Often the oldest child left in charge was no more than six or seven. When they were eight, they could work in the fields and add to the family income.

"Do you know why he is crying?" Lamorna asked patiently.

The child shook her head, her hair falling in her face. Lamorna stepped past the two of them and opened the cottage door. The only light inside came from two tiny windows, but she could see well enough to spy the baby in his crib. He was crying fitfully and the reason was evident. The smell of urine and feces was strong; Lamorna wondered when last he had been wrapped in a clean cloth.

She looked about for a basin and some clean linen. What she found was none too clean but it would have to do. Anything was better than the soaked filthy cloth now clinging to the baby. She wiped the little body clean as best she could and pinned the cloth about his little thighs and waist. Then she stripped the bed linen, found a blanket, and laid the baby on it inside his crib.

"I've changed your brother but I daresay he's hungry," she told Prudie. "You must give him some milk."

"Ais, miss."

"And you shouldn't let him lie in dirty linen. Do you understand?"

"Ais, miss," said the child listlessly.

Lamorna shook her head. It was too much responsibility for Prudie to look after a baby and a younger sister four years old.

"I must take this to Mrs. Martin, but I will be back. Then I will fix you something to eat. All right?"

A wan smile lit the girl's face. "Thank 'ee, miss."

Lamorna went further along the rough pony track, passing other granite hovels. The pungent scent of burning turf filled the air. At the Martins' cottage, she knocked on the door. Ill-fitting as it was, it offered little protection from the drafts.

A little boy opened the door. "Hello, Tim," said Lamorna. "I've come with some mixture for your brother."

"Let 'un in, Tim," called Mrs. Martin.

It was damp and chilly inside the cottage. The smells of cooking and burning furze did not hide those of unwashed bodies and rotten bedding. The floor was dirt and it was wet in places where the rain had leaked in.

This cottage, like all the others, had just two rooms, one up and one down. In the living area and kitchen was a table, stools, and one chair which belonged to the head of the household. The children had to sit on blocks of wood. The inside walls had once been white-washed, but years of accumulated grime and smoke had darkened them. In one corner a small cupboard held a few pottery cups, basins, and tin plates. Upstairs, the family slept together on mattresses on the floor, with only sacks and their clothes for covers.

"Some o' Deborah's mixsher, es et?" asked Mrs. Martin, coming forward. She was no more than thirty but looked fifteen years older. Her dark hair was thin and scraggly, her face careworn. Wiping her hands on her dirty apron, she took the crock.

"Just give him a little. Deborah says it's strong."

"Ais. He be frettin' with an ear ache all night long as well. I cut him an onion. Harry, hold that onion to your ear like I told 'ee."

Lamorna smiled at the boy, who lifted the onion to his head.

"Wild storm come up last night," continued Mrs. Martin. "Have two o' them sailors at the vicarage, do 'ee?"

"Yes, the only survivors." Lamorna hoped that Mrs. Martin was not going to repeat the notion about a stranger from the sea turning into one's enemy.

She didn't. Mrs. Martin had mentioned the sailors for only one reason. "Look 'ee, miss, at what Zeke took from the wreck." Her colorless voice was touched with unaccustomed excitement. "Heaven be thanked the wreck weren't on a Sunday like the last else he couldn't've gone til Monday for the pickins."

She held up several bolts of cotton cloth. "Tight inside a box they were with never a drop o' water on 'em. The children will get new clothes. 'Twas a blessing, that wreck."

"Not for the poor men who lost their lives," said Lamorna sharply.

Mrs. Martin shrugged. "Tes the will o' God, I reckon. The pickin's won't do they dead 'uns any good."

Lamorna nodded. Why shouldn't Mrs. Martin, living in a hovel with several children who rarely got enough to eat, plagued by sickness, rejoice over the good fortune the shipwreck had brought her family?

She was startled by a loud snore coming from upstairs.

"Tes Zeke," said Mrs. Martin a trifle defiantly.

"He's not working at Nanfanna today?" asked Lamorna, referring to a farm some miles distant.

"No, he be poorly today," said Mrs. Martin.

Drunk the night before on cognac from the wreck and now

sleeping it off, thought Lamorna. "Well, I'll be going, Mrs. Martin. I've got to stop by the Sauls' cottage. Where is Kate, by the way?"

"Her be workin' up Nanfanna farm, pickin' stones and tendin' the chickens," said Mrs. Martin proudly.

"Oh. I didn't think she was old enough."

"Her's gone ten year."

"Ten?" The small red-headed girl didn't look nearly that old. "They—they certainly grow up quickly."

"Ais, miss, that they do. Peter be there, too, singin' to the oxen to keep 'em in line."

"Mr. Poldirth is lucky to have them."

Mrs. Martin looked blank. "I reckon they be the lucky ones, miss." She did not add that she no longer had to provide their dinner because they now ate at the farm.

"Be they buryin' they sailors today?" she asked.

"Yes, once my uncle has read prayers for them."

"The vicar ought to send the live two straight off. Bad luck they be to they that takes 'em in."

"They are very ill, Mrs. Martin," said Lamorna impatiently.

Mrs. Martin pushed back a limp lock of hair. "When I were a girl, some folks took in a wrecked sailor. Before the year were out, one of the daughters took to laughin' and cryin' all at once and had to be ducked in St. Nun's Well off and on until she died."

Lamorna did not answer; she merely said goodbye and left the cottage, feeling relieved. In the Sauls' hovel, the children were all inside, the baby still fretting.

"What did your mother leave for your dinner, Prudie?"

"Bit o' pie from last night."

"Very well. You sit down and I'll get you some."

When the older children were eating their small portions of fish pie, Lamorna prepared some warm milk for the baby.

"What did you have for breakfast?" she asked them.

"Blue sky and sinkers, miss," said Prudie.

No wonder they were hungry. Blue sky and sinkers was a

weak concoction made by adding barley flour and skimmed milk to boiling water. The liquid, bright blue in color, was then poured into bowls over pieces of barley bread which remained at the bottom. Not at all a sustaining breakfast for men who put in five hours of hard labor before noon, or a woman or child who picked turnips or radishes from eight o'clock in the morning until six at night. But it was often all that was served for breakfast in the cottages, especially in winter. Lamorna would ask Deborah to bring some pilchards, carrots, and potatoes to the Sauls later that day.

It was time she returned to the vicarage; her aunt would be wondering what had become of her. And she was hoping to see the two sailors. Her belly clenched with anticipation as she set off along the headland, the wind whipping her curls, the gulls screeching overhead. Below, the sea battered the base of the slate-purple cliff. The air was fresh and tangy after the smells of the cottages. Lamorna hastened past the hedgerow of prickly brambles that formed a fence along the headland.

When she entered the hallway of the vicarage, her aunt was putting on her gray cloak. "There you are, child. Your uncle wishes to read the service now. You've been gone a long while."

"I know. I stopped at the Sauls' cottage. The baby needed to be washed and changed and fed. Prudie Saul is too young to cope."

Her aunt sighed. "She needs looking after as well as the other two. You were right to stop. But we must go to church."

Lamorna felt a twinge of dismay. She disliked funerals, despite the frequency with which they were held. There were many deaths every year at Rowenstow from illnesses and accidents. Yet she never got used to them.

"The two sailors—are they awake yet?" she asked wistfully.

"Yes. You may speak to them later, after luncheon."

Nine

The Rowenstow church dated back to Norman times, though sections of it had been rebuilt in the fifteenth century. Inside were carved moldings of a dolphin, a whale, and a lamb lying between two dragons. The ceiling was vaulted; a row of arches stood on both sides. On one wall a medieval mural depicted "Christ Blessing the Trades" in which blood dripped down from a crudely-drawn figure onto farming and fishing tools painted beside him. The figure's eyes were dark and dull; Lamorna considered the mural ugly. She preferred the stained glass windows that had been donated by a baron in the Middle Ages; they had escaped destruction from Cromwell's soldiers over fifty years before. Rowenstow was too isolated and remote, even for the Puritans who had sacked other Anglican churches throughout Cornwall.

One of the windows displayed a lamb, another a pelican and its brood, and one St. Peter and St. Paul. The bench-ends had been elaborately carved in the Tudor years with the figures of a jester, male and female saints, and, Lamorna's favorite, a mermaid clutching a large comb and mirror. The door in the northern wall was known as the Devil's Door. When a new member was christened, the door was thrown open to allow the devil to escape. No graves were dug on the northern side of the church where Satan and his hosts were believed to abide.

The Reverend Hall stood in his robes in the small wineglass pulpit, prayerbook in hand. Several men from the village shuffled restlessly. These were the gravediggers. Lamorna and her aunt entered a pew on the opposite side.

Samuel began to read. " 'But there the glorious Lord will be unto us a place of broad rivers and streams; wherein shall go no galley with oars, neither shall gallant ships pass thereby. For the Lord is our judge, the Lord is our lawgiver, the Lord is our King. He will save us. The tacklings are loosed; they could not well strengthen their mast, they could not spread the sail; then is the prey of a great spoil divided; the lamb taketh the prey.

" 'They who go down to the sea in ships, and occupy their business in great waters . . .' "

When the service was ended, they all filed outdoors. Will Pender said to Samuel, "We'll be buryin' the bodies now, sir." He held a battered woven basket in one hand. Lamorna shuddered, realizing its significance. It was for collecting the "gobbets"—the pieces of the bodies that had been severed by the slate rocks.

"Thank you, men," said Samuel. He was tired today. They touched their forelocks and headed over to the cliff path.

Lamorna walked back to the vicarage with her aunt and uncle. Deborah was laying the parlor table for dinner. Lamorna went upstairs and washed her hands. She slipped a clean organdy fichu in the square-cut bodice of her gown, smoothing her wind-tossed hair.

Dinner was squab pie, a delicious combination of apples, bacon, onions, mutton, and young pigeon, but Lamorna again had little appetite. When they had finished she said, "Shall I take the plates in to Deborah, Aunt Marya?"

Marya smiled. "Yes, do. She has her hands full looking after the sailors. Go ahead and make the acquaintances of our guests."

Lamorna collected the plates and pushed open the kitchen door. Her heart had begun to hammer. Deborah was kneading dough at the worn table. She glanced up as Lamorna set down the plates but said nothing. Lamorna stepped forward to where the two men lay.

The sandy-haired man lay on his side, asleep. The other man gazed into the hearth at the cheerful, crackling flames. He was vaguely conscious of approaching footsteps, but he did not look in their direction. His head ached where he had struck it when the ship was going down. But he heard a soft voice ask, "How are you feeling?", and turned his head.

It was she. He had not dreamed her. When he had seen no one but the vicar, his sister, and the housekeeper, he had assumed that the girl's face he had glimpsed between bouts of unconsciousness was a trick of his imagination.

This, their first meeting, would remain in his memory. He could never forget, though often he would curse it. He lay in rags at her feet, her standing above him fresh and lovely in a striped gown. The image of their two positions would torment him for a long time to come.

But Lamorna did not stand for long. When he did not answer, when he could do nothing but gaze into the blue eyes so remarkably tinged with the purple of heather, she knelt down beside him.

"Don't try to talk. You had a very narrow escape. You must be feeling poorly indeed."

Her voice was sweet and slightly husky. He tried to reply, clearing his throat. "Not too bad, miss."

"Do you know where you are? This is my uncle's house. He is the vicar of Rowenstow, in north Cornwall."

"I told him, Miss Lamorna," said Deborah. "What be I doin' here all mornin' but talkin' to he while I work? He b'ain't got the sense to sleep like the other 'un."

The sailor grinned. "I can't sleep with the smell o' good cookin' about me. But her will only give me broth."

"Your belly b'ain't ready for naught else. Bide your time." Deborah spoke curtly but Lamorna could tell she was pleased.

"What is your name?"

"Dirk, miss. Dirk Killigrew." He could smell the lavender water with which she rinsed her hair.

"And are you truly a smuggler?" she asked.

"Miss Lamorna, leave well enough alone, do," scolded the housekeeper.

His dark eyes took on a shuttered look. "Aye. I reckon I be. Zachy and me—we be all that were left."

"My uncle has read prayers for your captain and friends. I am sorry."

Dirk scowled. "He ought to 've saved his breath. All the prayin' in the world won't do they no good. The captain were an evil man and most o' the crew took after he." His voice had roughened.

Lamorna was taken aback. "But the man you saved . . ."

"Zachy? Aye, he be a good true 'un." He paused. "And now us be free from the black bastard."

"Here, we'll be havin' none of that talk in the vicar's house, lad!" cried Deborah. "Miss Lamorna be gently bred, and I'll not have her ears sullied with rough sailor talk."

Dirk flushed. "I beg your pardon, miss. I've had naught but rough company for many a year."

"That's all right," Lamorna said soothingly.

"Miss Lamorna, leave he to rest now. He has a sore head and shouldn't be answering questions."

Lamorna stood up hastily. "I hope I didn't tire you. Goodbye."

He didn't want her to go; he had forgotten his throbbing head, but naturally he could not say that. "Goodbye, miss," was all he said.

The following evening the Halls learned the story of the two shipwrecked men. Deborah had given them bites of solid food that day, washed down with strong milky tea. She had filled the large tin tub with hot water for them to bathe in, and brought them one of the vicar's razors. Marya had managed to fit them with old breeches and muslin shirts from two of the village men who were happy to take payment in return. They bathed, shaved, and dressed, still rather weak and wobbly. After a long rest and a supper of muggety pie, they sat round the kitchen table with the vicar and his family. The vicar poured them tumblers of port wine.

Dirk's face was dark in the shadowed room; his glossy black hair hung over his shoulders and down his back. His head no longer ached. From time to time he looked across at Lamorna.

"Have 'ee heard in these parts of the smuggler, Captain Trey?"

Samuel nodded, his brow puckering. "Do you mean that was his ship?"

"Aye. 'Ee wasted fine prayers on a devil, sir."

"Prayers are wasted on no one," said Samuel gently. "Even such a man as Captain Trey."

"All that 'ee's heard o' him be true, sir," said Zachy. "Terrible cruel and evil he were. He thought nowt o' cuttin' off men's hands, o' slittin' their throats."

"Did he beat you?" asked Lamorna.

Dirk flushed. So she had seen. "Aye," he growled, not looking at her.

"But my son, how was it that you and Zachy were a part of this man's crew?" asked Samuel.

It was Zachy who answered. Glancing at Dirk's rigid face, he said, "We were pressed into workin' for he. One night comin' home after our shift at the mine, we be struck down. When us came to, we were on his ship, in chains. That were six year ago."

Lamorna caught her breath in pity and horror. For six years they had been forced to work for the brutal smuggler. She had heard of men being taken aboard ships against their will, drugged or stunned into immobility. Even the British Navy was not above pressing men into service were it deemed necessary. Now she understood what Dirk had meant about being free.

Samuel shook his head sadly. "I'm truly sorry, my son. Where did you both live before?"

"Landrawna," said Zachy.

"Ah, yes, near to Kilworthy, further down the coast. But Sir John Roscarrock owns no mines. You worked at—?"

"Wheel Charity," Dirk said, and there was an almost savage bitterness in his tone.

The vicar did not appear to notice. "One of Matthew Tregarth's mines?" he asked.

"Aye." Dirk looked down, his two large brown hands clenching into fists in his lap.

"The mine is doing well, I believe. No doubt they'll take you on again when you have fully recovered. Until then you are to remain here."

Dirk's face relaxed a bit. "I haven't thanked 'ee proper, sir, for haulin' we out o' the sea and lookin' after we."

"We must let them rest now, Samuel," said Marya. Rising, she gestured to Lamorna, who stood up as well.

The sailors shifted to their feet, rather clumsily touching their forelocks. "Thank 'ee, miss, sir, for all 'ee done for we," Dirk said again.

Against his will he looked at Lamorna. Her eyes were dark with compassion. He stepped aside for her to pass, his gaze taking in her profile, the warm brown curls, the rise of her small breasts beneath the fichu, her narrow waist. Swallowing hard, he turned aside as she left the room with her aunt and uncle.

"That parson," began Zachy after a pause, "he be like no other I heard of. Lookin' after we, even sittin' at table with we. Like no gentry I ever seen afore."

"He be a rare man," said Deborah who was banking up the fire for the night. "He follows the Scriptures true. Poor as a mouse he be, though he gives away all he can so folk don't starve."

"Owns no mine or land, do he?" asked Dirk.

"I be tellin' 'ee he do not. His livin' comes from Sir John Roscarrock up Kilworthy. Not that Sir John worships here."

"He allus went to St. Petroc's, in Landrawna," said Zachy.

"I remember that scurvy parson there, the Reverend Poldew. He was another kettle of fish. Never one to care for the likes o' we."

"The vicar of Rowenstow be a true man o' God with holiness coursin' through his veins," declared Deborah.

"Miss Lamorna," said Dirk, gazing into the fire. "Got no parents, has her?" His tone was disinterested, cool.

Deborah regarded him sharply. "Not since they were took with sickness when she were two year old. Miss Hall and the vicar be the only folk her has. And don't think I didn't see the way 'ee looked at she tonight, lad."

Dirk's face grew hot. "I weren't meanin' no disrespect," he mumbled.

"Well, see that 'ee keep it that way. Her's a mere child and gently reared, as I told 'ee. Good night." Without a backward look, Deborah went through to her own room.

Zachy stretched out in front of the fire. He sensed his friend's embarrassment and talked idly. "It be good to lie down again. My head were startin' to spin."

Dirk said nothing. Humiliation seethed in him. He did not blame Deborah; she was right. He had no call to moon over the vicar's pretty niece. She was gentry, no matter how impoverished. Had he forgotten what members of the gentry had done to him? Lying there by the fire, he forced himself to recall his suffering at their hands. The hateful memories blotted out Lamorna's lovely face. A well of loathing surged in him. He had learned in no uncertain terms what a tremendous gap existed between those like him and the upper classes. It was a gap that could never be breached. And Miss Lamorna Hall stood firmly on the opposite side. He must not lose sight of that again. Weakness had caused him to think and act foolishly; now that he was gaining his strength he would not be so witless.

"Us have no need to go back to the mine, Zachy," said Dirk.

Zachy nodded, his eyes lighting up. "I be thinkin' the same thing. The captain's gold and silver."

"Aye. Enough to set we up."

Zachy frowned. "What do 'ee mean, Dirk?"

"What do us know, Zachy, other than minin'?"

Zachy shrugged. "Free tradin', I reckon."

"Aye." Dirk's deep-set eyes narrowed. "For six year we slaved for that devil, Trey, took beatin's and starved like rats whenever he took a notion. And sat in chains when he weren't needin' us to work. But us learned the trade, Zachy, learned the sea's moods, and the best coves and clefts to slip in and out of. Us know enough to sail a craft of our own. With the coins the cap'n stashed in the cave, and none but ourselves to know of it, us can buy and sail our own vessel to France and back."

Zachy leaned up on one elbow. " 'Ee'd be a cap'n, Dirk?"

"Aye. But not like Trey, damn his memory. I'll run a good ship and treat the men fair. What do 'ee say, Zachy? Will 'ee be my first mate and partner?"

Zachy grinned, his blue eyes bright. " 'Ee do know the sea, better'n I. It do sound a grand idea, lad."

"Us'll go to Landrawna and Pendreath for any men who'd care to make up the crew. And deal with the Frenchies in Roscoff as fair as with our own Cornishmen." He gazed into the fire. "Never again will us do another's bidding. Us'll be our own men, Zachy, subject to none."

Over the course of the next few days the men grew stronger. They ate heartily and with great relish; food such as Deborah cooked had not passed their lips in many a year. Her pasties and pies filled with meat and vegetables, her puddings, apple tarts, and heavy currant cakes she served them with clotted cream and bramble jam—all were devoured as though each meal were their last. Filled with purpose and determination, their bodies warmed, their bellies full, Dirk and Zachy made their plans.

Lamorna had begun to avoid the kitchen. She had realized

that she seemed to make both men uncomfortable. They would abruptly stop talking or bantering with Deborah when she entered, and the atmosphere in the room would become awkward and stilted. Lamorna was both hurt and puzzled; she performed the tasks her aunt gave her forlornly, and she continued to see to the children in Rowenstow whose parents had left them alone.

Samuel sat talking with the two sailors in the evenings, but Lamorna and Marya stayed in the parlor, occupied with their embroidery. Marya noticed her niece's woeful countenance and guessed a little of the cause. Dirk Killigrew must seem very attractive to the girl with his dark hair, deep-set brown eyes, and handsome face. But even she had no notion of the depth of Lamorna's interest. If she had, she would have insisted that the two men leave the vicarage.

About a week following the sailors' rescue, Lamorna was coming along the headland from the village. It was late afternoon, and she was tired from looking after the various children in the cottages. Her fichu was soiled and her green skirt dusty and spattered with milk stains.

To her chagrin, she saw Dirk standing up ahead. He was staring out to sea. There was no way she could avoid him, but she would hurry past as quickly as she could.

When she got close she murmured a greeting, her face downcast. He turned and seemed taken aback. "Hello, miss." She would have moved past him but he stopped her with a question.

"Where've 'ee been, Miss Lamorna?" With her tousled hair and simple work gown she looked like a village lass, except for her white stockings and black buckled shoes. Those no village girl could have afforded. His eyes did not miss the spots on her gown. "Fall down, did 'ee?"

Her eyes widened. Did he think her a child, slipping in puddles? "Certainly not. I've been in the village, looking in on the children left alone."

His brows drew together; he was astonished. " 'Ee does that?"

"Yes, I've just told you. Someone has to see that they come to no harm. In the past there have been fires, pigs attacking children . . ."

He nodded. Every village had those tragedies. "What do 'ee do, miss?"

"Oh, feed them, change the babies' linen, make certain the lower doors are bolted so no animal can enter, tell them stories."

Now he was astounded. In all his twenty-four years, he had never once heard of a young lady working in a laborer's cottage. He did not know what to say.

"You don't believe me?" asked Lamorna, frowning.

"Oh, aye, miss," he said, flushing. Suddenly he longed to reach out and take her hand, even to touch her glowing cheek. " 'Tis good of 'ee, Miss Lamorna," he said softly.

"Today I had an idea. Some of the children are quite bright. I was wondering . . . do you think it would be foolish if I tried to teach them to read and write?"

Dirk's narrow mouth tightened; he turned away, peering out to sea. There again was the enormous gap between them. And he had wanted to hold her hand. Fool! " 'Tis not for I to say, miss."

Lamorna realized instantly what she had said. Dirk himself had been one of those children; he could not read. Biting her lip, she sought to change the subject.

"My uncle is planning to write to the mine captain at Wheel Charity on your behalf, and to Matthew Tregarth. He wishes to help you find employment."

Dirk whirled to face her, his eyes blazing. She took a step back, flinching. "There'll be no writin' to they! I'd sooner work another six year for Cap'n Trey than for the likes of them!"

Lamorna regarded him in dismay. "I—I'm sorry—I don't understand—"

Dirk's jaw clenched but the fire in his eyes died. "No more do 'ee, miss. I spoke too rough again and I beg 'ee's pardon. But Zachy and me—us have far better plans."

"Oh." She waited but he did not enlighten her. "Well," she said lamely, "I daresay I should be getting back."

He could not let her go yet, not with his harsh words ringing in her ears. "I've a mind to see the church. Will 'ee show me?"

"Of course, if you like."

Inside the church it was cool and smelt damp. They walked down the center aisle past the carved bench-ends. He stopped before the one of the mermaid.

"Isn't she lovely?" asked Lamorna softly. The mermaid's long curls covered her breast; her scaly tail curved up beside her.

He wanted to tell her that the mermaid reminded him of her but he feared speaking so boldly. "Aye," he said.

"Perhaps you and Zachy will sit with us on Sunday?" she asked shyly.

His voice was abrupt, even curt. "Won't be here, miss. Leavin' on the morrow, we be. Sun up."

"Oh." She felt a piercing disappointment. "Well, you'll have a long walk ahead of you. You must take food for yourselves."

He shook his head. He needed nothing from her and her family.

Lamorna, gazing at his face with its strong bones, realized that again she had somehow offended him.

"I just thought you might get hungry . . . though if you'd rather have money I'm sure Uncle—"

"—Damn you and your bloody charity!" he cried. This time there was no containing his outrage. "Zachy and me don't need ought from 'ee. The parson pulled us from the sea and fed and clothed us. Let that be an end on it!"

In all her seventeen years no one had ever shouted at Lamorna that way. She winced as though she had been struck, turned, and ran out of the church. Her face was red; tears welled up in her eyes and spilled down her cheeks.

Dirk watched her go, unrepentant. Her offer of food, then money, had sorely offended him. How dared she lump him together with the poor wretches who survived on the vicar's generosity? He would be beholden to the Halls no longer. And before long he would be far richer than they, gentry or no.

Then he felt deeply ashamed. He had lived so long among brutes that he did not recognize true kindness when he saw it. This family had saved his life, seen that he was warm and well-fed. And this was how he repaid them—by shouting at Lamorna, who was only acting as her aunt and uncle had taught her.

It wasn't her fault that she was the loveliest thing he had ever seen in all his life. It wasn't her fault that she was the niece of a vicar and not of a miner or fisherman. It wasn't her fault that he had endured years of poverty and despair, while the Tregarths and those like them lived like kings.

Striding from the church, he saw Lamorna hurrying across the moor. He began to run after her. Her legs were no match for his; before long he had caught up with her.

"Miss, please forgive me. I wronged 'ee, I know. I be nothin' but a brute."

She turned to face him, tears streaming down her face. He stared at her, aghast. He had done this to her. Her, of all people. He was a lout while she . . .

Without realizing that he did so, he put out a hand and grasped her slender arm. Her small bosom was heaving, her breath coming rapidly.

"For six year I've lived with savages, miss. I were a savage to 'ee back there and I be that sorry for it. 'Ee's been very kind to we, and your aunt and uncle, too. But Zachy and me don't need the vicar's shillings." He spoke with a calm dignity, despite the fact that his heart was thumping in his chest. He wanted desperately to take her in his arms, to wipe away her tears . . .

Lamorna nodded. She had deeply wounded his pride. This man was no ordinary sailor or miner. He seemed very large standing beside her, his black hair blowing loosely in the breeze.

"I ask your pardon as well," she said in a low voice. "I will be sorry to see you go."

Dirk drew in his breath. His eyes gazed intently into hers. Slowly his hand slid up her arm to her shoulder. She trembled. A violent wave of desire rose in him. He had not been with a woman since that distasteful time in France when Captain Trey's first mate had brought a group of prostitutes aboard. His belly churned. My God, how could he even think of that now? That repellent episode had naught to do with this girl. He recalled the woman's foul breath and lewd jests. Neither had kept them from coupling like animals, but afterward he had felt revulsion for himself and for her. It was a miracle he'd not caught the French pox.

"Dirk! Dirk, lad!"

Abruptly he released her, breathing raggedly. "It—it be Zachy."

"Come on, Deborah's got the tea ready. Fuggan cake, too."

Lamorna and Dirk began to walk toward the vicarage. She felt warm and light-headed. As she wiped off her cheeks, her fingers shook.

What in bloody hell was I going to say? thought Dirk. That I'll be comin' into money, that I'll give her a fine house, furniture, silk gowns . . . ? That I'll spend my life lookin' after her if only she'll marry me? Aye, those words had filled his head and been on the tip of his tongue.

The realization was so absurd, so inconceivable and hopeless that his head reeled. Thank God Zachy had called out before he had spoken. For once the words were said, he would never have been able to take them back. God's blood, he thought bitterly, I've got to get away from Rowenstow . . .

* * *

When Lamorna awoke early the next morning, she learned that the two sailors had already left the vicarage.

"Before dawn it were," said Deborah. "Not that I were sad to see the backs of they. My kitchen be my own again and the goings-on back to what I be used to."

Lamorna said nothing. She could not eat the bacon and freshly baked bread Deborah had set before her. Inside she was aching and hollow. She got up from the table and went outside. Deborah watched her go and for once did not scold. Her broad face wore a rueful expression; she shook her head. It had to happen someday. The girl had no experience with men, and even she had to admit that Dirk was a fine specimen of young manhood. But he was no better than one of the cottagers at Rowenstow, far below her in station. A handsome face and hard body counted for little when it was enormously outweighed by breeding, class, and education.

And there was something else. Despite the playful teasing manner he sometimes had adopted in response to her grumblings, he was not an easy man. Not like Zachy. Something ate at him from within, a bitterness, a rancor. Zachy had undergone a similar ordeal with Captain Trey, but whatever seethed beneath Dirk's surface was lacking in him. That Dirk had become infatuated with Lamorna was all too clear to Deborah, hide it though he might. She was a pretty lass with a sweet nature. He had doubtless never met any such, just as she had met no one quite like him. Perhaps it was inevitable that they had been drawn to one another. Deborah was certain that Dirk himself realized the incongruity of the situation, and that had prompted their departure this morning.

Ah well, thought Deborah, 'tis the way o' life, I reckon. Miss Lamorna'll get over it after a bit. Resolutely she put the matter from her mind, concentrating on the morning's chore of scrubbing the hearth.

* * *

Lamorna had run out of the vicarage and across to the church. Hurrying around to the back of the building, she had leaned against the cold, weathered granite and wept. She was both bewildered and overwhelmed by the new feelings recently stirring inside her, and now to add to them was a sharp sense of anguish and loss. Dirk had deliberately not waited to bid her farewell. Last night he had barely looked at her, his face set in grim lines. In some way again he was angry and now she could not make amends. When he had taken her arm and they had looked into one another's eyes, a powerful tingling had at once thrilled and lulled her. She had assumed he felt the same. But today he had left without saying goodbye, without ever suggesting a future meeting.

Lamorna did not consider the difference in their classes. To her it was irrelevant. She knew only that she loved and trusted him. And he had betrayed that love and trust by leaving her.

Dirk and Zachy had a long day's walk ahead of them. Despite their protests, Deborah had packed a lunch for them. Dirk understood Deborah's relief in seeing them off; she had not beat about the bush with him.

When Zachy had gone out to use the privy, she addressed a few harsh words to Dirk. "I seen the way the wind be blowin', my lad. And her scarce more than a child. But child or no, her be a *lady.* Vicar's niece."

"I don't need 'ee to be tellin' me that," said Dirk, reddening. "I know I be dirt under the feet of all gentry."

Deborah had softened. "Sit down and eat. We allus kill a sow in the autumn and I have bacon for 'ee this morn."

"Thank 'ee, no," he said coldly.

She placed her hands on her hips. "Don't be daft, lad. I spoke strong words to 'ee, I know, but I be an old woman and 'tis been many a year that I've looked after Miss Lamorna. I only want to see she comes to no hurt or harm."

Dirk's angry eyes met hers. "I would not be hurtin' a hair

on her head, nor would I do any wrong to she. I'd cut off my arm first."

"She don't understand the world and its ways. 'Ee do."

"Aye," was his gruff response.

Zachy came in then and sat down, sniffing the food appreciatively. Rarely in his life had he tasted pork. On the ship the men had been fed conger eel stew and the everlasting pilchards.

"Eat hearty, do," said Deborah. "I'll fetch tea for 'ee."

When they had finished Dirk said, "Tell the vicar again we'll not be forgettin' his kindness, ever."

" 'Ee've been very good to we," nodded Zachy. "And I've never eaten better in all my life."

"Go along with 'ee," said Deborah, embarrassment making her irritable. "It'll be good to have 'ee two great lummoxes out o' my kitchen."

Zachy grinned; Dirk took the wrapped-up lunch she handed him. "Good luck to 'ee," she said. "And stay out o' trouble."

"Trouble do seem to come lookin' for I," said Dirk with a rueful smile. His anger had cooled. "Goodbye to 'ee."

The two men set out along the cliff path. Overhead the sky was a deep violet, but across the moors the horizon glowed like a fiery opal. Soon the rising sun streamed over the rough heath scarred with rocks and boulders, gilding the gorse and warming the sailors as they walked.

They were not headed directly for Landrawna. Though both longed to be reunited with their loved ones—Zachy with his sister and her family and Dirk with his mother—they were determined not to return as shipwrecked sailors of a press gang, but as men with money in their pockets and a bright future ahead of them.

Some miles up the coast from Landrawna in a remote part of the coastline was a hill fort of crumbling granite. No one knew how old it was; some said the Old Ones had built it many years before the birth of Christ. Dirk cared nothing for its age or history; for him it had a far different significance.

Under the outcrop of stone blocks protruding from the grassy headland was an opening. It had always been covered with a wilderness of thorns, bracken, and briars. But Dirk, along with the rest of the crew, had often worked to clear away the jumble of vegetation and reveal the entrance. Always at night by lantern light, and always at gunpoint. Captain Trey had trusted no one, especially his crew. Through the fougou were several chambers where the smuggled goods were stored, waiting for the land crew to pack them on their ponies and deliver them up and down the coast and across Whistmoor.

Yet what Dirk now sought was not inside the fougou. That was in a place as secret but far less accessible. A fortnight ago he had observed the first mate scramble down the cliff on a rope, his shirt bulging. He had been gone a short time before he had signaled to Captain Trey that the crew was to haul him up. When he reached the headland, his shirt was loose and blowing in the wind.

That morning Dirk and Zachy had met only a few people on the cliff path; it was the tracks on the moors that were used by farmers to convey their produce to market, and by the boys driving ponies that carried coal to nearby mines. When they reached the hill fort about noon, they had not seen a soul for miles. Standing on the headland, they peered down the cliff to the water and rocks below.

"There be a cave down there, Zachy, and I'll find it. Stay here, will 'ee, and wait for I to tug the rope. Give a whistle if it b'ain't clear."

Dirk uncoiled the rope he had taken from the beach at Rowenstow one day after the shipwreck. He laughed. "Black Trey, the old devil, he even left us the rope. The gold and the means to get it! But I still be hopin' his filthy hide burns in hell."

"Aye," said Zachy. "But take care, lad. 'Tis a fearful drop."

"That be why I reckon the treasure still be there," said Dirk. They secured one end of the rope, knotting it round a large boulder. Tying the other end about his waist, Dirk carefully went down the precipice. Zachy watched his head disappear over the cliff and then glanced about to make certain no one was approaching from a distance. The salt air was tangy in his nostrils and blew his sandy hair out of its confining piece of string at the back of his neck. The water pounded against the spiked rocks below. Be careful, lad, he thought. Whatever was in the cave was not worth the death of his closest friend.

About halfway down the promontory, Dirk slipped against the face of the cliff, scraping his face and tearing his breeches. Clutching a rock, he felt about with his foot for some small outcropping on which to stand. When he located one, he paused, trying to catch his breath. It would not do to hurry.

He began to search for a cave, peering this way and that. There was nothing to his right which could be called an opening; it was sheer, solid rock all the way down. Looking to the left, he noticed a long, narrow cleft. But he could not be certain that that was the place the first mate had gone; it seemed to be merely a hollow between two jutting surfaces.

Dirk frowned. He could not see any dark, gaping spaces in the side of the cliff, nothing but this fold. He decided that he could swing across to it easily, and perhaps from that position a larger opening might reveal itself. Gripping the rope with his callused hands, he flung himself off the outcropping and to the left. For a couple of instants a jolt of panic passed through him as his feet were suspended in midair. But then he landed on the ledge just in front of the cleft.

Impatiently he brushed the loose strands of hair from his eyes. The insides of his palms were bleeding, despite the calluses. The narrow opening was high and pitch-dark. Taking his tinderbox and a piece of hemp from his pocket, he lit it and felt his way ahead. Before he had taken more than six steps, the light revealed nothing but solid granite in front of him. Daunted, he looked about for a second opening and found it below his waist. He got to his knees and began to crawl.

After a short time, the tunnel enlarged and he was able to

walk again. He stood at the entrance to a huge vaulted room. The ocean sounded very faint. His light was burning quicker than he had anticipated; he had to find what he was looking for quickly and make his way back through the cave.

Scattered about the rock floor were empty brandy bottles. Dirk's bare feet were already bleeding from the sharp ledges; he had to be careful not to step on any shards. Men had died from simple cuts which had festered.

Captain Trey's crew had never seen this cave, except for the first mate, but they had all been aware of its existence. While the first mate had scrambled down the face of the cliff, the crew had waited in silence, wary of the captain and his two pistols. Yet the captain had rarely shot to kill; he preferred a slower means of execution for those who earned his wrath.

The most commonly used was the old form of Cornish justice dating back no one knew how far. The doomed man was fastened to a rock out to sea. He was given two barley loaves and a pitcher of water. When the tide came in, he was drowned. Dirk and Zachy had helplessly witnessed such horrors, the victims usually men who had sought to escape the ship's servitude, or a land smuggler Trey believed had cheated him. The men were flogged frequently at the captain's whims; he had considered that the best way to manage his crew.

The captain had had other pleasures as well. He had once crushed a man's fingers with his boots and slit a Frenchman's belly open with his knife. The man had believed he was going to dine with the captain. And then there was that hideous night when they had sat awake in chains listening to the screams of some poor woman the captain had taken aboard at Roscoff. Hardened as most were to the captain's savagery, the woman's shrieks had been ghastly to hear. The youngest of the crew had clapped his hands over his ears and moaned, rocking back and forth. Dirk, his knuckles white, his teeth grinding, had cried, "May the devil take the bloody fiend!"

One of the men had reported his words to the captain and Dirk had been lashed. But before that he was ordered to clean the woman's blood from the floor of the captain's quarters. He never learned what happened to the wretched creature, but he could guess.

Well, thought Dirk, the devil had him now. He caught sight of a box against one wall. It was padlocked; he took up a sharp rock to break the rusty metal. He wouldn't be able to carry the box back up the cliff; it was too cumbersome for that. He had to force it open now, no matter that the hemp was burning lower. Hammering at the lock with powerful blows, he finally managed to sever it. He flung the lock away and, with shaking fingers, lifted the lid of the box.

Zachy was uneasy. Dirk had been gone a long while. Again he looked over his shoulder to see if anyone was in sight. A woman had been gathering furze in the distance but she was gone now. Zachy waited for his friend, his feeling of helplessness growing by the minute.

He was just considering whether he ought to climb down the face of the cliff himself when he felt the rope grow taut in his hand. Dirk was climbing it as he used to climb the ship's rigging. Zachy stood, barely breathing, until he heard Dirk's voice. Then he hauled him up and over the promontory.

Dirk was cut and bruised. But he was grinning, and a look of triumph lit his eyes.

"I got it, Zachy, lad," he said. "It be ours now. Payment for six year in the devil's employ."

Ten

The remaining miles to Landrawna passed swiftly. They stopped briefly for lunch, well away from the hill fort. Both men were quiet, absorbed in their own thoughts. The realization that fortune had finally smiled upon them was nearly impossible to take in. By the standards of their class they were suddenly rich. And, as much as they had dreamed of locating Captain Trey's hidden store, now that it was theirs, they were more overawed than anything else. Bemused, they walked in rarely broken silence, numb to the cuts and scrapes on their bare feet. Dirk had bandaged his hand with a torn piece from his shirt.

At a crossroads, they passed a gibbet where the bloated, blackened carcass of a man hung in an iron cage. The stench was oppressively foul, carried downwind on the sea breeze. Yet neither man gave it a second glance.

Dirk was thinking of his mother, picturing the look on her face when she beheld him alive and well. Now he would be able to look after her, take her away from their hovel and ensure that she would want for nothing the rest of her days. He recalled her long, black hair; it would be laced with silver now, and her face lined with six more years of hard living. He would buy her fine gowns, pewter, furniture, and a new house in Padstow. She would never be poor or hungry again.

The village of Landrawna lay clustered above a half-moon-shaped harbor. The narrow streets were steep, the stone cottages set close together, marching in steps against the backdrop of the cliffs and headland. Beyond the village was the land owned by Sir John Roscarrock, who cultivated it for corn and wheat. In the spring and autumn the villagers worked in the fields. The wages were pitifully low, but there was the promise of a full belly as Sir John provided a noonday dinner for the workers. But the winters were harsh with little to eat but barley bread and the preserved pilchards. Most of the men and boys toiled at the local tin mines belonging to Matthew Tregarth, but unless a rich lode were being worked, their families were often hungry and cold.

A few children played in the dusty street or on doorsteps. They turned off one street and up another which curved away from the harbor. As they did so, Dirk nearly collided with a young woman. She wore a russet skirt and a green kerchief around her auburn hair. In her arms she carried a basket of eggs.

"Ye great lummox, watch where 'ee go," she cried sharply.

Dirk mumbled an apology and would have gone on had she not said, "Who 'ee be then? There be summat familiar about 'ee." Her long-lidded green eyes took in his tall, broad frame and the well-defined contours of his face, his deep-set eyes under black brows. Her gaze became arch as she smiled saucily.

"I believe 'tis Mary Ann Nance," said Zachy.

Turning to him, she shook her head. "I be Rosina Nance. Mary Ann, her be my sister."

Zachy grinned. "Rosina, es et? 'Ee were just a child when we left nigh on six year ago. Don't 'ee know us, lass? Zachy Sawyer . . . and Dirk Killigrew."

"Dirk Killigrew," she repeated, her green eyes gleaming. "Aye, I know ye both now. 'Ee've grown, Dirk Killigrew. And us be all thinkin' the two of 'ee dead long afore." She glanced back at Zachy. "But I can see 'ee b'ain't no ghosts."

"No fear o' that," said Zachy. "Just two sailors come home, tes all."

"Sailors? The lads I remember be miners."

"No more o' that for we," said Dirk gruffly.

Rosina tilted her head to one side. "I be a bal maiden up Wheel Charity," she said. "Why don't 'ee get your old jobs back? I could put in a word for 'ee. Reece Bodmin, he be the mine cap'n. He'd be pleased to take 'ee on again, I reckon."

"Thank 'ee, no," said Dirk and his voice was curt. "And now we best be on our way. Good day to 'ee."

She nodded. "Welcome back home, Dirk Killigrew," she said. "And 'ee too, Zachy. I'll be seein' more of 'ee, I reckon." Her basket on one hip, she watched them trudge up the street.

Dirk Killigrew. She remembered him now—a tall youth who had passed her father's cottage every day on his way to and from Wheel Charity. He had lived on the outskirts of Landrawna with his mother. Rosina gasped suddenly. The two men were now out of sight, over the hill. Well, she was not going to be the one to tell him. If he did not already know, he would learn soon enough. Excitedly she hurried along the street, eager to spread the news of Zachy's and Dirk's return.

Zachy was grinning good-naturedly. "She likes 'ee, I reckon. Scarce knew I were there."

Dirk said nothing.

Zachy went on, "She be a fair maid—well-shaped, too. Do 'ee remember she?"

"Aye. A spiteful thing, bullied young 'uns."

"Ah, well, that were six year ago. Mayhap she's changed. This here be my sister's street. 'Ee be welcome to come along o' me now."

Dirk shook his head. "Remember, Zachy, not a word about the money. It be our secret. But take these." He pressed a few coins into Zachy's hand. "Give they folks a rare treat. Tell 'em 'twere from the vicar who saved us."

Zachy nodded, gripping his friend's shoulder for an instant. Then he went down the street while Dirk headed out the village to his mother's hovel. Passing the grimy cottages, he imagined the small but handsome house he would buy for her. She would have lace curtains at the windows and a real bed, not a dirty, lumpy mattress. In the parlor she'd have a set of comfortable chairs, and a polished wooden floor with a hooked rug. And she'd drink coffee and tea out of china cups with silver spoons like those that hung on the parlor wall at the vicarage.

The image of Lamorna, never far from his thoughts, filled his mind. Angrily he tried to shake it off, looking ahead to the thatched cottage of cob he had shared with his mother until Captain Trey's men had pressed him into service.

Dirk was startled to see two children with runny noses chasing a small pig about with a stick outside Cherry's home. Was his mother looking after them, perhaps? Then he noticed that the flowers his mother had carefully tended about the hovel were gone. Scruffy, brittle weeds had taken their place. The windows which she had washed and wiped weekly were filthy. Dirk paused, frowning. Slowly a sensation of dread began to well up inside him.

He moved forward and knocked at the door. The two children had stopped teasing the pig to stare at him. The door was opened by a woman he'd never seen before. Her greasy hair was drawn back in a kerchief. She was missing several front teeth.

"Well? What do 'ee want?" she asked sharply.

"I be lookin' for Cherry Killigrew."

"Cherry who?"

"Cherry Killigrew. This be her cottage. Or were six year ago."

The woman's plain face stiffened. "This be my man's cottage and no other."

"For how long, missus?"

"Three year. Sir John Roscarrock gave it him. Now be off with 'ee. I've work to do."

She would have shut the door, but Dirk held it open with one arm. "Where be the woman who lived here afore?" His voice had hardened.

ECHOES OF THE HEART

The woman was not intimidated. "Who wants to know?" she snarled. "I don't know 'ee."

"I be her son, Dirk Killigrew," he said.

" 'Ee's a liar. Her son be drowned—or run off."

"I be alive and well, woman! Now answer me! Where be my Mam?" he shouted furiously.

The woman did not meet his eyes. "Yer Mam be dead these last three year," she mumbled. "Sir John gave us this place after her were buried." Once again she looked up at him, her eyes cold. "Don't 'ee be thinkin' 'ee can have it back. Tes my man's true and proper for three lives."

Dirk stared at her, his face white. His arm fell from the door as it was slammed in his face. Unsteadily he turned and stumbled up the path which led up over the fields. He tried to comprehend that there was nothing he could now give his mother. No new house and furniture, no fine gowns and silver-backed brushes.

He could not believe it. The woman was wrong. All this time he had been imagining her in her cottage, she couldn't have been dead. His mind refused to accept it. The thick fog in his head, the winded sensation as from a severe blow—none of it seemed real. He was dreaming, he *must* be dreaming.

He did not hear the old man's approach nor the voice calling his name. But when he felt a hand on his shoulder, he looked around.

"Dirk, my lad. Tes a blessed miracle to see 'ee."

Dirk stared at the old man.

"Don't 'ee know me, lad? I be Jonah, Jonah Sawyer. Zachy's granddad. 'Ee not be forgettin' ol' Jonah who taught 'ee how to use the pick, eh? We thought 'ee were dead, 'ee and Zachy, drowned many year back. Yer Mam found your cap on the beach."

"Mam—she—I went to her cottage. The woman there said—said her be dead. Tesn't true, es et?"

The old man nodded, his watery blue eyes filled with compassion. "I fear that be the way of it, my boy. I tried to catch up with 'ee—I be sorry 'ee had to hear the news from that mean-tempered besom."

Dirk shook his head. He felt dazed, stupid. "What happened, Jonah?"

The old man hesitated. "Her be at rest now, Dirk. 'Twas a sudden illness, and her not bein' strong enough to fight it. It were in the winter three year back. Folks were hungry, some took sick as well. Zachy's younger sister, us lost her a week before yer Mam died. Such a pretty little thing her were, too. Liked to hear me play the fiddle, her did." Sniffing, he wiped his nose on his sleeve.

Dirk said nothing.

Jonah cleared his throat and continued. "A bad harvest, it were. Ruined by rain. Salt tax were high as well so few pilchards could be put by. A terrible time, it were."

Dirk looked down at his trembling hands.

"Come back with I, my lad. Bessie'll fix us some supper and 'ee'll be among friends."

Slowly he shook his head.

The old man did not press him. "Come when 'ee've a mind to, then. Tes good to have 'ee and Zachy back."

Dirk did not reply, nor did he notice the old man had gone. He was remembering how his mother had changed in the year before his capture, how her open, buoyant nature had sunk into silent apathy. And he was to blame for it. What had she thought when he had disappeared? Did she wonder whether he might have abandoned her deliberately?

Dirk sank his head in his hands. It wasn't possible, not after everything else that had happened . . . He had been going to give her back the joy in living which she had lost. No, which he had taken from her. And now he couldn't ask her forgiveness.

When he was a small boy, Cherry had taken him to Wheel Charity. They had stood on the cliff looking down at the mine, at the black smoke billowing from the tall, narrow chimney. They had listened to the clatter and pounding of the engine workings and the shouts of the men.

"Know who that belongs to, do 'ee?" Cherry had asked her son.

He shook his head.

"To your father," she said softly.

He heard the unmistakable pride in her voice. "My father?" Dirk was bewildered. "Folk say I b'ain't got a father."

Cherry made an impatient gesture. "Don't 'ee listen to they. Of course 'ee's got a father. All children do. He do own that mine and another. He be a rich man with lace on his shirt and gold trim on his coat."

Dirk tried to imagine this. "Why don't he live with us?"

Cherry laughed. "Live with we! That be a fair joke, lad. He be gentry, not plain folk like we. But don't 'ee forget, Dirk, that 'ee be half-gentry. 'Ee won't allus live in a hovel with a dirt floor and eat pease porridge when there be nothing else. He do know he has a son. Some day, when the time be right, he'll send for 'ee, do right by 'ee."

"Will 'ee come too, Mam?" he asked nervously.

She seemed not to have heard him. Gazing down at the mine, she said, "Blood be thicker than water, even if it be on the wrong side o' the blanket. Remember what I tell 'ee, Dirk, and think on that when folks say 'ee've no father."

Dirk had many opportunities to do just that. From the village children he had learned that because his mother was not married, he himself was somehow set apart from them. The older boys bullied him until eventually he began to give more bloody noses than he got. They stopped calling him names as well.

He had asked her once, "Mam, what be a bastard?"

"Tes a word for a child whose parents b'ain't married," she answered matter-of-factly.

"Like 'ee and my father?"

"Ais. But there be no shame to 'ee. And I don't feel none

so there be an end on it. You be special, Dirk, no matter what they do say. Half-gentry, whereas they be common folk through and through. 'Ee must allus hold your head up."

"What be my father's name?"

"Matthew Tregarth of Tregartha."

When he had begun to work at the mine as an older boy, Dirk had never let on by a word or sign that his father and the owner of Wheel Charity were one and the same person. Cherry had urged him to keep silent; she had never revealed his father's identity to anyone in Landrawna. An orphan, she had gone to work at Tregartha as a maid when she was fourteen, and at sixteen she had left when her pregnancy could no longer be concealed by loose lacings of her bodice. Mrs. Tregarth, knowing full well who was responsible for her condition, accused the girl of consorting with the band of gypsies that had set up camp on Whistmoor some months earlier. And so had begun the rumors that Dirk's father was a gypsy. His dark coloring did nothing to dispel the tale. When Cherry left Tregartha, Matthew's steward was instructed by his master to give the girl a few guineas. And, as far as Matthew was concerned, that was the end of it. Despite what Cherry believed, he did not know she had borne him a son, and would not have cared in the least had he known. Cherry was not the first nor the last mistress to bear him an illegitimate child.

One harvest-tide Dirk had seen his father for the first time. Not yet old enough to work at the mine, he was helping with the harvesting of the fields owned by Sir John Roscarrock. Fishermen left their boats for six weeks of harvest-tide, and miners often toiled in the fields following their long shifts underground, enjoying the fresh air and taking advantage of the abundant food and drink Sir John's steward, Mr. Trenow, provided.

The women did the reaping, their hair tied back with gaily colored scarves, bending nearly double and slashing at the stalks of corn with sickles. Only strong, healthy women were up to the pace and arduousness of the work, and Cherry Killigrew was one of these.

The men followed behind, tying the shorn stalks in sheaves with straw binders. Coming last, the children gathered the remaining bits into "riskans," or little bundles.

At ten o'clock in the morning they would stop for a mug of cider and a piece of fuggan. Later the laborers were given an hour to eat their lunch—meat and slabs of white bread made from wheat rather than the cheaper barley flour—and stretch their aching muscles. Then they worked until six in the evening and heaped their plates from dishes set out on tables.

On the last day of the harvest, an enormous feast was prepared by the landowner's servants. There were lammy pies, squab pies, leek and pork pies, pies of fish and apple, goose and parsnip. Then came the rump of beef with onions, carrots, and potatoes, mutton, ham, and chicken. This was often the only time of the year that the villagers ate meat, and they made the most of it. The meal was followed by an abundance of desserts—plum and figgy puddings powdered with white sugar, rice pudding served with cream, gingerbreads, saffron cakes made from crocus flowers, and apple and blackberry tarts with clotted cream. To drink there was cider, ale, and homebrewed wines such as gillyflower, cowslip, elderberry, and metheglin. This was the "Gooldize," the Harvest Supper.

It was the day of the feast, the last day of the harvest. The sky was an enormous expanse of bright blue, the breeze mild and scented with wildflowers, herbs, and a hint of the sea. The last few handfuls of standing corn were cut and given to the steward, who lifted them high above his head.

The harvesters had divided themselves into three groups and had knelt down on the stubby ground. All was quiet and solemn.

When Mr. Trenow gave the sign, the first group chanted, "We have 'un, we have 'un, we have 'un." The second group, standing upright, asked together, "What have 'ee? What have 'ee? What have 'ee?" Dirk and Cherry were a part of the third group. They raised their arms over their heads, answering gravely and reverently, "A neck. A neck. A neck." An odd thrill passed through the people as they spoke the words of the ancient ritual. Then the three groups cried out together, "We yen. We yen. We yen," which meant, "We have ended."

In the resulting jubilation which followed the dignified ceremony, Cherry had bent down and whispered in Dirk's ear, "Look, lad. There he be. With Sir John, the new master."

"Who?" he asked.

"Your father." No one heard them; no one noticed their preoccupation with the two gentlemen on horseback. Dirk gazed across the shorn cornfield at Matthew Tregarth.

He sat on a magnificent chestnut horse. He wore a red, full-skirted coat embroidered with gold. Rich lacing foamed at his throat and wrists. On his head was a long, brown, curly wig and a black hat with wide brim.

The boy stared, awe and pride welling up in him. He was like a king. Dirk hugged his secret to himself. His mother had been right all along. He *was* special. He was this fine gentleman's son.

The crowd was shouting, "Huzzah! Huzzah for Mr. Trenow! Huzzah for Sir John!"

A few of the women were plaiting the neck and adorning it with cornflowers and poppies while the men passed around a crock of beer. In a bemused state, Dirk ate the neck-cutting bun that was handed to him. Sir John saluted his workers and he and Matthew Tregarth had ridden away. Dirk watched them go, his eyes shining.

Then the harvesters had processed merrily to the steward's stone house for the Gooldize. The neck was presented to Mrs. Trenow, who hung it over the chimneypiece in the great beamed kitchen. It would hang there until the next harvest-tide, for luck. No one understood its significance as the sacrificed corn spirit—that knowledge had been lost long ago.

Dirk had run off to play with Zachy and a few other boys.

He did not speak to them of his father, then or later. Zachy did not learn the truth until many years later on the smuggling ship. And it was not only an older Dirk, but a very different one, who told him.

The years passed; at age twelve Dirk became a tributer at Wheel Charity, digging for tin ore. He worked twelve hours a day, descending two thousand feet into the bowels on slimy, rickety ladders in dripping shafts. The only light came from the smoky hempen candle attached to his hat with a piece of clay. The temperature was ninety degrees or better, the air stifling. Yet Dirk did not question his lot, or shirk his work. He was paid only for the ore he found and sent up in kibbles to the surface, hoisted by horses above ground. Thus he worked as hard as he could, eager to strike a rich lode.

In the evenings, after an hour and a half climb to the surface, drenched with sweat, he would change into the clothes he had left in the open shed. In the winters his clothes were often wet and always cold as he walked the three miles back to Landrawna.

There was the constant danger of accidents from dislodged rocks, collapsed shafts, broken-runged ladders and air contaminated with gunpowder smoke and explosions. Yet the work was eagerly sought by those fully prepared to toil in almost intolerable conditions. They knew nothing else. It was recognized that smoke and dust ate at one's lungs, but none would have starved to save their lungs. And when they made no more than four shillings a week, they were very nearly starving anyway.

Each year the mines in Cornwall claimed many lives, but the tinners had no choice but to work them. In his early teens Dirk began to question why his father did not see to it that the ladders were repaired and the shafts better pumped of water. But his father did not go down into the bal. It was no place for a gentleman. It was the bal captain who was responsible for the underground workings. He was often resented by the tinners, yet none cared to lose their jobs in a dispute over the operations. The understanding was that each man worked independently, looking to his own safety and his own yield of ore.

The year Dirk was seventeen, the harvest was a poor one. Mr. Trenow needed only a small number of workers, and Cherry Killigrew was not hired. She managed to get a place in the fish cellar, salting the layers of gleaming pilchards laid out as high as the women could reach. This "bulking" work, smelly and loathsome as it was, continued far into the nights, the women working by flickering candles as the men carried in the boxes of fish and dumped them out on the floor.

One night Cherry slipped in the slimy ooze, the residue of thousands of fish, and badly twisted her back. Faint and nauseous with pain, she managed to make it home. By the next morning she could not get out of bed; there would be no more work in the fish cellar that autumn.

Dirk was working a poor pitch at the mine and earning even less than usual. By November they were subsisting on milky broth and barley bread in the mornings, more hunks of bread for lunch, and clumps of pease porridge for supper. It wasn't nearly enough to sustain a growing youth who worked twelve hours a day. Cherry began giving Dirk her portions without him knowing it, telling him she had already eaten. Yet before long he had realized she was eating next to nothing. Frantic with worry, his own limbs weak, his head swimming from lack of nourishment, he went to the Reverend Poldew to ask for parish relief.

It was Sir John's cousin who had the living at Landrawna. He was displeased when Dirk interrupted his dinner of mutton and potatoes. Still another to complain, to beg. Didn't they realize that God purposely gave them trials to bear? Not that this lad would know any such thing; he and his mother only went to church on Christmas and Easter. The mother was no better than she should be; everyone knew her son was a bastard. Some said a gypsy's brat. These people bred like rats, he thought disgustedly. And then they expected him to put matters right.

"Three shillings," he said to Dirk.

Dirk swallowed hard in dismay. "But—but sir, that won't pay for more than a few days' food." He flushed. "If 'ee please, sir, we be needin' a bit more."

"I don't please," said the vicar coldly. "That is all there is. Consider yourself fortunate."

"Sir John'd want 'ee to do good by her," said Dirk stubbornly. "She's worked hard for him for many a harvest."

The man flushed with anger. "How dare you tell me what my cousin would want? I am the priest of this parish. Now get out."

Dirk stared flint-eyed at the vicar with his florid face, the capillaries showing beneath his skin, and his heavy frame. "I can tell 'ee's never known what it be like to go hungry, sir. I reckon the stories I've heard of 'ee be true, that 'ee takes from the plate to add to your living, that 'ee visits the upstairs rooms of the White Horse in Redruth for bedsport. I'll be takin' the three shillings, sir, with many thanks." His voice was heavy with sarcasm.

Turning on his heel, he walked out, the clergyman's words flung at his back. "Don't come back, Dirk Killigrew! You'll get nothing from the parish again. Go and join the gypsies—they were good enough for your mother once. Any more trouble from you and I'll see to it that Sir John evicts you from your cottage."

Dirk had longed to rush back and smash his fist into the fat vicar's face. But he was weak from lack of food, and besides, he could not risk losing the roof over their heads.

He went to the open market and bought as much food as he could with the three shillings, but it wasn't long before the situation was desperate again.

He had had the idea in the back of his mind for some time. Gradually it grew, compelling him to acknowledge it was the only choice left to him. He was working as hard as he could, despite his weakened state and dizziness, and yet it was not enough. The other villagers were struggling to feed their own families. There was no option but to appeal to his father for help. Raised by a mother as naive as himself, he had never doubted that his father would help them if he knew they were in need. He did not wonder why his father had never displayed any interest or concern in them heretofore; that was doubtless the way of the gentry. But if Matthew Tregarth knew how Cherry and their son suffered, he would surely be charitable.

Instead of going to Wheel Charity, Dirk walked the eleven miles across Whistmoor to Tregartha. He knew the money he would earn would be docked for failing to report for work, but that did not trouble him unduly. His father would give him enough to more than compensate for what he lost. He had no intention of asking for more than was necessary to see them through the winter, but he was not going to watch his mother starve while his father lived and ate like a king.

The day was bitterly cold. Dirk's coat was thin and too small for him; his wrists stuck out and there were splits under his arms because the coat was too narrow at the shoulders. Despite his leanness he was muscular and sinewy. The gale cut through him as he trudged over the moors.

It was nearly midday when Tregartha came into view. Not as large as Kilworthy, Sir John Roscarrock's mansion, but older, built when the virgin queen was on the throne. He gazed at the granite house with its three protruding bays and decorated gables. He had been raised in a poor, simple home, but Dirk had an innate sense of what was aesthetically pleasing. Tregartha sat like a jewel on the rugged moor.

As he drew close to the house, delicious smells of food cooking reached his nostrils. His mouth watered; his head reeled slightly.

Sounding the black iron knocker on the front door, he waited. He knew he should not call at the front of the house, but he was afraid that if he went round to the servants' entrance they would send him away. A footman in a brown suit,

ECHOES OF THE HEART

white stockings, and buckled shoes opened the door. He stared in hostile astonishment at the dirty youth before him in patched clothing.

"Get on with 'ee! Are ye mad, rappin' at the door like 'ee's a right to?"

"I be here to see Mr. Tregarth," said Dirk evenly. "Tell him, if 'ee please, that I be wantin' a word with him."

The footman burst out laughing. "A word, es et? That be a good 'un. Go along. The master b'ain't got no business with the likes of 'ee."

Dirk's face hardened. Despite his youth, he was taller and broader than the footman. No manservant was going to prevent him from speaking to his father.

"I be askin' 'ee polite-like," he said crisply. "Tell your master Dirk Killigrew be wantin' a few words with him."

"I've told 'ee to get on," snarled the footman. "Tes no use—'ee won't be seein' my master."

"Tell Mr. Tregarth that I be the son of Cherry Killigrew who worked here," Dirk said firmly.

"Are ye daft, lad?" cried the footman. "Don't 'ee hear what I tell 'ee?" The man began to shut the door, but Dirk leaned heavily against it.

"Look here, my lad—" The footman broke off as another voice cried imperiously, "What is going on, Robert?"

The footman released his hold on the door. "Oh, Mr. Joshua, sir, this lad be tryin' to force his way in."

"What!"

Dirk looked over the footman's shoulder and saw a young man a few years older than himself. He came forward and Dirk stared at his long, curly wig, his purple satin coat and breeches, the diamond pin thrust into his cravat. His face was narrow, and even more angular than Dirk's. His eyes were blue and surveyed the younger man with contempt.

"How dare you come to my father's front door? What do you want?"

"To see Mr. Tregarth," said Dirk.

"A common lout like you! My father only receives his guests, and you are scarcely one of those. Get out before I have you thrown out." Behind Joshua stood a girl of about ten or eleven. She was watching the scene, wide-eyed. Her hair was almost black; she wore a red gown.

Joshua looked behind him impatiently. "Go upstairs, Tamara." To Dirk he said, "Get out, you filthy beggar. My father—"

"He be my father as well," said Dirk deliberately.

Joshua's face was suffused with red. "That's a bloody lie! You dare to come here—to my mother's house—"

"—Ask Mr. Tregarth if it be not so. Ask him about Cherry Killigrew who worked in this house and caught her master's eye."

Dirk got no further. The other young man had lunged forward, striking his jaw with his fist. Dirk fell back, groaning. Bleary-eyed, he looked up at Joshua who stood over him.

"So you thought to come begging, did you? Do you make a habit of this, going to gentlemen's homes with some cock-and-bull story about being their son?"

"It be the truth," said Dirk savagely.

"And what if it is? Do you believe my father knows or cares what happened nearly twenty years ago? He doesn't encourage beggars, especially those with sluts for mothers!"

Dirk bolted up, rage contorting his features. Hurling himself into Joshua, he began to pummel him with his fists. His half-brother gasped and cried out. The girl stood in stunned silence.

Dirk did not see the two burly men enter the hall, but he felt himself roughly grabbed and torn away from Joshua, who was doubled over, his face cut and bruised.

"Take him outside," panted Joshua. "You—you men know what to do with housebreakers."

"Aye, Mr. Joshua," one of the men said.

They dragged Dirk, still struggling, out the front door. It was fortunate that he was in a weakened, exhausted condition; he blacked out after only a few heavy blows to his face and torso. The men got no pleasure out of pounding an unconscious youth. They carried him down the gravel drive and heaved him, bleeding and insensible, onto the moor.

Eleven

When Dirk came to, the pain overwhelmed him. It jolted his head and racked his muscles. When he breathed, an agonizing sharpness pierced his chest. The lacerations in his skin stung and throbbed. One eye was grossly swollen; he could barely focus it.

As he tried to sit up, bile rose from his belly. Leaning over, he wretched helplessly. Spent, he fell back on the hard, rough heath. And blacked out again.

He woke in the middle of the afternoon. In another two hours or so it would be dark. He had to get up and begin the long walk home. If he lay here in the cold all night, he would die. It was then that he noticed the thick wool blanket which lay over him. To his amazement he saw a small glazed crock leaning against a nearby rock, and a bundle wrapped in blue cotton.

Reaching for the crock, he tried to draw the cork with his teeth but his jaw was too sore and swollen. He set it between his knees and managed to work it out with his grazed fingers. Tentatively he sniffed it. Brandy. Greedily he swallowed a large swig and felt it burning his throat. Within a short time he was warm, his aching body less sore.

Shifting his weight, he leaned across and gripped the blue bundle. He unwrapped it and was further astonished to see a large pasty inside. It smelled wonderful. The spasms of nausea were gone; he was ravenous. He lifted the pasty to take a bite and saw that beneath it were nine shillings.

At first he could do nothing but assuage his hunger. He wolfed down half the pasty. It was filled with beef and potatoes in a rich juice. He had not tasted anything like it in years. Taking another swig of brandy, he wrapped the rest of the pasty in the blue cloth. His mother would have something to eat after all.

His head felt pleasantly light and detached from his sore frame; the brandy had reduced the throes to mere discomforts. He flexed his legs; nothing seemed broken. Stumbling a little, he got to his feet. The blanket he left on the heath. He would not risk being transported or imprisoned because of it—no cottager owned such fine wool. If he were seen carrying it, or if it were found in the cottage, no one would believe he had not stolen it. The nine shillings he would take, though. It was likely that some servant, hearing of the scene in the hallway of Tregartha, had brought him the things. Perhaps someone who had known Cherry, and wanted to help.

Dirk knew he had to leave now, while the brandy still worked to deaden the pain. He would feel far worse later when it had worn off. His knees were weak; his head throbbed slightly, but the nourishment from the pasty gave him strength.

It was night by the time he fell against the door of the hovel and pushed it open. The room was dark and cold, but he heard his mother's voice.

"Dirk, es that 'ee?"

He was glad she could not see him. "Aye, Mam. I've brought 'ee some food. Worked a better pitch today. Bought a pasty and some brandy. Here." He handed her the crock and bundle.

She sighed. "I knew 'ee would come about, love. 'Twill be all right now, I reckon." Hungrily she chewed and swallowed the rest of the pasty and drank the harsh liquor from the crock.

Dirk climbed up to his cot and was asleep almost instantly.

Cherry woke first the next morning. It was Sunday, she remembered, so Dirk did not have to go to the mine. Turning on one side to look at her son, she gasped in horror.

He lay sprawled on his mattress, his face a mass of cuts and bruises, his hair crusted with blood, his coat torn and filthy. He had not bothered to take off his boots before he fell asleep.

She sat up, moaning in concern, and reached for his hand. His eyelids flickered.

"Dirk, lad, what happened to 'ee?"

"I had a bit o' trouble, Mam. Tes naught."

"But Dirk, who did this to 'ee? 'Ee've been beaten summat cruel."

He pushed himself up. Every muscle shrieked in outrage; there was a vise about his skull. Gritting his teeth, he said, "Let be, Mam."

" 'Twas it at the mine? Or—or did 'ee go to a wreck?"

"I've said tes naught," he growled.

She winced at the harsh tone in his voice. This wasn't at all like Dirk. His battered face was grimmer than she'd ever seen it; his eyes had taken on a cold, withdrawn look. Cherry recalled the beef-filled pasty and the nine shillings.

"Dirk, lad, 'ee didn't steal, did 'ee? Tes not like wreckin' when them that drown have no need o' things."

"I ain't no thief, Mam," he said. He would not look at her; his face was white beneath the cuts and scrapes.

Cherry, frightened and distressed, began to weep. Dirk was appalled. His mother never cried. Kneeling beside her, he put his arm round her shoulders.

"Don't cry, Mam. Please don't cry. Tes all right. Us can buy food now, and wood for the fire. Don't 'ee take on."

Cherry shook her head, wiping her cheeks. "Tesn't that. I be not sad for I, but for 'ee. 'Ee deserves better, more than I could ever give 'ee. 'Ee must never take what don't belong to 'ee for I. 'Ee's no common village lad, ee's half-gentry and—"

A tremendous wave of bitterness and revulsion swiftly bore away Dirk's resolution not to tell his mother what had happened at Tregartha. "Stop it!" he cried viciously. "Stop it! I never want to hear 'ee say that again! I never want 'ee to talk of my father!"

Cherry's lips went white. She shrunk away from a son she did not recognize.

Yet Dirk could not stop. "Do 'ee know who beat me? Do 'ee? 'Tweren't anyone at the mine. 'Tweren't no wrecker. 'Twere *my father's* men."

Cherry, aghast, gave a whimper.

"Aye, Mam."

" 'Ee—'ee saw your father?"

He shook his head. "No. They wouldn't let me. Mr. Joshua Tregarth ordered me beaten and left on the moor for dead. And now there finally be some sense in my head. Now I know there won't be aught comin' to we from Mr. Matthew Tregarth. My father don't care nothin' about I or 'ee. Do 'ee understand that, Mam? 'Ee should have known that when 'ee were sent packin' after he'd had his bit o' fun. You were nothin' but a kitchen wench he took for pleasure. I be a stupid lummox not to have seen it afore now. Matthew Tregarth don't care whether we be alive or dead. I ain't half-gentry. There be no such thing. I be plain Dirk Killigrew, bastard son of spinster Cherry Killigrew. And that be an end on it!"

This time when his mother began to cry, he did not comfort her. He climbed down from the shelf rigged under the rafters where they slept and went out of the cottage. He was filled with disgust for the conviction she had harbored all these years since his birth, that Matthew Tregarth would take his illegitimate son under his wing. For nearly twenty years she had believed this. And how on earth could he have been so credulous, so stupid as well? How could he have been taken in by his mother's foolish hopes and dreams? He was seventeen; he had been doing a man's work for five years. He should have realized the way of the world long before now. His mother's gaiety, her cheerful optimism he now saw as impractical gullibility. Her belief that some day Matthew Tregarth would recognize Dirk as his son was a ludicrous fantasy.

In the months that followed, Cherry began to age. She had always looked younger than her years, and her merry, girlish nature had contributed to this. She had looked more like Dirk's older sister than his mother.

But a change came over her. She no longer sang to herself or ran over the headland to meet Dirk coming home from the mine. Their circumstances improved and once again there was enough to eat. She tended the cottage, and, in the spring, planted flowers from the moors about the house. But the light was gone from her, the enthusiasm she had always had for day to day living. There was nothing left but a joyless resignation.

Dirk knew he was to blame and loathed himself for it. He had destroyed his mother's fantasy world, her faith in a golden future. Wretched with remorse, he now understood that her dreams had shaped the essence of her character. Without them she was an empty shell. She spoke little; she no longer teased or laughed. At first Dirk had made attempts to draw her out, to coax her into her old nature. But she did not respond. Dirk began to spend his evenings drinking at the kiddleywink where the gin was cheap and effective.

Until the day he and Zachy Sawyer were ambushed on the beach and taken aboard Captain Trey's ship.

Dirk spent the night out on the headland, shielded from the damp wind by a large boulder. Before dawn he rose and set off across the fields, making his way to the cliffs above the sea.

The sun was rising over the water when he halted abruptly, gazing down at the bulk that was Wheel Charity. The engine house glowed mellow in the pale light; black coal smoke and dust rose from its chimney. He stood there a long while, ignoring the hunger gnawing in his belly and the chill wind blowing his long, black hair wildly about. He watched the men changing shifts, too far away to recognize any of them.

With one hand he gripped the bag filled with gold and silver coins he had taken from the cave. Gulls shrieked over his head, swooping and soaring.

Finally he spoke. "I hope 'ee can hear me, Mam, wherever 'ee may be. I ain't no miner any longer, nor no poor wretch at the mercy of any folk. I'll never live by another's leave again. And someday I'll be takin' my revenge on they bloody Tregarths, I swear that to 'ee."

Elias Pollard was a solitary, well-respected merchant in Padstow. He owned a shop which sold pewter made from the local tin. It was a small shop but stocked with fine pieces. His customers could also order items made to their specifications.

He was unmarried and content to be so, enjoying a particular relationship with his accommodating housekeeper. Mrs. Roscoe looked after him very well, never aspiring to become Mrs. Pollard. She was a buxom widow in her late forties, still attractive and fortunately now past the age of child-bearing. Elias was fond of her for she was a woman of sound good sense, an excellent cook, and a pleasing mistress.

They lived in Elias's comfortable townhouse with its whitewashed stone walls and cobalt-blue trim about the door and windows. His shop was on the ground floor of the house, in the front. Mrs. Roscoe's parlor and bedchamber were at the back, as was the kitchen. Elias occupied the upper two stories. Below the ground floor was a labyrinth of cellars which few had seen.

Elias lived quite well, far better than the people of Padstow supposed. His private apartments were filled with the finest furniture, crystal, and silver. There was not a piece of pewter to be seen. He and Mrs. Roscoe enjoyed the best foods and French wines, port and madeira. Had other pewter merchants visited his chambers, they would have been startled at the very least. So would his neighbors, all merchants in a small way themselves. For that very reason Elias Pollard kept to himself.

Yet that October he was filled with anxiety and frustration. At night he walked the handsome carpet; during the day he ignored the dishes prepared by Mrs. Roscoe. He also ignored her other charms.

" 'Ee's got to eat, Elias," she told him one morning when she came to collect his untouched breakfast tray. " 'Ee be terrible pale and drawn."

"Leave off, woman!" he cried impatiently. "Damn, where is the fellow? I've orders to fill! Tes two weeks ago the ship was due. Two weeks—and not one word! Blast it all! Well, I cannot wait any longer. I must be making inquiries."

Mrs. Roscoe began to tidy the bedlinen. " 'Ee cannot be makin' inquiries, Elias. 'Ee do know that. Who would 'ee go to?"

Elias stared morosely in front of him, acknowledging the truth of her statement. They had always sent word to him, informing him of the landing and cargo. His own men, those in Padstow and the surrounding area who shared his good fortune, stored the ship's smuggled cargo and distributed it to his customers. It was a very good living and there was little risk involved; the Queen's excise officers rarely ventured as far north as Padstow, though it brought a zest to his day-to-day existence he would never have had selling pewter bowls and goblets.

"Tes likely they be delayed, Elias. No good will come o' frettin'. Now, how about a nice lammy pie?"

"Oh, take your pie and be off with you! I must think, and I can't with you yammering at me."

Mrs. Roscoe, not at all offended, picked up the tray and left the room. Inwardly she was as concerned about the whereabouts of the smuggling ship as her phlegmatic nature would allow. She, too, enjoyed the comfort Elias's secret business dealings provided and she would be loath to see them reduced.

Mrs. Roscoe washed up the breakfast dishes. She was polishing the silver tea set, as she did every week, when there was a knock on the door which connected her rooms with the shop. Setting down the cloth and sugar bowl, she wiped her hands on her apron and went across to open the door.

It was the young man who helped Elias in the shop. Elias himself had not looked in in days; Mrs. Roscoe had said he was ill.

"Tes a man to see Mr. Pollard."

"Mr. Pollard be ill, 'ee do know that," said Mrs. Roscoe. "Iffen he wants a piece of pewter, 'ee can take the order."

The young man shook his head. "He don't want pewter, Mrs. Roscoe. He be wantin' to speak to Mr. Pollard on a private matter, he says."

Mrs. Roscoe frowned. "Private, es et? Well, lad, bring 'un through. I'll see him for myself. Perhaps the master be feelin' a bit stronger today . . ."

Into her parlor strode a tall, broad-shouldered man in his twenties. He moved with a fierce grace which she recognized as peculiar to a sailor. Yet this man was no common salt. He wore a leather coat buckled at the waist, brown breeches, and glossy black boots. His black hair was tied back with a ribbon.

"What private business do 'ee have with Mr. Pollard, sir?" she asked after he had shut the door behind him. Her voice had an edge of suspicion.

"The same as he had with Cap'n Trey," was the crisp response.

Mrs. Roscoe started. The man's deep-set gaze did not waver from her face. "Wait here," she said.

Upstairs, she began, "Elias, tes a man below. He be bringin' news o' the ship, I reckon."

Elias turned from contemplation out the window, his face glowing with relief and excitement. "What? Well, don't leave him below to cool his heels! Bring him up, woman! He's the answer to my prayers."

She hesitated. "Aye. But tes not the usual man. I've never seen this 'un before."

"What matter, what matter? If he's been sent by the excise officers, he'll not find anything here. He must have news, news I've been waiting a fortnight for! Go on, woman!"

"But 'ee ain't dressed, Elias," she protested. "I'll tell 'un to wait."

"You'll do no such thing," blustered Elias. "Just hand me my wig. I'll not wait another minute for news."

Still attired in his flamboyant embroidered silk dressing gown, he adjusted his powdered periwig and went through to the elegant sitting room.

There were sounds of footsteps on the stairs, and Mrs. Roscoe opened the door. "Mr. Dirk Killigrew to see 'ee, sir," she said, standing aside for him to enter.

"Thank you, Mrs. Roscoe. That will be all. Killigrew, eh? Can't say I've heard your name before. What business matter do you wish to discuss with me?" None of the urgency Elias felt showed in his voice or manner. He surveyed the tall young man, his eyes narrowing.

"The same business, sir, that 'ee had with Cap'n Trey."

"Captain Trey? Who might that be, eh? And what sort of business did I have with that gentleman?"

Dirk's tone was cool. "The distribution of certain cargo—Cousin Jack, tea, salt, lace, tobacco."

"And what do you know of my dealings in these goods? You yourself came through my shop. I sell pewter."

"For nigh upon six year, sir, I were a part of Cap'n Trey's crew," was the blunt answer. "I know 'ee orders the land traders to deliver the goods."

Elias did not respond for a moment. He lifted a small china bowl from the table and traced its pattern with his finger.

"Did Captain Trey send you?" he finally asked.

"Cap'n Trey be dead, sir."

"What's that you say?" Elias abandoned the play-acting. His questions came hard and swift.

"Aye." Dirk smiled crookedly.

"The ship—the crew?"

"Wrecked, drowned. Save me and one other."

"When did this happen?"

"More'n two week since."

"Where?"

"North. Off Rowenstow."

Elias sighed. "I feared something like that had occurred. But you—how was it you were spared?"

"I floated in on some timber with another lad."

"The cargo?" snapped Elias.

"Wreckers."

Elias uttered a bitter exclamation. "A damned wicked loss—and 'twill cost me dear." He glanced around at the gracious sitting room with its fine appointments. Then he turned sharply to Dirk. "You don't look like a seaman, not in those clothes. How did you come by them?"

"I have money. It were Cap'n Trey's. I won't be lyin' to 'ee. But the devil's gone now and I reckon it be mine well enough. I were pressed into his dirty crew six year ago. I can steer a ship as well as he himself. I know Roscoff—the dealers, the goods. I know the sea twixt there and Cornwall. And I do know the trade, where to make landings where the soldiers don't look, where to store the cargo, the coves, the clefts."

"Well? How does your expertise concern me?" asked Elias brusquely.

Dirk spoke coolly and deliberately. "It be my aim, sir, to buy a ship. Not a big 'un, but a fast sailin' sloop. I'll fit out my own crew, not by pressin' they, but by fair dividin' the profits. Mevagissey's the place to get a ship and I'll be headin' there soon. I've come to ask 'ee, sir, if 'ee'd do for I what 'ee did for Cap'n Trey—buy the goods and haul 'em away once my lads bring 'em on land."

Elias keenly scrutinized the younger man before him, the cool determination in his deep-set eyes, his proud, though not arrogant, bearing, the ease with which he stood in Elias's parlor waiting for an answer.

"Tell me about yourself, Killigrew."

He saw the handsome, well-contoured face harden. "All 'ee needs to know, sir, is that I can run a vessel and land a cargo as well as any. And I'll vow to deal only wi' 'ee."

Elias had suspected that he wasn't receiving the whole of Captain Trey's cargo for distribution. At times certain runs had seemed slim, and Elias had had difficulty filling all his orders. Captain Trey's man had offered explanations of kegs washed overboard in rough weather and packages of lace ruined by wet. Still, he knew next to nothing about this Dirk Killigrew.

"I'm to have my own ship, Mr. Pollard, no matter what 'ee do say. I can deal with 'ee, or another 'un," said Dirk.

Still Elias said nothing.

Dirk glanced about the sitting room, noting the red brocade curtains, the oil paintings, the crystal decanters, and mahogany furniture. " 'Twill be a pity to let the business go, sir, but I can tell 'ee not be interested. Good day to 'ee."

"Wait, lad."

Dirk's hand was already on the doorknob. Releasing it, he turned around, his level gaze on Elias's flushed face.

"Go to Mevagissey and order your sloop. Pick your crew. And I will go into partnership with you."

Dirk's expression did not change. " 'Ee won't have cause to regret it, sir."

"No, lad," said Elias thoughtfully, "I don't believe I will."

When Dirk had gone, Mrs. Roscoe went upstairs in answer to Elias's eager ring.

"Ah, my dear," he said, "I believe you said there was a lammy pie. I'll have a good slice of that now, and some ale to wash it down." He rubbed his hands together.

"So it's pleased 'ee be now? And all because o' that young man?"

"Aye, my dear. He's ambitious, that one. He'll be most successful—I'll wager anything you like on it. I foresee an excellent partnership."

"He be a fine figure of a man, I'll say that for 'un," said Mrs. Roscoe.

Elias waved away this irrelevancy. "According to him, Captain Trey was cheating me blind."

"And how do 'ee know this 'un won't do the same?"

Elias's eyes narrowed shrewdly. "Killigrew is very different from Captain Trey. That man was a bloodthirsty rogue. Killigrew called him a devil, and I daresay he was right. As for our Mr. Killigrew, he's not merely after the profits."

"What else, then?" asked Mrs. Roscoe skeptically.

Elias paused. Then he said seriously, "Unless I'm very much mistaken, and I'm certain I'm not, Dirk Killigrew is out to prove something. To himself—and, I daresay, to others as well."

Dirk had one more stop in Padstow before hiring a horse and riding to Mevagissey. Walking down a winding street, he stopped in front of a white-washed cottage. Flowers fluttered brightly in the windowboxes. He knocked on the door, but there was no answer. Then he heard a sound behind the small house and went round to investigate.

Behind the cottage was a tiny garden. A little white-haired man knelt on the ground, his hands caked with dirt.

"Mr. Penwen, sir?" asked Dirk.

The man did not turn around. Dirk repeated the name, louder this time. Then the old man looked up, smiled, and got to his feet, brushing his hands together.

"Yes, I'm Christopher Penwen. What can I do for you, sir?"

"I heard 'ee used to be a tutor, sir," said Dirk.

Mr. Penwen realized the man before him was not a gentleman, as he had first assumed from the sober, but well-cut, clothes.

"Yes, that is true," he answered, puzzled. "I've taught many a young gentleman in my day. How does that interest you, my boy?"

Dirk hesitated, his cheeks tinged with color. "I—I want to learn to read and write. And to reckon with long figures. I'll pay 'ee well, sir."

"Do you live here in Padstow, lad?"

"I will, some o' the time. I be from Landrawna, up the coast."

"Landrawna. Sir John Roscarrock's land, eh? But you can't be a farmer, or a miner."

"I've done both kinds of work, sir. Now I be a sailor and soon to have my own vessel. But I want to learn my letters while I be outfittin' the ship and hirin' a crew."

The old man's brow cleared. His eyes lit up. Now the situation was plain to him. "A smuggler, eh?" he said with glee. "Well, well! I could never afford my pipe tobacco or tea if it weren't for you lads. I'll teach you, my boy, and gladly."

A number of months went by before Dirk was ready to leave for Brittany on the ship's first run. It was a vessel of fifty tons armed with light carriage guns. He and Zachy had recruited old friends and acquaintances to make up the twelve-man crew. These men were only too eager to leave their fishing boats for what promised to be far greater earnings. Elias Pollard had gone to Mevagissey himself to look over the sloop and was highly satisfied. He was already counting the profits a good run would bring in. A cargo of brandy alone could be purchased across the channel for fifteen hundred pounds, but would be sold for double that in Cornwall. And that price was still far below the one charged legally, once the government had levied its heavy tax on the imported brandy. Elias wished Dirk good luck and fair seas.

Two nights before the ship was to sail, Dirk rode up the coast from Landrawna to Rowenstow. A fierce March wind blew in from the sea; below the headland the water surged and lashed at the slate rocks.

He had come for a reason, and he had managed to half-convince himself it was the only one. Entering the stone church, he took out a handful of coins and dropped them into the collection box. Then he went back outside and gazed across at the vicarage. It was dark, and the wind drowned out any sounds he and his horse made.

Stealthily he crept across to the house until he was close enough to see clearly through the parlor window. The vicar was asleep in his chair, his head lolled to one side. His sister's face was bent over some needlework. But it was neither of them that he yearned to see.

Lamorna sat very still, staring into the fire. Her brown curls gleamed in the firelight. Dirk's hungry gaze caressed her delicate profile—the smooth, pale brow, her long-lashed eyes, small nose, and full rosy mouth. He looked at her white neck and throat. She wore a simple gown, untouched with ruffles or lace.

Then Marya spoke to her, and he saw her look up, a faint smile on her face. She shook her head and picked up her embroidery from her lap. Dirk watched as she made intricate stitches in the white cloth. She had ceased to be an unassuming young woman gazing into the fire; in that brief moment she had become what she was—a lady trained in the skills of a gentlewoman.

Abruptly Dirk turned and stalked away from the vicarage to where his horse was secured. Fool, fool, he told himself savagely. She is out of your reach, no matter what you do. She can never be anything to you. Forget her. For God's sake, forget her.

Twelve

It was the following Christmas, and Lamorna was eighteen years old. It had been over a year since she had seen Dirk last, and she had gradually willed herself not to think of him. There was another storm that October, but no ships wrecked off the coast at Rowenstow. She had lain awake that night listening to the gales, the waves rearing and crashing below her window. She could not help but recall the night Dirk and Zachy had been carried into the vicarage kitchen, more dead than alive. There was a hollow ache in her, and when she finally fell asleep, she dreamed of Dirk.

In her dream he did not wear the loose muslin shirt and old breeches he had worn at the vicarage, but an odd-looking dark suit. And his black hair, rather than being long and tangled, was cut close to his head. He was gripping her tightly, his deep-set dark eyes gazing intently into hers. "It's no use," he said. "You belong to me. We belong together. I know that now." And then he was kissing her with passion and urgency, his body hard against her own . . .

Lamorna awoke trembling. There was a yearning in her body which shocked her. The man in her dream—he could not have been Dirk, so why had she assumed he was? And why had his touch, his mouth, felt so familiar? Her own desire had risen to meet his . . .

By the next morning she could remember little of the disturbing dream. Yet a lingering melancholy remained with her all that day, and Marya had to repeat herself several times when speaking to her niece.

Wool-gathering, thought Marya indulgently. Yet she was faintly troubled by the wistful look in the girl's eyes. Marya was not reminded of the shipwrecked sailors; she had ceased to think of them for many months. Lamorna had moped when they had left the vicarage, and Marya thought she understood why. The rescue and nursing back to health of the two men had brought excitement into Lamorna's life. For a week, their usual quiet existence had altered perceptibly; it was only natural that once the normal routine was resumed the child would suffer the blue devils. Wisely, Marya said nothing.

Unfortunately, Deborah was not so tactful. For days she had observed the girl's low spirits and knew their cause better than did Marya. For Marya did not realize that Lamorna's affections were involved. To her it was inconceivable that a gently-bred young woman could fall in love with a man from the laboring classes.

" 'Ee's no cause to pine for that sailor any longer," said Deborah one evening, concern and fondness for the girl making her impatient.

Lamorna had not realized her feelings were so evident. Mortified, she had turned away from Deborah.

"There, my pet, I'm not meanin' to upset 'ee, but 'ee must see this frettin' must stop. That young man, 'ee won't be seein' him again and there be no reason why 'ee should. He's gone back to where he belong while 'ee stays where 'ee belong. Don't 'ee see that there be an end on it?" There was a tender note in Deborah's voice which was rarely heard.

Lamorna nodded miserably and climbed the stairs to her room. Deborah was right—this mooning over a man she barely knew was foolish. He had had no difficulty in leaving her, so why was she making herself wretched by continuing to pine for him? From now on she would try her best to forget Dirk Killigrew.

When the windfall of silver was discovered in the box, no one thought of Dirk, not even Lamorna.

She continued to mind the village children in the spring and autumn months when their mothers were helping with the planting and harvesting. She had enlisted the help of a girl of fourteen whose face had been badly scarred by the smallpox. Maggie took to her duties zealously and did exactly as Lamorna instructed her. Lamorna allowed no unkind remarks about her appearance and treated her with more thoughtfulness than she had ever known. Lamorna taught the children rhymes and songs; she told them stories from the Bible, and tales of good Cornish brownies and spiteful piskies. She also taught a few of them their letters.

That Christmas she showed Maggie how to make the Christmas bush for the front hall. The two girls went out with baskets and cut branches of evergreens and furze blossoms. In the vicarage kitchen, Lamorna fastened the greenery to the two wooden hoops which intersected one another at right angles. She secured a candle to the base, and Maggie strung lady apples below.

They also stuck sprigs of holly above all the doors and windows to keep out evil. In the church Marya helped them fill each deep-set windowsill with armfuls of yew and box. From Deborah's dried herbs, Lamorna took rosemary and bay, arranging them on the altar cloth in honor of Mary.

Maggie was thrilled to be included in the preparations. She adored Lamorna and took a new-found pride in being her helper and companion. She began to forget about the ugly marks on her face. She helped Lamorna and Deborah bake gingerbread, saffron and seedy cakes, fig and plum pudding soaked in rare madeira. Every Christmas they made a cake for every family in the village. Maggie's parents could not complain that she spent too much time in the company of the vicar's niece, because Lamorna often sent baskets of fruit or scones home with the girl. Maggie's mother accepted the goods gratefully.

One morning less than a fortnight before Christmas, a boy knocked at the back door of the vicarage. He carried a letter addressed to the Reverend Samuel and Miss Marya Hall. It was of heavy parchment, folded and sealed in oxblood wax with the Roscarrock imprint.

Lamorna took it from the boy and brought it to her aunt in the parlor. " 'Tis from Sir John Roscarrock, I believe," she said.

Marya broke the seal and spread open the letter. "No, 'tis from Miss Denzella Roscarrock."

"Who is that?"

"A cousin of Sir John. It appears she is now living at Kilworthy as well. Lady Constance's health grows poorer, I fear. Perhaps Miss Roscarrock has gone to look after her."

"Why does she write to us?"

Marya perused the letter. "Why, 'tis an invitation. To a Christmas house party at Kilworthy. She and Sir John would be most glad if we would be their guests for a few days. She writes that she appreciates your uncle's duties on Christmas Eve and Day so they will expect us the following afternoon."

"Oh, Aunt! A house party . . . and at Kilworthy. I've longed to see it. You've said 'tis a grand manor house. May we go?"

Marya looked at her niece's face, her shining violet eyes. This was what she herself had been wishing for her beloved niece—the opportunity to mix with the members of the Cornish gentry. Lamorna was eighteen; it was time she met people of her own class, despite the Halls' impoverished state. She had beauty and grace, and was better educated than most young ladies. She deserved a life preferable to the simple one at the vicarage.

Yet for some reason Marya hesitated. She felt a curious reluctance she could not account for. "We must consult your uncle, Lamorna," she said.

"But the boy, he's waiting for an answer, and Uncle is in the village visiting," protested the girl.

Marya was at a loss. There was not one good reason why they should not accept the invitation, and several reasons why they should. Miss Denzella Roscarrock honored them with it, and it would not do to offend Sir John, who held Samuel's living. The visit was sure to bring Lamorna pleasure, and Marya was honest enough to admit that she herself would enjoy a few days of gracious living.

"Very well, child, I'll write and accept. Fetch me your uncle's quill, ink, and paper."

Lamorna awakened early on the day after Christmas, St. Stephen's Day. Yet it was not of that martyred saint and his arrows that she thought. She was filled with excitement; this morning they were riding to Kilworthy. Sir John Roscarrock was sending three of his horses and a groom to convey them to his estate.

Marya had helped Lamorna to make a new gown. The fabric had cost dear but Marya had no qualms about sacrificing some of the housekeeping expenses. The gown was of lavender silk, the skirt full, the sleeves elbow-length and festooned with lace. A deep frill of lace trimmed the low, square-cut bodice as well. Marya had also sewn a woolen tippet for Lamorna to wear on the ride. She had a new pair of gloves and white stockings. Marya took no pride in herself, but she was determined that Lamorna not be shamed before the more fortunate gentry.

But when she went down to breakfast in the blue woolen gown she was to wear on the journey, Marya greeted her with a doleful expression and hushed voice.

"Your uncle is ill, dearest. Only a head cold, but he cannot travel today."

Lamorna's heart sank. She dared not ask the question uppermost in her mind.

"In the light of this, I fear we should not go to Kilworthy."

"Now, Miss Marya, I told 'ee I'd look after the vicar," said

Deborah. "There be naught 'ee can do for 'un. He be needin' rest, tes all. You and Miss Lamorna go to Kilworthy."

Marya looked uncertain. "But Samuel—he may need us," she said somewhat feebly.

"If he's took worse, I'll send 'ee word and 'ee can come straight away. But 'ee ought to go. Miss Lamorna's new gown and things ought not to go to waste. And tes time she met those of her own station," she added with a certain deliberation.

Marya sighed. "I believe you are right, Deborah. Very well, if you are certain you can manage here . . ."

Deborah bridled. "I can look after the vicar as well as any," she said.

"Yes, of course," said Marya hastily. "I know he will have the best of care."

Lamorna let out her breath in relief. She finished her breakfast and brought down her bag. The groom arrived with the three horses. Marya eyed them warily, but the man assured her they were all docile mounts. He strapped their bags onto the third horse. In her tippet and flat, broad-brimmed hat, Lamorna rode happily alongside her aunt. Her cheeks were rosy in the damp air and her violet-blue eyes sparkled with anticipation.

She was a pretty maid, thought the groom. He was anxious to reach Kilworthy before the mist began to rise on the moors; he didn't like the look of the lowered sky nor the clamminess in the air. The ladies were not moving quickly enough for him. They stopped once to rest the horses and eat the pasties Deborah had packed. There was no wind to penetrate the heavy dampness, and coils of vapor were already forming.

"Still a few miles to go, miss," he said to Marya. "Us ought to hasten. We don't want to be caught in the mist."

So they quickened their pace, and soon reached a village spread in a half-circle above the sea.

"What place is this?" asked Lamorna. She had never been so far from Rowenstow. The landscape had grown lusher as they rode south. The bleak, rock-scarred moors had gradually softened to grassy headlands and fields.

"Landrawna, miss," said the groom.

Lamorna caught her breath. Landrawna, where Dirk Killigrew lived. Or used to live. She stole a glance at her aunt, but it was obvious that she did not connect the name with the sailors they had looked after over a year before.

" 'Tis a pretty place, the way it nestles above the sea," was Marya's reply.

The groom grunted. He had scant interest in views of the sea. He wished only to get back to Kilworthy where he could continue the Christmas revels in the servants' hall. There was a buxom dairy maid who had caught his eye; he would position her beneath the mistletoe that evening during a dance. He resented this errand on which he had been sent while most of his fellows had gone hunting with Sir John and his male guests.

They rode up the steep streets of Landrawna while Lamorna's heart beat wildly in her breast. She did not know whether she feared meeting Dirk or longed to see him. But in neither way was she satisfied; they passed a number of people but none was Dirk or Zachy.

Once out of the village, they crossed several fields awaiting cultivation in the spring. As they were climbing a hill thick with beech trees, the groom said, "Kilworthy be on the other side, Miss Hall."

And then it came into view: a sprawling granite mansion with hundreds of narrow windows, crenellated roofs, and numerous sprouting chimneys. On the front lawn were yew trees shaped like giant urns.

Just ahead sat the massive gatehouse, crosses and niches cut into its stone walls, projecting bays on either side of the arched entrance. As they drew close, their horses' hooves crunching on the gravelled drive, an intense wave of panic overwhelmed Lamorna. She swayed in her saddle, trembling.

A man's voice spoke. "Rather hideous, isn't it? Diana's grandfather remodelled it and built on."

The mare suddenly whinnied nervously, raising her head. The groom swore and reached across for her bridle. "What's got into 'ee, m'dear? We be home," he said to the horse. He glanced at Lamorna, noticing her pallor and the undisguised fright in her eyes. "Tes all right, miss. She likely saw a mouse or summat."

Lamorna gazed at him in disbelief. Hadn't he heard the man's voice? Where on earth had it come from? She turned to her aunt. Marya's face mirrored her concern but nothing else.

" 'Tis been a long ride," she said soothingly. "The horses are tired. As am I. We'll rest before dinner, Lamorna."

Lamorna nodded abstractedly, giving no answer. She looked down at her gloved hands gripping the reins. The words had meant nothing to her; she knew no one named Diana. But there had been something distinctly familiar about the man's voice. Her eyes were dark pools in her white face. She tried to ignore the clutch of dismay in her belly and still her trembling frame.

The groom helped them to dismount, and the great doors were opened by two footmen in powdered wigs and green satin livery. The floor in the hall was not of wood, but of marble, great squares of black and white. Like a chessboard, thought Lamorna. Her fear was evaporating as she looked about, awestruck.

They were shown into the drawing room. The ceiling was high and decorated with ornately carved molding. Huge portraits hung on the walls in the vast room. At each end was an enormous fireplace with a white marble mantel and blue and white tiles. Garlands of laurel draped the long windows, and the sills were arranged with holly, boxwood, apples, oranges, and lemons. Set in each window was a tall white candle.

" 'Tis beautiful," Lamorna gasped. She wandered about, too restless to sit beside her aunt in one of the blue and white striped chairs.

"Good afternoon, and Merry Christmas." A tall, full-breasted woman had entered the room. Her hair was powdered and coiled high on her head, and she wore a wine-red velvet gown. She made an imposing figure; Lamorna felt suddenly shy and uneasy.

"I am Denzella Roscarrock," she said.

"How do you do?" said Marya, rising from her seat. "May I be permitted to present my niece, Lamorna."

The woman nodded as Lamorna dropped a curtsy. "Please sit down. I regret that the Reverend Hall was not able to accompany you today, Miss Hall."

"I'm afraid he awakened feeling poorly this morning. He has been busy with many duties recently."

"Nothing serious, I hope?"

"No, merely a cold, but the journey . . ."

"Yes, of course. And how was your long ride? Were the horses to your satisfaction?"

"Yes, indeed, Miss Roscarrock. Sir John was most kind to send them."

"You must both be tired and cold. I will have you shown to your room and some refreshment sent up. We will dine in two hours' time. I have instructed that the food be set out in the Great Hall so that the servants may be permitted their own celebrations of the season. So we will be rather informal tonight. In the meantime I will have hot water brought up to you. If there is anything you need, you have only to ask one of the maids."

"Thank you, Miss Roscarrock," said Marya. " 'Tis a great honor for us to be at Kilworthy."

Denzella smiled graciously. When the maid came, Marya and Lamorna rose. "I will see you both tonight," said their hostess.

I don't like her, Lamorna thought to herself. Yet there was nothing to account for her dislike. She followed her aunt upstairs, the feeling of dismay returning.

Denzella thoughtfully watched them go. It was obvious they were ill at ease at Kilworthy, but that was to be expected. Constance had grown very lax in her responsibilities, and she had ceased to entertain. The Halls were gentry, despite their simple means, and Sir John owed them his condescension. He provided the living at Rowenstow, after all, but with his wife practically an invalid, he did not invite ladies to Kilworthy.

Lady Constance suffered from headaches which had grown increasingly worse over the years. She had little energy, even when not plagued by them. That was the reason Denzella had come to Kilworthy. She despised Lady Constance, and didn't think much better of her daughter, Kitty, a pale, puny miss. The Roscarrocks—her family as well—needed some rich, healthy blood. Sir John needed a male heir. Lady Constance was not past the age of childbearing yet, but Denzella despaired of her producing a son.

Since coming to Kilworthy, Denzella had rarely seen them together. Sir John was not in the habit of visiting his wife's sickbed, so they met on the rare occasions she appeared for dinner. Denzella had remonstrated with Constance, urging her to leave her bed and assume the duties of the wife of a great landowner. She had scolded, bullied, and cajoled her, all to no avail.

"You see to matters, Denzella," she had replied feebly in response when the older woman had pointed out several household affairs requiring her supervision. "I can't think . . . my poor head . . ."

"If you interested yourself in something besides your health, Constance, perhaps your headaches would improve," she had stated coldly. Her own health had always been excellent; she had no sympathy with habitual illness.

Constance had closed her gray eyes wearily. "You don't understand. No one knows the way I suffer."

"You ought to take an interest in your daughter, Constance. She needs a mother's care." When Constance did not reply, Denzella became angry. "Doesn't Kitty mean anything to you? Or John? Or Kilworthy?"

Lady Constance's lips trembled, and Denzella pressed what she thought to be her advantage. "John needs an heir. You are his wife. You must try to give him a son."

A visible wave of revulsion crossed Lady Constance's countenance. Her nostrils distended, and two spots of color appeared in her sunken cheeks. "You do not know what you are asking, Denzella. I'm ill . . . please leave me be."

Disgusted, Denzella had swept out of the room. Constance was a tremendous disappointment. Mistress of one of the most magnificent mansions in Cornwall, and she withdrew into the four walls of her chamber. She was content to let the servants go about their business any way they pleased. She did not seek her husband's company nor that of her only child. It did not surprise Denzella that they, in turn, avoided her. Sir John refused to hire a governess for Kitty; she was tutored by the curate from Landrawna. She was a quiet, timid child, clearly intimidated by her father and Denzella herself. So far she had spoken to few of the guests, sitting in corners with her head bent. Another disappointment to the great name of Roscarrock. Perhaps Lamorna Hall would be able to draw the girl out, thought Denzella, but with little hope. Kitty was as impossible as her mother.

That evening Lamorna sat in the Great Hall at Kilworthy. She wore her new lavender silk gown and a lace cap on her brown curls. The room was filled with guests, and Lamorna was content to watch them. She had never seen such splendid gowns, embroidered and gathered in loops to reveal silk petticoats with double flounces. A few had even painted their faces.

The men were no less flamboyant. Their coats were heavily trimmed with gold down the fronts and about the flap pockets. Some wore powdered wigs, and jeweled rings sparkled on their hands.

"Such finery," she said to Marya, her eyes full of wonder.

Privately Marya thought that Lamorna was far more lovely in her simply-cut pale violet gown than were these powdered and patched ladies. She was relieved that the girl had recovered from whatever had ailed her. A fit of nerves, likely.

Sir John had greeted them when they had first entered the Great Hall. He was an elegant figure in brown wig and crimson full-skirt coat and breeches with a gold embroidered waistcoat. He was of medium height, in his early forties, a proud man but rather indolent by nature. He smiled at Lamorna and complimented her aunt on the girl's fairness. "You must meet my daughter, Kitty," he said.

Marya had said they would be pleased, and Sir John moved on to speak to other guests. Marya and Lamorna had taken seats along one side of the vast room, panelled in dark glossy wood. Marya looked about the room, recognizing some of the guests by sight. There was Matthew Tregarth, a corpulent heavy-jowled widower, and his son Joshua, a tall, thin-lipped young man. Marya supposed the girl of about Lamorna's age to be Joshua's sister, Tamara. She had dark hair and wore an apple-green gown. The woman at Joshua's side must be his wife. She had heard he had married the heiress Isolde St. Aubyn. She was fair, and her throat and hands sparkled with jewels.

There was a commotion at the door; Denzella announced, "The curl singers are here."

The curl, or carol, singers were a group of local men. They trooped into the Hall in their well-worn, patched clothing and scuffed boots. Pulling at their forelocks before all the company, they waited for Sir John to formally welcome them. When he had done so, they tuned their fiddles.

"Are 'ee ready, boys?" said the leader. "Sound for it, then!"

> Welcome Christmas which brings us all good cheer,
> Pies and puddings, roast pork and strong beer.
> Come let me taste your Christmas beer
> That is so very strong,
> And I do wish that Christmas time
> With all its mirth and song
> Was twenty times so long.

They sang "The First Nowell," "The Holly and the Ivy," "The Holy Well," "Born is the King of Israel," pronouncing it "Isery-hell." The four part harmony was well done, the fiddle accompaniment merry. Yet Lamorna noticed the men eyeing the servants who carried in huge succulent joints of beef, pork, and mutton, and platters of geese baked crisp and brown, setting them down on the long tables. She wondered if any of them ate the roast pork they sang of.

The leader passed the dash-an-darrus, or stirrup cup, to Sir John, who tossed in a handful of coins. "Go around to the kitchen," said Denzella to the men. "You will find food and drink."

The men bowed, touching their forelocks again and thanking their host and hostess. "A Merry Christmas to all here," cried the leader as they left.

Marya and Lamorna joined the line forming at the long table. Denzella came up to them, her arm about a young girl. "Miss Hall," she said to Marya, "pray look after Kitty for me. See that she eats something, and don't permit her to be tongue-tied tonight."

Marya smiled at the girl whose white face had flushed a painful scarlet. "How do you do, Kitty? Allow me to present my niece to you, Miss Lamorna Hall."

Lamorna smiled at Kitty and the girl nodded in return. Denzella shouldn't have embarrassed her so cruelly, thought Lamorna. Despite the fact that Kilworthy was her own home, she was obviously overwhelmed by the assembly. Her timidity gave Lamorna confidence. Kitty was thin, no doubt the reason for her relation's words, but she had a sweet face and delicate features, almost like a doll's.

"How is Lady Constance?" asked Marya. "I am sorry that she did not feel up to joining us this evening."

Kitty murmured something polite. People were always asking after her mother. Most of them were merely curious; they were not truly concerned about her state of health. Her reclusiveness was cause for speculation and censure in North Cornwall. She had no intimates. It had been Denzella's idea to invite the local gentry to a Christmas house party, and her father had readily agreed. Kitty herself had dreaded it; she was highly uncomfortable around groups of people. But she knew better than to voice her feelings.

Denzella had taken over the running of Kilworthy, and her mother seemed content, even relieved, that she do so. She had gradually relinquished all interest in household affairs, retreating into the confines of her bedchamber and sitting room. She's hiding, thought Kitty bitterly. She doesn't care to see me or anyone else.

Kitty remembered when she used to go to her mother's room only to be told by Rose, the maid, that no, she couldn't see her mother; she was feeling too poorly.

But one day Kitty had refused to be turned away; she had cried and hammered on the door. It had taken two of the maids to drag her down the hall and up the stairs to her room on the floor above. Kitty had had a nurse then, a kindly woman, but she had departed soon after the episode, and Kitty was told that it was because of the disgraceful, hysterical way in which she had behaved. Her father never employed another nurse. She was left to her own devices except when she had lessons with the curate, the Reverend Simon Pettinger.

Neither enjoyed the hours they spent together; he considered

Kitty a dull, unimaginative child who absorbed little of what he tried to teach. Her spelling was abominable; the adding and subtracting of figures confused her; and she showed little interest in music, history, or geography. In desperation he had several times set her up with paints and easel, hoping to light a spark of interest in *something*. But the pictures she executed were so bizarre and unsettling, not at all the placid still lifes and gentle pastoral scenes he had had in mind, that he soon abandoned the pursuit. Kitty did not object.

Serving their plates, Marya, Lamorna, and Kitty took seats near the Tregarths. Tamara knew Kitty, but she had never met Lamorna. The two girls liked one another on sight. Tamara was lively and easy to talk to, far easier than Kitty.

"See that young man over there?" said Tamara. "Doesn't he have the face of a fish? He's Isolde's cousin and my brother would like us to marry. Can you imagine? I told him nothing would induce me to marry Frederick."

Lamorna giggled. "What did he say?"

"Nothing, but Isolde told me to hold my tongue. She was furious, I daresay because she resembles Frederick! She has a great deal of money, so I suppose Joshua doesn't care much about her looks. Frederick has a lot of money as well, but there isn't enough money in the world to make me marry him!"

Lamorna noticed that Kitty had eaten only a few bites of the food on her plate. "Aren't you hungry?" she asked. "I thought I would be too excited to eat, but it's all so wonderful. I've never eaten such food as this!"

"Look, Kitty," cried Tamara excitedly. "The musicians have begun to play and your father is coming this way. I believe he must want you to partner him since your mother isn't here."

Kitty reddened. "Oh, no, I couldn't. I—I don't dance very well. And I couldn't in front of all these people!" She shrunk back in her chair.

But Sir John was standing before the three girls and making them all a gracious bow. "I vow you three ladies are the prettiest here tonight," he said, smiling. " 'Tis good to see more young faces at Kilworthy. Kitty, my dear, I ask the honor of the first dance."

"Please, Father, not now, I don't feel very well . . ."

"You must, Kitty. I will not take no for an answer. Come, everyone is waiting for us. They cannot dance until we do."

"But there are so many people here, Father," she protested in dismay.

"They are all our friends, my dear. Come." He held out his hand. Without another word she put hers into it and permitted him to lead her into the center of the room.

"Sir John is rather handsome, is he not?" asked Tamara. "And what elegant manners he has." She looked over at her own father, who was eating and drinking noisily, a mark of grease on his florid cheek. Isolde had risen to dance with her husband. Marya was talking pleasantly with another lady.

"You live with your aunt and uncle?"

Lamorna nodded. "Yes, at Rowenstow. My uncle is the vicar there."

"Is this your first time at Kilworthy?"

"This is my first time anywhere," said Lamorna with a rueful smile. "Rowenstow is rather isolated, and we have only one horse."

Tamara was startled. The girl was well-spoken and wore a lovely silk gown, but it sounded as though she and her aunt and uncle were poor by the standards of the gentry. She was curious about Lamorna and wanted to get to know her better. But they had little opportunity to talk that night; both of them were claimed for the reels and country dances. Lamorna danced once with Sir John, and he entertained her with a droll tale of two fishermen who tried to catch a mermaid. She danced with a few young men who were charmed by her face and figure. Mr. Pettinger, Kitty's tutor and the curate at Landrawna, was most taken with her. A girl reared in a vicarage, lovely as a flower, she might be just the wife for him. He doubted there would be much of a dowry, though, as the Halls were known to be impoverished. Still, "her face was her fortune," as the old rhyme went. He began to entertain fond hopes.

Lamorna knew nothing of what was going on inside Simon's head. She enjoyed the dancing, though none of her partners sparked her interest. One of them, full of mead, had planted a wet kiss on her cheek and she had pushed him away. Another had whispered a bawdy song in her ear which had shocked and revolted her. Tamara Tregarth would have known just how to respond, with a witty rebuff, but Lamorna, sheltered all her life, was at a loss. Her cheeks hot, she had said nothing, but eluded the young man's attempts to convince her to leave the Great Hall for a breath of fresh air. She had rejoined Marya and then danced one final time with Mr. Pettinger before they retired for the night.

Lamorna, Kitty, and Tamara spent much of the following days together. They walked in the extensive gardens, played cards in one of the sitting rooms, and visited the new litter of puppies in the stables. They went "a-gooding" with Denzella, taking baskets of food and niceties to local widows. Lady Constance had not done so in years, and the women were grateful to Denzella. The three girls rode with her in a carriage about Landrawna, stopping at cottages along the way, but Lamorna never saw Dirk. Yet she could not help but think of him, knowing that this village was his home. *I wonder what he is doing now,* she thought. *Perhaps he is married . . .* She bit her lip. When Mr. Pettinger passed them and smiled at her, she did not even notice him.

Denzella relished her new role as bounteous mistress. She had resolved to reinstate all the traditions at Kilworthy—the Christmas house party and goody baskets were only a beginning. She was determined to see that the Roscarrocks became the most respected family in Cornwall.

As a child she had visited Kilworthy and wished passionately that it were her home. Her parents' townhouse in Penzance was a far cry from the splendid mansion that belonged to the main branch of their family. Despite her own straitened circumstances, she was enormously proud to be related to the Roscarrocks of Kilworthy. Without consciously doing so, she spurned the young men who might have asked for her hand. She had no wish to lose the link she shared with her cousin John, her surname. She remained at home, looking after her ailing parents who lingered for many years longer than was expected. She had undertaken the long, uncomfortable trip north to Kilworthy for Kitty's christening, turning a deaf ear to her parents' shocked protests that it was too far and she could not possibly travel alone. She longed to be mistress of such a house and bitterly envied John's new wife, Constance. Not that she was the least in love with John; it was the house itself which inspired her devotion. At night she often visualized herself walking the long corridors, giving orders to the staff, entertaining guests in the beautiful drawing room. Her parents knew nothing of this secret longing. To them she was a dutiful daughter, cool and competent. She herself knew she was capable of far more than managing her parents' simple household, and often felt stifled and oppressed. But she kept these feelings to herself.

After her mother's death, she was alone—a handsome, though no longer young, woman. She wrote to Sir John and he had rather vaguely extended an invitation for her to visit. She swiftly accepted.

It had not taken her long to realize the state of affairs. The house was sloppily run; the servants needed a firm hand. There were obvious signs of neglect—dust on the furniture, holes in the draperies, meals badly prepared and cold by the time they reached the dining room. Sir John was often away from home, dining and playing cards with friends, while Lady Constance lay in her bed complaining of weakness and headaches. Denzella's own parents had been none too well, but Constance was still fairly young and she was fortunate enough to be the mistress of Kilworthy. Denzella felt nothing but contempt for her self-imposed seclusion. Yet it was Constance's poor health which caused the idea to grow.

To her there was only one clear remedy. For Denzella to live permanently at Kilworthy and take the running of the household in her cool and capable hands. Denzella did not doubt for a minute that she could do it justice. The house was in a neglected state and would only get worse. Yet Sir John seemed not to notice. He was rather lazy and spent much time away. As for Kitty, she was frail and withdrawn. It was a sorry state of affairs for one of the finest houses in Cornwall.

The intensity of her desire grew to an obsession, but she had always been good at masking her emotions. She approached her cousin with tact and caution, speaking with professed concern for Constance's health. Poor lady, she was unable to cope with the running of the house, suffering as she did with dreadful headaches. And Kitty needed a woman's care just as Kilworthy did. Denzella would be happy to be of any use she could. She remembered the house in earlier days when Sir John's parents had been alive. It was a pity that Constance . . . well, she could scarcely be blamed, poor soul.

Sir John had agreed with her that the household had run better in his mother's day. Yet he did not voice the question she so longed to hear. All that night Denzella chafed and agonized. To be so close to fulfilling the desperate longing of her life but to have nothing resolved. Had she said too much or too little? Was her meaning plain enough, or her offer to help too vague? Had she sounded critical rather than merely solicitous?

But the next morning Sir John asked her to join him for a glass of madeira. And he had asked if she would like to make her home at Kilworthy. He would be most grateful to her if she were to assume the duties which Constance had not the strength for. She was, after all, his closest relation and he did not like to think of her living alone in Penzance.

Denzella had kept her head bowed for a few moments so her cousin would not see the glitter in her eyes. The hand which held the wineglass was trembling. Her dream, so long elusive, was now to be realized. Lifting her head, she gazed coolly across at Sir John.

"I would be most pleased to do anything in my power for you, Cousin, and for Constance. I accept your gracious invitation." Vaguely she was pleased that her voice did not quiver with emotion.

"Then I am in your debt, Cousin," he replied. He understood her passion for his home far better than she realized. There had been no real reason to hesitate, he told himself. Denzella would manage the house superbly. His comforts would be restored without any effort on his part. As for Denzella, her gratitude would work in his favor. Had he not just fulfilled her dearest wish?

Thirteen

The Christmas celebrations at Kilworthy culminated in an elaborate Twelfth Night ball and supper. For days Marya had longed to be back at Rowenstow. Once the New Year began, she told Lamorna it was time for them to leave. But Denzella urged them to remain until after Twelfth Night, and Tamara Tregarth added her own entreaties as well. Not wishing to seem ungracious, Marya gave in. Lamorna was enjoying the company of her new friend and the unaccustomed lavishness of her surroundings; Marya did not have the heart to begrudge her the final festivities.

Contrary to her expectations, Marya had not found their stay at Kilworthy a pleasurable one. She was gratified that Tamara Tregarth had befriended her niece; the girl was high-spirited yet thoughtful and without conceit. But Marya, charitable though she was, could find little to admire in the rest of Tamara's family. Her father, Matthew Tregarth, shamelessly ogled all the pretty women; he was still a notorious lecher despite his sagging jowls and heavy frame. Marya disliked the greedy look in his eyes as they feasted on Lamorna. And his coarse jests and crude table manners put Marya off her food when she was seated near to him.

His son, Joshua Tregarth, was very different, his manners formal and fastidious, yet Marya could like him little better. His deep-set eyes showed no warmth; his thin lips rarely smiled nor did he bestir himself to be convivial. He spoke of his position as local magistrate, announcing, not without satisfaction, that in his few months in that role he had transported and hanged nearly as many people as had his predecessor in two years. He was married to a great heiress, Isolde St. Aubyn, who was quick to show Marya that she considered her and her niece far below the rest of the guests in station. Put out by Tamara's obvious interest in the girl from the humble vicarage, she had unwisely rebuked her.

"Why must you spend all your time with that girl? I wonder at Miss Roscarrock's inviting them here—an impulsive gesture, no doubt. The girl has nothing at all to recommend her except a pretty face. Why, Sir John had to provide the very horses that conveyed them here! Anyone can see that they are not at their ease in a house such as Kilworthy."

"No?" asked Tamara coolly. "Then perhaps they will feel more comfortable at Tregartha which is not nearly so large or grand."

Isolde flushed to the roots of her powdered hair. "You have not asked them to Tregartha!"

"No, but I mean to."

"I forbid it, do you hear? I am mistress of your father's house and I refuse to entertain them. The relatives of an obscure parson—they are beneath our notice, Tamara."

Tamara gave her sister-in-law a long derisive look. "Perhaps you are right, Isolde. 'Twould doubtless be preferable if I visited them at Rowenstow. That way they would not be subjected to your company."

"How dare you—how—" Isolde sputtered furiously.

"She has a name, you know. 'Tis Lamorna, as pretty and sweet as herself. And that rankles, does it not? Are you apprehensive, Isolde, that she will turn my brother's head?"

Isolde was speechless with rage. She stood, rigid, while Tamara turned and left the room. She could have gladly throttled her sister-in-law for accusing her of jealousy. Jealous of that insignificant chit—it was absurd! She, a St. Aubyn, wed to a Tregarth, jealous of some poor orphan raised in a simple vicarage! It was outrageous. Tamara had gone too far this time. As though Joshua had even noticed the girl! Despite his father's lascivious nature, Joshua's dignity and high sense of propriety would never allow him to regard a young woman in that way. Tamara must know how ridiculous her words had been; Joshua was simply not that sort of man. Sometimes Isolde wished that her husband was not so fastidious, that his visits to her bedchamber were more frequent. Her body craved his much more than he realized or would have found acceptable. She sensed this and curbed her own passions. Joshua was not a passionate man; he kept a tight rein on all emotions, all hungers. As his father was ruled by his urges, so did Joshua seem to subjugate his. Isolde sighed, her anger abating. She was very fortunate that her husband was not like his father. But there were times when she longed for his self-restraint to give way, at least for a few moments. Perhaps if she herself were as pretty as that girl . . . In a rare instant of honest appraisal Isolde observed her appearance in the glass. She was splendidly dressed and bejeweled; no one could deny that. Her maid had curled and crimped her limp hair most satisfactorily, and her complexion was enhanced with powder and rouge. Yet neither paint nor finery could straighten her crooked, prominent teeth, soften a chin that was sharply pointed or shorten her long nose. Surely it was preferable to have a husband like hers rather than one with sensual appetites. At least she did not have to share him with the maidservants or worse. And she had already presented him with two healthy sons. If that was the only desire he took to their marriage bed, well then, he was not disappointed.

Tamara was well aware of her father's visits to the brothels in Newquay and Padstow, and his dallying with numerous female servants and village women. In years past, her mother had dismissed every maid who had caught her master's eye. Not only was this a formidable task, but one that ensured a shortage of female servants. Tamara had realized at an early age that it was not the fault of the maids, something her mother had never acknowledged. What could they say when the man who paid their wages pressed them to more intimate duties? A few left of their own accord, but many submitted. Girls whose parents wanted to protect them did not send them into service at Tregartha.

Tamara had not been fond of her mother any more than she was of her father. She had had a governess for many years—a kind, sensible woman, already middle-aged when she came to Tregatha—who was to be commended for the balanced, goodhearted girl Tamara had become.

Joshua had not fared nearly so well. Considered by his father to be too attached to his mother, he had been sent away to school with only yearly visits home. When he had returned for good and gradually taken over the management of the two Tregarth mines, Wheel Charity and Wheel Faith, from his father's careless hands, they had begun to show a much greater profit. His mother had died one spring while he was still at school, and when the news reached him she had already been laid to rest. Matthew thought that Joshua had greatly benefited from his schooling even though Matthew himself had had no formal education. He was delighted with his son's business sense. "Never liked being troubled with all those figures myself," he had said. "You're a wonder, m'boy."

Yet when Joshua had chosen Isolde St. Aubyn to be his wife, his father had objected. "Don't do it! Just think of looking across at her for the rest of your days. Rich as Croesus, I'll grant you, but not a morsel I'd wish to take to bed. Not with the candles lit!" He had laughed while Joshua disdainfully remained silent. Isolde's comeliness or lack of it meant little to him. He wanted heirs, and he could put aside his distaste for the pleasures of the flesh enough to assure that they be conceived.

Isolde managed Tregartha very well, and her dowry had swelled the family fortunes considerably. He knew that she loved jewelry and occasionally presented her with elaborate pieces. It was his way of conveying his approval.

As for Tamara, she had not yet met a man for whom she was tempted to leave Tregartha, despite her lack of affection for her family. And she had so far resisted her brother's attempts to choose a suitable husband for her.

Marya's high hopes for her niece had begun to sink when it became plain that none of the young men at the house party who admired Lamorna were anxious to arrange further meetings. Money and property were the most important considerations in marriage, and she had neither. One could not fault a man for wishing to make the most profitable match he could. If the lady was comely, then all the better. But one did not look for that first. In most cases it was the parents who arranged marriages for their sons or daughters, and Lamorna, despite her grace and beauty, was not on a list of suitable brides. Most of the company was amiable to the Halls, but no invitations were forthcoming.

For several days Marya had enjoyed being idle, taking pleasure in the splendor of her surroundings and talking with several gentlewomen present. Sir John and his cousin, Denzella Roscarrock, were a gracious host and hostess. Yet soon Marya was ready to return to the quiet routine of the vicarage. She realized she had little taste for the lifestyle at Kilworthy and other such houses, in spite of their luxuries and comforts. The rich, heavy food began to disagree with her, making her sluggish. At the vicarage their diet consisted mainly of fish and vegetables; her belly began to rebel at the spiced beef and mutton and her head to ache from the strong mead and other wines. She had no interest in the gossip which happily occupied the other women, and she deplored the drunken ribaldry into which each evening sank. The men were too free with their lewd jests and the women often little better. There was much flirting and what Marya considered unseemly behavior; she discerned inappropriate interest in a number of people, each of whom was married to another. Marya saw to it that she and Lamorna retired early, leaving their fellow guests to their revels.

Though Denzella had urged them to ask for anything they wished, Marya recognized that the maids were not prepared to wait on them with the attention and vigilance they gave the others. She had not brought a maidservant herself to go down to the servants' hall and assert their needs. The Halls had been swiftly sized up by the maids. Therefore, their morning tea was tepid and the water for washing even cooler. They did not speak of it, but these slights convinced Marya even more that they ought to go back where they belonged.

And there was something else that unsettled Marya. Lady Constance, Sir John's ailing wife, made but two appearances in the course of their visit. The first time, Marya was deeply shocked at the change in her—she looked far older than her years. There was no doubt she was ill. Her languid weakness was evident and the pain, doubtless from one of her headaches, was all too readable in her face. Neither time did she linger, staying just long enough to greet her guests and drink a glass of wine. She sat at one end of the long table while Marya regarded her in dismay, conscious of something in the atmosphere which she could not grasp but which troubled her. Her desire to leave Kilworthy mounted. Yet she did not speak of this to Lamorna. Upon examination, her random apprehensions appeared foolish. And she had to admit that Kitty, Sir John, and Lady Constance's shy, frail daughter, seemed to be benefitting from the company of the two older girls. Except when her mother joined the company. Then Marya noticed she became withdrawn, her head bent. She neither spoke to her mother nor embraced her.

On the Twelfth Night Lamorna again wore her lavender silk gown. Tamara herself arranged her hair, drawing back the long curls that swept her cheeks and winding them into a knot at the back of her head. The rest of her hair was left down. She gave Lamorna a set of teardrop pearl earrings which she insisted she had no use for. At first Marya and Lamorna had protested this gift, but Tamara, hardheaded, had her way.

The entertainment that evening was provided by a group of gaudily dressed masked guise dancers. The girls wore the raiments of sailors, while the young men were attired as coy maidens in lace veils and old-fashioned gowns. Cavorting about the banquet hall to the sounds of drums, mouth organs, and concertinas, they swept a number of the company into the dance with them.

After the departure of the guise dancers was "St. George and the Dragon," a play presented by travelling mummers. There was Father Christmas with long, white wig, the comical doctor in a three-cornered hat, the maiden wearing a gown decorated with ribbons, the Turkish knight looking villainous in black, and St. George, the Christian knight who slayed both the Turk and the dragon with its long, sharp teeth. The party shouted their praise of St. George, denounced the infidel Turk, and laughed at the doctor who was able to bring back to life the fallen Turk only to have St. George slay him again. At the end St. George took the maiden for his bride and there followed many cheers and broad jests.

The masque was succeeded by the drinking of "lamb's wool"—delicious spiced ale seasoned with roasted apples—for the continued health of the apple trees. Dancing resumed to gay, whirling tunes, and Lamorna was claimed by the curate of St. Petroc's, Simon Pettinger. She found him pleasant company; his obvious shyness gave her confidence. As for him, his affections were already engaged. Her lack of dowry had ceased to be of any importance.

"Shame to waste so delicious a lass on the curds-and-whey cleric," said Matthew Tregarth to Joshua before he lumbered up to dance with her. Mr. Pettinger's face hardened. Stepping aside with a cool nod to Matthew, he hoped the old goat would not offend her. He watched in helpless anger and revulsion as the man's large, red hands held hers tightly.

Marya was also watching Matthew with her niece. Thank heaven they were leaving on the morrow! The last few days had seemed endless, characterized by long meals and people who bathed rarely but who drenched themselves in scent. When the dance was over she saw with relief that Matthew had left her niece's side, doubtless in search of more accommodating company, while the nice young curate hastened to partner her again.

Lamorna's aunt observed him with far more approval. A personable, quiet man in his late twenties, he was known to be diligent in the executing of his duties as curate of Landrawna's parish church. Far more diligent than the vicar, the Reverend Poldew. If he were a bit stiff in manner, that could, Marya was certain, be set down to diffidence rather than coldness. He was solemn and something of a scholar and surely would appreciate Lamorna's upbringing and education. If he offered for her it would be a good match. His income would not be as high as that of a successful farmer, but they were equals in station. Perhaps marrying a cleric would be best for her. Having been reared in a vicarage, she knew what was expected. She would make an admirable wife for a curate, and, later, vicar. And Mr. Pettinger might someday rise even higher, perhaps to the rank of archdeacon. Marya allowed her thoughts to run unchecked, which she rarely did. It was known that Mr. Pettinger did the real work of the parish. Mr. Poldew, the fat vicar, spent his time in more worldly pursuits. The living at Landrawna was far greater than at Rowenstow, justifiably so when Sir John, the man who held them both, was a member of St. Petroc's. Marya was aware that the Reverend Mr. Poldew had taken holy orders at his family's insistence; he had no interest in his vocation. His attentions were fully taken up by the shares he held in various mines, by cardplaying and hunting. The bishop was surely aware of Simon's worth, Marya mused. Perhaps it would not be long before he was sent to another parish, this time as vicar.

At midnight Tamara sought out Lamorna and Kitty for the burning of the rushes, an old Twelfth Night custom. She took their hands and led them to the fireplace.

Lamorna smilingly shook her head. "You do it, Tamara. I've no cause for such foolishness."

"Oh, you've no interest in love or marriage, Lamorna? Don't be coy; 'tis to see into your future, after all. You must toss in two rushes, one for yourself and one for another you shall name privately, and watch how they burn. If they lie apart in the fire, you must look elsewhere. But if they burn together, you will marry him."

" 'Tis nonsense," Lamorna protested feebly. But she took the two rushes from Tamara and, closing her eyes, threw each into the hearth. Into her mind came Dirk's face, his dark, deep-set eyes, aquiline nose, the furrows on either side of his square jaw. Then Tamara's voice broke into her abstraction.

"Well, whoever he is, he's not the one. Poor Mr. Pettinger!"

Kitty giggled. Opening her eyes, Lamorna saw that the two rushes had landed apart. She flushed. " 'Twas not Mr. Pettinger I thought of! 'Twas no one at all."

"Ah, well, 'tis only a game," said Tamara. "Now 'tis my turn. What a relief—I won't be wed to Frederick St. Aubyn, in spite of Isolde's efforts! Won't she be disappointed when I tell her!"

Lamorna was not listening. Her gaze was fixed on one of the burning rushes as it swiftly shrivelled and was consumed by the flames. She felt a sickening lurch of fear. The fire danced before her eyes as a wave of heat wafted over her. She uttered a soft moan.

"Lamorna, you've gone green," said Tamara. " 'Tis only a farmhouse custom, you know." She put her arm about her friend's shoulders and drew her away from the fireplace.

Kitty studied Lamorna's pale face. The violet-blue eyes had darkened, her breathing had quickened. She looked more frightened than ill, though of what, Kitty could not fathom. Lamorna's life seemed uncomplicated enough. Yet what did one truly know of another's life? There was the life one showed to the world, but it was not all. Kitty knew that better than most.

"My head aches," said Lamorna. "I'm going to sit with my aunt a little while."

When Mr. Pettinger came over to them a short while later, Lamorna did not look up.

"I fear my niece is tired," said Marya, smiling. "We are not used to the late hours nor the constant merrymaking."

Simon nodded. It was what he would have expected, and his admiration of her rose even higher. Her nature was neither giddy nor frivolous; Tamara Tregarth, however, he had quickly and inaccurately summed up as both.

Simon's light brown hair was tied back with a black ribbon; he wore a blue coat and breeches which contrasted somberly with the satins and laces of the other men, including those of his own vicar. He felt less than comfortable at these affairs; indeed, he would not have come at all had it not been for the desire to see Lamorna before she returned to Rowenstow.

Flushing a little, he embarked on the speech he had prepared. "Pray allow me to say, Miss Hall, that my own enjoyment of the festivities has been largely due to your presence and that of your niece. I have not had the honor yet of meeting the Reverend Hall, though his character is well known." Here Simon took a breath and then plunged on with the crux of the matter. "Perhaps one day soon I may ride up to Rowenstow, with your leave."

"We would be most pleased to receive you, Mr. Pettinger," said Marya warmly, sensing the earnestness behind his rather prim words. She glanced at Lamorna; the girl's face was pale, her expression remote. " 'Tis time, I think, that we retired. Pray excuse us, Mr. Pettinger." She rose.

Simon was disappointed; he had hoped for a little more time with Lamorna. But he said, "By all means, Miss Hall. It is getting late; I should return to Landrawna myself." He was assuring her that he had no further interest in the proceedings.

"Come, dearest," said Marya, "you look most fatigued. And we are leaving early in the morning." What a blessed relief that will be, she thought. Though if Mr. Pettinger contemplated a certain proposal, then the journey south had been worth it after all.

Lamorna rose listlessly.

"Good night, Miss Lamorna," said Simon. "A safe journey back to Rowenstow."

She smiled faintly. "Thank you. Good night, Mr. Pettinger."

Simon watched them leave the banquet hall, his face revealing his tender feelings.

Denzella stood nearby, observing the curate's doting look as she had Marya's approval. This would not do at all, she thought, exasperated. Over the last few days she had conceived a far different future for the vicarage girl. Lamorna would be wasted on Simon Pettinger. Yet, she assured herself, there was no danger. If necessary, John could write to the bishop with the request that Simon remain single for the present. Young curates had little autonomy.

Following their return to Rowenstow, Marya became ill and was forced to stay in bed. Her throat burned fiercely, her head and limbs ached, and she alternately shivered and sweltered beneath the bedclothes. Deborah boiled elderflower and mixed the liquid with treacle to bring down the fever, and later administered vinegar and honey for her cough.

Tamara visited, bringing a basket of oranges and costly spices off the ships at Newquay. She and Lamorna took tea in the parlor, eating Deborah's heavy cakes with clotted cream and bramble preserves. Tamara had not seen Kitty Roscarrock since the house party; she had heard that Lady Constance had worsened and the family was keeping to themselves. Samuel was delighted his niece had made a friend; knowing Matthew Tregarth's reputation had made him apprehensive about the daughter, but upon meeting Tamara his doubts were laid to rest. She was a dark-haired, dark-eyed beauty who seemed to have remained blessedly untouched by the harmful influences of her household. She was willful and spoke her mind, but there was nothing sly or malicious in her manner. As for Tamara, she found Samuel kind and gentle. She envied Lamorna. The Halls were poor and Rowenstow a bleak place, but in the austerely-furnished vicarage there was warmth, peace, and affection, qualities wholly lacking in the atmosphere at Tregartha. Tamara began to visit often.

One mild day in late February, Lamorna and the village girl, Maggie, were outside clearing Deborah's patch of garden and turning the earth for spring planting. The winter had been a soft one and was yielding genially to the next season.

Lamorna's skirt was drawn up to her knees and knotted, her sleeves pushed above her elbows. Both girls were bent down and pulling old roots from the dirt. At the sound of approaching horse-hooves, they looked up. Lamorna was startled to recognize Simon Pettinger in his three-cornered hat and black suit. Getting to her feet, she brushed her hands together. Maggie stared at the strange gentleman and bobbed a curtsey.

From a distance Simon had assumed they were two village girls. It was a rather unpleasant shock to realize it was Lamorna who stood before him with streaks of grime on her bare arms, her hands and nails gritty, her gown drawn up in an unseemly fashion. There were smudges on her face and neck and her brown hair was tousled, the curls rippling and gleaming in the sunlight. She was a far cry from the demure girl in lace cap and fichu he had met at Kilworthy not two months before.

Lamorna saw his confusion and was amused. She smiled, showing her teeth and a dimple in one blotted cheek. His heart turned over; her appeal could not be denied.

"You have taken us by surprise, sir," she said. "Maggie and I are readying the garden for planting."

Simon had understood the Halls were impoverished, but he had never imagined Lamorna doing the work of a servant. He remembered to take off his hat, his voice slightly uncertain. " 'Tis a fine day for it, Miss Lamorna."

"Have you come to see my uncle? He is inside, I believe. Go to the front door—Deborah will show you into the parlor."

So they did have at least one servant, he thought in relief.

Two, perhaps, if one counted the pock-marked girl. He was slightly annoyed that Lamorna be allowed to sully herself like this; never would she have to perform such tasks were he fortunate enough to marry her. Bowing, he rode round the vicarage to the front door.

Lamorna giggled. "I must look a fright. Did you notice his expression?"

"Ais, miss," said Maggie. She smiled but her eyes were wary. She had indeed noticed the young gentleman's expression, which had mirrored more than disapproval. He loves her, thought Maggie. This was no mere call upon her uncle.

"We'll finish this section now and do the rest tomorrow," said Lamorna. Maggie assented; they did not speak of Simon again.

When, later, she went into the kitchen from the scullery, Deborah was preparing a lavish tea. "Today of all days," she grumbled, eyeing Lamorna with disfavor. "Look at 'ee! A raggle-taggle gypsy! Go wash and change your gown. I brought up hot water for 'ee. No more diggin' up the garden; I'll do it myself."

"But, Deborah, I've done it every year," protested Lamorna.

"Aye, but 'ee be a young lady now and ought to act like 'un. Be quick, child! The tea'll soon be ready."

Lamorna entered the parlor a quarter of an hour later, her hair brushed smooth and threaded with a green ribbon. She wore a green bodice with matching overskirt opened down the front to show her yellow-and-white flowered petticoat. On her feet were stockings and black buckled shoes.

"My dear, there you are," said Marya. She had been flustered when she greeted Mr. Pettinger, realizing he must have seen Lamorna working in the garden. Yet it was good work and the girl enjoyed it. Even so, it was not exactly a chore for a young lady, however poor she might be or how necessary the task.

But in the last few minutes all thoughts of Lamorna's dishevelled appearance and Mr. Pettinger's reactions to it had fled her mind.

"I fear Mr. Pettinger has brought us some very sad news," she said, handing her niece a cup of tea.

" 'Twas good of you to ride up and tell us," said Samuel. "We get little news at Rowenstow. I will write to Sir John today, if you will kindly take the letter back with you."

"Of course, sir," said Simon.

Lamorna glanced at each of them. "Why, what has happened?"

" 'Tis Lady Constance Roscarrock," said Marya. "She is dead."

"Kitty's mother? Oh, no!"

"I fear so."

"Tamara said she was worse, but I did not think . . ."

"Dr. Pendarvis attended her but he could do nothing," said Simon. "She grew weaker and weaker—bleeding her helped not at all. At the last she spoke her daughter's name. Miss Roscarrock and I tried to assure her that she would be well looked after."

"Poor Kitty," said Lamorna. "I will write to her. How is she?"

Simon frowned. "In truth she seemed scarce affected. She did not shed one tear at her mother's bedside nor at the service." He did not add that he considered her detachment callous and unnatural.

"Grief takes us all differently, Mr. Pettinger," said Marya but without reproof. Could it be that I had a premonition of Lady Constance's death and that was what unsettled me at Kilworthy? she wondered silently.

" 'Tis a good thing Denzella is there," continued Marya. "And Kitty and her father can comfort one another."

Simon nodded, though he reflected that Sir John had appeared no more grief-stricken than had his daughter. Lady Constance's passing had been observed in the manner befitting her station, but there had seemed to Simon to be little actual mourning.

After a while Samuel excused himself to write the promised note, and Marya carried the tea tray to the kitchen, leaving the two young people alone.

"Perhaps you will be good enough to take my note to Kitty," said Lamorna.

"I would be pleased to do so," he replied. He longed to tell her he would do many things for her if she allowed him to, but now was not the time to speak his heart.

"The girl in the garden—is she your maid?" he asked.

"Not really," said Lamorna. "That was Maggie; she lives in Rowenstow and helps us sometimes. I've been teaching her to read."

"To read!" he repeated, astounded. "What—what on earth for?"

"Because she wishes to learn," said Lamorna simply.

He was nearly at a loss. "But—what good will it do her, a simple village girl? What books will she ever see?"

"Well, she will be able to read signs and perhaps someday get a position in a shop or as a lady's maid." Her voice had become a trifle defensive.

Simon did not ask her what lady would want a maid who could read. "I beg your pardon, Miss Lamorna, but the only result I see is that the girl will become dissatisfied with her station in life. You are to be commended for your efforts, but 'tis not perhaps . . . wise."

Lamorna's chin rose. "There is more shame in ignorance than in learning, Mr. Pettinger."

Again he was taken aback by her response; she had not been so outspoken at Kilworthy. But she was young; she could be persuaded to relinquish her extraordinary notions, those that did not fit in with his own. His conviction that she was the wife for him did not waver. When he thought about holding her in his arms he felt light-headed. Mr. Pettinger had never before been in love. He had always planned to wait until he became a vicar before he married. But he had now thrown this careful design to the winds.

"I—I hope you will permit me to call again, Miss Lamorna," he said quietly.

"Certainly, Mr. Pettinger, though 'tis a long ride, is it not? My aunt and uncle will always be happy to see you."

"And you?" he asked, holding his breath, his gray eyes shyly hopeful.

"Of course, sir, if I am here."

"Why, where would you be?"

"Soon the village women will go to work in the fields at the nearby farms. I look after the young children who are left on their own."

Again he regarded her with ill-concealed disbelief. "You tend the cottage children?"

She nodded, her gaze steady.

"But surely—the—the filth in those hovels, the vermin—I cannot believe your aunt allows—"

"—Do you not visit the cottages in Landrawna, Mr. Pettinger?"

"I? Yes, but . . ."

"Some children are left alone all day. They can, and do, come to harm."

"But 'tis always been so," he said dazedly. "Children everywhere stay home with no one to tend them."

"Yes, and many tragedies have occurred which might have been prevented. Even now I cannot be at every cottage at once, but Maggie and I try to make certain the children are fed and do not sit in sullied cloths."

The thought of her changing the babies' linens, working as a scullery maid who tossed out chamber pots, appalled him. There would be none of that when they were wed; she would change none but their own children. And the sooner that came to pass, the better. He now wanted to take her away from Rowenstow as soon as possible. The life he could give her was preferable and more suited to her station than this isolated, harsh existence in the northern wilds.

"If you will excuse me, Mr. Pettinger, I will go and compose the letter to Kitty now," she said, rising.

He got to his feet as well. "As you wish, Miss Lamorna." Simon was conscious of anticlimax. The visit had not gone the way he had envisioned it all these weeks. Yet he could not condemn Lamorna for her unorthodox behavior; her motives were of the purest. She was not impervious to the sufferings of others as Mrs. Poldew was, and, for that matter, the Reverend Poldew himself. She would quickly earn the villagers' respect and liking.

When Lamorna returned he had regained his composure, and thanked both her and Marya for the tea. "I would like to call again before long, Miss Hall," he said.

"We shall be delighted," promised Marya. She longed to ask her niece how she felt about their guest; the girl appeared unaffected by his visit and insensible to the implications. She decided to hold her tongue for the present; it would doubtless be unwise to fill Lamorna's head with mere speculations. Mr. Pettinger would have to speak for himself if he so desired. Lamorna was still young, and seemingly unconcerned about the future. Marya doubted whether she even thought about marriage and her own family yet. But it was her aunt's wish that she and the curate of Landrawna would make a match.

Mr. Pettinger rode up to Rowenstow several times that spring. On only one occasion did he miss Lamorna, who generally was back from the village by tea-time. She had casually mentioned these visits to Tamara, who smiled knowingly.

"My uncle enjoys talking with him. Mr. Pettinger has asked his advice on various matters relating to the parish."

"And naturally that is the reason he rides so many miles up the coast," laughed Tamara. "My innocent lamb, he comes here for one reason."

"What is that?"

"To see you, of course. Haven't you guessed?"

Lamorna colored. "Oh, no, Tamara, you must be mistaken."

"On my honor! It was obvious at Christmas that he was fond of you."

Lamorna regarded her in dismay; she did not want Simon to be fond of her.

The next time he appeared on the vicarage doorstep, she recalled Tamara's words and hoped she was wrong. She liked Mr. Pettinger well enough, and her aunt and uncle did as well. He was kind and thoughtful, and had ceased to censure her behavior after that first time. But she could not regard him as a husband. At night it was not his face which rose before her nor his gray eyes she beheld.

After tea Simon spoke privately to Samuel. What he said came as no surprise to the older man. He heard him out and then said gently, "If she wishes to marry you, my boy, you both have my blessing. It would make her aunt and me very happy."

"Do I have your permission to speak to her, sir?"

"By all means, Simon. I hope you will have the answer you seek, even if it does mean she will go away from us."

As though walking on air, Simon returned to the parlor and asked Lamorna to walk with him. She bit her lip and cast a fleeting look of distress at her aunt. Marya saw it and her heart sank. Watching them leave the room, Marya felt Simon's forthcoming disappointment keenly—as well as her own.

It was unfortunate that Simon suggested they go in the church. For once inside, there came to Lamorna the memory of another young man with whom she had walked across the smooth stone floor. He had said she was like the carved mermaid on the bench-end. She couldn't imagine Mr. Pettinger saying anything of that sort; he seemed too conventional and formal. Not that she desired to hear such talk from him. Tensely, she awaited his next words.

Simon cleared his throat. "Miss Lamorna, by now you must

be aware of the nature of my feelings for you. I—I would regard myself as the most fortunate man on earth were you to consent to be my wife."

He had said it; the terrible burden of the unspoken words was finally gone. Relief soared through him, swiftly followed by new anxiety. His mouth felt parched. "I . . . I love you, Lamorna," he said softly, and reached for her hand.

She did not remove it from his grasp. To his surprise and dismay he saw her eyes were full of regret. "I am fond of you, too, Simon," she said unsteadily, "but I cannot wed you."

His world plummeted. Stricken, he groped for words. "You—you say you are fond of me. Then why not . . . ?"

" 'Tis not enough to build a marriage on," she said. "Forgive me, I've no wish to hurt you. If only I could . . feel for you what you do for me, I would gladly say yes. But 'tis no use."

He clutched her hand tighter. "But we are friends, are we not? Is there not mutual respect between us? Surely these are adequate grounds for marriage. If 'tis because I was critical early in our acquaintance, I assure you that—"

She had shaken her head; she had no wish for him to continue and embarrass them both. " 'Tis not that, Simon. Pray do not press me again. We would not suit."

His grip had grown limp; she withdrew her hand. "I am sorry," she whispered.

It was a heartsick Mr. Pettinger who rode the long miles back to Landrawna.

Marya tried as best she could to conceal her disappointment when Lamorna related her conversation with Simon. "I regret I cannot make you and Uncle happy in this," she said. "I know you would gladly welcome Mr. Pettinger as my husband."

"We are not so eager to lose you, dearest," Marya assured her. "Yet I am sorry, too—for Mr. Pettinger. I believe he would make you a fine husband and I know his feelings are deeply engaged. But you are both young—there will be another someday for each of you." But whom, thought Marya unhappily. It would have been a good match; there would likely be none better. Yet she would not press her niece, having no wish to see her married to a man not of her choice.

Lamorna was in low spirits for some time afterwards. Simon's proposal had brought back all the memories of Dirk, and the same hollow yearnings. No matter that a year and a half had passed since last they met. She was haunted by the image of him and often imagined she could feel the clasp of his large brown hand on her arm. It was the only time they had touched, yet Lamorna visualized further sweet intimacies and knew the dark sailor was the only man she wanted for her husband. Telling herself over and over that she was being ridiculous did little good. Why, she had been a mere child at the time of the shipwreck—what could she possibly have known of love? And she knew just as little of him. She had created a dream for herself, that was all. And it wasn't fair to Simon Pettinger. Yet the dream persisted.

One day in the village she poured out her heart to Maggie, unable to bear her misery alone. It was a tremendous relief to tell someone who would not berate her or betray her confidence.

"I know 'tis foolish," she concluded. "I have tried to forget him. After all, 'twas long ago. But when Mr. Pettinger asked me to wed, I could not help but think of this other man."

Maggie stared at her, wide-eyed. "But miss, do 'ee truly wish to wed the sailor?"

"Oh, I don't know. I said 'twas all nonsense. I scarcely know him. So why can I not forget?"

The younger girl was dumbfounded. That the young lady from the vicarage had fallen in love with a rough sailor—it was incredible. "I knew summat were troublin' 'ee, Miss Lamorna. But even were 'ee to see that man again, 'ee couldn't wed him. 'Twouldn't be right. 'Ee must marry a gentleman."

"Oh, Maggie, I hoped you of all people would understand. That is not the reason I want to forget him. What he is—can't you see that it does not matter?"

"Mayhap not to 'ee, but would matter for sure to your aunt and uncle," said the girl frankly. "And 'twould matter to *him*. If 'ee don't know 'tis wrong, he would."

Lamorna swallowed hard, not answering nor meeting Maggie's pitying gaze. Then she said, "If only I knew how he fared, then perhaps I might stop thinking of him."

This was something Maggie understood. " 'Ee ought to ask the holy well. 'Twould be better to know, I reckon, were he alive or drowned."

Lamorna winced. "Perhaps I will, though Uncle does not approve of such things."

" 'Ee have only to say, 'in the name of God,' and no harm will come of it."

Late that very afternoon Lamorna left the straggling cottages of Rowenstow and walked to the well marked by a wheel-headed cross. There was no longer any building which encircled it, nothing but a low pile of granite to one side. Kneeling down, she bent over the stone basin filled with flowing water and recited softly:

> Water, water, tell me truly
> Is the man that I love duly
> On the earth or below the sod,
> Sick or ill, in the name of God?

For a few moments she held her breath, her belly contracting. Then there came a sudden gush of bubbles and she sighed in relief. So he was alive. He was safe and alive—the holy well had said so. Now if only she could cease to think of him, and stop wondering whether they would meet again. And whether he ever thought of her . . .

* * *

Every May a fair day was held at Grove, some miles to the east of Rowenstow. In days past, it had been a saint's day, in honor of a Celtic Christian priest who had sought to ward off the ill luck long associated with the month of May. The phrase, "a hot May, fat church hay," meaning many burials, was still chanted throughout Cornwall, and that May was ominously warm.

On the morning of the fair, a robin fell down the chimney into the hearth. Deborah fished it out with the fire tongs, her hands shaking badly. It was dead, its red waistcoat stiff. For a robin to enter a house, alive or dead, meant dire misfortune. Deborah said nothing to the Halls as she served them breakfast, but she was filled with dread. She would go to see Old Rose, who lived in a thatched cob hovel on the moor, and ask her to work a charm to "backen" the omen. Old Rose was said to be over a hundred years old and the seventh child of a seventh child. A white witch, she had worked many cures during her long lifetime. All of Rowenstow knew her powers to be indisputable.

There had been that time some years ago when a boy had sickened through no apparent cause. The mother had gone to Old Rose, who told her that he had been "ill-wished" by a neighbor. She had advised the anxious mother to scratch the woman's arm until it bled, "for 'twill cause her power to leave her." The mother had taken up a rusty nail and gone to the neighbor's cottage where she drove it into the woman's arm despite her shrieks of innocence. That evening the boy had begun to mend, and within a week he was fully recovered. As for the neighbor woman, a peculiar thing happened. Her arm, indeed all her bones, locked in place. Before long she died. People nodded wisely and declared that her own evil spell had backened into her.

Old Rose was said to hear fairy voices; she kept a basin of fresh spring water by the hearthstone so that the Small

People could wash their children. The trivet for baking was turned down at night to prevent them from sitting on it and burning themselves. In return they lent power to her charms. The Small People were believed to be the spirits of an earlier race of men who had inhabited Cornwall before the coming of Christ. They had refused to give up their idolatries and so were refused entrance into heaven. Since Christ's birth they had been getting smaller; one day, it was expected, they would dwindle away altogether. But in the meantime it was wise not to incur their wrath. They could be helpful to those humans to which they took a fancy, and were not to be feared as were the Spriggans and the Piskies. Those were also fairies but with evil intents. Fallen angels, *they* were, who had escaped to earth in ugly, tiny incarnations to torment poor Christian folk.

Old Rose had a cat—the same cat, all of Rowenstow believed, as old as she was—whose tail would cure eye ailments. Anyone with a red or swollen eye would go to Old Rose's cottage with an offering of food or fuel and request to draw the cat's tail across the offending lid. A farmer's dying cows had been cured when he had followed Old Rose's instructions to build a bonfire and push his best calf into it. She claimed it was a very ancient remedy, sacrificing the best for the good of the rest.

So the people of Rowenstow had faith in Old Rose, and Deborah was determined to visit her without delay. Naturally she would keep mum; the vicar's disapproval of Old Rose's practices was well known. After the Halls departed for the fair, she baked a special saffron cake. When it had cooled, she wrapped it up and followed the pony track round the ancient barrow and across the moor to Rose's cottage.

But as she approached the lone hovel, Deborah was surprised to see the chimney bare of smoke. Old Rose was too infirm to walk much, and kindly villagers took turns bringing her meals. Deborah knocked and called out but no answer came. Gingerly opening the door, she felt a cold draft sweep over her while the cat rushed past and outside.

Old Rose sat in her chair by the hearth, but the pipe she was fond of smoking had fallen to the dirt floor and her unkempt head hung forward. The old woman would work no more charms or cures. Trembling, Deborah stumbled out of the cottage, halting abruptly on the scraggly path. Before her was a white hare. For a few moments it watched her with unblinking red eyes. Then it ran off over the heath.

" 'Twas the old witch herself," murmured Deborah, more chills washing over her. She hurried toward the village, mumbling an old prayer in garbled English and Latin. Everyone knew that the sight of a white hare foretold disaster. That was now two—the robin and the white hare. Despite her earnest praying, she had little faith in it. Some grievous calamity was in the wind; there was no denying it.

Lamorna had always looked forward to the Grove Fair and she had resolved to enjoy herself this year as well. She couldn't continue to mope, nor was she content with her fascination for a man she had not seen in nearly two years and would likely not meet again. Confiding in Maggie had forced her to realize her languishings were senseless and her vague hopes futile. Just because she could not regard Mr. Pettinger as a possible husband she had no cause to pine for a man she could never have. He was handsome; he had nearly drowned; he had saved his friend—all these things had made him intriguing to her. But it was all in the past.

It was an enjoyable five mile walk to Grove; there were many on the track going to the fair. Maggie walked beside Lamorna in one of Lamorna's old gowns, periwinkle blue printed cotton. The girl had not ventured from Rowenstow since contracting the smallpox; she had dreaded being among strangers because of her disfigured face, but Lamorna had urged her to accompany them. Maggie had carefully washed her hair the night before; she was learning much from Lamorna and followed her example in many things.

The moor near Grove was famous for its healing stone. Mothers would bring their weak or ailing children to be passed nine times against the sun through the large round hole carved thousands of years ago from its center. There was also a hermitage chapel where, in medieval times, people had left food and drink for wandering lepers who could not enter towns or villages lest their hideous disease contaminate others. That practice had gradually died out as leprosy became rarer, and now the chapel crumbled quietly on the moor. An air of pathos still clung to it; perhaps the desolation felt by the forsaken lepers had somehow become imprinted on the atmosphere. People kept their distance. None of its granite blocks was ever chiselled off and carted away for use elsewhere.

The fair was noisy and colorful, reeking with all sorts of smells, pleasant and unpleasant. Lamorna and Maggie watched a play about mistaken identities that entailed much boxing of ears; they stood before a conjurer who made white doves appear. After that there was a marionette show about a shrewish wife and her lazy husband, and then they paid a penny to peep at the dwarfed man and woman who stood inside a wooden crate with one tiny window cut out of its side.

There were boxing and wrestling matches, and on a hill above the grounds was a bear tied to a tree for baiting. Its cries and growls could occasionally be heard above the din of the crowds. Wandering musicians played their instruments and sang sad ballads about cast-off lovers and selkies and the good King Arthur. Booths set up by tradesmen displayed their wares—boots, clothing, saddlery, pitchers, pans, knives, plates, basins, fabric, jewelry, baskets, flint-lock pistols, handkerchiefs, and various trinkets.

Marya bought a roasted goose and a loaf of bread which they shared on the heath some yards away from the bustling crowd. Maggie's family had goose only twice a year, at Michaelmas and Christmas, so she was grateful for the luxury. She watched the delicate way in which the two ladies ate and tried to do the same. At the vicarage she had learned to use a fork and now sat proudly with the gentry family who treated her nearly as one of themselves. She could scarcely believe her good fortune and had forgotten to be ashamed of her blemished face.

As the day wore on, many people became drunk on the locally brewed beer which was of very poor quality. Intoxicated men, even a few women, lay in the street. A fight broke out between two rough men and Marya swiftly ushered the girls away from the shouted oaths and crashing fists.

A boy was crying piteously, struggling in the grip of a burly tradesman with heavy black brows. The child was woefully thin, his eyes bulged with terror.

"Got 'ee, little wretch!" cried the large man. " 'Twill be seven years transportation for 'ee, and good riddance!"

"Please, sir, please, I'll never take from 'ee again! 'Tis only that I'd nothin' to eat all day." He squirmed, sobbing.

" 'Ee'll not steal again from any 'un! I'll have 'ee up before a magistrate, I tell 'ee."

"No, no," cried the lad, who was no more than seven or eight.

"What has the boy done?" asked Samuel.

The burly man glanced up and saw the vicar in his sober, dark raiment. He spoke respectfully but did not loosen his hold on the boy. " 'Tis a thief I have here, sir. Twice he took a pasty without payin' for it. He'll be sailing to the West Indies afore long."

"Pray release him. He's too young to face transportation," said Samuel.

The man scowled. "But sir—"

"I'll pay for the pasties. Only let the boy go."

"He be a little limb of Satan," said the man gruffly, but he released the trembling boy.

"You know 'tis wrong to steal, do you not?" asked Samuel. "If you are hungry, 'tis better to ask."

The boy looked at him, too young and relieved to show the

scorn an older boy might have felt, gabbled a hasty assent, and fled.

"I fear that last transaction has depleted my purse," said Samuel, smiling ruefully.

" 'Tis time we were leaving anyway," said Marya. " 'Twas enough excitement for one day, and we have the walk back." She was not feeling well; perhaps the goose had not agreed with her. She popped a peppermint into her mouth which she hoped would settle her queasy belly.

But it did not. Dragging herself home, she felt light-headed and dizzy. That night she began to vomit and purge, a high fever raging throughout her body. All Deborah's nostrums and remedies were of no avail; she suspected typhoid and knew it was hopeless. She had expected misfortune and it had come. Within a few days Marya was dead.

Just before the end she was calm and lucid and no longer in pain. Lamorna and Samuel stood at her bedside, both of them weeping as Samuel read from Psalms. Marya groped for Lamorna's hand.

"My dearest one," she whispered, "if only you had wed. Then I could rest. What will . . . happen to you . . . you must be provided for somehow."

"Oh, Aunt, don't worry about me," sobbed Lamorna. "I shall be fine."

"Look after her, Samuel. Do what is best," said Marya faintly. Then she closed her eyes.

All of Rowenstow attended the funeral service. Pieces of black crepe were draped over the beehives; the flowers blooming in the vicarage garden were covered in mourning as well, for it was believed that they, too, might wither and die. Marya was buried in the churchyard with her feet towards the east.

Simon Pettinger rode up from Landrawna; Tamara came from Tregartha. And Rowenstow was greatly honored by the presence of the great landowner, Sir John Roscarrock, and his cousin, Miss Denzella Roscarrock. Kitty did not accompany them.

The villagers left the church after the service; only the gentry, Maggie, and Deborah attended the burial. Deborah had cooked a funeral luncheon, assuaging her own grief and loss by preparing dishes far more elaborate than those ordinarily served at the vicarage. She was highly gratified by their guests' acceptance of Samuel's offer to dine.

Simon had not seen Lamorna since she had turned him down, and he felt awkward and embarrassed in her presence. Yet her dazed grieving wrenched his heart and he wished he might comfort her. She looked white and lost and barely spoke to anyone, even Tamara. Samuel tried to be a dutiful host, but he was numb with shock and misery as well. He had loved his sister very much and she had been an unfailing source of quiet strength. He did not begrudge her her place in Paradise, but he felt her loss keenly. And Lamorna was now solely his responsibility. If he were to be taken as well, she would be left with nothing and no one to look after her. The house would go to the new vicar and Deborah would remain as housekeeper. If Lamorna were not married, she would have to seek some sort of employment. But what on earth would that be? Perhaps Mr. Pettinger might again press his suit and Lamorna would reconsider. Samuel prayed fervently for guidance.

Studying Lamorna, Denzella thought that the girl was like a boat without a rudder. Her aunt had been the strong one and might have proven an obstacle, but Denzella had no doubt about the mild, forbearing uncle. Marya Hall's death might be considered a good thing, she thought. The Reverend Hall would be easily persuaded when the time came.

Denzella glanced about the simple vicarage, which seemed crowded with the few guests. She did not believe much persuasion would be necessary. The girl's uncle would be gratified to see her placed so well. As for Lamorna herself, Denzella foresaw no difficulties. She would surely be overwhelmed by her good fortune. Besides, she was dutiful; she would wish to please her uncle. And he must earnestly want to see her safely provided for. Yes, thought Denzella complacently, the death of Miss Hall had been providential. Events were moving deliberately toward one outcome. And the result would be what drove Denzella at all times—the continued good of the Roscarrocks, and of Kilworthy.

Fourteen

It was in the autumn of that year when Lamorna received her second invitation to Kilworthy. Denzella wrote that a change of scenery would doubtless be beneficial; the past few months must have been very hard on her. Kitty, too, had suffered: would Lamorna consider coming to Kilworthy? The two perhaps might find some consolation with one another.

Samuel thought it an excellent notion and most goodhearted of Miss Roscarrock. And it was a worthy reminder that he and Lamorna were not the only despondent ones. He urged her to accept; he would miss her but he would not be selfish. Denzella had known precisely how to appeal to the good vicar.

" 'Twill do you good, my dear child. And Sir John's daughter as well. Surely she could do with a friend just now, and you will be closer to Miss Tregarth staying at Kilworthy."

Lamorna was reluctant, recalling that the only other time she had been a guest at Kilworthy was in the company of her aunt. "I do not like to leave you, Uncle. Perhaps another time."

But Samuel was firm. "My dear, I want you to go. Deborah will look after me very well. And the change will do you good. It has pained me to see your misery these last few months. 'Tis not what your aunt would have wished, to be mourned in this way."

"But what of the children? 'Tis nearly Harvest-tide."

"Cannot Maggie look after them?"

Lamorna shook her head. "She will be working in the fields as well."

"Then they must get along without you—they do in all other parts of Cornwall. You must go to Kilworthy, Lamorna. You cannot refuse so kind and gracious an invitation."

Samuel was not aware of the vague misgivings Marya had felt during the Christmas festivities. She had never confided in him, deeming it both uncharitable and of little consequence once they were home at Rowenstow. Samuel knew only that Marya had hoped for their niece to be welcomed into Cornish Society, and there was no higher circumstance than to be a guest at Kilworthy

"Very well, Uncle," said Lamorna without enthusiasm. She would have preferred to remain at Rowenstow, but she had neither the heart nor the energy to protest further. Her uncle rarely asked things of her, and together he and Deborah were determined that she make the journey south.

A groom came north to escort her and, as they rode down the coast, Lamorna told herself that Marya would have been pleased.

" 'Tis the best thing," said Deborah to Samuel. "Her'll come back with roses in her cheeks and meat on her bones."

Samuel nodded, a little forlorn.

It was a beautiful September day, the sky a brilliant blue untouched with clouds, the breeze mild and sea-scented. The young groom thought Lamorna a fair young lady, despite her pallor and thinness, and did not resent his errand as had the other man. He had not yet learned to look down on those members of the gentry who were far poorer than his employer, Sir John.

When they stopped and dismounted to eat the pasties that Deborah had packed, Lamorna found she was actually hungry. She had begun to notice the changing landscape as they travelled the pony track, the bleak moors with their outcroppings of rock and scruffy gorse gradually softening to green headlands strewn with purple flowers. Rather than riding through the village of Landrawna, the groom took a different route, crossing lush meadows and penetrating a thick copse of beeches which grew on a hill above Kilworthy. When the massive house came into view, she was conscious of a surge of excitement, very different from the feeling of dread she had experienced on St. Stephen's Day. Indeed, Lamorna had forgotten her earlier inexplicable revulsion.

Denzella welcomed her warmly, bending to kiss her cheek. She and Kitty showed her her room in the guest wing, a much grander one than that which she and Marya had been allotted. The furnishings were hung in rose-colored silk embroidered with flowers, and the view looked out over the elaborate formal gardens which still bloomed with roses, hydrangea, and myrtle. Red berries glowed in hedges and on slender trees. On the hill in the distance the copper beeches were a soft, shimmering amber.

One of the maids unpacked her things while Lamorna bathed in a copper tub, easing the muscles unaccustomed to riding long distances. A tea tray came, and again she had an appetite for the gingerbread and comfits. In one corner of the room was a tall looking-glass which showed Lamorna her whole reflection for the first time. Sweet-smelling potpourri filled small silver bowls about the room.

After tea she unlaced her stays and fell asleep on the vast featherbed, waking more refreshed and content than she had in months. As Denzella had hoped, the uncommon luxury of her surroundings was working its spell. Before she dressed for dinner in her lavender silk gown, she used the rose-scented toilet water and powder set upon the silver tray.

At dinner she was placed to the right of Sir John in the smaller dining room the family used. He spoke to her considerately of her aunt while Denzella echoed his sentiments. Lamorna warmed to them, her diffidence diminishing.

"We are a quiet house just now," said Denzella, "as no doubt is your uncle's vicarage. There will be no balls or parties, naturally, as we are in mourning. But you girls will find ways to amuse yourselves. There will be the Gooldize for the harvesters in a few weeks' time."

"Doesn't Kitty have lessons?" asked Lamorna, thinking uneasily of Simon Pettinger.

"No, I have decided they are no longer necessary," said Sir John smoothly.

"Mr. Pettinger, I fear, was not the best of tutors," said Denzella. "And he is busy with parish affairs. A conscientious young man, but rather commonplace," she added dismissively, alert to Lamorna's reaction.

But Lamorna was looking at Kitty, who toyed with the pieces of roast beef on her plate. "Then Kitty and I shall entertain one another. It was most kind of you to invite me to stay, Miss Roscarrock."

"Nonsense, my dear. I can tell you've not been well and Kitty, too, has been poorly. I hope you will both benefit from your time with us."

That night when Lamorna went to bed she slept soundly, enveloped in soft, finely-woven sheets which smelt of lavender. Though she missed her uncle, she was lightened by her new circumstances and resolved to do her best to hearten Kitty as well.

At breakfast the next day Denzella announced, " 'Tis time Kitty had some new gowns made. I have sent for my dressmaker in Padstow and she will no doubt arrive shortly. Lamorna, it would give me great pleasure to order something for you also."

"Oh, no, Miss Roscarrock, I couldn't—"

Denzella held up her hand. "Just one or two things—a small gift, nothing more. Pray indulge me, my dear."

The dressmaker came and the girls were measured and wrapped in fine cottons, woolens, and silks. Wisely, Denzella stuck to her word, ordering only two gowns for Lamorna, one for day and one for evening. More would have distressed and embarrassed her. Flushing with pleasure, she thanked Denzella gratefully. Kitty, who received far more, was apathetic.

ECHOES OF THE HEART

Kitty and Lamorna rode about the countryside, climbing Rough Tor to see the Virgin Sisters, a circle of standing stones, and the holy well at St. Isaac's oratory, roofless and rippling with vines. Tamara rode over several times from Tregartha, and one afternoon Mistress Poldew, the vicar's wife, came to tea at Kilworthy. They sat at a table in the garden under an apple tree while Mistress Poldew, who was as corpulent as her husband, talked about her children, of whom she was excessively proud. Her only daughter had made an excellent match, marrying into an illustrious family with a title and an estate on the southern coast of Cornwall. Lamorna found her patronizing manner unpleasant, and was diverted when a few bees began to circle about the rotund lady.

"Shoo, shoo," cried Mistress Poldew, flapping her arms about.

"You must call, 'browney, browney,' " said Lamorna, "for 'tis said only the browneys can settle bees when they begin to swarm."

"Ridiculous!" said the vicar's wife with contempt. Her high color deepened.

"Perhaps it would be better if we went inside," said Denzella, rising. "Kitty, you and Lamorna may walk about the gardens, if you prefer."

Behind the rhododendron bushes the two girls burst into laughter they had stifled until the older ladies entered the house. Lamorna realized she had not laughed like that in ages.

"Mistress Poldew had better watch she doesn't offend the browneys," said Kitty. "When she's piskey-led someday in the darkness she won't have them to aid her. I could not believe it when she asked you if you were my new paid companion!"

"Oh, well, 'tis unimportant. And your cousin was most gracious in her reply. I confess that at first I did not want to come but now I'm glad I did. If at any time you wish to talk about your mother, Kitty, I will listen and understand."

Kitty gave her a rather curious glance before stiffly nodding and dropping her gaze. She was a moody girl, quiet and reserved. At times Lamorna found her hard to fathom; her grief for her mother was well in check. Although Lamorna began to speak often of her aunt, Kitty did not once mention her mother.

Sir John took his daughter and their guest to Padstow on Market day. They wandered among the stalls, purchasing trinkets and comfits with the coins Sir John handed them. They took luncheon at the Bull and Clover, a treat for Lamorna, who had never before dined at an inn. Sir John put himself out to be a pleasant and considerate host; he had ceased to intimidate Lamorna despite his station and years. She found Denzella, too, more agreeable than on her previous visit to Kilworthy when the older woman had seemed grandly forbidding.

For all the magnificence of Kilworthy, its atmosphere was tranquil. Lamorna felt very comfortable after awhile, which was exactly what Denzella had wished. She ate well, walked and rode often, and slept deeply at night. Gradually her spirits rose; she began to glow. Denzella observed this with increasing approval. She spoke highly of the girl to John, but never too often or with marked implications. It was not yet time for him to be made aware of her plans. When that time came, she did not believe he would refuse. He would be forced to acknowledge the merit of the undertaking, no matter what his inclinations. A naive, vicarage-bred girl, overawed by her good fortune, by the life which would be hers, knowing little of men and women, grateful, pliable . . . nothing could be better.

When Simon Pettinger learned that Lamorna had come to stay at Kilworthy, his sore heart had quickened, his hopes had revived. He had not ceased thinking of her, only the strictures of polite behavior had prevented him from riding up to Rowenstow to again further his suit. As far as he knew, she had no other serious admirers, and these last months he had consoled himself with the prospect that she might be persuaded to accept him as a husband at some future date.

He had come to admire her efforts on behalf of the Rowenstow cottagers, but he had to admit that he preferred to think of her at Kilworthy rather than in some filthy hovel. Perhaps Miss Denzella Roscarrock would prove an ally to him; were she made aware of his hopes she might induce Lamorna to reconsider his offer.

It was just as well for Simon's peace of mind that he knew nothing of Denzella's own schemes.

Simon waited for an invitation to Kilworthy. As he was no longer Kitty's tutor he could not simply come and go at will. When Sir John had relieved him of these duties, he had been grateful, but now he sorely regretted an end to the daily visits.

Every Sunday Lamorna attended church with the family, yet there were no opportunities for private conversations. On a few occasions she greeted him civilly at the end of a service, but more often than not Denzella swept her out of the box and from St. Petroc's before Simon could make his way to them. Denzella was fully aware of his interest in Lamorna—though she knew nothing of the proposal—and she was taking no chances. Simon was out of luck.

On the afternoon of the Gooldize, all the household at Kilworthy went to the shorn fields to observe the laborers Crying the Neck. It was a damp, gray day, the clouds low and swollen with moisture. Wisps of mist rose from the ground and a fog bank had begun to creep in from the sea.

Lamorna stood beside Kitty as the harvesters divided themselves into three groups for the traditional ceremony. Their voices, chanting in unison, were eerie in the coiling vapor. When the last group intoned, "A neck, a neck, a neck," there came the usual cheers for Sir John and his steward, followed by the decorating of the neck by a few of the women. Crocks of cider and beer were passed about from mouth to mouth; the celebrating had begun. Lamorna recalled Samuel telling her once that Crying the Neck was a pagan way of saying,

"Give us this day our daily bread." While she and Kitty ate a neck-cutting bun, Sir John wandered about, greeting his workers and discussing the harvest. Denzella did her part with the women of the village.

A man took up a fiddle and a few couples began to dance. Still ahead was the work of pitching the sheaves onto the ricks to dry, but the crucial corn-gathering was over. All of Landrawna, even the miners and fishermen, were in the field that day to share in the merriment and the upcoming feast.

Rosina Nance abruptly left her partner when she spied a familiar figure in the faint mist.

"Why, tes Zachy Sawyer! Us heard the *Cormorant* were back. Had a good run, did 'ee?"

"Aye, Rosina," said Zachy. "A fair 'un."

"And where be the cap'n'? Tes an age since I've seen 'un. He'll not be forgettin' his friends, I trust."

Zachy grinned. " 'Ee be a lass not easy to forget, Rosina." He noted with approval her bold green eyes, russet curls, the shapely ankles and calves revealed by her drawn-up skirt, the full, round breasts swelling above her blue bodice. Yet he knew she was not interested in him; it was Dirk she was wild about, and his indifference seemed only to intrigue her further.

"Tell that to the cap'n himself, would 'ee? Tell him Landrawna be still his home."

Zachy shrugged. "He be content to stay these days in Padstow."

"Oh, aye, he be almost a gentleman now, I do hear. Thinks he be too good for the likes of we, does he?" she asked, nettled.

"No, Rosina, tes not that at all. He don't ever forget what be past. If he wanted some learnin' 'twas not because he be proud."

The smuggling venture undertaken two years ago had proven to be highly successful. All of Landrawna had profited from the fair-trading as had the nearby village of Pendreath. The *Cormorant* brought rare luxuries to the villagers—tea and coffee, French lace for curtains, tablecloths, and gown trimmings, fine eggshell tea cups, salt for the fish cellars used in preserving the pilchards for the winter months, rum, and Cousin Jack, the cognac. The men who made up the crew received a cut of the profits, and their families prospered as never before. Zachy's sister, Bessie, had a spinning wheel and his uncle Jonah was never without tobacco from the American colonies for his pipe. Best of all, after a good run no one went hungry. There were still lean times in Landrawna, but none so severe as in memory.

Zachy himself wore a fine muslin shirt, well-cut breeches, and a coat with silver buttons. He was hailed in a friendly fashion by many of the harvesters. There was no resentment or disapproval; the moonlighters who had brought some prosperity to Landrawna were held in high esteem. It was difficult and dangerous work that many would have shunned, so the smugglers themselves were admired and appreciated. As for their trade, it was deemed a perfectly honest one, despite the laws of the Crown.

"No revenue cutters sail after 'ee?" asked Rosina.

"Not this time," Zachy replied. The risk of being spotted and fired at by the Queen's men, whether at sea or on land, was one all fair-traders undertook. But the danger, Zachy thought, was minimal. Their sloop could outrun the larger cutters, and excisemen rarely patrolled the northwestern Cornish coast. There was plenty of activity for them on the southern shore at places such as Penzance and Mullion.

Zachy took a crock of beer and lifted it to his lips. After a long swallow he turned to hand it to the man nearest him. As he did so he noticed Kitty Roscarrock standing on a slight rise near them.

"So Lady Constance be gone to her reward," he said. "Poor skinny mite, her daughter be."

"Aye," shrugged Rosina, who had no interest in Kitty. "Now, Zachy, when might Dirk—" She broke off, her brow furrowed. It was obvious Zachy was not attending. Instead he was gazing through the thickening mist.

"Zachy?" she repeated. She was not used to being ignored.

Without looking at her, he said slowly, "That maid beside her . . . who is she?"

Rosina glanced over to Lamorna. "Do 'ee mean the vicar's niece from someplace north?"

Zachy let out a long, low whistle under his breath. "Aye. I thought 'twas her, even in this mucky air."

"Do 'ee know her, Zachy?" Rosina asked, puzzled. She stared at Lamorna, who wore a straw bonnet and a coral-colored bodice and skirt. She had noticed her once or twice in the company of Sir John's daughter but had paid her no heed. How did Zachy come to know her?

He had taken a few steps forward; Rosina watched as Lamorna looked across at him and tensed. Curious, she followed behind Zachy.

Lamorna's eyes were wide with shock and recognition. She remarked his changed appearance, his good clothes and glossy boots.

"Good day to 'ee, Miss Hall," he said, taking off his hat.

She smiled uncertainly. " 'Tis you, Zachy. At first I thought my eyes were playing tricks."

"My circumstances be much improved since last we met at your good aunt's house," said Zachy without pride. "Be the lady well?"

"My aunt died in May. 'Twas typhoid."

He was dismayed and saddened; it was a terrible way to die and she had been an admirable lady. "I be sorry to hear that, miss. Your uncle . . . and Deborah?"

"They are both well, thank you." Lamorna was desperately wanting to ask about Dirk but the words would not come. She was flushed and tremulous.

Rosina touched Zachy's arm lightly; he turned to her. "Miss Hall, this be Rosina Nance."

Lamorna smiled and nodded; Rosina bobbed a curtsey. She

had been swift to perceive something between the two of them which she could not comprehend. The young lady seemed almost agitated while Zachy looked self-conscious.

"Well, miss," he began, "it were good to see 'ee." Touching his forelock, he would have turned away had not Lamorna stopped him.

"Your—your friend . . ." she said breathlessly. "How is he?"

Rosina stiffened; she glanced sharply from Lamorna to Zachy.

"Dirk?" A slight constraint came over his face. "Oh, he be well, miss."

"He is not here with you?"

"No, Miss Hall." Zachy looked at Rosina. " 'Twas Miss Hall's uncle who dragged us from the sea two years ago."

Rosina's eyes narrowed as she studied Lamorna's blushing face under her demure bonnet. After a few more words, Zachy moved away to talk to two other men, but Rosina stood her ground. Abruptly she said, "When I see Dirk Killigrew I'll tell 'un 'ee were askin' about 'un."

Lamorna was bemused. "I'm sorry, what did you say?" Her tone was vague and remote.

Rosina was only too glad to repeat her words. "I said I'll be seein' Dirk Killigrew soon. We be special friends, he and I."

Lamorna's gaze grew keener; she appeared to see Rosina for the first time. Nor were the young woman's implications lost on her. Lamorna took in the red rippling hair, provocative wide mouth, and voluptuous figure. Her eyes dropped. "Oh. I—I am relieved to learn that he is well. My uncle and I have wondered from time to time."

Rosina bobbed another curtsey, her expression hardening as Lamorna moved away. So that was the lay of the land, was it? The young lady's feelings had been easy to read. She had been besotted with the near-drowned Dirk, had she? Him a penniless sailor and her a vicar's niece. 'Twas shameful, unthinkable! Only now Dirk Killigrew was no longer poor, and he had learned to read and write and speak like the lady did herself. But he was still not of her class, no matter how he had improved himself. The girl could be no rival to her; the notion was absurd. She was out of his reach whereas Rosina herself was convinced Dirk was her property. He had only to come round.

Meanwhile Lamorna was still dazed, though her heart beat wildly in her breast. To see Zachy, to hear news of Dirk after all this time . . . What had happened in the last two years? Were Dirk's own circumstances improved as well? She recalled his angry spurning of her uncle's offer of money, his recoil from the suggestion of work at the Tregarth mine. He had evidently had something quite different in mind.

And what of the girl, Rosina? Was Dirk in love with her? Why not—she was certainly alluring. A wave of misery swept over Lamorna, her stunned confusion giving way to the despair that until recently had marked her days. Dirk would likely wed Rosina; perhaps they were already lovers. The lower classes did not always prize virginity as did the gentry. The thought filled her with pain; she shivered in the damp, chilly air.

"How do you do, Miss Lamorna?" said Simon Pettinger.

She had not noticed his approach. Startled, she began huskily, "Oh, Mr. Pettinger. I'm well, thank you."

"It pleases me to hear it," he said automatically, though he saw the unhappiness in her eyes. He frowned. "That man over there with whom you were speaking a few minutes ago. Do you know him?"

"Do you mean Zachy Sawyer? Yes, I know him."

Perplexed, he said, "I did not imagine that you had acquaintance with any of the 'gentlemen'."

"The gentlemen?" she repeated.

"Smugglers, Miss Lamorna. That fellow is known to be in the trade."

She shook her head. "I know nothing of that, sir. We were speaking of my aunt and uncle. We had occasion to meet once, at Rowenstow. I can assure you that Mr. Sawyer was not taking part in smuggling then."

Simon nodded but he was still in the dark. "Are you coming to the Gooldize?"

Lamorna was not attending. So that was the story behind Zachy's well-turned-out appearance. Did this mean that Dirk had become a smuggler as well? Not an unpaid member of a crew, but one of authority and stature?

"Lamorna?"

"I beg your pardon, Mr. Pettinger. What did you say?"

"May I sit with you at supper tonight?"

She bit her lip. "I regret that I won't be attending the Gooldize, later. I'm not feeling well—I must return to the house."

" 'Tis a long walk. Permit me to accompany you."

She shook her head. "I—I wish to be alone, sir. Tomorrow I am returning to Rowenstow. 'Tis time I went home."

To his consternation he saw her eyes had welled up with tears. Before he could respond, she was gone, hurrying across the stubby cornfield.

Samuel was overjoyed at Lamorna's sudden arrival the following afternoon. In her absence he had found the loss of Marya doubly hard to bear, yet he was sincerely pleased that his niece had been a guest at Kilworthy for several weeks. She was not nearly so thin and pale upon her return, but to his dismay he soon realized that something was troubling her. At times there was a blighted look on her face and her eyes were dark with melancholy.

Ever so gently, Samuel tried to probe. Had they been kind to her at Kilworthy? Oh, yes, very kind. Had she seen Tamara? Several times. How did Kitty Roscarrock seem these days? Quiet, often remote . . . She was no longer being tutored by Mr. Pettinger.

Ah, thought Samuel. And did you see Mr. Pettinger? In

church every Sunday, she answered. And, very tentatively, did she perhaps regret what had passed between them? Oh, no—and now if he would excuse her she must help Deborah with the wash.

Samuel remained both mystified and distressed.

Lamorna threw herself into the homely tasks at the vicarage. She took down all the curtains and washed them; she scrubbed and polished, dusted and swept.

"Well," said Deborah, hands on her hips, " 'ee didn't come home too fine to dirty your hands, I'll say that for 'ee." But she too was perplexed by the girl's flurry of activity; her constant labors were unsettling. At times Deborah would send her out to the moor to collect herbs and furze so that she might have a little peace.

Maggie came to see her to hear about the grand doings at Kilworthy, but Lamorna disappointed her by having little to say. Instead she enlisted the girl's help in scouring the scullery and sewing lavender in the corners of the freshly laundered bedlinens.

But one night as Lamorna sat with her uncle in the parlor she blurted out her secret, though he was not to realize the significance.

"Uncle?"

"Yes, my dear?"

"While I was at Kilworthy . . . I saw one of the sailors."

He looked up from the text he was reading. "Which sailors?"

"One of the two men you saved from the shipwreck two autumns ago. They had been pressed into a smuggler's employ for six years and then the ship foundered off the coast."

"Oh, yes, I recall now," said Samuel. "You say you saw one of them? How was he?"

" 'Twas Zachy Sawyer. He—he was very well. I asked after his friend, the one called Dirk."

"Miners, weren't they?" asked Samuel absentmindedly.

"Not any longer. Mr. Pettinger told me Zachy was a fair-trader as well."

Samuel raised his brows. "I would have thought that he had had enough of that life."

She was quick to defend him. "Oh, 'tis not like before when the crew were starved and beaten. Zachy has prospered."

"Which one was this Zachy? The tall, black-haired fellow?"

She flushed. "No, the other."

"And what of that one? Is he fair-trading as well?"

"I don't know."

"Well, I daresay 'tis to be expected. Fair-trading, if successful, earns men far more than tinning. 'Tis little shame in it if done justly, with taxes high as they are. Where did you meet Zachy?"

" 'Twas at Kilworthy—he'd come for the Gooldize. He spoke warmly of my aunt and asked after you and Deborah."

"What of I?" asked the plump woman entering the parlor with two candles.

"Miss Lamorna met one of our shipwrecked sailors, Deborah, during her recent stay with the Roscarrocks."

Deborah's gaze grew keener; she gazed at Lamorna, who had suddenly taken up her embroidery. "Eh? Which one?"

"Zachy Sawyer," Lamorna answered in a muffled voice.

"And the other?" she asked sharply.

"I did not see him, Deborah. It was Zachy who asked to be remembered to you and my uncle."

" 'Tis time 'ee were in bed, Miss Lamorna," said Deborah.

She raised her chin, a pucker in her brow. "I'm not a child, Deborah."

"No, my dear, but it is late," said Samuel, rising. "I confess I'm weary."

Lamorna went over and kissed his cheek. He took up the candle, wished both of them good night, and left the room. Lamorna folded her embroidery.

" 'Ee did little enough on that pillowcase," declared Deborah.

"I shall work on it all tomorrow afternoon," said Lamorna irritably.

Deborah made an impatient sound. " 'Tis that sailor again, es et? 'Ee still be thinkin' of he."

Lamorna's face flamed. " 'Twas only because I saw the other one," she said defensively.

"And that be the reason for your constant toil, to mask your broodin'. Oh, don't think us haven't noticed. The vicar be fair worried about 'ee. He sent 'ee to Kilworthy to mend and all that do happen be that 'ee exchanged one blue devil for another. 'Tis foolish of 'ee, Miss Lamorna—if your good aunt knew, her heart would break."

"Don't say that!" fired the girl. " 'Tis cruel of you to talk as though I would shame my aunt."

"Aye," nodded Deborah. "But 'tis cruel of *'ee* to make your uncle fret so. Cannot 'ee see he's not as well as he was?"

"What do you mean?"

"Open your eyes, Miss Lamorna. Your aunt's death were a severe blow. He tires easily, and sometimes 'tis hard for him to catch his breath. He were never a strong man."

Stricken, Lamorna stared at Deborah.

"Well, now 'ee do know if 'ee didn't afore. So stop worryin' 'un with your foolish pinin'."

Tears of humiliation and shame pricked Lamorna's eyes. As she took her candle to go upstairs, Deborah said, "Well, what did 'ee hear of the other 'un, that Dirk?"

"Only that he was well. And . . ." she faltered, "that he must be fond of a certain young woman. She—she spoke of him and was on friendly terms with Zachy Sawyer."

"A village lass?"

"Yes."

"Then that be that, Miss Lamorna. 'Tis as it should be. Now 'ee ought to forget all about 'un and cease your uncle from worryin'."

"I will," she answered dully. "Good night, Deborah."

"There, pet, 'ee be fair worn out. Sleep well," said the old woman mildly.

* * *

Lady Constance Roscarrock had been dead for a year when Sir John rode north to the vicarage at Rowenstow. About him the landscape grew increasingly desolate and wild, the narrow track plunging down stony valleys and up slopes topped with stunted, windswept gorse and bracken. Ahead of him rose the scarred slate cliffs cut by jagged coves and promontories. He passed long barrows which marked ancient graves, and lichened, wheel-headed crosses that long ago reassured travellers that Christian men were to be found nearby. The sun shone palely through swaths of clouds, light and shadow staining the heath.

Deborah was outside and saw the elegant Sir John approaching on his black horse. She curtseyed deeply despite the distance, and then hurried inside to the vicar's small library.

" 'Tis Sir John Roscarrock, sir. He be comin' here."

"What, now? Sir John, you say?"

Deborah nodded. "I'll fetch the madeira and glasses once I've shown him inside." Without waiting for another word she left the room. The vicar set down his book, wondering nervously what reason was behind Sir John making such a journey. Samuel adjusted his wig as he heard the rapping on the front door.

"This is an unexpected honor, sir," he said, bowing to his guest.

"Your servant, Vicar," said John, smiling. He was splendidly dressed in a blue satin coat and breeches and yellow waistcoat; his hair was unpowdered, curled into pigeon's wings on either side of his head. A large ruby glowed on his right hand.

" 'Tis a rough journey from Kilworthy, sir. Pray join me in a glass of madeira. You will dine with us, I trust?"

John acknowledged this with a word of thanks. "I have

come to see you, Mr. Hall, on a matter of great importance to me."

Samuel nodded. "Pray tell me, sir, what I may do for you."

Sir John told him.

"You—you wish to marry Lamorna?" the older man said faintly. He was astounded.

"If she will do me that honor," said John smoothly. "I had not thought to marry again, but your niece's visit last autumn gradually caused me to reconsider. Naturally I said nothing to her at the time, but these last few months I have contemplated little else, Vicar."

"You must forgive me, Sir John. This comes as a great surprise to me."

"Not an unpleasant one, I hope?"

Samuel sought to reassure him. "Not at all. You do my niece and myself a tremendous honor. I scarcely know what to say." He stared at the madeira in his glass.

"When Miss Hall, Lamorna, if you will permit me, stayed with us, we derived much pleasure from her company. Kitty and my cousin grew very fond of her, as did I. She is a lovely and charming young lady. I realize the difference in our ages is more than she might wish, but I assure you that she would have every care and luxury as Lady Roscarrock. And, were we blessed with a son, he would naturally inherit Kilworthy. As a female, my daughter is unable to do so."

Bemused, Samuel nodded. "This—this is a vast compliment you have paid my niece, Sir John. If my sister were here . . ." He faltered, overwhelmed by what he had never imagined. Lamorna, wife to Sir John Roscarrock, mistress of Kilworthy! Great landowners did not wed the daughters or nieces of impoverished vicars; they married heiresses whose blood flowed as blue as their own. The Halls had never been an important family in the scheme of things, despite their gentry status.

Sir John smiled. Denzella had been right—the Reverend Hall was overcome. John was rather enjoying himself.

"You . . . you have given me much to think on, Sir John."

"And you have no objection, I trust?"

"Indeed not, no, indeed not."

"Then will you plead my case with your niece?"

Samuel blinked. "You do not wish to speak with her yourself?"

Sir John put the tips of his fingers together. "I think not. She is, after all, very young and inexperienced. Perhaps she would prefer to hear it from you; I have no wish to disconcert her."

"Yes, most tactful, most tactful. I will, naturally, commend you to her. I am certain she will be as gratified by your offer as I."

Sir John rose. "Then I have nothing further to say; my suit lies in good hands."

"Will you not stay to dine?"

"On second thought, no. You and your niece will have much to discuss. I will bid you good day."

After Deborah had shown him out, she hastened back to the library. "Tes not bad news, sir?"

"Bad news? Oh, no, no indeed."

She stared at his flushed face, his dazed expression. "Be 'ee well, sir? Shall I go for Miss Lamorna?"

"By all means, Deborah. This cannot wait. Sir John has just asked for her hand in marriage."

Deborah's plump hand rose to her throat and fell back. "Heaven be praised! Tes a blessed miracle and no less."

Lamorna gripped the side of the table. "But Uncle, I can't believe . . . never did I imagine such a thing."

"I believe he did not know his own mind until after you had left Kilworthy, my dear. He could not woo you until his period of mourning was over, after all, and certainly not while you were a guest in his home."

She nodded mutely, a slight giddiness in her head. She took

a swallow of tea and set the cup down shakily. "Do—do you wish me to wed Sir John, Uncle Samuel?"

"That is for you to say, Lamorna. He is a fine man, and he spoke most highly of you today. He even admitted that he had not thought to wed again. Oh, my dear one, this makes me so very happy. If only your aunt were here to see this day—how she worried herself over your future. Never could she have hoped for a more ideal one."

Lamorna regarded him in confused dismay.

He went on, "I have very little to leave you when I am gone, my child. You will be homeless. Yet, if you were wed, you would be provided for. I confess I have regretted that you did not accept Simon Pettinger's offer. If you married Sir John, you would be mistress of a fine home and your son would one day inherit; he has told me this. You would want for nothing for the rest of your days."

Lamorna nodded. "I am not ungrateful for the honor done me by Sir John, Uncle. But I have never thought of him as a husband. I scarcely know him."

"I will not press you, Lamorna. But I believe you will never have a better offer than this one. Pray think on it seriously. I wish your happiness above all else, but I also desire your security. As Lady Roscarrock your future would be assured." He sighed. "I wish that your aunt was here to advise both of us."

Alone in her room, Lamorna was filled with uncertainty. Nothing her uncle had said could be refuted; she knew the perils of being penniless, homeless. Marriage was the only sanctuary. Marya had never wed, but she had had a brother to look after her as she had looked after him. Lamorna would be alone someday. She hated to think of her uncle worrying about her future welfare, and she knew it pressed on his mind. And who was she to spurn one of the greatest men in Cornwall? What did it matter whom she married, after all? She had refused Simon Pettinger—it was unlikely that she would get another offer. Yet what did she know of Sir John, other than he could be a genial host? Kilworthy was a magnificent house; she would take great pleasure in her surroundings and who could blame her? But were these things enough to base a marriage on? Many would find them so—why should she not be one of them? Deborah was wild with joy, and her uncle was just as pleased. There was no earthly reason why she should not do as they both wished.

When the news of Sir John Roscarrock's upcoming marriage to Lamorna Hall reached Tregartha, Isolde was thunderstruck. If Tamara had felt less disquiet herself, she would have been amused by her sister-in-law's violent reaction.

"The man's deranged, I cannot otherwise countenance it! That chit, scarce older than his daughter . . ."

"I seem to recall you and my brother suggesting a husband for me who was twice my age," said Tamara.

Isolde ignored her. "Her family is inconsequential, not an acre of property, no dowry, nothing! 'Tis madness. Unless he has got her in the family way and her uncle has threatened to make a scandal."

Tamara flung down her napkin. "That's ridiculous, Isolde. How dare you! Lamorna has not visited at Kilworthy in many months. And I can assure you she is definitely not expecting a child. That's a slanderous thing to say, and totally undeserved."

"That girl, mistress of Kilworthy. 'Tis unthinkable." Two spots of color stained her sallow cheeks.

"Well, you had better think of it for 'tis not long off. Denzella, I understand, is delighted with the match."

Isolde made a derisive gesture. "And who is *she,* pray, but a poor relation who owes her elevated circumstances to her cousin's benevolence?"

Tamara surveyed her outraged sister-in-law coolly. "For some reason I've never been able to understand, Isolde, you don't like Lamorna. Perhaps 'tis because she is beautiful, kind, and clever—qualities you possess in meager quantities."

Isolde struck her across the cheek. Wincing, Tamara touched her stinging face. The two young women glared at one another.

"I should not have spoken so, Isolde," said Tamara. "But Lamorna does not deserve your scorn and contempt. She will make Sir John an admirable wife. I confess I look forward to the day when you will be forced to acknowledge her as Lady Roscarrock." Turning on her heel, she swept from the room.

But privately Tamara had reservations. It was a splendid match for Lamorna, so why had she not written and told her? To have had to learn the news from Isolde was galling. She was dismayed, even a trifle hurt. They were not even invited to the wedding, which was actually being held during Lent at the Rowenstow church. She was surprised at Lamorna's uncle going along with it. "Marry in Lent you may live to repent," they said. Why, then, could the wedding not wait? Was it perhaps because either or both of them feared they might change their minds? Why the haste? It was a very brief engagement. And Lamorna's continued silence about the news was somehow significant. No happy, excited bride acted thus. Was Lamorna fond of Sir John or was this merely a marriage of convenience on her part? And Sir John . . . was he fond of her? His first marriage had been arranged by his parents; he was doubtless now choosing his second wife to please himself. Certainly he had no need of more property or fortune. So why, then, did these qualms persist? Why could she not merely rejoice for Lamorna's sake?

Denzella rode up to Rowenstow with two grooms a few days before the wedding. They were laden with gifts for Lamorna and the household at Rowenstow, including a new gown Denzella had ordered made for the ceremony.

" 'Tis lovely, Miss Roscarrock," said Lamorna. She lifted

the gown of gold brocade from its wrappings, fingering the heavy folds of lace at the elbows and the satin shirring down the front.

"You must now call me Denzella, my dear, for we are soon to be related. And that makes me very happy."

Lamorna bit her lip. "I—I hope I will not disappoint you, Denzella, or my—my husband," she said in a strained voice. None of it seemed real to her; she passed the days in a benumbed state.

"Have no fear of that, Lamorna. Your marriage to John will not only benefit him but Kitty as well. She will be glad of your friendship."

"I have a favor to ask, Denzella. You have already done so much, but I regret I must impose on your good nature again. I wish to bring a girl from Rowenstow as my personal maid. She is willing and hard-working, and I am fond of her."

Denzella was taken aback. "But Lamorna, there are already many maids at Kilworthy. Surely one of them would suffice."

"I am certain that they are well trained, but I would prefer Maggie."

"Oh, very well, child," said Denzella. She would give way in this, though she resented the girl asking favors after all she had received. In the future Lamorna would learn that her whims would not be indulged so easily. Except, of course, when she was carrying a child. When she was pregnant with an heir, Denzella would gladly fulfill her most trivial wishes, provided that they did not conflict with Denzella's own.

Fifteen

On the eve of her wedding, Lamorna was awake most of the night. Toward dawn she drifted into a fitful sleep, and dreamed. In her dream she was wandering a succession of long, dark corridors. There were others with her but their forms were shadowed and indistinct. By wavering candlelight they drifted in and out of rooms whose furnishings were filthy and rotting. She grew increasingly uneasy and longed to leave the group and the place, but she could not. The air reeked of mildew; her head ached. Moving forward, the group paused on the threshold of yet another room. Lamorna was swept along with them, gazed ahead, and froze. A nameless dread swelled in her. A woman's voice was speaking, it asked, "What is wrong with this room?" Her feeling of horror mounted. Somehow she knew what was wrong with the room, but she did not want to acknowledge it, did not want to see inside. She would not look and covered her face with her hands. It was horrible, monstrous . . . she began to scream.

With a jolt Lamorna was awake, shuddering and gasping in her bed at the vicarage. She glanced wildly about the familiar room, now lit with a dawn-pink radiance. The lace curtains Marya had made many years before blew softly at the windows; there was her china pitcher painted with violets; there was the oak wardrobe and chest. Shakily she sat up to get a better look. On the chest was draped a gown of gold brocade—her wedding gown. Today she would be wed to Sir John Roscarrock in her uncle's church. There was near-relief in that thought, anything to blot out the lingering traces of the nightmare. She was awake now, and this was real. Whatever had so terrified her, it was not real and had vanished in the pearly light of the new day. There was no longer any cause for the tremors or the panicky sensation in her belly. With the movements of the day they would fade altogether.

Lamorna stood in the Great Hall at Kilworthy beside her husband of one day and one night, receiving the guests who had come to wish the bridal couple well. Some were there for a look at Lamorna, whom they did not know, and some purely for the feasting and dancing, rare during Lent. Unlucky, too, it was said. The affair was rather odd, the bride a nobody from somewhere north. A farmer's daughter, claimed some. No, a doctor's niece, said others. Not so, her uncle was a vicar. She was very young; no, she wasn't; she was a friend of Kitty's; no, she had been her governess or companion for a short while. It was all very irksome and mystifying.

For some, a glance at the new bride told enough. She was most charming in a peacock-blue silk gown, the stiff, full skirt supported by *paniers* at her small waist. At her throat was a magnificent diamond necklace, a wedding gift from Sir John. More diamonds sparkled in her hair, which fell in long spiral curls over her shoulders. Whatever she had been—there was still some perplexity—she was gracefully suited to her new role.

Hundreds of candles glowed in the vast room. For days Denzella had supervised the preparations, the scrupulous cleaning, the roasting and baking of many delicacies including a wedding cake dotted with currants and iced in white. The Great Hall was draped in ivy and early spring blossoms. On this grand occasion the musicians were not local men but had come all the way from Launceston to play for the ball.

Lamorna nodded and smiled at countless people, forgettable faces beneath powdered wigs, their satin suits and silk gowns merging into the gaudy, glittering spectacle all about her. It was her ball and yet she felt strangely detached.

When Samuel had waved goodbye to the wedding party on their way to Kilworthy, he had been beaming with pride, his voice gone hoarse with emotion. "You've made me very happy, my child," he said, "you and Sir John. May your union prosper."

Lamorna rode to her new home on a white mare—her own horse, Sir John had assured her. She was delighted with the gift and her spirits took a surge. But it began to drizzle before they were halfway to Landrawna, and Sir John surprised her by riding away at a gallop. The drizzle became a steady downpour and all of them, including Maggie who trudged behind, were drenched and dishevelled when they finally reached Kilworthy. It was a regrettable beginning.

Kitty, shivering, was sent directly to her room with instructions to the maids about hot bricks and broth. Denzella led Lamorna to her bedchamber on the same corridor. It had been entirely redone, the walnut bed now hung in claret velvet secured with gold tassels. The same fabric blotted out the wet darkness through the windows.

Maggie helped her peel off her sodden clothes. A reassuring fire burned in the hearth; she sat down in the chair beside it, wrapped snugly in a new dressing gown. Denzella had opened wardrobes and chests to reveal an extensive array of new clothes, telling her they would dine in an hour.

Lamorna had no appetite for food and no energy for conversation. Yet she was now mistress of this great house. Uncertainty filled her, then anxiety. Had she done the right thing? Everyone seemed to think so, and she had allowed their pleasure to sweep her along. But how could Sir John have ridden off, leaving them to struggle along the soggy, rough track? Kitty and Denzella had not seemed at all surprised, but Lamorna had been severely put off by what she saw as a show of rudeness. A small thing, perhaps, but it rankled. He had left the women to fend for themselves without so much as a word. She longed to discuss her feelings with Maggie but her loyalty to her husband would not permit it. She owed him respect, and far more.

Attired hours later in a lace-trimmed chemise of softest lawn cotton, she waited for him to come to her. She waited for a long while before eventually falling into an exhausted sleep. At some point in the night she awoke to the sound of heavy breathing and her legs being drawn apart. The candles had all burned out and the room was in darkness.

She started, tensing. "John?"

"Shhh," came his voice in the blackness.

Stifling a cry, she tried to lie still and pliant while he moved above her. It was over very swiftly. She waited for him to speak. Instead, he rose from the bed. Before she realized what he was doing, he had left the room. She lay there, bewildered. Had she done something wrong? Was there something she had not done? But surely she could not know; wasn't it for him to guide her? No soft words, no kisses or caresses. Just that rapid act and then he was gone.

Mr. Pettinger did not attend the ball. He had sent his regrets, claiming a sudden indisposition. Sir John would not notice his absence any more than he would his presence, not with so many important guests filling the banqueting hall at Kilworthy, the hall where Simon himself had danced with Lamorna. The Reverend and Mrs. Poldew would attend, of course, although the vicar had resented the wedding not taking place at St. Petroc's. For his part, Simon was grateful. He might have had to assist, and that would have been even worse than attending the wedding ball.

He was not surprised that she had accepted Sir John; refusing a lord of the realm was vastly different from refusing a curate. Looking about his cottage with its mere five rooms, he thought of Kilworthy, the marble floors, the ornately-carved panelling and mouldings, the rich tapestries, the army of servants . . . The contrast was staggering. Simon was mortified when he contemplated his own proposal, his presumption that he would provide for her and ensure her happiness. How smug he had been!

He told himself he wished her well. She was now Lady Roscarrock and he had to think of her as such. It was disconcerting to realize that while he had been cherishing his fond hopes, the master of Kilworthy was forming his own resolve to marry Lamorna. Had she accepted him some months ago, she might never have known that Sir John wanted to marry her himself. Would he have spoken up had she become engaged to Simon?

Mr. Pettinger had a sudden ridiculous image of himself and Sir John fighting a duel over Lamorna. Pistols? Swords? He was not proficient in either. Sir John would have defeated him and gone home to eat his breakfast. And Simon, wounded, would have given way. They all had to, all who were under Sir John's influence. Even the gentle old vicar up at Rowenstow. Even Lamorna herself.

But it solved nothing to think that way. She had made her choice and was now ensconced in the splendor of her new home. It was absurd, and futile, to wonder whether she was feeling lost and forlorn. Sore at heart, Simon snuffed out his candle and got into bed.

"You were a success tonight, Lamorna," said her husband. "I was proud of you." The guests had all departed and she was sitting with John and Denzella in the drawing room.

"I am unused to large groups of people," said Lamorna. "I fear my tongue was tied in knots much of the time." She stifled a yawn. Tonight had been a great strain and she was longing to retire. But what of her husband? Was it for him to suggest?

"You did very well, Lamorna," said Denzella. "Go to bed now, my dear. I can see you are exhausted. Tomorrow you can be as idle as you like, and begin to get accustomed to your new home."

Rising, Lamorna looked at her husband, who was smoking a long clay pipe. "Thank you, John, for the ball. 'Twas a brilliant affair—I have never known its equal. My only sorrow is that my uncle could not come, but he is not strong these days . . ."

"You must write him all about it," said Denzella.

"I shall. Good night." Her gaze flickered uncertainly to her husband who sat indolently, one leg crossed over the other.

He glanced up. "Good night, Lamorna. Sleep well."

Nodding, she left the room. And that night her rest was undisturbed.

On the next day she and Kitty slept very late, later walking in the extensive gardens, sitting with their needlework and making a fuss over Millie, Kitty's dog, who howled in protest when Kitty played some tunes on the harpsichord. Denzella was occupied elsewhere and Sir John had gone out for the day.

"Oh, Papa is often away, playing cards or hunting," said Kitty.

Lamorna nodded as if it were perfectly comprehensible that a bridegroom should spend all day away from his bride without even leaving a message. But what had she expected? Did she truly wish him to act the ardent lover? She did not know whether to be relieved or piqued by his lack of attention. They had spoken but little since their marriage two days ago, and then only in trivialities. He was still a stranger to her. Yet perhaps this was natural; he had never mentioned love between them; she knew he wanted an heir and she had been his choice for its mother. Yet it was most disconcerting to still feel like a guest in her husband's home.

He joined them for dinner, sitting at the opposite end of the table from Lamorna, who was dressed in one of the new evening gowns and weighed down with jewels. She made an effort at conversation, trying to ignore the discomfort she felt caused by the cane hoops of the farthingale under her skirts. She had never worn one before and doubted Denzella's assurance that she would become used to it in time. The crystal sparkled, the silver gleamed, the lavish courses continued, but overall there was an illusory quality. She felt more like a spectator than an actual participant while John talked about his good luck at cards and a new foal that had been born that morning.

Lamorna had the notion that the scene would go on like it did whether she were there or not, that she had little or no impact on the other three . . .

They left John to his port and took tea in the drawing room. There was lemon to go with it, a very rare luxury at Rowenstow. Somehow its tartness seemed another indication of her separateness.

And when Sir John woke her that night, again without words or caresses, she felt more removed than ever.

On waking one morning a week or so after her marriage, she resolved to breach that distance, to plunge into her new life and new responsibilities. She was not merely a visitor at Kilworthy; it was time she undertook pursuits which would determine her effect on the household.

The kitchen was the obvious place to begin, the heart of all domestic activities engaged in by the women. She found her way there and greeted the servants cordially. Their easy chatter had ceased abruptly at her entrance and she could not help but notice their startled expressions.

She smiled at the cook. "Mrs. Quill, I should like to speak with you privately."

"Aye, my lady." The woman gestured to the maids, who filed from the room, casting curious glances at Lamorna.

"I have been giving some thought to the menus, Mrs. Quill. And I have a few small suggestions to make."

"You're not pleased with the food, my lady?"

"Oh, no, that is not it at all, Mrs. Quill. It is delicious, the best I have ever tasted. But there appears to be a great deal of waste—so much of what you work so hard to prepare is barely touched. Naturally there is the rest of the household to feed, I understand that, but perhaps we could do with fewer dishes, especially at the midday meal. Sir John is rarely here and Miss Kitty is a very light eater."

She paused, studying the woman's face for a reaction. There was none. " 'Tis the same at tea. All those cakes and tarts—they are enough to feed a small garrison of soldiers." She laughed, dismayed by the cook's blank gaze. "Do you understand what I mean, Mrs. Quill?"

"Aye, my lady," was the stolid response. "May I call the girls back in now, my lady? We have work to do."

"Of course, Mrs. Quill. A good morning to you."

Some time later Lamorna was shocked to see the large array of dishes brought to the dining table. Frowning, she looked at the three maids who carried the platters and bowls.

"Mrs. Quill instructed you to bring all of this?" she asked.

"Ais, my lady," said one of the maids, exchanging glances with the other two.

"But—"

"—That will be all," interrupted Denzella. "You may go."

Bobbing curtseys, they left the room. Lamorna turned to Denzella inquiringly. "I saw Mrs. Quill myself this morning. I explained to her that surely there was no need for so much food at one meal. I thought she understood, but I daresay I should have been more specific."

To her further surprise Denzella's face, which had never been anything but benign, hardened. "You must not trouble yourself about such matters, Lamorna. I am here to run the household, to oversee Mrs. Quill and the rest of the servants. I have been doing precisely that since coming to Kilworthy three years ago. My cousin has never found fault with my endeavors, I assure you."

Lamorna flushed, realizing she had unwittingly offended the older woman. "I'm sorry, Denzella—I did not mean to appear to be criticizing the way things are done. 'Twas only that such copious amounts of food are a waste. Mutton and chicken and ham at luncheon—surely 'tis not necessary . . ."

"You and Kitty could both do with a bit of extra weight. And one never knows when company might descend on us." Denzella's tone took on a slight edge. "Certain standards are kept at Kilworthy, Lamorna. There is no need for the penny-pinching enacted in lesser households such as your uncle's vicarage. From now on I must insist that you not go to Mrs. Quill or any of the others with orders to change the way matters are seen to here. These things do not concern you. Now, may I give you some of Mrs. Quill's special pheasant pie?"

Lamorna sat very still in her chair. As Denzella chatted idly with Kitty she could feel the hot color staining her cheeks. So she was to have no say in the managing of the household. She was not to issue orders to the servants or make any changes of any kind. She was to have no influence in the managing of Kilworthy whatsoever. Gazing about the table at the numerous dishes for three people, she felt suddenly ill. Standing up, she murmured to be excused, not waiting for a response. What response was required by someone who was a mere nonentity?

And that was exactly what she was. No longer a guest to be pampered and entertained, but not a person who belonged, no one of merit. She had no authority, no consequence, no use except to dress in finery and submit to her husband's infrequent visits to her room.

It struck her then that on those occasions she seemed to have as little importance as in all other areas. At night when John possessed her, he did so with little awareness of her as a person. She might have been anyone, or no one.

One misty evening they rode over to Tregartha for dinner. At her husband's request Lamorna wore a large emerald pendant with matching earrings; to set off the set was her pale green gown with ruffled sleeves and flounces in the skirt.

Denzella complimented her on her elegant appearance; she looked just as she ought.

Tregartha sat in a walled garden of green lawn, boxwood, and sycamores. Lamorna liked its pleasing symmetry, the shaped gables above the three projecting bays. Beyond the stone walls was the sweep of Whistmoor, its barrenness softened by the blooming yellow gorse and wild anemones.

The banqueting hall was painted a buttery white. The ceiling was beautifully coffered, and a minstrel's gallery with twelve openings was set high in one wall. An enormous bank of tiny-paned windows looked out to the front across from the two recently-executed portraits of Joshua and Isolde framed in heavy gold.

"Dreadful, aren't they?" hissed Tamara to Kitty and Lamorna. "Joshua looks positively sinister, and as for Isolde, well, one can never call her a beauty. I daresay even 'pleasant-looking' is beyond her as well. Joshua gave her the diamond and sapphire necklace she's wearing."

The rest of the party had gone to the drawing room for early refreshments while Tamara showed Kitty and Lamorna about the house and grounds.

She had studied Lamorna rather critically. "I vow, I scarce know you, Lamorna! You are quite the Lady of the Manor, is she not, Kitty? And how do you like having Lamorna for a stepmamma?" Not waiting for answers, she chattered on. "That ball Sir John gave for you—people are still talking of it."

"I hope you enjoyed yourself, Tamara," said Lamorna. She felt uncomfortable with her friend and dreaded the intimate inquiries she might make. At least she would not dare do so in front of Kitty.

"Oh, I did. Though Lord Trevanion *would* keep pestering me and he's old enough to be my father!" Instantly she realized what she had said and flushed scarlet, hastily changing the subject.

Before long they were summoned to dinner. To Lamorna's

dismay she was seated to the right of Matthew Tregarth and was forced to endure his bantering and bold leers at her throat and bosom. They sat at a long, gleaming table laden with crystal, silver, and porcelain. Coming through the openings in the minstrel gallery above their heads were the strains of violin, recorder, and clarinet. Isolde had ordered an elaborate feast—a marvelous assortment of meats, fish, fowl, side dishes, fruits imported from the tropics, and numerous wines. She had been determined to show the Roscarrocks that they were not the only ones who entertained on a grand scale.

"Will you sell your corn abroad this year?" asked Joshua of Sir John. "The profit will be far greater."

"Tinners won't like it," grunted Matthew, his lips blotted with grease. "Serve 'em right though. When I think on the times they've left the mines to clear a wreck—'tis enough to make my blood boil."

"We dock their pay, Father," said Joshua coolly. "Though I wonder what they'd say if we told them they could clear wrecks for a living."

" 'Tis only that they are in need of the goods a wreck provides," said Lamorna.

Joshua glanced at her, his narrow mouth tightening. Matthew guffawed. "You sound like the mine captain at Wheel Charity, my dear. The fellow's too soft by far; he blames their misfortune on the rain we had this winter. The men could not tin, he says, and so they were not paid. Well, what of it? I'm not such a fool to pay wages for tin not dug!"

"You must forgive my wife, Matthew," said John with a slight smile. "She does not understand these things."

She turned to her husband, a crease in her brow. "But I do, sir. At Rowenstow the coast is especially treacherous; there have been a great many wrecks over the years. And my uncle has never sought to prevent the villagers from taking what they can salvage."

"I am surprised to learn that the Reverend Hall is so lax and permissive," declared Isolde. "The lawlessness resulting from a wreck is well known. The wreckers themselves are no better than savages, scavengers picking at the bones of a ship."

"They use the wood for fires, Mistress Tregarth. What good is the ship left to the waves? And my uncle is never lax in his care to his parishioners," Lamorna said, a tremor in her voice.

Isolde raised her brows. Hastily Tamara announced, "The Reverend Hall is well-loved by his flock."

"That is because he has their interests at heart," said Lamorna.

"Your uncle's benevolence contributes to his poor judgment at times," said John dismissively.

Lamorna's face flamed; she stared at her husband, mortified. How could he speak so discourteously of her uncle before all these people? Just then his gaze met hers and she was taken aback by the sudden cold fury in his eyes.

"No, now, my dear, don't sulk," said Matthew, patting her hand. "These matters are better left to gentlemen, I'm certain you'll agree. You mustn't worry your pretty head about the miners; they're all tarred with the same brush and mustn't be allowed to get above themselves." Barely suppressing a belch, he loosened his waistcoat and took another helping of lamb.

Isolde regarded Lamorna's downcast face with scorn. Lady Roscarrock, wife to Sir John, mistress of Kilworthy—and she was championing the wreckers! She might be all done up like a peacock, but her foolish remarks had betrayed her common origins. She looked forward to passing the story on to others of her acquaintance.

" 'Tis no wonder the rest of England considers us wild barbarians," said Joshua as he cut his roast beef in precise cubes. "The lower classes simply cannot be restrained except by bringing them before the bench. As a magistrate I show no leniency. Just this week a boy was hauled up for stealing a gold watch. His father claimed he was a half-wit and hadn't meant to steal, that he just liked the shiny gold color. As though that should excuse him. If I had let him go, we'd have every thief pretending to be dim-witted! He'll hang tomorrow."

Lamorna winced; she laid down her fork. She glanced down the table at Tamara, who directed a swift sympathetic look at her.

"The soldiers are a useless lot," Matthew was saying, "especially when up against the moonlighters."

"They're well paid, Father, to look the other way," said Joshua. "They make a show of searching but come up with nothing."

Sir John smiled. "I've no doubt the excisemen would prefer to be anywhere but on those cliffs at night when the smugglers make their landings. They want to save their skins, after all, and they are always far outnumbered."

"In my opinion the laws have been flagrantly defied for too long. The moonlighters believe themselves to be above the law simply because the revenuers rarely patrol these shores. I have resolved to do everything in my power to see that smuggling is stamped out in my jurisdiction."

Lamorna's head shot up. *Stamped out,* she thought. That means arrests, jail sentences, perhaps even transportation. That is, if he could get a jury to convict them. The Cornish were notoriously protective of the "gentlemen." Even so, Lamorna did not underestimate Joshua Tregarth's resolve. Zachy was a fair-trader—Dirk might be as well. If they ever fell into the magistrate's hands, he would show no mercy. Lamorna deeply pitied those unfortunate souls who stood in the dock before him.

Tamara was feeling very sorry for her friend, who had merely been defending her uncle. But the Reverend Hall's views were not those commonly held by the gentry. There was no changing the rigid, uncompromising attitudes of those in positions of wealth and authority. Tamara considered her family callous and arrogant, but so were most others of her acquaintance. Joshua believed it his solemn duty to punish every transgressor to the fullest extent of the law. Otherwise, he was convinced, the lower classes would become even more unruly than they already were. They must be kept in their place, cowed and tractable. They must never presume that Jack was as good as his master. Her friendship with Lamorna had exposed her to ideas similar to those held by her former governess, ideas of kindness and charity as opposed to condemnation. Lamorna had been reared with vastly different notions from those of her husband, and that had been one reason for Tamara's misgivings about her marriage.

"Well," said Isolde to her husband after their guests had departed, "Sir John will regret this ill-advised marriage before long if he does not already."

Joshua shrugged. "She's young. He'll take her to task a few more times and she'll leave off her odd notions. Her uncle's parish is isolated; they mixed little with Cornish Society when her aunt was alive."

Isolde set down her silver-backed hairbrush with a snap. "And 'tis she who becomes Lady Roscarrock. What was Sir John thinking of? If he desired a young wife, why not Tamara? She is far more suited to it."

"Tamara is flighty. Whatever you may think about the new bride, she is not."

"You had better be careful, Joshua, or you will never marry off that girl."

On the ride home, John rode ahead. Denzella leaned across and said, "When you are alone with John, ask his pardon. He did right to admonish you, Lamorna. You shouldn't have contradicted our hostess."

"Not even when she spoke so disparagingly of my uncle?" Lamorna cried.

"You were at fault by talking about the wreckers the way you did, justifying their violence. We will speak no more on the subject. Mind you ask John's forgiveness."

Lamorna said nothing else. John had not looked at or spoken to her since dinner. She dreaded what the night might bring. While she got ready for bed, she composed an apology that did not compromise her defense of her uncle. But she could have saved herself the strain and energy; Sir John did not come.

As the days passed, his neglect grew more pronounced. When they were together in the same room, he had always been polite, asking how she had spent her day and sharing news he had heard. But now he seemed not to notice her. He was away from home frequently and sometimes at night he entertained a party of gentlemen long after she had retired.

Denzella grew impatient; she considered that the girl had seen the error of her ways and that this deliberate avoidance was pointless. This was no way to father an heir. Lamorna had been shown what was not to be condoned and that ought to be the end of it.

One night about a week after the dinner party at Tregartha, Lamorna was awakened by her husband crawling into bed beside her. Again the room was in total darkness; she felt his smooth hands pushing aside her nightgown. Lying still, she was silent, relieved that there was no roughness in his gestures. Perhaps she was back in his good graces.

But this time there was no swift satiation on his part. His efforts continued until she began to chafe. Yet she was not hindering him. Suddenly he moved away and got up.

Bewildered, Lamorna asked, "John? Is there anything wrong?"

"Damn you," came his icy voice in the darkness. "Damn you."

Kilworthy was to host a Beltane festival on the eve of May first. The people from the nearby villages were invited to the old celebration which Denzella declared was for them and not the local gentry. The men built an enormous pile of wood and furze for the bonfire. In the vast Kilworthy kitchen the women baked and roasted for days. There would be music and dancing and feasting and blowing of the shrill "May" whistles made from narrow sycamore branches. On May Day sycamore branches would be cut to adorn the cottage doors and windows to herald the start of summer.

The morning of April 30 dawned clear and cool; the air was freshly scented with dew-drenched wildflowers. Huge, wispy cobwebs draped the hedges and the spiders scurried over them, foretelling fine weather to come.

Lamorna rose early and dressed in a blue laced bodice and skirt printed with tiny yellow flowers. She had sent Maggie ahead to the fields to join the other women of the household and the nearby villages; she was concerned that Maggie was not happy at Kilworthy though the girl had said nothing. But Lamorna feared the female servants had not been welcoming. Going down the hall and around the corner, Lamorna went up the three steps to Kitty's bedchamber.

She knocked several times but received no answer. "Kitty?" she called, and opened the door.

The girl was still sound asleep. She wore a thin cotton nightdress; her hair was plaited. She looked no more than a child.

"Kitty, wake up!" Moving across to the three banks of windows of the six-sided room, she drew aside the curtains.

Kitty frowned, opened her eyes, stared uncomprehendingly at Lamorna, and shut them again.

"Kitty, 'tis time to get up. Beltane has begun—we're to go to the meadow."

The younger girl whined, struggling to keep her eyes open.

Grinning, Lamorna said, "You're a slugabed today! Come, 'tis time to be up and dressed. We don't want to miss it."

"Miss what?" asked Kitty irritably.

"Why, making the Green Lady, of course. Don't you remember?"

"Oh, that," murmured Kitty.

"Yes, and I've never seen such a thing. Come along, get up, I'll help you dress." She poured some water into a basin for Kitty to wash her face, and then took a gown from her wardrobe.

Kitty's movements were slow and clumsy. Lamorna fastened her gown and brushed out her hair, tying a ribbon in it. The girl seemed still half-asleep.

Outside, the breeze was delightful. They strolled through the gardens to the fields beyond. Bluebells bloomed in the tall grass. A large crowd of women had already gathered and were working busily. They wore brightly colored skirts and scarves on their heads. Denzella was in their midst, a tall, imposing figure with an eye to the proceedings.

Out of a rough framework of sycamore boughs, the buxom shape of a female had been fashioned and was now being densely padded with greenery. The women chatted and laughed as they worked, armed with ropes of vines and boughs thick with leaves. Lamorna and Kitty sat on a rise nearby and watched.

Getting up from her place on the grass, Rosina Nance moved toward Denzella, her heart beating rapidly. "Might I have a word with 'ee, miss? A private word?" she asked.

Denzella turned to the young woman, whose hair glowed bright copper in the sun. "What is it, Rosina?" She prided herself on knowing all the villagers by name.

"I've heard tell, miss, that 'ee sometimes makes up mixshers, potions for—for makin' things happen. Tes known 'ee gave summat to Emma Lister and she were wed not a month after."

Denzella noted the young woman's voluptuous figure beneath her brown skirt and green bodice. "I cannot imagine why you would require such a thing, Rosina. Are the men of Landrawna blind? Surely you have scant need of a love potion."

Rosina flushed. "The man I want—he . . ."

"Is taking his time declaring himself? But there must be others who would gladly take his place."

There was sudden fire in the girl's eyes. "I want no other,

miss. I want only him." Her full lower lip pouted. "Will 'ee help me, miss? I've money."

"Keep your money, my dear. I'll make up a powder for you. Then when next you are with this man, slip it into his wine or ale. The ingredients have been known to make men amorous. But the most potent charm is your affection for him. If you truly want him more than anything—"

"—Oh, I do, miss!" said Rosina passionately.

"Well, then, you must do all in your power to win him. If you desire something bad enough, Rosina, it may indeed come to pass. Come to the kitchen this afternoon; I will have the powder ready. Just ask Mrs. Quill."

"Thank 'ee, miss," said Rosina, curtseying. "Thank 'ee truly."

Lamorna had observed the two women conversing. She had recognized Rosina at once and could not help thinking of Dirk. Perhaps they were already wed. Quickly and impatiently she dropped a curtain down on these stray thoughts and turned her attention to the making of the Green Lady once again.

By noon it was finished. It had a round face, an impressive bosom, graceful arms of boughs, and a bell-like skirt. A sash of red anemones was wound around its small waist. On its head sat a wreath of white flowers; several flower chains of various lengths hung from its neck. The Green Lady stood on a slight platform and was surrounded by the women, who were admiring their handiwork.

Denzella praised them, saying, "I'm certain she will bring us all good luck. May the summer be a fertile one to ensure a fine harvest."

Lamorna glanced at Kitty, wondering at her listlessness. "You ought to take a nap this afternoon," she suggested. They would all be up late to welcome in the May.

She was startled to see a look of sullen resentment come over Kitty's pale face. "You are not my mother, Lamorna. I do not have to do what you tell me."

Lamorna was stunned; she had never heard Kitty speak so

to anyone. Nor had she heretofore beheld that hostile expression in her eyes. Before she could speak, Kitty had risen and begun to walk away. Lamorna followed her.

"I'm sorry, Kitty, 'twas only that you seemed so weary—"

She broke off as Kitty whirled round. Contempt flared in her eyes. "Leave me alone, Lamorna. Just leave me be."

Sixteen

At midafternoon, Dirk, Zachy, and the rest of the crew strode into Landrawna, weary, hungry, but in good spirits. Those who had families and sweethearts living in the village were eager to be reunited with them and bestow the articles they had brought from France—fine calfskin gloves, necklaces of coral from the West Indies, silver shoebuckles and buttons, trifles for the children.

One lad, the youngest of the crew, kept reaching into his coat pocket to make certain a ring was there, a ring which he fervently hoped would adorn a certain girl's finger that evening. He took the broad waggery of his friends good-naturedly; their banter in no way discouraged him or shook his resolve. Were he not one of them and earning a share of the profits, he would not now be rehearsing his speech to the girl's father.

Upon entering the village, the men went their separate ways, but not before calling last jests to the young man as he stopped before one of the cottages. Red-faced, he took off his hat but did not knock.

Dirk gripped his shoulder for a moment. "Good luck, Ralph." And, when the lad did not move or speak, added, "Well, go on then—and be glad she's waiting for you."

Ralph nodded somewhat bemusedly and raised his fist to the wooden door. Dirk and Zachy continued up the steep street to the cottage where Zachy's sister Bessie lived with her husband Paul and their children.

"I hope ol' Elizir lets Ralph have his Pearl," said Zachy, "else there'll be a heartbroken lad on our next run."

"I'll speak to Elizir myself if he scorns the boy," said Dirk. "Ralph will make Pearl a good husband, none better."

Zachy made a sound of agreement. He's thinking of *her* again, he thought, the vicar's niece. When he had casually mentioned to Dirk last autumn that he had seen her at Kilworthy, his friend's feelings had been revealed to him in one sudden, naked look. A look of starved, eager ardor, swiftly hardened by a studied indifference. Yet Zachy was not fooled. Now he thought he understood Dirk's moodiness, his reluctance to discuss the past, specifically the shipwreck which had freed them from Captain Trey's bondage, his disinterest in women such as Rosina Nance, even his determined attempts to better himself. But to what purpose? He could never marry the young lady; none of his recent accomplishments could alter the facts of his birth. Surely Dirk realized his yearnings would never be fulfilled. Zachy felt very sorry for his friend, but he was loath to understand his obsession as well. He hoped that with time Dirk would accept the futility of it and Miss Hall would fade from his mind.

Rosina was elated; the *Cormorant* was back from Brittany, just in time for the Beltane festival. They had been away for several months, holed up in Roscoff while the ship was repaired and various orders filled. And before that he remained in Padstow, only coming infrequently to Landrawna. To her frustration he did not seek her out on those occasions but she made it her business to learn his whereabouts and turn up there. Rosina had received several offers of marriage already; Dirk Killigrew's indifference galled her and fueled her determination to have him. The more he kept her at arm's length, the more she wanted him. In the past two years they had exchanged one or two kisses, at her instigation rather than his, and Rosina was wise enough to recognize that his heart wasn't in them. He was altogether too casual, too remote, for her liking.

So she had resolved to ask Denzella Roscarrock for a love potion, and even now it was burning a hole in her apron pocket. Surely Dirk would be at the Beltane celebration that night—it was one of the great events of the year. Somehow she would slip the powder in his drink and then he would be hers.

Dirk had intrigued Rosina on the first day after their six-year absence from the village when he and Zachy had trudged into Landrawna. Despite his grim demeanor and tattered, ill-fitting clothing, she had found him very attractive. As his fortunes gradually improved and he became the successful captain of his own smuggling vessel, someone who could read and write and talk like a gentleman, she became obsessed with winning him. His cool aloofness only served to inflame her further. The fierce grace with which he moved, the proud carriage of his head and shoulders, the chiselled features of his face enthralled her.

And, if she were to wed him, she would never have to work another day at the mine nor cook and clean her own house. It was known that Dirk employed two servants, a husband and wife, to see to his house and his needs. Once they were married, Rosina could be as idle as she chose, besides having fine things to wear, plenty to eat, and handsome furnishings. She had been inside his house once when he was away, stealing a glance into the beamed parlor with his banister-back chairs, tapestry curtains, and porcelain tiles below the carved mantel. The woman who kept house for him had made short shrift of Rosina's flimsy excuse to enter, and had swiftly bustled her out of the house. She longed to put the old cow in her place, which she would certainly do were she to become Dirk's wife. She would also drink chocolate in bed in the mornings before going out to buy anything she desired from the shops.

He'll come tonight, she thought desperately. He must. Rosina vigorously pumped water from the well into a tin basin and carried it into the kitchen. She scrubbed her face, neck, and hands. Then she began to prepare supper for her father and brothers. Rolling out dough for several large pasties, she filled them with spinach, parsley, pepper-grass, and mustard before setting them in the oven to bake. Then she climbed up the crooked narrow stairway to her room under the eaves. Midnight tonight would mark the beginning of summer, a time of warmth and plenty and long, light nights. And surely of love. It will happen this summer, thought Rosina.

Unlacing her bodice and untying the drawstring of her skirt, she slipped out of them. Across her rope bed lay her best gown, newly washed and pressed. It was moss green with a plunging neckline and full skirt. Tonight she would be at her most alluring. Brushing out her red hair, she took the irons and wound the lengths into curls. With her little finger she patted a mixture of tallow and berry juice onto her lips. Then she dabbed some carnation scent on her throat and the bare round tops of her breasts. Taking the packet of Denzella's powder, she slipped it into her chemise.

Bessie handed round the filled plates to the men sitting around her table. "Tonight be the Beltane festival up Kilworthy," she said. " 'Ee came back just in time. 'Twill be a merry night—we spent all morn makin' the Green Lady."

"Aye," nodded Paul. "I mind the one last year, 'twere a good time. Like Beltane when I were a lad, before Lady Roscarrock took to her bed."

"Tes a new Lady Roscarrock now," said Bessie. "Sir John wed again not many weeks ago. She be young and comely, not much older than Miss Kitty."

"Speakin' of comely maids, Rosina Nance be askin' after 'ee, Dirk," said Paul, grinning. " 'Ee's made a conquest there and no mistake."

Dirk shrugged.

"What be the matter with 'ee? She be the best-looking girl for miles around."

Bessie frowned. "Give over, Paul. Rosina be too brazen to my way o' thinkin'. *And* gives herself airs. She never had a mind to speak to me 'til Dirk began comin' here."

Paul winked at Zachy and Dirk behind Bessie's back. "Well, there be more'n one lad who'd like to make her his own."

"More fool they," said Bessie scornfully. "She'll bring 'un nothin' but grief."

"There were searchers about last week, I heard," said Paul. "Up and down the cliff, two nights runnin'."

Dirk's black brows drew together. "Excisemen in Landrawna?"

"Aye," said Bessie. "They got wind somehow."

" 'Tis one way I know of to deal with them," said Dirk.

Zachy cocked a knowing glance at him. "The Gauger's Pocket?"

"Aye. We fill it."

Some time later, dressed in their best, Zachy's family joined a large procession making their way up the hill and across the fields to Kilworthy. Dirk had agreed to stay the night and walked with them. A few villagers sang the May song as they went.

> Unite and unite, and let us all unite
> For summer is a-cuman today;
> And whither we are going we all will unite
> In the merry morning of May.

> With the merry ring, adieu the merry spring,
> For summer is a-cuman in today;
> How happy is the little bird that merrily doth sing,
> In the merry morning of May.

Rosina was one of those who sang. She had caught sight of Dirk and tossed him a provocative smile even as she held on to the arm of the man walking beside her. She wanted to remind him how sought-after she was. Perhaps she had been too bold in the past; most men liked to do their own pursuing, her mother had told her years before, seeking to curb her wayward daughter. But jealousy might kindle his amorous feelings were he to see her dancing with others. She would be high-spirited and carefree and encourage all her admirers tonight. Then Dirk would realize that she was not to be lightly regarded. If he still proved elusive, there was always the powder, secure in her bosom.

It was nearly dark. The bonfire was not lit but rose like a mountain of brush in the meadow. The music and dancing had already begun amidst the throngs of people from the nearby villages who milled about, shouting and laughing and greeting one another. Above the din could be heard the sounds of fiddles and drums and recorders. Several groups were dancing six- and eight-handed reels. Children chased their cronies, squealing cheerfully. No food had yet been served, but there was plenty to drink: the traditional May junket made with cream, metheglin, elderberry wine, beer, and brandy.

Soon the bonfire went up with a tremendous roar. The crowd cheered as the flames spat and crackled, consuming the hill of wood, bracken, and furze. The deepening purple sky took on a tawny glow.

Dirk wandered about with a tankard of beer, nodding at those who hailed him. Zachy had urged him to find a partner and join in the reel, but he had no interest in dancing just then. Rosina was creating a stir with her various partners but Dirk was not tempted to become one of them. In Roscoff there were women who could have been his for the asking, but he was not interested in them nor in the respectable daughters of merchants and shopkeepers. The troublesome needs that arose in his body from time to time he restrained. He would think of Lamorna and grow furious with himself for so doing.

Dirk set down his tankard on one of the long tables, suddenly weary of the noise and confusion around him. Threading his way through the crowds, he saw Ralph with a blond maid of sixteen or seventeen. Beaming from ear to ear, Ralph cried out, "Cap'n Dirk, I be the luckiest man! Pearl's father agreed to our weddin'."

Dirk smiled and said, "As if I couldn't hazard a guess! He's a good lad, Pearl. Not that I have to tell you that."

"No, sir," said the girl shyly, flushing with happiness.

"My best to you both," said Dirk.

"Be 'ee leavin' then?" asked Ralph in surprise. "But there'll be supper, and the Green Lady to follow."

Dirk shook his head, moving away. Ralph and Pearl watched him go.

"Your Captain Dirk be a sad man," she said.

"Sad?" chuckled Ralph. "What do he have to be sad about? Why, he be captain of the best sloop out o' Cornwall."

"Mayhap he be, but b'ain't enough to make him happy," replied his sweetheart. "The look in his eyes be forlorn."

Ralph was not convinced, but he shook his head and said, "If what 'ee do say be true, then I hope tes soon remedied. Now dance with I." They soon forgot about Dirk, immersed in their own gaiety.

Dirk had decided to get his horse from the blacksmith's stable and ride to Padstow. He longed for the peace and solitude of his home. And, in the morning, he would call on Elias Pollard. A little boy stumbled and fell across his path. Setting the child on his feet, he brushed off his leg, saw that there was no cut or scrape, and sent him off to find his mother.

As he moved further away from the bonfire, the light grew dim. There was a young woman standing quite alone, away from the groups of revelers. His glance steadied, then deepened. Stopping in his tracks, he stood still as his heart lurched. It could not be; the fatigue and depression were in league together, mocking him. It could not be she. Yet he knew that profile; hadn't he carried it with him everywhere for the past two and a half years, forcibly pushing it from his mind only for it to intrude again and again?

He could scarcely breathe; he felt a thudding in his chest, and a constriction. With unsteady movements he drew closer to her. It was she, he was certain now. The bonfire's faint glow revealed her delicate features, her dark curls. His hungry gaze took in the changes that nearly three years had wrought. A wistful, vernal loveliness had characterized her then; the wistfulness was still there but her face and form were more defined, the promise of beauty fulfilled.

Something very like pain shot through him. "Lamorna."

He was not aware that he had spoken, but she turned and their eyes met in the flickering gloom. A slight sound escaped her parted lips. In the glint of the bonfire she whitened and swayed. He closed the distance between them in three long strides and took her arm. She was trembling. In her shadowed face her eyes were large, dark pools; in the dusky hollow of her throat a pulse beat violently.

With a dazed fascination she noted his chocolate coat and tan breeches, the brass buttons, the starched white neckcloth and ruffled cuffs at his wrists. For reassurance her eyes again flew to his face which she remembered as well as her own. The deep-set dark eyes, hawk-like nose, high cheekbones with their slanted grooves framing his square jaw.

Reaching for his hand with both of hers, she whispered, "It . . . it is you, is it not? Dirk?"

As she spoke his name his grip tightened about her arm, his other hand clasping hers.

"Aye," he answered hoarsely, and then, "My love."

"I—" She broke off, swallowing. "I thought for a moment I was dreaming. I did not think to see you again."

"Nor I you," he said, "Though not one day has passed when I haven't longed to." He did not stop to question why he was speaking so openly; he had no control over his words.

The shock of seeing her again had left him exposed, without defenses. Then, gradually, reason reasserted itself. "What are you doing here? Are you a guest at Kilworthy?"

In bewildered dismay he witnessed a change come over her. She seemed to shrink; she dropped his hand. The radiance left her face as she took a shaky step backwards into the shadows. Dread clutched at him; he released her arm but again narrowed the gap between them. Her eyes were wide with panic and what he identified as shame or guilt. This last baffled and alarmed him most of all. He could sense her withdrawal from him after the initial joy she had displayed. His eyes did not leave her face. He said nothing, waiting, terrified she would leave him as swiftly as she had appeared.

And then the fearful moment passed. "Let's—let's dance," she said, again taking his hand.

His apprehension dwindled before her sweet smile. Lamorna was thinking wildly, desperately, he mustn't find out, he mustn't, but I can't let him go, not yet, just a dance or two and then I'll slip away to the house . . . But they continued to dance, hands clasped, apart from the crowd. Lamorna, dressed in a simple gown, wearing no jewels, had been recognizable to few as Lady Roscarrock; she was thankful the dimness obscured her face. She knew she ought to tell him; it was wicked not to, but still she put it off.

The music finally ceased and Dirk said, "May I get something for you? Some food or drink? 'Tis thirsty work, dancing." He grinned. He had nearly forgotten her earlier behavior; she had been flushed and happy while dancing.

She should tell him *now*. She opened her mouth but said only, "Some metheglin, perhaps. I—I'm not hungry."

He looked intently into her face. "You won't disappear, will you?"

Coloring, she shook her head. That would be too cruel, and too easy for her. She did not deserve such easiness as he did not deserve to be further deceived as to the true state of things. She was married to another, despite the fact that Dirk was her own true love as she was his. There was no longer any denying it; their eyes had revealed all to one another in the first few moments of their unexpected encounter. Unexpected, but inevitable. She had barely noticed the difference in his speech and manner; that had not heightened her rapturous feelings in the slightest. Her speculations that he had prospered along with Zachy Sawyer were now realized, but the change in him was greatly overshadowed by her own cowardice and recoil from confessing the truth.

Her eyes stung. What was he doing here tonight? Why had he come, when all those other times she had looked for him in Landrawna, still free, unmarried . . .

Dirk had reached the table and taken up two tumblers of metheglin. Some called it lovers' mead because its heady potency was said to produce those blissful feelings in the imbiber. Yet he and Lamorna needed none of its intoxicating qualities. His head was already pleasantly light; he barely noticed anyone or anything around him. He had found her again. And, to his amazement, she seemed to return the feelings he had long considered hopeless. It was a night wrought by magic; he could barely take it all in.

"Why, tes the famous Captain Dirk Killigrew," said a voice at his side. "I were hopin' 'ee'd join me for a drink."

Dirk looked over at the young woman beside him. For an instant or two he could not think who she was. His head was consumed by thoughts of Lamorna.

Rosina cocked her head, smiled, and reached for one of the tumblers he held. "Have 'ee been dancin'? I've scarce stopped all evenin'. Not one minute I be havin' to myself with they lads." That was said in case he had not noticed her popularity; she had looked in vain a number of times for his face in the crowd.

Dirk nodded impatiently. He felt no inclination to talk with her; he only wanted to return to Lamorna. Taking another tumbler of metheglin, he would have walked away had she not taken his elbow.

"Shall we go somewhere quiet and drink together? Mead be just the thing on a night such as this." Her voice had softened, grown husky.

He shook his head. "Good night, Rosina."

Her jaw dropped. "Good night? Be 'ee leavin' then? Tes early yet. First have a drink with I."

He pulled out of her clutch, some of the mead spilling on his hand and ruffled cuff. Without another word he was striding away while she gazed after him in rising indignation. It was only after he had been swallowed up by the crowd that she was struck by the significance of the two tumblers.

Recklessly she pushed through the horde of revelers, searching for a sight of Dirk's tall figure. He wouldn't be among the dancers, not with two drinks in his hands. Nor was he with those gathered about the bonfire. Where was he? More importantly, who was he with? She had to know . . .

A short while later she spied him away from the mob, on the edge of the night shadows. He was sitting cross-legged on the ground beside a young woman. They were drinking together. Rosina could not see the girl's face, only her dark hair and slender waist. As she drew closer, she looked at Dirk and observed the adoration and longing she had desperately wanted for herself. The two were not touching, but the intimacy between them was unmistakable. Rosina seethed. Who was this wench who had taken her man?

Her cheeks hot, her heart hammering, she circled the two beneath the tree, careful to keep her distance. She did not wish to be seen, but she was determined to find out her rival's identity.

The young woman lifted her face, and Rosina watched as Dirk brushed her cheek with his fingers. She did not look happy—that was obvious. Rosina saw her shake her head slightly and drop her gaze. There was something familiar about her, Rosina thought, though her face was in semi-darkness. She crept a little closer. Who on earth was she? Not a lass from Landrawna. Pendreath then? No, most of the young women there worked at the mine and she knew them all. Was she someone Dirk had brought from Padstow, or perhaps someone employed up at Kilworthy?

Rosina drew in her breath sharply, her eyes nearly starting out of her head. A villager, a servant—why, the girl was none of these! She was none other than Lady Roscarrock, Sir John's new bride! The same maid that Rosina herself had spoken to last Harvest-tide, the one who had asked Zachy Sawyer about Dirk. Rosina glanced about her. No one else was paying the couple any mind; they had attracted no attention. Miss Denzella and Sir John were not in sight. And the two seated together were oblivious to their surroundings.

Dirk in love with Sir John's wife! A hot spurt of anger rose to blot out Rosina's shock. When she had heard that the landlord had married the vicar's niece she had been pleased, confident that the girl's interest in Dirk was over. But no, she was Lady Roscarrock—and that was not enough for her! She had to have Dirk as well! And he—did he know? He'd been in France at the time of their marriage and he had only returned today. Their reunion could not have been foreseen, and must have stunned them both. Had she confessed to him?

Rosina did not wait a moment longer; she moved toward the couple, her eyes glinting with scorn. The frustration threatened to choke her; she had to confront them. When she had reached their side, they looked up at her, puzzled. Then the girl's look turned to fear and Dirk's to anger. Her own fury mounted. So he could not bear to be interrupted, she thought. Mooning over that girl who could never be his. She'd bring them back to reality.

Mockingly Rosina made a low curtsey. "Pardon me, my lady. Tes a grand night and we be grateful to 'ee."

All the color drained from Lamorna's face. She stared at Rosina in horror and dread. Dirk scowled. "Leave us be, Rosina."

"Leave the two of 'ee alone, do 'ee mean? Sir John wouldn't be too happy about that, I reckon." She smiled broadly.

Lamorna made a moan of protest; she twisted a fold of her gown around one finger.

"Why should Sir John care who Miss Hall is with?" asked Dirk irritably.

"Miss Hall, es et?" She went off in a peal of laughter. "I never figured 'ee for a fool, Dirk Killigrew, but 'ee be mazed as a curlew."

Lamorna stiffened. This girl would not have the pleasure of breaking the news to Dirk; she would do it herself, right now. "Dirk, I must tell you—"

"—Ask her what be her true name now, for it b'ain't Miss Hall no longer," cried Rosina gleefully.

Dirk turned to Lamorna, whose eyes were full of anguish. It clutched at his belly; again in their depths he perceived shame and guilt.

Lamorna blurted out, "It's true, I'm not—"

But Rosina was determined to be before her. "She be the wife of Sir John Roscarrock, Dirk Killigrew. Ask her to show 'ee the ring on her finger. They were wed in March. Her be Lady Roscarrock now, not Miss Hall!"

Lamorna covered her face with her hands. The night, before likened to a dream, had become a nightmare. She should have told him before, dealt the blow herself rather than leaving it to this cruelly taunting village girl. What could she say now? How could she explain? She couldn't, not in front of Rosina. She staggered to her feet, tears scorching her cheeks. One look at Dirk's thunderstruck face and she was stumbling away in unbearable torment.

Dirk was white to his lips, his features harshly sculpted in the murky light. Rosina glared down at him. She no longer jeered; her expression had turned sullen, her voice peevish.

"What do 'ee want with she? Her be gentry, Dirk Killigrew." When he did not respond, she added tightly, "And 'ee be nowt but the bastard son of a village wench. The new fine ways 'ee have don't change that at all."

Dirk rose, still reeling from the blow he had never seen

coming. He barely heard Rosina, was barely conscious of her. There was a drumming in his ears and he had the odd sensation that he was watching himself from above.

Lamorna . . . married. No, he could not accept it. Lamorna wed to Sir John Roscarrock, a man twice her age, a man who owned the fields where his mother had toiled, the hovel they had lived in . . . Lady Roscarrock.

And why not? Had he actually believed she was *his*? Rosina was right; he was a fool to think that a miracle had occurred tonight, that his hopeless yearnings had been fulfilled. She had been beside him in the flesh, no longer untouchable, unapproachable. He should have recognized that for what it was—one of life's brutal jests.

Now he saw that the truth had been as plain as day had he not been so besotted. Her presence at Kilworthy, the bleakness which had flitted over her face, her wish to linger in the gloom, far off from the bonfire's blaze. These things should have alerted him, but he had been too easily pacified. When the smile had returned to her face and the warmth to her eyes, his apprehensions had subsided. He had not wanted to challenge his good fortune for fear it would shatter.

And now that was just what had happened. Lamorna was more unattainable than ever before.

Where had been his armor of aloofness, the tight restraint that had become second nature? The answer was pathetically obvious—it had crumpled as soon as he had laid eyes on her again. There had been times in the past few years when he almost convinced himself he had got her out of his blood. What was she, he would ask himself, but a dream-image, the memory of a sweet, lovely face that he had at first taken for an angel's? She was part of the past and would hopefully grow more distant with the passage of time.

But just a short while ago he had seen her again. And was lost. His love and longing had surged forth, overpowering him, making a mockery of his dogged denial. Bemused, he had dared to believe that they would not be parted again, that somehow the boundaries of class and birth might be breached. All this he had half-presumed, only to learn that there was a new barrier. And one wholly impenetrable.

She had married Sir John, the rich landowner, friend to Matthew Tregarth. The Tregarths and people like them now made up her circle. He ground his teeth. What good was the gold and silver in his pockets, the education he had striven for, the successful business ventures, the ability to speak like a gentleman? To what purpose was it all? He was not a gentleman and never would be.

Why had he come tonight, why had he seen her? Why had she not let on, acted like the lady of the manor? Instead she had been his own Lamorna, reaching for his hands, her eyes filled with wonder and delight as they gazed on him. She ought to have forgotten him, ignored him . . . that would have been easier to bear than this bitter agony.

He wanted to cry out, to strike something, to release some of the tension and pain consuming him. But he stood as rigid as one of the stone megaliths on the moors.

"Come along, Dirk, do, and take a drink o' this," urged Rosina, holding out a tumbler of metheglin.

Abstractedly he shook his head. The thought of swallowing anything was repellent.

" 'Twill do 'ee good, lad, drink up," she continued. His brain is in a muddle, she thought. 'Twas a shock I gave him. She regretted reminding him of his illegitimacy, and sought to make amends. Lifting the glass of mead to his lips, she tilted it downwards. He sputtered, and his helpless rage found a target. Knocking the tumbler roughly from her hand, he growled, "Damn 'ee, woman, haven't 'ee done enough this night? Leave me be!" In his fury he had inadvertently lapsed into his former way of speech.

Rosina gave a mournful cry. "I only wanted to give 'ee a taste o' mead," she said. " 'Twould've helped 'ee. But no, 'ee would rather pine and brood and boil like a bear with a sore head! Well, mayhap someday 'ee will stop wantin' summat that 'ee can't have, Dirk Killigrew. Mayhap 'ee'll look to what be right in your grasp. But one thing be for sure. Her be Lady Roscarrock and not for 'ee. Her do have a husband, and tes his bed she shares."

Wrath twisted Dirk's features; in his eyes was suddenly the savage, maddened look of a wounded animal. Rosina flinched and stepped backwards. She knew she had gone too far. Her jealousy had overwhelmed her, made her spiteful and vicious. That was not the way to win him, to let him see her contempt for his feelings.

Regretfully she said, "I be sorry, Dirk. I oughtn't to have spoken so to 'ee. But her be wrong for 'ee, married or no, can't 'ee see that?"

"Leave me, Rosina," he answered furiously, "or by God I'll throttle 'ee!"

She fled, conscious of a bitter defeat she might never overcome. And Denzella's precious powder lay dissolved in the golden liquid that Dirk had dashed to the ground.

Zachy located Dirk some minutes later. "There 'ee be, lad. Tes nigh on midnight and time for the Green Lady. Find a lass, why don't 'ee?" Then the smile was wiped clean from his face; he faltered before the look of naked misery in his friend's eyes. What in God's name had caused it?

"Dirk, what be wrong with 'ee? Bad news . . . the ship, the goods . . ." He broke off, baffled and distressed. No mere business setback, he was certain, would provoke such suffering. What then?

Dirk's voice was flat, dull. "She's wed, Zachy. She wed Sir John Roscarrock not two months ago."

Zachy stared at his friend, uncomprehending. Then it suddenly struck him; *she* could be one person only, the Reverend Hall's fair niece. Zachy cursed himself for not knowing, for not listening closer to Bessie's gossip. He might have shielded Dirk from this, though how he knew not.

" 'Ee saw her?" he asked, moistening his lips.

Dirk nodded.

"Well, tes a sorry life, dark as a shaft, hard as iron." He did not know what to say, how to console the blighted man before him. Had Dirk actually aspired to marry the young lady himself? Zachy knew that Dirk's course of determined and difficult improvement had been motivated by the terrible years with Captain Trey and also by the outrage he had felt on learning his mother had died in abject poverty. But had there also been another impetus, one that perhaps Dirk did not even acknowledge to himself? Had he been striving to make himself worthy of the vicar's niece? Had he hoped that someday he might approach her again, this time on a much firmer footing? Zachy was speechless before such self-delusion.

There were any number of respectable girls he might have, but none of them ladies. Ladies did not marry smugglers, and they most certainly did not marry bastards. Surely Dirk knew this. Knew, perhaps, but accepted? Had he cherished secret hopes, secret even to himself? Otherwise why should the news of her marriage be so devastating?

"I'm leaving, I'm off to Padstow," said Dirk curtly.

"Tonight? Wait til morn. Tes a long ride and dark as pitch," protested Zachy in dismay.

Dirk shrugged.

"Well, I'll go with 'ee then," he offered.

Shaking his head, Dirk said, "No, you stay here. I'm no fit company tonight. I'll send word of the next run, after I've seen Elias Pollard."

Zachy nodded unhappily. He pressed Dirk's shoulder somewhat awkwardly and watched him move away. It was indeed a sorry state of affairs but, after all, gentry wed gentry. Lamorna's marriage did not surprise him, though he thought she must find life at Kilworthy vastly different from the Rowenstow vicarage.

Dirk did not see the Green Lady lifted by four of the older women, raised three times in the air, and then heaved into the fire. He did not hear the cheers of the crowd, the bawdy quips, the laughter. The ancient ceremony of fertility marking the onset of summer meant nothing to him. In the future he would avoid Landrawna like the plague. Never again would he set foot on Kilworthy land. Perhaps he would one day settle in Brittany for good.

There were footsteps behind him, coming toward him. Glancing over his shoulder, he tensed. Lamorna was running in his direction, but, to his surprise, she flew past him and into the darkness, her face twisted in terror. Looking about rather wildly, he saw no one in pursuit and wondered where she was going. Without another thought, he set off after her, his bitterness and anger fading.

"Lamorna! Lamorna!" he called, and seized her. Initially she struggled, her eyes unseeing, but as he spoke to her again she uttered a tremulous sob and pressed against him.

His arms went round her protectively, his hand stroking her tumbled curls. There was such piercingly sweet bliss in holding her that he asked no questions, but instead whispered endearments, "My love, my dearest one, my own." His mouth bent over her hair, lightly brushing it. His trembling fingers touched her cheek.

She took a ragged breath and abruptly drew away. "N—no, forgive me."

Dirk raked his fingers through his hair. "What happened? What frightened you so?" His voice was unsteady.

She hung her head. "A foolish fancy, no more. I—I did not know they were going to *burn* the Green Lady . . . at Rowenstow we had not such a custom." There was lingering shock and horror in her tone.

He frowned in perplexity. Her undeniable anxiety, the desperate retreat was due to that fatuous observance? He could not credit it, especially when he ached to take her back into his arms.

" 'Tis naught but an old custom," he said.

"Y—yes, I see that now." She bit her lip.

For a few moments they were silent, then Dirk heard himself asking, "Sir John—is he good to you?" and wished he had not. Whatever her answer, it would be intolerable.

Looking up, she could barely see his face in the darkness. Her voice was choked with unshed tears. "Oh, my love, forget me," she murmured, and then she was gone while the scent of her hair and the impression of her body against him were still fresh.

During the evening Simon Pettinger had wandered about, observing the merry-making. He considered the burning of the Green Lady regrettably pagan, but such rustic customs were popular. It wasn't as though anyone actually *believed* that fashioning a female out of greenery and then casting her into the flames would bring about a fertile growing season. His parishioners were well aware that these matters were left to the will of God. And he had to admit that the massive, glowing fire was a powerful image, its fascination rooted in a distant past when man had honored the sun.

When the Green Lady was committed to the flames, there followed the usual kisses, cheers, and lewd jests. All quite in keeping with the festivities. At first Mr. Pettinger did not notice the couple some distance away from where he stood at the edge of the shadows. When he drew closer he gave them a cursory glance and would have passed on had he not heard the girl's stifled cry of relief as she threw herself into the man's arms.

Mr. Pettinger halted in his tracks, astounded. In the man's close embrace was Lady Roscarrock, and his arms offered both strength and solace.

Simon gazed at them, his chest pounding. Lamorna, married these last two months to Sir John, was clinging to another man! And though the two were not kissing, it was no brotherly embrace. The tall man, his head bent, held her like some infinitely cherished belonging. Simon's own bruised heart twisted. Doxy! he thought, taking refuge in anger and disgust. This was a young woman he had prized above all others, wanted to look after . . . But then Lamorna pulled away and the man's arms dropped stiffly to his sides. Some words passed between them and Lamorna lifted her face. Then she was gone.

Mr. Pettinger stood very still, stricken by her tragic expression. This was no depraved tryst, not the stolen embrace he had assumed. There had been more despair in their attitude than passion. He was honest enough to realize that his moral indignation had been fueled by jealousy. Though he had often imagined it, he had never held Lamorna in his arms. And not since her marriage had he allowed himself such thoughts.

Who, then, was this man who had attained what he had not? He had clasped her to him like a treasured possession only for her to melt away.

And now the fellow was coming toward him, moving in fierce, long strides. He came within a few feet of Simon, engrossed, oblivious to his surroundings. The glow of the bonfire illuminated his face for an instant, and Simon frowned. He knew him; that is, he knew who he was. The smuggling captain.

Simon was far more cognizant of village affairs than was the Reverend Poldew or Sir John. He knew that a sloop worked by Landrawna men sailed to France and back, bringing contraband. Simon did not condemn fair-trading; it was preferable to wrecking, after all, and to some of the other pursuits of the lower classes as well. He himself never purchased smuggled goods, deeming it unbecoming to his calling, but he never reproached the villagers for doing so.

Simon recalled the day last autumn when he had seen Lamorna talking to another of the "gentlemen"—Zachy Sawyer. How was it she knew these men? Simon pondered what he had heard of Dirk Killigrew. The illegitimate son of a village woman who had died some years back, before he had come to St. Petroc's as curate. No one seemed certain as to who his father was though there were rumors, mostly culled from his housekeeper. A handsome roving gypsy, perhaps even a rich gentleman who had seduced and then abandoned her. Both were colorful stories and likely neither of them true. More like a plain man who had had no inclination to marry Cherry Killigrew, or one who was already wed. It was a common tale and one Mr. Pettinger deplored. As for her son, it was said he had been part of a smuggling crew before returning to Landrawna and somehow becoming captain of his own vessel—an extraordinary feat, considering his origins. Today no one could take him for a village lout, but how in God's name did he come to be cradling Lady Roscarrock in his arms?

No one else appeared to have noticed them, for which Simon was grateful. He had no desire to see Lamorna embroiled in an ugly scandal. Should he broach the subject with her, warn her to take care? No, he could not imagine himself doing any such thing. Not even in his role as cleric. He had tried to suppress his feelings for her, to regard her as Sir John's wife, but the scene he had just witnessed made a mockery of his efforts.

The pain in him was real, and with it came an acute fear for Lamorna.

Seventeen

Not long after the Beltane festival, Kilworthy hosted a dinner party for some of the local gentry. Among the guests were the Tregarths, the St. Aubyns, Isolde's brother and sister-in-law, and the Nancherrows, who brought along their youngest son, a bashful lad with a slight stammer.

Lamorna had not seen Tamara since the night at Tregartha; she had put off her invitations to tea with rather feeble excuses.

Isolde was with child for the third time and looked and felt the worse for it. Not only that, Joshua now avoided her bed, claiming she needed her rest. She was not deceived; she knew that her body revolted him during pregnancy, but at least she was doing her duty which could not yet be said of Sir John's new wife.

Her father-in-law was squeezing Lamorna's hand and speaking to her in a low voice. The old goat, thought Isolde with disgust. But she had to admit that Lamorna did nothing to encourage him. Sir John was talking to Mistress Nancherrow and took no heed. It did not escape Isolde's notice that he never glanced at his bride. So the bloom was already off the rose, was it? Isolde's gaze shifted to Kitty; the girl did not look well—there were smudges beneath her eyes and her mouth had a pinched look. But Philip Nancherrow did not seem to mind. The two youngest people were seated beside one another and Philip was overcoming his own shyness enough to speak to her. Not bad looking, thought Isolde; he might have been spotty or had a weak chin. A stammer was preferable to either of those.

"I hear there is illness in Pendreath," said Mistress St. Aubyn.

"There is always illness in the villages, of one sort or another," said Joshua.

"Aye," his father nodded. "I said as much to young Dr. St. Cleer only yesterday when I passed him on his way to Pendreath. 'Turn round,' I advised him, 'there's nothing you can do for them. Let the sickness run its course and take the ones who are marked for death. Save your efforts for those who can pay you!' " He gave a rumbling chuckle.

"And did he take your advice, Matthew?" asked Sir John.

Matthew snorted. "The young fool bade me good day and good health. I may as well have saved my breath."

"Perhaps he has a new cure, Father," said Tamara.

"And perhaps pigs can fly, girl! 'Twould take a miracle to stop sickness sweeping through a village. Those people live like rats!"

John cracked a nut and took out the meat with his long, white fingers. "I hear he's a pleasant enough fellow, grandnephew to Dr. Pendarvis."

"He won't make his fortune tending the cottagers," announced Joshua.

"I doubt they will trust him," said Denzella. "They have their own ways of treating illnesses—and they mistrust doctors."

"Surely that is because doctors are so reluctant to treat them," said Lamorna. "Most cannot be bothered with the ills of the villagers. Perhaps if a doctor had been near to Rowenstow, my aunt would not have died."

"Doctors cannot cure typhoid, Lamorna," said Denzella dismissively.

"If you ask me, they can't cure anything," said Matthew. "My foot was so swollen with gout last winter I couldn't walk, and there wasn't a damn thing Dr. Pendarvis could do about it. 'Eat and drink less,' was his foolish advice. 'Damn it, doctor, I can't move,' I told him. 'What else is there to do *besides* eat and drink? A man must have sustenance.' "

Tamara looked at her father's bulk. He ought to be able to sustain himself for weeks, she thought scornfully.

"Well, Father, you know what they say. 'If the doctor doesn't kill you, he will cure you,' " said Joshua.

Matthew reached over and patted Lamorna's hand. "You mustn't distress yourself unnecessarily, Lady Roscarrock. 'Tis highly doubtful a doctor could have helped your good aunt."

Lamorna nodded faintly and withdrew her hand, putting it in her lap. It took all her efforts to be civil to her husband's guest. Heaven be thanked that Sir John was not like Matthew Tregarth with his gross appetites. Lamorna felt nothing but relief now that John no longer claimed his rights as husband. But still she was his.

She thought of the night of Beltane when she had hastened back to Kilworthy and up to her room. To her surprise Maggie was there, asleep; she had supposed her to have been down at the bonfire. Maggie had wakened with a jolt, her bleary gaze growing keener as it focused on her mistress's face.

"What—what is it, Miss Lamorna? What's happened?" she had asked, slipping into the old mode of address.

And Lamorna had told her. Maggie listened and tried to comfort while her mistress wept piteously. The girl was aware that Sir John no longer came to her, though Lamorna had not referred to it. Maggie was in a quandary, wondering whether she ought to tell her mistress her suspicions. She had decided against it; Lamorna's knowledge would likely make little difference and it was sure to make her life at Kilworthy unbearable. So Maggie held her tongue, and Lamorna eventually cried herself to sleep.

Maggie had grasped certain particulars unfathomable to Lamorna. Brought up in a village, where little, if anything, was secret, she was acutely familiar with the ways of the world.

ECHOES OF THE HEART

After dinner the ladies withdrew to the drawing room.

"Tamara is looking very well," said Denzella to Isolde. "I confess I am surprised she is still unclaimed."

Isolde's mouth tightened. "Joshua is quite annoyed with her. She has refused several suitors over the last year and seems perfectly willing to drift aimlessly into spinsterhood. Yet Joshua is determined that shall not happen." She shifted uncomfortably in her chair, wishing she might loosen her corset stays. "I would like a daughter, but not one so troublesome as Tamara."

"Doubtless the result of losing her mother at so tender an age," said Mistress St. Aubyn. " 'Tis a pity, Isolde, your father-in-law did not marry again."

Tamara was seated near to Lamorna, but the opportunity to converse privately with her never came. Lamorna seemed determined to speak of nothing but trivialities, and Tamara had no wish to disconcert her. Sensing her friend's quiet despair, she chafed to know its cause. She, too, had noticed that Sir John paid no heed to his wife, as though she were not in the room at all.

Philip Nancherrow and Kitty were talking diffidently with one another, their conversation rather stilted and uneasy. But Tamara noted that Philip's stammer was scarcely apparent and Kitty's cheeks were flushed. Well, thought Tamara, at least someone is having a good time tonight.

After their guests had gone, John regarded his daughter ironically. "It appears you've made a conquest, my dear."

She colored painfully. "I—I don't know what you mean, sir."

"Come, Kitty, don't be coy. Young Philip Nancherrow, of course. He seemed m-m-most t-t-t-taken with you." He laughed. "A pity he's so unpromising."

Lamorna saw Kitty's face fall and said, "I thought him very sweet."

Sir John's gaze flickered to his wife. "Your opinion, Lamorna, is of no consequence whatsoever. Kindly hold your tongue." His voice was coldly contemptuous.

Lamorna bit her lip, staring down into her lap. He sounds as though he *hates* me, she thought miserably, and yet what have I done but speak my mind on occasion?

"A foolish whelp," continued John, "and a younger son at that. If he thinks to ally himself with my family he is much mistaken."

"Goodness, John," said Denzella lightly. "Kitty did nothing more than her duty as hostess. If you ask me, it was good for her to be with someone her own age—she so rarely is."

John shrugged. "I doubt that Kitty would wish to continue an acquaintance with a lad who would call her 'K-k-k-kitty' all the time. I thought he sounded rather an imbecile. Am I right, my dear?"

Kitty nodded, avoiding her father's amused eyes. Later, alone in her room, she opened her cupboard and took out a blue bottle. Pouring a little into a tumbler, she drank it. There was no need to add water; the taste did not bother her. It was a blessing, as was the feeling of lassitude that began to creep into her limbs and dull her brain. Soon she lay in a drowsy stupor, remote from the body clothed in the nightdress.

She was barely conscious of the opening of the door.

The illness in Pendreath was found to be measles, and soon the disease had spread to Landrawna with the onset of high fevers which preceded the appearance of red sores on the sufferers.

When Lamorna heard the news from Maggie, she wanted to know what was being done to look after the sick.

"Tes like always," Maggie told her. "Take a cat and cut off its left ear. Add three drops of its blood to water and drink it. Tes likely all the village cats'll be losin' their ears afore long."

"The poor beasts—and my aunt had no faith in that remedy! She always gave elderflower tea to bring down a fever. I'll gather some and we'll take it to Landrawna."

"You, my lady?" gasped Maggie.

"Why not? I had measles as a child and so shan't catch it again. Fetch one of my old gowns and an apron. And we'll need two baskets for gathering. If we can prevent the fevers from rising too high, perhaps some tragedies will be prevented." It was well known that measles, though not often fatal, caused blindness and deafness.

"Miss Denzella won't like it," declared Maggie "Her has given orders no one is to go to Landrawna while they be sick."

"Miss Denzella is not my gaoler," said Lamorna.

In a few hours, the kettles in the hearths were boiling with elderflower and treacle, and Lamorna and Maggie had done what they could to make the sick more comfortable. They had changed soiled linens, bathed feverish faces, and held cups of the herb tea to parched mouths.

"Bless 'ee, my lady," said one woman who was ill herself. "Bless 'ee for comin'. I be too poorly to tend to Peter and Luke here myself. My man be at the mine—he didn't like to go, but how we be goin' to live if he don't work?"

"Don't worry, Mrs. Sennen. None of you shall go hungry. If you are in need, send someone to Kilworthy who has already had measles, and you will be given food," said Lamorna.

Mrs. Sennen's expression was grateful but uncertain. "My Jack—he won't like to go beggin', my lady."

"Nonsense. It is not begging at a time such as this. You need your husband to look after you and the boys. I am going to ask Dr. St. Cleer to call as well."

"I don't know, we've never had no doctor," said Mrs. Sennen, alarmed. "Their fees'd ruin we."

"This doctor has been treating the villagers at Pendreath and they are over the worst of the epidemic there. He will not ask what you cannot pay, Mrs. Sennen."

It was late in the afternoon when Maggie and Lamorna

wearily climbed the steep street, passing the miners returning from their shift.

"They don't know 'ee," chuckled Maggie. "Not in that plain skirt and kerchief."

Lamorna smiled. "And here I was thinking I haven't felt more myself in a long while—since coming to Kilworthy, in fact." She was reluctant to return there now. These last hours she had felt productive and useful, even free. Ahead of her was a formidable task but one she would not shirk. This time she would brook no refusal; this time her requests would be heeded, her orders carried out.

Simon Pettinger was walking towards them; she bade him good evening. He looked with surprise at her pale face framed by the blue kerchief, the obvious strain in the violet-blue eyes. She looked exhausted; her white apron was spotted and streaked, the laced bodice soiled. He was reminded of the time he had come upon her working in the vicarage garden. I disapproved of her then, he thought remorsefully.

"Some of the people here are very ill, Mr. Pettinger," she said. "The Reverend and Mistress Poldew have done nothing. They are in need of parish relief and heartening. Would you call tonight at the cottages?"

Simon flushed; she seemed to be reproaching him. "I had every intention of doing so, my lady. But it is my superior who doles out the parish relief."

"Then that should be changed," said Lamorna. "I will speak to Sir John."

He nodded dumbly. In her voice was a new note of grave authority.

"I'm going to send for the new doctor," she said. "Pray do what you can to convince the people to trust him."

He watched her trudge up the street, her shoulders stiff with purpose. Then he turned and went on his way, his heart heavy.

Lamorna and Maggie passed through the labyrinth of sculleries, larders, and pantries to the kitchen. The maids looked up from their chores, gaping as they recognized their master's wife dressed like one of themselves.

Mrs. Quill stiffened, but her round face remained impassive. "Good afternoon, my lady," she said.

Lamorna did not waste words. "As you know, there is measles in Landrawna. A few of the families will require almost constant nursing, and thus the adults who are not sick will not be able to go out and work. Because they will receive no wages while they are tending to their children, they may not have enough money to buy food. I have told the villagers that Kilworthy will make provisions for them—they have only to call at the kitchen door. Also, I want jars of mallow made up and distributed as quickly as possible."

Mrs. Quill found her tongue. "I've received no such orders from Miss Denzella, my lady."

"Nor will you, I daresay. That is not to the point, Mrs. Quill. These instructions come from me; I will speak to Miss Denzella myself." She turned to go, adding, "I will return later to make certain you have done what I've asked."

When she and Maggie had left the kitchen, Mrs. Quill trembled with fury. "So I'm to cook for all Landrawna, es et?" Her heavy cheeks had reddened.

"Miss Denzella won't like it, I reckon," said one of the maids.

"Well, my sister be ill," said another. "Tes just as bad when grown people come down with measles, worse even. I be goin' to count the jars of mallow in the pantry." She walked briskly out of the kitchen and two other girls, exchanging glances, followed her.

"Tes shameful," declared Mrs. Quill. "Her don't know her place. I won't take orders from two mistresses. Tes Miss Denzella who tells I what to do, not that chit. Afore her came here, Miss Denzella did say that nowt was to change."

One of the women tittered. "What her be doin' comin' through the scullery door, mind? And lookin' like a scullery maid herself!"

"I'll tell 'ee what her be doin'!" said Maggie sharply, standing in the doorway. "Lady Roscarrock did go to every cottage today where there were sick 'uns. But afore that she picked elderflowers and boiled 'em down for medicine. Her tended all o' they with her two white hands! Where were your precious Miss Denzella then? Any that recover'll know who to thank! What do 'ee say to that, eh?"

No one said anything; Mrs. Quill turned to stir something in a pot.

"Now I'll be gettin' hot water for my lady's bath," continued Maggie. "And then her'll be writin' to the new doctor to ask his help. Mayhap the rest of 'ee'll quit blathering and do like my lady says."

Determined to have the last word before the maids, Mrs. Quill said of Maggie, "She got brass enough to make a copper kettle, but no one'll stop their horse from gallopin' to take a second look." But the words were uttered once Maggie was gone from the kitchen.

When Lamorna had bathed and dressed for dinner, she sat down and wrote to Dr. St. Cleer. If he would come to Landrawna the next morning, she would meet him and take him to the cottages where he was needed. She folded and sealed the parchment, handing it to Maggie, who took it below to one of the grooms to deliver. He was happy to go to Pendreath for her, and willing to have his supper late. By now all of the servants had heard about Lady Roscarrock's efforts in Landrawna, and most applauded her.

"Her do have a plucky, kind heart which be even better than her pretty face," declared one of the gardeners.

In the small dining room Lamorna had taken her place at the table with her husband and Denzella. Kitty did not join them. Lamorna discovered she was very hungry, and helped herself to the mutton with cucumber sauce.

"I understand you went to the village today," said Denzella.

"That is so," Lamorna said calmly.

"What were you thinking of, Lamorna?" asked John. "I will not permit my wife to play nursemaid to the families of tinners and fishermen!"

"Your duties do not include looking after sick cottagers," said Denzella.

"Are you referring to my duties as a Christian, or as Lady Roscarrock? As to the latter, I have no duties, have I? You have not allowed me any, Denzella. I have been idle these last months and I have not liked it. Today was a welcome change, in spite of the suffering I witnessed."

Denzella's pale eyes flashed. "I did not think it would be necessary to remind you of your position here, my girl. My cousin bestowed on you a great honor when he made you his wife. An honor you hurl back in his face when you disgrace him like this."

"The villagers saw no disgrace in it. I was merely doing as my aunt would have had me do."

"Your aunt did not live in a house such as Kilworthy. You had no right to give the servants instructions to feed all and sundry."

"I did not say that, Denzella. I merely assured the people that they would not go hungry had they to leave off work during the epidemic. Surely you and John will not allow your tenants to starve."

"There is the parish relief, Lamorna," said John. "I do not get personally involved in these matters."

"Nor, I have observed, does the Reverend Poldew. Perhaps you will allow Mr. Pettinger to distribute the relief fund. He is painstaking and honest, as you know. In any case, I believe we have an obligation to make certain that the present hardships do not increase. Those who may watch their children become deaf or blind should not be allowed to worry about where their next meal is coming from."

"No, you've made it perfectly clear to them that it's coming from Kilworthy," said John. "And I am weary of this talk. If you prefer to sully yourself in the hovels rather than sit in your own drawing room, then by all means please yourself. But Kitty is not to accompany you on any of these outings. And do not be so hasty as to make promises to my tenants in the future."

Later when they were alone, Denzella said icily, " 'Tis a pity you have chosen to displease your husband so early in your marriage, Lamorna."

Lamorna flushed. "You speak as though my wish was to annoy John rather than to see to the sick."

"I am telling you that it is not your place to change the bed-linen of his laborers' children!"

"Just what is my place then, Denzella? You have made it clear I have no responsibilities in managing Kilworthy. Kitty stays much to herself these days and my husband does not seek my company. What do you suggest I do with myself?" Her cool control had left her; there was a note of desperation in her risen voice.

Denzella regarded her deliberately. "You are to give John an heir. That is your one responsibility, to provide him—and Kilworthy—with a healthy boy. Do not make me wish I had chosen another bride for him."

"You—!" Appalled, Lamorna could not finish.

"He might just have easily married your friend, Tamara Tregarth," said Denzella, "but I considered you more suitable, despite your impoverished upbringing." She rose. "Do not prove me wrong, Lamorna. You will most certainly regret it."

Alone in the drawing room, Lamorna sat, marble-like. I was carefully selected and purchased like a brood mare, she thought. My uncle was led to believe Sir John was fond of me; he wooed us both, patronized us. And not because he truly wished to make me his wife. Because Denzella decided that I was the one to give him a son.

Suddenly Lamorna wanted to laugh aloud. Poor Denzella— she was the one to be pitied. She had chosen a bride for her cousin who was not to his taste, and therefore he had ceased to claim his marital rights.

There was slim chance of an heir.

Mark St. Cleer had grown up in Newquay, but rather than acting as an apprentice to one of the doctors there, he had left Cornwall to study in London. For several years he pored over heavy tomes, listened to lectures on the latest medical findings, and worked in a London hospital. But all that time he longed to trade the crowded, noisome streets for purple-slate cliffs and fresh ocean air; he missed Cornwall. Newquay did not need another doctor, even one who had braved the horrors of a London hospital, and he no longer had family there; his parents were dead and his elder sister had long ago married and moved to St. Ives. So he wrote to his mother's uncle in Pendreath, Dr. Pendarvis, and asked if he might join him in practice. He had not seen his grand-uncle in many years, but he hoped his offer to assist the older gentleman would not be denied.

Dr. Pendarvis was delighted; he did not mind admitting that he wasn't the man he used to be and would welcome Mark's taking over some of his practice. But when he realized that it was his nephew's intention to treat the laborers as well as the merchants, professional class, and gentry, he had attempted to dissuade him.

"Believe me, my boy, they won't thank you. They are content with their wise women and midwives. Take my advice and devote yourself to those who will appreciate and pay well for your efforts."

When Mark would not be swayed from his resolve, the older man shrugged his shoulders. Mark's time was his own affair; if he chose to squander it on those who could not afford the fees then there was no more to be said. He was young, earnest, and conscientious. The young were often full of unrealistic ideals; he would learn. The common people were convinced that the way to cure scrofula was not to eat citrus fruits, which they could ill afford, but to pass the hand of a dead child over the affected skin. And that cutting a live pigeon in half and placing the bleeding parts against the patient's feet would rid one of an unknown illness. These superstitions went back many centuries, and the villagers were loath to give them up. That the remedies seemed to work only seldom did not discourage their adherents' loyalties.

Soon after Mark was settled in a small but pleasant cottage in Pendreath, near to the stream which flowed past the stone church, measles struck. There was, simply, no cure; one had to wait for the crisis point, but some patients responded to attempts to bring down the fevers, and there were medicines to dab on the painful, itching sores. At the very least, these methods afforded more relief than drinking the blood from a cat's left ear.

And now the disease had spread to Landrawna. No one understood how diseases moved from place to place; there was nothing in the prevailing belief of the body's four humors to explain this. Most doctors insisted on bleeding, administering leeches to the patient's body to release the excess assumed to be causing the illness. It was this practice which horrified the laboring classes and was at the root of their distrust and dislike of doctors. Mark, therefore, seldom bled anyone, though often the gentry expected and insisted on it.

When Mark received Lady Roscarrock's letter, he was gratified by her appeal to him. He knew nothing about her, and was vaguely surprised that she had written on behalf of the villagers. Most often they were left to their own devices by the landowners. He had heard of Sir John, of course—an older man with a teenage daughter. And so when he rode into Landrawna the following morning, he was taken aback at the sight of a young woman, her hair confined in a kerchief and an apron pinned to her serviceable dress, who introduced herself as Lady Roscarrock. He swept off his hat, attempting to conceal his surprise. When he realized she was planning to assist him, he was astounded.

But she brushed away his objections. "My husband is aware that I am here, Doctor. I visited these people yesterday; I believe, I hope, they trust me. If I accompany you they may be more willing to submit to your ministrations."

He could not deny the wisdom of her argument, but he was still uncertain. He had expected someone far older; she looked no more than nineteen or twenty. In her present attire no one would have taken her for what she was, the wife of a very rich and titled gentleman. Still, he would be grateful for her help.

They went from cottage to cottage. Mark praised her use of the elderflower tea, but mentioned that there was an ointment superior to mallow for the sores. A chemist was preparing it according to his specifications, and he would bring some along on the morrow.

Lamorna liked Mark St. Cleer very much; she was full of admiration for his gentleness and concern. He played finger games with the children, coaxing smiles from wan faces, even feeble giggles. The wariness of the mothers gradually turned to acceptance and then gratitude.

Bessie Trotter's little girl was one of those who were sick. Bessie was beside herself because she had lost a daughter to influenza years before. Mark assured her that the girl's case was not a desperate one, and Lamorna insisted that Bessie sit down while she made tea.

"Paul won't believe it when I tell him," she said shakily. "Lady Roscarrock in my kitchen fixing tea for we! I be that grateful to 'ee, my lady, and the doctor."

"You must bathe her face every hour, Mrs. Trotter," said Mark. "Her fever will likely not climb any higher. But if there is any change for the worse, send your husband to my house tonight and I will come."

Bessie nodded. She was calmer now. "Her be my brother

Zachy's favorite," she murmured. "And the only girl left to Paul and me."

"She will be all right, Mrs. Trotter. She seems a strong lass. But she must drink plenty of Lady Roscarrock's elderflower brew."

"Aye, sir, I'll see to that."

"Your brother, Mrs. Trotter, is he Zachy Sawyer?" asked Lamorna.

Startled, Bessie said, "Ais, my lady."

Lamorna gazed into her mug of tea; she understood Bessie's sudden wariness. Zachy was a fair-trader, a criminal to some such as Joshua Tregarth. She longed to ask about his—and Dirk's—whereabouts, whether they had gone back to Brittany. But of course that was impossible. She was Lady Roscarrock; she could not show an interest in the doings of smugglers.

There were no deaths from measles in Landrawna. It was reckoned to be milder than other epidemics in the past. Grudgingly the villagers admitted that the young doctor had done well by them, and those who could pay him with a catch of fish or a sack of potatoes did so.

Mark met the vicar of St. Petroc's in the street one day astride a chestnut gelding. The florid, corpulent vicar scrutinized him from under bushy brows before he spoke. He wore a powdered periwig and a suit of poppy-colored satin with a waistcoat of cornflower blue.

"Dr. St. Cleer, is it?"

"Your servant, sir," said Mark.

"So you are the new doctor who's been calling at the cottages. I've never heard the like before, sir. 'Tis a wonder they let you in the doors."

Mark smiled. "I owe that to Lady Roscarrock."

"Indeed," said the vicar coolly. "I won't disguise from you, Doctor, that I find her behavior both incongruous and unwise. Yet I hear her uncle is much the same, given to sentimental feelings about the lower classes. She was not bred to her present lifestyle, you see."

Mark frowned slightly. "As she was raised in a vicarage, no doubt her actions should be understandable to you."

The Reverend Poldew grunted. "Not in the least, I assure you. 'Tis unnatural, unseemly for a gently-bred lady to be amidst the filth and vermin in those hovels. I cannot understand my cousin permitting it."

"Your cousin, sir?"

"Sir John is my cousin," was the answer.

"Doubtless you have heard that fortunately no tragedies occurred from this attack of measles. You may not realize, sir, that this was due in part to Lady Roscarrock's swift response when the disease first surfaced. I assure you that the mothers of the recovering children did not regard her behavior as unnatural nor unseemly. Good day, sir."

Insolent young pup, thought the Reverend Poldew. And misguided in the bargain. He could not have made more than a few shillings for all the time he had spent in the village of late. He would soon tire of his righteous notions. There was no virtue in being poor, despite what the Bible said. The vicar's belly rumbled; he urged his horse to a trot. His wife had ordered the cook to prepare his favorite, roast pork, for dinner tonight. Then he was due at the Bull and Clover for a night of whist. He had won the last game and made a fair sum. He was a well-contented man, and had nothing but impatience for the fools who declared that life was unfair. Let Simon deal with their grumbling and whimpering.

After the measles epidemic was over, Tamara wrote to Lamorna urging her to come to Tregartha for the afternoon; Kitty was welcome, too. But when Lamorna asked Kitty to join her, the girl said she did not feel up to the ride. She was content to sit on her windowseat and embroider.

"But Kitty, 'tis an age since you've gone out! And Tamara will be disappointed if you refuse."

Kitty stubbornly shook her head. "Another time, perhaps."

Lamorna scrutinized Kitty's face. "Are you feeling poorly? I believe you've grown thinner these last weeks. I can send for Dr. St. Cleer to have a look at you."

"I'm well enough," said Kitty.

"Still, perhaps Dr. St Cleer—"

Kitty's eyes suddenly blazed. "Don't you dare ask him here, Lamorna. If you do, I'll refuse to see him. I won't be prodded and poked like a sick cow! Doctors—what do they know? Not one could help my mother."

Lamorna said defensively, " 'Twas only that I was concerned about you, Kitty. But naturally I will not send for him if you are so against it. Goodbye."

Kitty did not answer; she had turned away and was gazing out the window. What is wrong with her, Lamorna wondered, and why so often is there contempt in her eyes as she looks at me? Is it because she knows her father regrets marrying me? Doesn't she realize how I've tried to be a good wife, to please him? It was he who turned from me. But she could not tell Kitty that.

As she rode to Tregartha, her spirits gradually lifted. The heather was in full bloom on Whistmoor, the breeze sweet. In the beauty of the afternoon she shook off her dejection.

Tamara greeted her joyfully. " 'Tis been an age, my love," she said. "We heard you'd been helping the new doctor. Isolde was aghast, of course." She took Lamorna's arm and the two went upstairs to Tamara's bedchamber.

"Thank you for coming; I need your counsel. My brother has received another offer of marriage for me, and this time they are pressing me to agree."

"Who is the gentleman?" asked Lamorna.

Tamara grimaced. " 'Tis Lord Trevanion again. But, Lamorna, he has already worn out two wives with breeding and I've no wish to be the third! I—I can't marry him!"

"Then do not," said Lamorna before she had thought. She colored. "I would not like to see you make the same mistake I have, Tamara. Surely you have realized by now that I am most unhappy in my new life."

Tamara clasped her hand. "Oh, my dear, I knew something was very wrong. Is—is he cruel to you?"

"He does not beat me, if that is what you mean. But neither does he pay me the slightest attention, except when I do something to anger him."

"Perhaps when you have children they will make up for his neglect," said Tamara.

Lamorna shook her head. "I fear that consolation is to be denied me as well. You see, when I say that John pays me no attention, I mean it in every sense."

Tamara was appalled; certainly she had not guessed that. She regarded her friend in pity and dismay.

"Indeed, I think I am fortunate in that—matters could be far worse. Yet there is so little to occupy my time. And Kitty has turned from me, why I know not." She shook her head. "I should not speak this way. When I compare my state with others I am consumed with shame."

"Does your uncle know?"

"Oh, no! At least he no longer frets about my future. But Tamara—" she broke off in some confusion.

"What is it, Lamorna?" asked her friend softly.

"I merely wish to say that if there is someone you would like to wed, do not allow anyone to dissuade you."

Tamara frowned. "There is no one, on my honor. But you, Lamorna, was there someone else?"

She said nothing; the answer was clear in her woeful face.

Eighteen

On the high cliff near the Iron Age fort, two men crouched over a small heap of furze and brush. "Well, that be done," said the bulkier of the two. "And Heaven grant us won't need to light 'un." The fire was only lit as a warning to those on the ship.

"Do 'ee think the searchers be nigh?" asked the other.

The first man spat. "They be wearin' fog-spectacles with bank-note shades. Mr. Pollard saw to it that the Gauger's Pocket were filled," he said, referring to a large boulder out on the moor. In it was a deep crevice, highly convenient for persuading the excise men to keep off the cliffs. The revenuer had only to reach in and shift the contents into the capacious pocket of his scarlet coat, and all were content.

"Still, I don't like it. Soldiers never used to come to Landrawna. Why they be botherin' we now?"

"The magistrate." He spat again. "Mr. Joshua Tregarth."

"No! Ol' Matthew Tregarth never troubled the gentlemen!"

"Well, this be his son and another kettle o' fish. He be boastin' that he'll put an end to the trade in these parts. Faugh!"

"I'll never understand the gentry—what do he want to interfere for? Us b'ain't no bother to he."

"Shhhh! Do 'ee hear summat?"

They moved down the headland, listening and looking out over the silver-black sea. Below the cliffs the waves tossed and broke over the jagged rocks.

"I don't hear nowt."

"There—do 'ee hear now? That be the sails flappin'. Hold up the lantern while I call to 'em below." Cupping his hands, he imitated the harsh cry of a gull.

In the pebbled cove below, the men heard and were alerted. Peering over the water, they soon made out the outline of a ship.

"There she be, and afore time, too."

"In this wind tes likely the captain made the crossin' in eight hours."

"Put to, lads," said another of the land crew, and they pushed their small boats into the water, waded in, and clambered aboard. Soon they were rowing close to the anchored sloop.

The unloading of the cargo took several hours. Bales of wool, ankers of rum, and kegs of "Cousin Jack" were shifted into the boats. The false bulkhead was emptied of its muslin, lace, snuffboxes, trinkets, and silk handkerchiefs. They worked by the light of lanterns and the pewter radiance of the moon. Gradually the cargo was rowed ashore and shifted to the backs of the hardy moor ponies led by Elias Pollard's land crew. The animals knew their way up the hazardous paths that rose from the stony beach to the headland and the fort above.

"Tes a right good haul," said one of the men.

"Aye. Us'll be usin' all the hidin' places this time, I reckon."

"Mr. Pollard said we were to leave a few ankers in the stream-bank on the moor north o' Pendreath. 'Twill give they searchers summat to report to the magistrate."

"Tes a waste o' good spirits to sit in the custom house, but I reckon he be right."

The hiding places for the contraband goods were varied and widespread. There were the wells and bogs and streamlets in isolated locations on the moors, and caves beneath the cliffs, and the granite formations such as Boscivey Quoit. But at the latter were known to lurk the Spriggans, evil fairies, and so the smugglers were always careful to turn their coats inside out as they drew near to ward off any evil spells.

Some of the cargo was stuffed beneath mattresses, behind false backs of cottages, and in the reeking fish cellars. The barns of sympathetic farmers provided more shelters, under ricks or haystacks.

Dirk had organized a complex network of storage places. The goods which were to be carried on horseback to innkeepers and other customers in Launceston and Bodmin were hid out on Whistmoor. Into the fougou beneath the ruined fort were rolled scores of ankers and kegs which were later distributed to Padstow and the nearby villages. The mines, Wheel Charity and Wheel Faith, manned by local men, provided their own dens and nooks for storage. There was almost no chance of discovery, for neither Matthew nor Joshua Tregarth nor their shareholders ventured deep down in the mines. It was a source of great amusement that the magistrate's own shafts furnished havens for the trade he was seeking to abolish.

Reece Bodmin, the mine captain at Wheel Charity, turned a blind eye to any goings-on and was a customer himself. His foreman worked the night shift and saw to it that the fair-traders' requirements were vouchsafed.

When all the cargo had been unloaded onto the small crafts and conveyed to shore, the *Cormorant* lifted anchor and sailed a short distance up the coast where an overhanging outcropping of cliff concealed a small cove below. Here the ship would stay until her next run. The anchor was again lowered and the remaining crew went ashore with Dirk. Zachy was already inside the fougou, supervising the counting and sorting of the goods.

Some time later the men on the headland who were unfastening the cargo from the ponies' backs to lug it into the fougou were startled by the whinny of a horse not far away.

"Gawd!" cried one. "Be it the searchers after all?"

"They be at the kiddleywink drinkin'. Come along, us'll have to see to 'un."

Stealthily they crept along the crumbling walls of the fort and saw a stocky figure coming toward them. He was gripping someone to his barrel chest, his large hand covering the captive's mouth.

"Well, knock 'un down, knock 'un down! What be 'ee waitin' for?"

"I can't," grumbled the captor. "Tes a lady."

"What? Have 'ee lost your wits, man? What'd a lady be doin' on the cliffs this time o' night? Tes a spy! Knock 'un down and be done with it!"

"Hold up your lamp, you fool. Be this the face of a man?"

The two men stared as the man shifted his hand slightly; they saw two terrified eyes in a white face. The light fell on her silk gown which gleamed between the folds of a dark cloak.

"Gawd! Tes a lady!" came the dumbfounded response.

"Ain't that what I be tellin' 'ee? Her horse be over there. Tes lame—she were walkin' beside it."

"What's to be done? We can't let her go. Here, man, let her breathe. If 'ee smothers her ther'll be hell to pay!"

"Now don't 'ee cry out, mistress—I'll knock 'ee out, be 'ee lady or no. Do 'ee understand?"

Lamorna nodded frantically, taking a gulp of air as his hand dropped. "Let me go. I'll say nothing, I promise you. I must get home."

One of the men peered closely at her face, lit up by the lantern. "Why, tes Lady Roscarrock of Kilworthy!"

The man who held her scowled. "Es et? 'Ee did a foolish thing passin' by here tonight, my lady."

" 'Twas she who helped in Landrawna when there were sickness. Don't 'ee worry, my lady, we wud'n hurt a hair of your head."

"But what's to be done? What if folk from Kilworthy come lookin' for she?"

"Nobbut'll come here—the word be out. When the gentlemen be abroad, folk know better than to come to the cliffs."

Tamara had entreated Lamorna to stay for dinner, saying that her father and brother would not be dining with them. Despite the lateness of the hour, she would have reached home hours before had her mare not stumbled in a rabbit hole on the moor. Then somehow she had got off the track and it wasn't until the moon rose later that she realized she had gone far out of her way. Still miles from Kilworthy, she had stopped to rest by the ancient fort when suddenly she was grasped from behind and nearly smothered by a large, none-too-clean, calloused hand.

" 'Ee must come with we, my lady. And we can't permit 'ee to see. Don't fret."

She opened her mouth to plead with them again when a cloth of some sort was abruptly drawn over her eyes and knotted at the back of her head. Both of her elbows were grasped and she was led forward a number of paces. The salty air of the sea whipped her cheeks; she took a gasping breath, panic welling in her. They couldn't be planning to push her over the cliff! She gave a piteous cry and instantly a hand was clapped over her mouth.

"We told 'ee not to make a sound. No harm will come to 'ee if 'ee do as we say."

"Come along, my lady, and take a step down. Aye, and another. Now 'ee must bend forward. I'll guide 'ee."

Where in the world were they taking her? She could no longer smell the sea or feel the gale on her face. Instead the air had turned musty and chilled. They were walking on stone; the men's heavy boots stamped and echoed in her ears. Lamorna stumbled but was supported by one of her guides. She heard the sound of men's voices, and also creakings and clatterings and scraping noises.

"All right, my lady. 'Ee can stand up straight now."

The talk ceased; then came exclamations of amazement and confusion. "Well, don't stand there gawkin', lads, someone fetch the captain!"

"Tes a lady!" cried a young man.

"Why, 'ee do win the prize, I reckon, Ralph," said a man sarcastically, and there was uncertain laughter.

Lamorna felt fingers fumbling behind her head and then the blind was off and she was blinking in the sudden bright light of torches. Before her was a group of men, eyeing her with suspicion. She was in a round stone chamber piled with kegs and barrels and oilskin sacks. Smugglers, she thought. And then her heart gave a leap. Was Dirk a part of this crew? Was he nearby? She realized they must be beneath the ancient fort; the domed walls of the room had not been formed by nature.

"Lady Roscarrock!" said someone. Glancing over, she gave a sob of relief.

"Zachy! 'Tis you! I'm sorry, I never meant to—" she broke off, gazing over his shoulder at the man behind him.

"Get on with your work, lads," said Dirk. "We have nothing to fear from this lady."

"But her has *seen,* sir," said one man with dirty gray locks. "Tes Sir John's bride. Her'll have the soldiers after we!"

A few others echoed him gruffly.

" 'Ee heard what the captain said," cried Zachy sharply. "There be nowt to worry any of 'ee. And tes more work to do afore the night's over."

Yet Zachy was uneasy. This chance encounter was likely to complicate more matters than fair-trading. He watched Dirk take her into the narrow stone passageway which led to the second corbelled chamber. It was fortunate for her that she had not come across the men earlier when he and Dirk were elsewhere. She might easily have been dealt a blow on the head and knocked senseless.

"Did they hurt you?" Dirk was asking Lamorna in the small, round room. He had dropped her arm and stood by, a frown on his face.

"No, I was just frightened," she said, looking around. " 'Tis the old fort, isn't it?"

"The fougou beneath. Why are you out on the moor at this time of night?"

She was surprised at the edge in his voice. "I wasn't looking for moonlighters, I assure you. My horse went lame and we lost our way."

"It's dangerous—you might have been hurt. Why were you riding alone?"

"I'd been to Tregartha."

His eyes narrowed; he stiffened. "Why did you go there?"

"To—to visit my friend, Tamara Tregarth."

One of the Tregarths—her friend! He turned away, clenching his jaw. Lamorna regarded him in dismay; his stony reaction hurt and bewildered her. Too, she felt a fresh shame from the night of the Beltane festival.

She untied the ribbons of her cloak and drew back the hood. "I—I have not seen you in Landrawna," she said softly.

He eyed her elegant silk gown beneath the cloak, its seams trimmed in gold braid. About her white throat was a pearl necklace. "No," he said curtly. "I thought—'twas better not."

She flushed. "You are the captain?"

He nodded.

"You know I won't say anything, Dirk, about . . . any of this." His black hair had come loose from its ribbon, his muslin shirt had a slight tear, his breeches and boots were dusty. She desperately longed for the grimness to leave his face, grimness she was aware she had caused.

"One of my men will see you safely back to Kilworthy," he said, not looking at her.

Her lip trembled. "Forgive me, Dirk . . . that night . . . I couldn't bear to tell you."

"That you were wed?"

There was silence between them. Then she said, her face bent, "I—I should go. I must go."

He heard the break in her voice and uttered a stifled exclamation. Clasping her to him, he murmured, "Forgive me, my love. But 'tis agony to see you, knowing you belong to another now."

Lifting her wet face, she said, "I don't belong to him, Dirk. We do not live as man and wife—we are strangers." She gave a harsh laugh. "He did not even wish to marry me—it was Denzella . . ."

Tenderly he stroked her hair. "Hush, 'tis all right—I'd no right to be angry with you. Do not weep, my dear one."

As he held her close, the feel of her against him, the scent of the sweet moorland in her hair, caused his pulses to throb madly. A searing hunger blazed in him as his lips took possession of hers. For so long he had imagined kissing her, and now his body cried out the joy, wonder, and triumph crowding his mind.

She drew back, touching his face, exploring the planes and hollows, threading her fingers through his dark mane while he trembled. He kissed her eyelids, her temples, the fluttering at the base of her throat, murmuring her name, before he again covered her mouth with his.

But soon he regained some measure of sanity. This was no place or time for love-making; she could not stay—her presence endangered them all should anyone come looking for her.

"You must go, my love," he said hoarsely.

"I don't want to leave you," she whispered.

He kissed her again, his heart turning over. "I love 'ee, Lamorna." He had never thought to say it and his voice quivered.

"And I love you, Dirk Killigrew," she said. "And I feel no shame for it."

"We will meet again soon, my dearest one. Until then I'll dream of this." He kissed her once more, swiftly, and then they moved together to the stone tunnel.

Denzella sat in the drawing room at Kilworthy. It was now nearly two o'clock in the morning, but she would wait up all night if she had to. Lamorna had sent a message that she was dining at Tregartha, but had said nothing about passing the night there. Kitty had retired hours before, and fortunately John himself was away.

Her exasperation was now a cold, hard fury untouched with weariness. Several times throughout the evening she had debated the wisdom of sending a servant to Tregartha to inquire after the girl, but her natural pride prevented her. Were the girl not there, Isolde, whose antipathy towards Lamorna Denzella had noticed, would be swift to attribute all sort of wild speculations to her disappearance. In twenty-four hours, all of north Cornwall would be convinced of her perversity, her infidelity to her husband.

Denzella was not concerned for Lamorna's safety; she merely deplored the thoughtlessness of the chit's behavior. She could not believe she was spending the night at Tregartha, not with Matthew under the same roof— his reputation was well known. Lamorna would not be so foolish or careless. No, there had to be another explanation for her failure to return home.

The older woman could not yet admit to herself that she had made a grievous error in her choice of a bride for her cousin, though she was increasingly dissatisfied with her observations of their union. John's frequent absences, his cool indifference, the girl's imprudent actions during the measles epidemic, and now this reprehensible contretemps . . . The entire situation was frustrating in the extreme. Together the two of them were thwarting her carefully-laid plans. The girl was young and lovely, John must see that; he could not be totally insensitive to her appeal. Denzella cared little for their happiness together, but Kilworthy required an heir. If, at John's death, the estate passed to a distant male relative, she would no longer be its chatelaine were she herself still alive. She would be forced to leave. Her cousin's marriage had to succeed, if only for the time necessary to conceive a son or two.

The notion that she might be forced at some time to leave Kilworthy was an intolerable one.

Sounds in the hallway alerted her. Rising, she moved toward the tall, panelled door. Lamorna was hastening past in her stockinged feet, her buckled shoes in one hand.

"Oh, Denzella!" she cried, startled. "I—I assumed everyone was in bed. It's quite late . . ." She colored under the woman's cold gaze.

"Where have you been, Lamorna?" Denzella asked, her eyes flickering over her wind-tossed hair, torn cloak, and filthy skirt hem.

"The mare went lame soon after I left Tregartha. She stumbled in a rabbit hole. I was walking her, and somehow we lost our way on Whistmoor. I'm sorry to have worried you, but there was no need for you to stay up."

"There was every need, Lamorna. Your maid has been frantic with concern for you. I sent out a party of men with torches but they returned a short while ago with nothing to report. Perhaps you will think twice about riding alone after dark."

"Yes, Denzella, I'm sorry," murmured Lamorna. "Good night," and hurried up the stairs.

Up in her room a sleepy Maggie took one look at her mistress's radiant face and said, "You've been with him—Captain Killigrew."

"You knew he was the smuggling captain? Why did you not tell me before?"

"Well, 'twas only puttin' two and two together. Tes lucky for 'ee the men sent to look for 'ee steered clear of the cliffs, as they do when the gentlemen be abroad."

" 'Twas his men who found me, Maggie. I was afraid for my life at first." She gave a hiccup of laughter.

"There be no danger for 'ee from they, my lady. Tes Miss Denzella I mistrust. Her be sharp as a tack, and as hard."

"Yet I'm certain she suspects nothing, Maggie. How could she? He loves me, and love such as ours cannot be wrong."

Not wrong, perhaps, thought Maggie. But perilous.

* * *

Joshua Tregarth regarded the three soldiers who stood before him with contempt. "You are asking me to believe that you have patrolled the cliffs these last weeks and seen nothing?"

The men in their uniforms shifted uneasily. "We did find five ankers in the streambed, sir," said the most senior.

"Five ankers!" repeated Joshua scornfully. "Don't be a fool, man! There were hundreds more—that was a decoy. I wanted the entire cargo located, not a few barrels! *And* the men responsible caught and put behind bars. You men are a disgrace to your uniforms and to the Queen!"

The men flushed. "Beggin' your pardon, sir, but there ain't enough of we to patrol all they miles o' headland. And even if us did catch 'em, tes likely no jury'd convict. The gentlemen be desperate men, sir, when they be interfered with. The folk o' Landrawna be in league with 'em. The whole damn countryside's against us!"

"Don't call them gentlemen! They are no more gentlemen than you are. They are criminals, common thieves, cheating the Crown of its rightful revenues. If you cannot hunt these men down—or at least learn a few of their names—I will find someone who will. Now get out."

Sheepishly the soldiers filed from the room. Cowards, dunderheads! thought Joshua. They know more than they're letting on, I'll warrant. They were doubtless bribed to stay away from the headland.

Isolde came in a short while later and found him dusting sand over a freshly written letter.

"Tamara and I are going to Padstow," she said. "Do you care to accompany us?"

He hesitated, considering. "Perhaps. I must see that this is delivered myself. I daresay even our own servants are not to be trusted where the wretched smugglers are concerned."

"To whom have you written?"

"To the commanding officer of the garrison at Launceston. I want a new group of soldiers sent here to rout out those men. As long as the people here persist in their shameful activities, Cornwall will forever lag behind the rest of England and continue to be viewed as lawless and uncivilized."

"I doubt Cornwall is the only area where smuggling goes on."

"No, but here it's a flagrant disobedience—the common people actually believe there's nothing dishonorable in the trade. They have been allowed to persist in that way of thinking and in supporting the moonlighters all too long."

"I'm certain you are right, Joshua. The gentry should uphold the law rather than turning a blind eye to it."

"As has my father in the past."

"Your father, my love, was never a magistrate."

No, he thought, my father would never bestir himself to take on such duties. He has always been too busy with other pursuits such as women and gaming. It was a wonder he had not died from the French pox, thought Joshua in distaste.

Once, many years ago, he had wandered into the stables and glimpsed his father in the hay atop one of the dairy maids. He had heard him grunting his pleasure and seen the woman's plump red thighs. Pigs, thought Joshua. He had run off, sickened and repelled. He had stayed away from Tregartha all that day, avoiding his tutor and the rest of his family. For that his father had later ordered him caned, and he had submitted without a cry. He could not stop seeing those stout pink thighs wrapped round his father's bulk.

When he was older Joshua never visited brothels—the notion was repugnant to him, though it was expected of young gentlemen. He had determined never to be ruled by his appetites as Matthew was. Yet he was resolved to marry; he was the only son—it was for him to carry on the family name.

Before his wedding, he had broken his long abstinence and paid a call on a certain widow in Newquay. He left wiser but unmoved. The experience had been perfunctory. At least the woman had been clean. And she was not foolish enough to prolong the act with fondling and kisses, neither of which could he have tolerated.

Isolde laid a hand on her husband's arm. "I'm pleased you're coming with us. We can take luncheon at the Bull and Clover."

"As you wish," he said coolly, turning away.

Her arm dropped. Can he not bear me touching him? she wondered miserably. But she merely said, "I have ordered that the horses be ready in one half-hour."

"I told you we should have brought one of the maids," complained Isolde as they stepped out of the millinery shop.

"Give me your boxes," said Tamara, "I'll carry them. 'Tis only a short step to the inn. There you can rest."

Isolde handed the boxes containing her purchases to the younger woman. They were not heavy but they were awkward. Tamara's arms were laden with parcels; slowly she followed her sister-in-law down the street past the fabric store, the glassblower's, the chemist's, the printer's, and the shop that sold pewter.

Isolde paused at the corner and then started to cross the street. She was weary and knew that Joshua would be waiting impatiently to dine. It was past the time they had agreed to meet at the Bull and Clover; Tamara always took too long to make decisions regarding purchases.

"Come along, Tamara," she called sharply.

Tamara was having difficulty cradling the numerous parcels. One in particular kept creeping across her arm and threatening to fall. Halfway across the street it began to slide and she staggered to catch it, stumbling. She did not notice the horse-drawn cart which had turned the corner and was bearing down on her.

"Tamara!" shouted Isolde.

Tamara looked up with a startled shriek. The boxes spilled

ECHOES OF THE HEART

on the dusty street as the horse snorted and reared, its hooves coming near to her terrified face. Just then she was yanked to one side, her arm nearly wrenched from its socket. A tall, dark man, a stranger to her, had pulled her out of harm's way.

"Are you all right, miss?" he asked.

She let out a shuddering sigh. "Yes, sir. Thank you—for a moment I feared I'd be trampled on."

"I'll get your parcels," he said, releasing her elbow.

She smiled, still trembling. With her gloved hand she adjusted her wide-brimmed hat and tried to brush the dirt from her gown.

Isolde was beside her. "That was most careless, Tamara. I nearly swooned to see that horse so close to you—you might have been killed!"

"Do you live nearby?" asked the man who now held her boxes. "I will take these home for you."

"You are very kind, sir," said Tamara, "but there is no need. There is my brother now; he will relieve you of them."

Nodding, Dirk glanced over at the gentleman standing in the entrance to the Bull and Clover. He went rigid, his face darkening. The man was Joshua Tregarth; there was no mistaking him, despite the years which had passed since he had ordered Dirk beaten senseless and thrown out on the moor to live or die.

"This gentleman came to my aid most bravely and quickly, Joshua," said his sister. "I was nearly struck down by a horse and cart."

"Your servant, sir," said Joshua. He surveyed the man before him who was as tall as he but broader through the shoulders. His wine-red breeches and coat were well made, his black boots highly polished and of the best leather. Joshua was puzzled. Who was the fellow—a merchant? A lawyer? Yet Joshua thought he knew all of them in Padstow. Besides, neither occupation seemed to fit him. Joshua felt at a disadvantage and he did not like it; he was used to swiftly summing up people he met.

"Have you bespoke a private room, Joshua?" asked Isolde. As far as she was concerned, the drama was over.

The landlord had come out to join them. "If the ladies will come with me, I will show them into the parlor."

Tamara turned to Dirk. "Thank you again, sir. You saved my life, I daresay."

"Come along, Tamara. I simply must sit down," said Isolde.

Joshua signalled for two of the inn's stableboys to take the parcels from Dirk. "Good day," he said, bowing slightly, and followed the ladies into the inn.

Dirk strode away, his face set in fierce lines. The memory of his last encounter with Joshua Tregarth burned like bile. The loathing and bitterness threatened to overwhelm him. Damn that family for all eternity!

And he had risked his own safety to pluck the young lady out of the cart's way! That must be the sister, Tamara, who was Lamorna's friend. What a shock for them to meet as he was coming out of Elias Pollard's shop—a shock for *him;* they, of course, had no earthly idea who he was. He had remarked his half-brother's perplexity as he had tried to identify him. The blond lady must be his wife; what a sour creature she looked. Dirk's lip curled as the irony of the situation struck him. He turned down the street to his house, contemplating a new scheme. The next time he sailed to France, it would be with a full cargo—a cargo consisting of tin from the Tregarth mine.

Tamara did not connect her handsome benefactor outside the Bull and Clover with the thin, big-boned youth in the dirty, patched clothing who had once appeared at Tregartha asking for money. She had found his announcement that they all three shared the same father bewildering. Then Joshua had said some ugly things and knocked him to the ground, refusing to call their father. Tamara had been frightened to see him lunge at Joshua, dealing him blow after blow until the men came to drag him from the house.

She had found him later, bleeding and crumpled on the moor. He was hungry, he had said, and she had every intention of helping him. She had wrapped up a pasty hot from the oven, filled a small crock with brandy, and taken the cook's wool blanket while she slept. She had found a few shillings upstairs in one of her drawers and then had slipped outside, knowing the men had tossed him somewhere. When she found him, she set down the food and drink and covered him with the blanket. He was badly cut and bruised, his face already swelling from the blows, and he did not stir.

Tamara had not thought of the incident in a long while, and she certainly was not reminded of it as she ate luncheon with her brother and sister-in-law.

Joshua was silent through most of the meal; he seemed preoccupied. When the landlord came and asked, "Is everything to your liking, sir?" he had answered, "Perfectly." Then he added, "I wonder if you can tell me who the man was standing with us outside the inn a short while ago. He was holding Miss Tregarth's parcels."

The landlord's brow creased. "I'm afraid I did not get a clear look at him, your honor. I was anxious to show Mistress and Miss Tregarth inside. What was he like?"

"Tall, dark, well dressed, but a stranger to me."

"No, I regret I cannot help you, sir."

Joshua shrugged. " 'Tis no great matter. Have the man bring the reckoning."

"Yes, your honor," said the landlord, bowing himself out of the parlor. He signalled to the waiter that the Tregarths were finished and went through to the taproom, his heart thumping uncomfortably.

He was not about to identify the man as Dirk Killigrew, captain of the *Cormorant*. He himself was a satisfied patron; much of the liquor he served had paid no custom duty. He owed his higher profits to Dirk and Elias Pollard. The magistrate would have to look elsewhere for the information he sought.

Nineteen

From a distance Dirk could see that something was terribly amiss at Wheel Charity. It was not the smoke billowing from the chimney column nor the vibration of the heath beneath his horse's hooves which alerted him, but the obvious signs of panic and confusion. All work on the surface had ceased, and there were audible cries and shouts and men staggering about. Fiercely Dirk urged his mount to a gallop.

The bal maidens stood in small groups, the long-handled hammers they used to chip apart the ore flung to the ground. Their supervisors, the grass men, too old to penetrate the mine's vast depths, did not order them to resume work. Nor did they rebuke the dozen or so children whose job it was to wash the ground ore.

Dismounting, Dirk caught sight of Jonah Sawyer, who was one of the grass captains. "What is it? What's happened?"

" 'Tis one o' they new shafts," the old man said gravely. "It be badly flooded—one o' the ropes on the horse-whim snapped while they were drainin' it. And the whim dropped down into the shaft."

Dirk pushed through the crowd of men gathered outside the engine house. There he saw the mine captain, Reece Bodmin, speaking to the foreman, Daniel Polwin.

"How many men still be down in the shaft?"

"Six or seven, I reckon. 'Twere a terrible sound when that chain went," he said grimly, wiping his face with a dirty handkerchief. "Us called down a warnin' but with the clatter o' the fallin' whim, I doubt we was heard. They be likely crushed by it or drowned in the rush o' water."

"One or two may be alive. We've got to climb down after them," said the captain curtly. "I'll go. Who else?"

His gaze roamed the sea of faces while the men before him shuffled uneasily or looked back at him somberly.

"And I," said Daniel.

"Well?" snapped Reece. "We need at least three men."

One man cleared his throat and began, "It be this way, sir. We don't know how to swim. If we was to fall into that flooded shaft, too, none of us would be no help even to ourselves."

Snarling an oath, Reece acknowledged the truth of the miner's words. The men weren't cowards, but neither were they eager to risk their own lives for those that were likely dead.

"I'll go," said Dirk. Shrugging off his coat, he began to roll up the sleeves of his muslin shirt.

The miners watched him, exchanging glances and terse words amongst themselves. Reece nodded. "You, David, fetch the new doctor in Pendreath. If the men be not dead he'll be needed. And you, Luke, go to Tregartha and inform Mr. Matthew and Mr. Joshua." Not that they'd concern themselves with the plight of a few tinners, he thought morosely. "All right, lads, let's go."

"How far down?" asked Dirk.

Reece had tossed his own coat on the heath. "Nearly one hundred fathoms," was the grim answer. The three men went inside the engine house, took a felt hat and lit the hempen candle attached to its brim.

"Tes been a long while since 'ee climbed down a shaft," said Daniel to Dirk.

He shrugged. Reece had already begun the long descent into the deep workings. Stepping down the first few rungs himself, Dirk gripped the sides of the ladder. All was quiet now except for the sound of dripping water. When they had climbed down only a few fathoms, the surface light was gone. The dim flicker provided by the candles on their hats lit the rungs before their eyes but little else.

The air was bad; it smelt of foul water and gunpowder. They had blasted a new shaft only recently and then it had swiftly flooded, requiring the use of the horse whim. As they continued to descend, the temperature rose. The men began to perspire, pausing now and then to wipe the sweat from their brows. Dirk's shirt clung to his back. He had thought never to climb down these shafts again, and bitter memories rose in him of the hazardous, laborious work which had occupied so many of his days for so little reward. *My father's mine,* he thought with loathing. And yet had Matthew ever desperately clutched the sides of the slippery ladders, or breathed the sulphurous air for hour after hour, or dodged the fall of rocks?

Reece called up warnings from time to time: "A rung be missin', lads," or "It be slimy here." Dirk gritted his teeth, shirking the fear that each subsequent rung would not hold his weight. Above his head Daniel's boots groped for the wooden slats; Dirk could hear him cursing as he nearly lost his footing a few times.

They had been climbing down for what seemed a very long time. The heat was oppressive and the blackness above and below them absolute. Then Reece called, "Eh, lads! Be anyone below? Can 'ee hear me?"

There was a still, breathless pause while the three men stood poised. And then came a sudden splashing sound and a man's voice crying, "Praise be!"

"One be alive," said Daniel gruffly.

"Hold on, man!" shouted Reece. "Us be comin' for 'ee. How many be down there?"

"Two—just two," came the faint mournful answer. "All else be dead."

"Then tes as many as five that be gone," said Reece and swore.

The two survivors were floating on pieces of broken wood, their faces eerily white and anxious in the poor light.

"Where are the others?" asked Dirk swiftly.

One of the men shook his head, his wet hair plastered to his skull. "When the kibble came crashin' down it struck Abe, Timothy, and Ned. Terrible the sound were—terrible," he shuddered.

"And the rest?" asked Reece.

"There were a great splash of water. When I came up for air there were only Saul and I here. Saul's leg be very bad—he's fainted dead away."

Dirk handed his hat to Daniel and then jumped into the water. He swam below the surface, reaching and groping for something solid. He dragged up one body after another, some hideously cut.

"Daniel, go up to grass and let down a kibble. We'll put in a body at a time and 'ee can hoist 'em up," said Reece.

"Aye, Cap'n," replied Daniel as he began to climb.

"Can 'ee climb at all?" Reece asked the miner.

"I fear I be too weak, sir," he said.

"Well, don't 'ee fret. We'll hoist 'ee up in the kibble as well. 'Ee'll be up in the sunlight afore 'ee do know it."

"Us—us feared we were done for," said Matt with a long sigh.

It was a long while before the men in the flooded shaft heard the clanking and grinding of the kibble being lowered. Reaching up, Dirk grasped the chain and gave a hard jerk to alert the men on the surface. Then he took hold of Saul who had just regained consciousness and lifted him into the large iron barrel. "You'll be fine now, Saul. They've sent for a doctor and he'll see to that leg."

Another long while passed until the kibble was again lowered and this time Matt was lifted into it. "Bless 'ee both," said Matt before Dirk gave the signal for the kibble to return to the surface.

Gradually the grindings of the chains grew faint. "Five

good men lost," said Reece harshly. "Christ, 'tis stifling down here. I be indebted to 'ee, Dirk. This business b'ain't naught to do with 'ee, not anymore. What made 'ee come here when 'ee did? Mayhap Providence?"

Dirk smiled crookedly. "I know nothing of Providence, Reece. I was coming to see you."

"To see I? What about then?"

Dirk glanced about the flooded pitch. In the dank water floated the battered bodies of the dead men. The air was hot and fetid; shadows from their candles wavered on the rough, dripping walls.

"Cornish tin would fetch a good price in Roscoff—tin that was taxed neither by the Crown nor the Frenchies."

Reece's brows drew together. "Aye?"

"Wheel Charity is producing a great deal of ore these days—yet the men and their families do not share in the profits. Everything goes into the pockets of the Tregarths and their shareholders." He paused, his face hardening. "There is a way in which more could benefit. My ship can hold a fair quantity of tin. Give me leave to take some of the ore to France, rather than sending it all to be smelted."

Reece was shaken. He had forgotten the bobbing bodies, the evil-smelling water. Dirk's offer was a tempting one; he had no more liking for his employers than had the younger man, but he was proud of his position and wanted to keep it. He had risen through the ranks to foreman and then to his present job as mine captain; he and his wife had their own box at church; his house was snug and comfortable; he was referred to as "Mr. Bodmin" by hundreds of miners. These were not things to be taken lightly, and things he stood a good chance of losing were he to permit tin to be smuggled to Brittany in the *Cormorant*.

Yet the idea had its merits. He knew Dirk was completely trustworthy and that his fair-trading ventures were successful. Matthew Tregarth saw little of what went on under his nose and would not notice a slight dip in the profits, but his son

Joshua was another matter. He had a nose for trouble and was a magistrate to boot. His suspicions, once alerted, would not be easily put off.

Were he to give Dirk the nod, he would get a share of the profits along with the men he chose to hide the ore in the unused shafts before loading it onto the ship. But the risk was too great, he told himself. Reluctantly he shook his head.

"I fear I cannot help 'ee, lad," he said.

Dirk had watched Reece's face as he had thought matters through and was not entirely discouraged. He could wait, and hope that later the mine captain would reconsider.

"Should you change your mind," he said, "the offer still holds." Pressing him further would do no good. He had planted the seed; perhaps one day it would take root.

Reece nodded somewhat uncomfortably. He liked Dirk and admired him, and was very grateful for his help these last few hours. But his customary cautiousness outweighed all other considerations.

He sought to change the subject. "The chains on that whim were as old as Methuselah. I've told Mr. Tregarth we be needin' money for repairs. Now he'll be forced to take notice."

Dirk said nothing. When the last body had been loaded and sent up the shaft, the two men began their long climb back to the surface. Neither mentioned the fair-trading or the Tregarths again. They ascended in silence, pausing only to wipe their faces, beaded with moisture, and their palms so they could better grasp the rungs of the series of ladders. It was slow going and treacherous; the ladders creaked and shuddered unsteadily under their boots. Reece cursed himself for not realizing that even more repairs were needed than he had thought. When one of the rungs snapped beneath him, he let out a shout and gripped the sides, his legs flailing. Hastily Dirk reached up to steady him, clenching his jaw and praying they would not lose their balance and topple downward.

"It be the damp," Reece said, panting. "It be rottin' the rungs."

ECHOES OF THE HEART 395

As they climbed from one shaft into another, a section of wall suddenly broke off. "Look out!" cried Reece, bending to one side.

But Dirk did not move swiftly enough. A cluster of rocks dislodged from the wall, sending a shower of gravel and stones over him. A sharp flag struck his forehead, and one shoulder was painfully lashed by the onslaught.

"Dirk, lad, are 'ee hit?" called Reece in alarm.

The blood was already streaming from the gash in his head; he rubbed at it with his sleeve. "A scratch," he said, grimacing. "Keep going." They climbed on. Dirk's head throbbed and he began to grow giddy. It took all his concentration to clutch the sides of the ladder and keep his balance. The blood, mixed with sweat, ran into his eyes; he had to continually stop and wipe it away.

He was nearly spent when Reece called down, "We be nearly there, lad. Hold on a little longer."

And soon there was white light above their heads and the sound of voices. Taking deep breaths, he leaned against the ladder until strong arms reached down and hauled him out of the shaft. "Careful with his head, lads," he heard Reece say, and then the light dissolved into blackness.

On the surface Rosina waited for Dirk to emerge. Most of the other bal maidens had gone home during the long hours that Reece Bodmin and Dirk had been in the mine, but Rosina had stood her ground. She watched the injured miners laid out and heard the wild weeping of the wives whose husbands' bodies were slowly brought to the surface. The crowd remaining was strained and silent. The young doctor had come, and was bent over Saul, whose leg was bleeding badly.

Late in the afternoon someone shouted, "They be comin'!" and Rosina hurried over to the engine house. When she saw the mine captain stagger out, she rushed forward. "Mr. Bodmin, be Dirk Killigrew with 'ee?"

Reece nodded abstractedly. "He's hurt his head. The doctor must see to it."

A short while later Dirk, supported by two men, stumbled down the steps of the engine house. He was haggard and filthy, and there was a jagged cut below his hairline from which the blood streamed. His long, loose hair was streaked with dust, his shirt ripped and stained with grime and blood.

Rosina uttered a sharp cry. "Dirk—thank heaven! I were afeared for 'ee. But 'ee be hurt, come home with me and I'll see to it."

Before Dirk could respond—Mark St. Cleer was before him, gently moving Rosina aside. "That gash needs cleaning," he said and proceeded to wash Dirk's forehead carefully. Too weary to argue, Dirk stood silently while Mark examined his face.

"I'm Dr. St. Cleer," said Mark.

"This is the first time I've seen a doctor attending to miners," said Dirk.

Mark did not answer. While he worked he studied the man before him. At first he had assumed he was a common tinner like the others, but he realized now that that was not the case. The fellow's clothes, while rent and muddy, were of good cloth, and his boots, though badly scuffed, had cost far more than miners could pay.

"Your head will require five stitches, sir," he said simply.

Dirk looked at him blankly.

"The skin must be repaired," explained Mark. "The wound is deep and will continue to bleed unless the opening is sutured, sewn together."

Rosina gasped. "Sewn together, did 'ee say? That be daft! Don't listen to 'un, Dirk. I'll fix 'ee right as rain myself."

The people were watching curiously. A few sniggered; others regarded the new doctor with scandalized repugnance.

Mark's eyes did not waver from Dirk's face. "It must be stitched, sir. If not, it can turn poisonous."

"Pay 'un no mind," said Rosina. "What do he think 'ee be, a piece o' cloth?"

Mark ignored her. He gestured to where Saul lay on the

heath, covered with a blanket. "This man has lost a great deal of blood. His wound requires stitching as well."

Dirk glanced over at Saul, who was watching them fearfully, stanching the wound in his leg with a blood-soaked cloth. Saul's face was white and drawn, his gaze bleary, feverish.

"He could lose the leg," said Mark quietly.

Everyone was waiting for Dirk's reply; he realized that Saul would not likely submit to the young doctor's ministrations if he did not himself. With another glance at Saul, he looked back at Mark and saw the entreaty in his blue eyes. Dirk nodded curtly.

"Very well, doctor," he said.

A murmur went through the crowd of onlookers. Appalled, Rosina began, "But Dirk—" only to have him shake off her arm.

"Perhaps you'd like some brandy," said Mark as he knelt down and rummaged through his black bag. "And you must sit down—you're nearly dead on your feet, sir." He was profoundly grateful to this dark man who was held in noticeably high esteem by the others. Saul's wife had been reluctant to allow Mark to tend to his leg wound, but he sensed that if this fellow was seen to trust him, so would she.

Reece handed Dirk a flask and he took a swallow. The mine captain's eyes registered dread mixed with respect; he doubted that he would have had the courage to consent to the doctor's sewing *his* flesh. His belly constricted unpleasantly.

"Take another," he urged.

Dirk shook his head and gave him back the flask. "Have a drink yourself," he said. "You look as though you can use it."

Dirk sat down on the ground before Mark, who cleansed the cut and then set to work. Rosina gave a stifled cry as the needle pierced Dirk's skin. Reece suddenly went light-headed and turned away. Some of the onlookers watched in fascinated horror while others grimaced or moaned. Dirk's jaw was clenched, his face hideously pale except for the angry red gash closing with small, black stitches.

Mark worked expertly and swiftly, well aware of the pain he was inflicting on his patient and his iron control. Liquor was an unsatisfactory deadener unless one drank enough to bring on unconsciousness. He had feared that the man might jerk away at the needle's first invasion. Had he done so, it was likely that Mark might never have overcome the villagers' abhorrence. But his patient sat very still, his only reaction to the completion a sudden sagging of the broad shoulders.

Now that Mark was finished, the crowd surged forward to gape at the row of black crisscrosses on Dirk's forehead. He rose unsteadily.

"Come home with I, Dirk," said Rosina. "I'll fix 'ee a pasty."

Dirk shook his head. "Thank you, Doctor."

Mark smiled. " 'Tis I who am in your debt, sir, as I am certain you know." He glanced over at Saul, who had once again lost consciousness. The woman beside him regarded the doctor imploringly. "Do summat, sir, afore it be too late!" she cried.

Ignoring Rosina, Dirk moved toward his horse. Abruptly a harsh voice cut into the excited murmurings of the crowd. Startled, they looked up to see Joshua Tregarth on a brown horse, his eyes narrowed to slits.

"What is the meaning of this? Why are you all standing about idly? Shut up, woman!" he shouted to one of the keening widows. "Where is Bodmin?"

"I be here, sir," said Reece, coming forward. "There's been an accident—five men be dead. The doctor's come to look to the two survivors."

"What happened?" asked Joshua curtly.

" 'Twas the horse whim, sir—the old chain snapped when the men were drainin' the new shaft. A man were sent to Tregartha to let 'ee know."

"I was not at Tregartha," said Joshua. He glanced about

the crowd and saw Dirk mounting his horse. His dark brows drew together. It was the man he had seen in Padstow. What on earth was he doing at Wheel Charity and looking so disreputable?

"If I could have a word in private with 'ee, sir," Reece was saying.

Joshua turned to Reece and nodded. "You there, see to my horse," he said to one of the men. Following Reece inside the engine house, he told him, "I want all work resumed tomorrow. That shaft must be drained. Send for the blacksmith to repair the chain."

" 'Tis about the whim I want to speak to 'ee, sir," said Reece.

"Well?" asked Joshua.

" 'Twere a bad accident today, sir, and we be lucky more men weren't lost. I hear there be new pumps worked by steam for drainin' shafts. Wheal Vor, the Godolphin mine, do have one." He hurried on, noting Joshua's tightening face. "These new pumps be reckoned safer, sir, no need for chains or whims. If 'ee would buy a fire engine for Wheel Charity, the shafts would be dry in half the time, and there'd be less danger to the men. All in all it be a sensible solution."

"Solution to what, man?" asked Joshua, a glint of amusement in his eyes. "To the men's carelessness? I think not. Those pumps burn coal at an enormous rate. The notion is absurd."

"But, sir, the mine be producin' well now. The expense wouldn't be hard to bear, and the work done faster."

Joshua studied the man before him. "What is your position here, Bodmin?"

Reece reddened and ran a grubby hand across his brow. "Mine captain, sir."

"And is it a position you wish to keep?"

"Aye, sir, but—"

"Then," went on Joshua coolly, "we shall have no more ridiculous talk of steam pumps. Do I make myself clear?"

"Aye, Mr. Joshua. I beg your pardon."

"I will overlook this as I can see you have had a most trying day. Goodbye, Bodmin."

"Wait, sir, if 'ee please. There be other things I wish to talk of. Needed repairs, for one. The ladders be in bad shape—I saw that today for myself. Some ought to be taken down and replaced with new."

"And how long do you figure that job will take?" asked Joshua.

"Not more'n a week, sir, mayhap less."

Joshua's voice took on an ominous note. "And during that time not a single ounce of ore will be produced. Your excursion into the depths has addled your wits, man. What you suggest is out of the question. Get the horse whim seen to and tell the men to be more careful in future. Good day to you."

Angry and humiliated, Reece watched him go. For some moments he stood unmoving, his mouth drawn in a bitter line. So be it, he thought. Dirk Killigrew would have his tin.

Joshua walked over to the doctor, who knelt beside an unconscious man. "Dr. St. Cleer," he said.

Mark did not look up. "Your servant, Mr. Tregarth," he said.

"Will the fellow live?" asked Joshua, glancing distastefully at his blood-soaked breeches.

"I am endeavoring to save him," Mark said.

"Doctor, I would like to know the identity of the man who was just here—the dark one who had his own horse."

"I'm afraid I cannot help you, sir. I have no idea who that man was."

Joshua scowled and his gaze fell on Saul's leg where the flesh was bare. "Good God, man, what are you doing?"

"Stitching his wound," was the calm reply.

Joshua gave a stifled oath and turned away. But as he was mounting his horse, a red-headed young woman came up to him.

"I know who he be, your honor," said Rosina.

"Well?"

"His name be Dirk Killigrew," she said. Joshua gave a curt nod, handed her a shilling, and rode away. Serve 'ee right, Dirk Killigrew, she thought. His careless rebuff of her hospitality had infuriated her. All day she had waited in fear for his safety and that had been her reward! She did not know why Joshua Tregarth wanted to know who Dirk was and she did not care. It was satisfaction enough to give him away when the rest refused. But she had been careful to go unnoticed by the crowd. Absorbed in what the doctor was doing to Saul's leg, they had neither seen nor heard her speaking to Joshua.

Dirk Killigrew, mused Joshua as he rode away from the mine. The name was oddly familiar. The man's horse had been a fine animal, and Joshua recalled his polished appearance outside the Bull and Clover. Who in God's name was he? And why had he been at the mine today? Frowning, he repeated the name to himself. Dirk Killigrew. Common-sounding, but the fellow wore good clothes and spoke passably well. He looked to be a few years younger than Joshua himself. Who was he and why did he seem familiar?

The answer eluded him until the following day when he sat on the bench in his magistrate's robes. In the dock stood a fourteen-year-old boy with greasy, dark hair, attired in ill-fitting, patched clothing. It was a common sight, except for the hot defiance in the youth's eyes. Rather than cringing or cowering as many did before sentence was passed, he radiated hostility.

And then Joshua knew. The boy wavered before him in a flash of red and became another boy, also dressed in filthy rags. But not in the court, in the hall at Tregartha! He had come to beg, not for charity but for what he considered his due. "He be my father as well." Joshua heard the words again, his face frozen. And he recalled the way the youth had attacked him, battering him with blows until the footmen hauled him off.

It wasn't possible! That brute of a boy, that wretched lout—and the man who had assisted his sister in the street in Padstow. *His* sister as well, thought Joshua with a jolt. "I be Dirk Killigrew, son of Cherry Killigrew." Cherry Killigrew, doubtless one of the many trollops his father had slept with over the years. Joshua gave a shudder, repelled by the memory and by the realization of how the youth had prospered. Joshua was incredulous that the man and boy were one and the same.

The magistrate on his left nudged him again. With a jerk he came back to the present. They were all waiting for him to pass sentence.

The boy's gaze was insolent; Joshua could not discern the misery and hopelessness in it as well.

"You are to be hanged by the neck until dead," he said. "You will be taken to gaol until sentence is carried out one week from today."

The next case concerned the trade of three prostitutes, Joshua ordered them to be taken outdoors and publicly flogged. Their pleas and screams went unheeded.

"I will no longer brook your defiance, Tamara. You will wed Lord Trevanion in the autumn."

"You cannot force me to marry that man, Joshua! Father, pray tell him."

Matthew smiled uneasily. "Now, my girl, 'tis a fine match. Lord Trevanion thinks highly of you. You will be a titled lady as is your friend, Lady Roscarrock."

Tamara's cheeks burned scarlet. "No! I will not marry a man who has daughters nearly as old as I! The whole idea is repugnant to me, as is Lord Trevanion himself!"

"Oh, Tamara, enough of these histrionics," snapped Isolde. "You are acting as if Lord Trevanion were some sort of monster."

"I scarcely know him—how can I know what he is truly like?"

"Well, you will have many years in which to improve your acquaintance," said Isolde. "Your brother knows best."

"Father, please—you would not force me against my will, surely?" Tamara, trembling violently, had turned imploring eyes on Matthew.

"Father is as much in favor of your marriage to Lord Trevanion as I," declared Joshua. "When you are calm and rational again you will see the wisdom of the match yourself."

"Never! Though 'tis clear to me why you wish to saddle me with that gout-ridden, repulsive toad—"

"—Tamara!" cried Isolde.

Tamara faced her family defiantly. " 'Tis not because you believe he will be a good husband to me. 'Tis only because you wish to acquire shares in his copper mines. You care nothing about my future—you wish only to gain more property. Well, I will not do it!"

Joshua regarded her disdainfully, his voice edged with ice. "You persist in the delusion that you have some say in the matter, Tamara. I assure you that nothing could be further from the truth. Father has already written to Lord Trevanion, accepting on your behalf. The deed is done; you are officially engaged and will wed in two or three months."

Tamara let out a wail of horrified disbelief and covered her face with her hands. Just then a maid knocked on the drawing room door.

"Yes, Mary?" asked Isolde.

"It be a gentleman to see Mr. Joshua and Mr. Matthew, Mistress."

"Who is it, girl?" cried Matthew, glad of the diversion.

"Tes Dr. St. Cleer."

Joshua's brows rose. "Dr. St. Cleer. Very well, Mary, show him in. Tamara, compose yourself."

She moved across to the window, opening the casement. The sweet night air, blowing in from the moor, fanned her hot face. Impatiently she realized that weeping or pleading would do no good; her family had made up their minds. But somehow she would thwart them.

Mark St. Cleer entered the room and bowed. "Good evening, Mistress Tregarth. I hope I am not calling at an inconvenient time; I found myself near to Tregartha and took the liberty of stopping."

"Sit down, doctor," said Matthew heartily. "Have a glass of port."

"Thank you, sir." Mark turned to Joshua. "You will be pleased to learn the man is recovering."

"What's this? What man?" asked Matthew, pouring out a glass of wine for himself.

"One of the miners, Father," said Joshua. "Now Dr. St. Cleer, what may we do for you?"

"The miners don't trust men of your profession," said Matthew. "If I were you I'd leave well enough alone."

"Had I done so, sir, the fellow would have bled to death," said Mark, though there was no sting to his voice. He had not come to quarrel. Glancing about, he noticed a dark-haired young woman standing at the window. He returned her gaze, realizing that she was highly overwrought about something; he must have interrupted a family discussion. What could be troubling her in this house of wealth and ease? She was pretty, and elegantly dressed. A pampered, spoiled girl who had likely failed to get her way on some trivial point—it was what he expected from this family.

Dismissing Tamara, he turned to the two men. "As you may know, I have recently come from London, where I studied medicine."

Matthew gave a guffaw. "Does one truly *study* medicine, my boy? Books, d'you mean? Must be dreadfully dull."

Mark smiled faintly. "Over the course of several years I made a comprehensive study on the various diseases of the lungs."

"Very commendable," said Joshua. "But how does this concern us, sir?"

Tamara was watching Mark closely. His manner was polite but it was apparent he had something to say which her father and brother were not going to appreciate. By the set of Joshua's face it was evident he thought so, too. So this was Dr. Pendarvis's grand-nephew, whom Lamorna had assisted during the measles epidemic in Landrawna. He was not as tall as her brother, but his bearing was good and she liked his air of quiet determination. His fair hair was drawn back with a black ribbon, his suit was dark gray, his waistcoat pale gray.

Mark was answering her brother's question. "The miners suffer from such lung diseases as tuberculosis and silicosis, brought on by the smoke and dust in the shafts. These diseases are commonly fatal—many miners do not reach the age of thirty. In my research I have observed that since the practice of blasting with gunpowder was introduced at the end of the last century, the cases of lung disease have far increased."

"Surely, sir," said Matthew, "you are not suggesting that we return to the old way of digging shafts with picks, an inch or two a day!"

"No, sir, I realize that would be impractical," said Mark. "But the blasting badly contaminates the already poor air down in the shafts. It is hazardous for the men to breathe. Yet after only a few days the air begins to clear and is less harmful to the lungs."

Joshua's eyes narrowed. "Just what are you saying, Dr. St. Cleer? I presume there is a point to all of this."

Mark met his gaze fully. "I am suggesting, Mr. Tregarth, that in the future you wait several days after blasting before sending the men down to dig. This way the air would be better and the men's health not as much at risk. They would live longer and thus produce more ore for the mines."

"And the men sit idle in the meantime? It's clear you're not a shareholder, my boy," said Matthew, chuckling.

"When compared with the lives of your laborers, surely a few days now and then is not too much to ask," said Mark, trying to speak evenly; he had no wish to sound righteous and presuming.

"I suggest, Doctor, that in the future you tend to your business and allow us the same courtesy," said Joshua.

Mark flushed. "It was not my intention to give offense, sir, I assure you. I am merely concerned with the health of the miners, who toil for very long hours."

"Your concern is touching, Dr. St. Cleer," said Joshua. "But there is never a shortage of labor; there are always many to replace the ones who sicken and die."

Mark's expression became steely. He rose. "Unfortunately you are right, Mr. Tregarth. There will, I fear, always be an abundance of labor to be wronged and exploited by men such as yourself. I see now that I have wasted my time and yours. Good night." With a curt bow, he turned on his heel and left the room.

"How dare he?" sputtered Isolde. "The effrontery of him! Telling you how to run your mine and then insulting you—"

"The fellow's a bloody Nosey Parker!" snorted Matthew. "Ought to be taught a lesson, sticking his nose where it don't belong!"

"I am shocked that Dr. Pendarvis allows him to share his practice," said Isolde.

Joshua made a dismissive gesture. "The man's a fool—pay him no mind. His head is full of ridiculous notions from his studies, that is all. I doubt he'll suggest them to any others now. And if he does, he'll receive the same response—and be a laughingstock."

"I'm certain you are right, Joshua," said Tamara coolly. "You have shown him how useless it is to appeal to the better nature of a mine owner." Rigid with contempt, she stalked out.

* * *

ECHOES OF THE HEART

Just before noon on Midsummer Eve, Lamorna knocked at the door of Kitty's room. It was already hot and sultry, the air nearly motionless. Lamorna had slept later than usual herself, but there was still no sound from behind Kitty's door. Twisting the knob, she went in and a stale odor wafted toward her. The room was in semi-darkness, the heavy curtains drawn against the sunlight.

"Kitty?" she said softly, moving across the floor to the three banks of windows. The heavy, still air from outside was preferable to that in the room. Kitty lay curled on one side, her nightgown bunched round her knees, her brown hair covering one cheek.

"Kitty, wake up." Still she did not stir. Lamorna, herself a light sleeper, did not understand how Kitty's slumber could be so long and deep. She shook her gently but there was no response, just the girl's even breathing. She felt the thinness of her beneath her nightdress, her bony shoulders and arms.

On the dresser was a china basin and a pitcher of water. Taking her handkerchief, she moistened it and went over to the bed. "Wake up, Kitty, 'tis Midsummer Eve. Wake up, my dear."

Kitty shifted, mumbling something. Lamorna pressed the wet handkerchief to her brow and the younger girl moaned, opening her eyes. For a few moments she looked blankly at Lamorna, her pupils strangely no bigger than pinpricks.

" 'Tis Midsummer Eve, Kitty. We are going to Padstow later for the festival, remember?" Lamorna once again dipped the cloth in the basin and touched it to Kitty's throat.

"Stop it, Lamorna," Kitty suddenly wailed. To Lamorna's shocked dismay, she flung out her arm, knocking over the basin and spilling the water on the bedclothes.

"Now see what you've done!" Kitty cried. "Why did you come in here, Lamorna? No one else minds me sleeping late! They leave me alone—why can't you?" She cast off the wet linens, trembling with fury.

Lamorna, stricken, hurried out of the room. What on earth

had she done to so anger the girl? And in Heaven's name why did she act as though she hated her?

Yet at luncheon, Kitty was her own placid, remote self. Stealing glances at her, Lamorna found it difficult to equate the quiet girl dressed in a demure white gown with the one who had turned on her so violently not two hours before, her face contorted, her eyes burning with contempt. These sudden and rare bursts of temper were alarming, yet they seemed to be aimed at her alone. Lamorna had never seen Kitty act that way in front of her father or Denzella. Kitty avoided her—indeed, avoided them all whenever possible—staying in her room or taking walks in the gardens with only Millie, her dog, for company.

It was seven o'clock that evening when the Roscarrocks rode into Padstow. The ostlers took charge of their horses while they entered the front room of the Bull and Clover. The inn was crowded and noisy, but the landlord spotted them immediately and led them through the public rooms to a private parlor. He spoke of pheasant and roast lamb, and, with John's approval, left to order their dinner.

Soon wine was brought and dishes laid before them, but Lamorna had little appetite.

"You will offend mine host's sensibilities," said John.

" 'Tis too hot for soup," said Lamorna.

"And you, Kitty, does the heat bother you as well?"

"There are the Tregarths," said Denzella, glancing out the window at the side street. "We should ask them to join us, John."

"By all means, cousin," he said and went from the room. When he returned, Isolde and Tamara were with him. The landlord bustled in, pulling out chairs for the ladies and sharply motioning to the waiters for more settings and food. Matthew entered, followed by Joshua.

"This is most pleasant," said Matthew. "How d'you do,

Miss Roscarrock, Lady Roscarrock? And Miss Kitty. 'Tis a hot Midsummer Eve this year."

Tamara's face was downcast; she had barely spoken and there were dark circles round her eyes. Lamorna now knew of her engagement to Lord Trevanion as did all of Cornwall. She had been terribly shocked and distressed when Denzella had told her, and had ridden over to Tregartha only to be told that Miss Tamara was indisposed and could not see anyone. With Tamara shut up in her room, Isolde had given strict instructions that Lady Roscarrock was not to be admitted; the girl needed no ally in her sulks and tantrums.

The men were deep in conversation about estate matters, and Isolde and Denzella were happily trading bits of gossip. Lamorna leaned across to speak to her friend.

"Tamara, did they tell you I came to see you?"

Tamara glanced up and Lamorna winced at the weary misery in her eyes. She had obviously not eaten or slept well in weeks. "I knew nothing of it," she whispered. "But I am not surprised. Do not worry about me, Lamorna. I am not going to marry Lord Trevanion—I'll think of something. The date is still months away; there will be no wedding until Isolde's child is born. Something will turn up." She gave a ghost of her former smile. "At least that is what I tell myself. If I have to leave Tregartha for good, I will do so."

Yet where would she go? Lamorna wondered. She was dependent on her family and had no money of her own. She could sell her jewels, but what would she live on once the price they fetched was gone? Lamorna desperately wanted to help her friend but was at a loss to know how.

Denzella's voice interrupted her musing. "Kitty, Lamorna, 'tis time to go. They will be lighting the barrels soon."

On Midsummer Eve barrels of tar were lit throughout the streets of Padstow, the town's answer to the bonfires raging on the cliffs and moors. They burned from the outskirts all the way down to the quay overlooking the river Camel. Outside the inn the crowd had gathered and begun to move slowly toward the river. Midsummer Eve was a festive occasion; the girls and young women wore wreaths of flowers on their heads and their best gowns. Boys carried handfuls of furze and sycamore, collected since May Day, to be burned later in the fires. Excitement ran high in the teeming, bustling streets.

Tamara and Lamorna managed to stay together, shunted down the sloping street by the crowd. But they had lost sight of John and the rest of the Tregarths, though ahead of them Lamorna saw Denzella's head covered by her lace cap and assumed she had charge of Kitty. It was growing dark and soon would be nearly impossible to find anyone. They were all to meet back at the Bull and Clover in several hours.

The two young women watched as, one by one, the barrels dotting the street were lit and the flames shot up with a roar. The crowd clapped, cheered, and moved on. Musicians played fiddles and recorders, and the beat of drums reverberated through the town. The sky above was purple-black, a breeze swirling the warm, heavy air.

When they were close to the quay, the throngs divided on two sides of the street. Lamorna and Tamara stood at the edge of the crowd while those about them said, "Do 'ee hear they? Be they comin'?" And then came the sound of running feet before the young men came into view, a long line of them racing down the center of the street, bright torches held high and swinging in a circular motion in imitation of the sun's movement in the heavens. Much skill and dexterity was required of the torch-bearers as the torches themselves were awkward and heavy. The people cheered as they passed, calling out to the young men.

One glanced over to respond to a jest and lost his balance. He fell heavily against Lamorna, the torch spinning out of his hand and hitting Tamara's sleeve. She screamed as the flames burned through the fabric and seared her skin. Swiftly a man gripped her arm and put out the flames, but Tamara was near to swooning with terror and pain.

"Clumsy lummox," said a woman to the youth. " 'Ee could have killed this poor lady. 'Ee ought not to be a torch-bearer!"

The young man looked horrified as he gazed at Tamara; he mumbled something and fled, pushing his way through the crowd.

The woman turned to Tamara. " 'Ee must cover the burn with wet bramble leaves and say the rhyme. Do 'ee know it?

> There came three angels out of the east
> One brought fire and two brought frost;
> Out fire and in frost,
> In the name of the Father, Son, and Holy Ghost!"

"No," objected the man who had doused the flames. "Goose grease be what 'ee wants, miss."

Tamara gave a moan and Lamorna said quickly, "Thank you both for your help. I'll take her to the inn. Come along, Tamara." Putting her arm about her friend's shoulders, she led her up the street. "I know it must hurt terribly. Drat that careless lad. But surely the landlord's wife will know what to do. Does it hurt very much?"

"More than I would wish," murmured Tamara.

They trudged away from the noisy quay and gradually the crowd thinned; the streets grew empty and quiet. Passing the shuttered shops and darkened houses, they made their way to the inn.

The Bull and Clover looked nearly deserted. A solitary boy was sweeping a broom across the stone floor; he stopped and stared at the two ladies.

"Where is the landlord?" asked Lamorna.

"Gone to the quay."

"And his lady? Is she gone as well?"

The boy nodded.

Lamorna bit her lip. "This lady needs help—she was burned by one of the torches and is in great pain."

The lad glanced at the charred fabric about Tamara's wrist.

"I be sorry, miss, but there be no doctor t'home tonight. The whole town be at the quay for the festivities." He would have been down there himself had he not broken a tray of glasses and incurred the landlord's wrath.

Tamara leaned against Lamorna, whimpering. "I feel ill," she mumbled. "I fear—I fear I'm going to be sick."

Lamorna helped her into a chair. In the lantern-light of the tap room, Tamara's face had a pale, greenish tint. What am I going to do? thought Lamorna frantically. She must have help. The rest of them would not return for hours yet and there was no hope of finding them in the host of merry-makers. "Don't worry, Tamara, it will be all right," she said.

The girl's answer was another pitiful moan. She had leaned her head back against the wall, her eyes closed, desperately trying to fight her panic and nausea. Lamorna turned to the boy again. "There must be someone you can send for—or tell us who we—"

She never finished her sentence. The door of the inn opened and Lamorna gave a wild sob of relief. "Dirk!" she cried, flinging herself into his arms. They tightened about her and his lips pressed against her hair.

The boy, still holding his broom, goggled at them. Tamara's eyes opened; dazed with pain, she regarded her friend locked in a tall man's embrace.

"Tamara's wrist is badly burned. She needs a doctor."

Dirk looked past her to where his half-sister sat. Swiftly he was at her side and gently taking hold of her arm, examining the blackened fabric and the red, blistered skin beneath it. Tamara moaned again.

"Fetch brandy and scissors," Dirk said over his shoulder to the boy. Relieved to be given an order he could follow, he quickly did as Dirk asked.

Lifting the glass to Tamara's lips, he said, "Drink this. It will numb the pain some. I must cut away your sleeve—it will only be worse if we delay."

ECHOES OF THE HEART

Tamara nodded, drinking a swallow of the brandy. "Once again, sir, you have come to my aid."

He made no reply. Taking the scissors from the hovering boy, he carefully began to cut her sleeve, drawing it away from her injured wrist. She gave an agonized cry and bit her lips. Lamorna took her other hand and squeezed it, watching anxiously.

Dirk rose. "I'm sorry to have hurt you, Miss Tregarth, but the pain would have been worse had you waited for the doctor to remove the fabric." He turned to Lamorna. "There's a doctor in Pendreath. I'll go for him now; my horse is outside."

"Dr. St. Cleer? Oh yes, Dirk, thank you!" said Lamorna. Pressing her hands hastily, he was gone.

"Who—who is that?" asked Tamara weakly. "I saw him once before in Padstow—he pulled me away from a horse and cart."

Flushing, Lamorna turned to the boy. "You may leave us now, and get on with your duties."

When the boy had left them alone, she said, " 'Tis a very long story, Tamara. He . . . is the man I love. His name is Dirk Killigrew. He was shipwrecked once off Rowenstow and was brought to our vicarage to recover."

"He is a sailor?"

"A—a fair-trader," whispered Lamorna. "But you shouldn't talk, Tamara. Have a little more brandy."

Tamara did not argue. She took another sip and leaned back against the wall. And Lamorna told her everything. The lantern-light shone on the beamed ceiling, on the polished surfaces of the small tables, on the rows of glasses, tumblers, and tankards lining the shelves. The boy did not disturb them again though they could hear the sound of dishes clattering off in the kitchen.

It was over an hour later when Mark strode into the inn. "Good evening, Lady Roscarrock," he said.

"Miss Tregarth is in severe pain, Dr. St. Cleer," she said. "We're most grateful to you for coming."

He took Tamara's wrist in both of his hands. "I'll need clean strips of gauze and a basin of cool, clean water."

"Yes, there's a boy somewhere," said Lamorna. "I'll ask him."

Tamara sighed. "Thank you for coming, Doctor. I—I feared you might not wish to."

"Your brother and father did not accompany you?" he asked.

"Yes, but they are somewhere in Padstow. Lady Roscarrock and I became separated from them, and then one of the young men stumbled and his torch fell against my arm."

"You are fortunate the injury is not far worse, Miss Tregarth, though I know it is vastly uncomfortable." Lamorna returned and held the pewter basin while he washed the burns. Tamara pressed her lips together, whimpering again.

Mark wrapped the strips of cotton gauze around her wrist. "Instruct your maid to do this once a day—remove the gauze, bathe the skin, and then apply fresh gauze."

"Is there not some ointment?" asked Lamorna.

Mark shook his head. " 'Tis better the skin remains clean and dry for now. I will call at Tregartha the day after tomorrow, Miss Tregarth, to see how it is healing. Unless, of course, you would prefer to send for my uncle."

Tamara flushed. "I would prefer you to call, Dr. St. Cleer; my brother is generally out all day so you would not be forced to see him. The truth is he cannot be told anything—he is convinced that he is infallible, that he always knows best."

Mark was startled by the bitterness in her voice. He scrutinized her face in the lamplight. She did not look nearly as well as she had on the night he had called at Tregartha; her face was pale and drawn, the corners of her mouth turned down. Her dark eyes were desolate. Evidently she was troubled by much more than a burned wrist; he found himself wondering what it was.

"Do not distress yourself on my behalf, Miss Tregarth," he answered. "The fault was undoubtedly mine for attempting to interfere in the business of mining. Your brother, I daresay, is no different and no worse than the rest of the mine-owners and shareholders." He shrugged. "They see figures in a ledger and little else."

" 'Twas brave of you even so. There are not many who care to cross swords with Joshua. I assure you he shows the members of his own family no more consideration than his miners."

He regarded her thoughtfully. Glancing away, her color higher, she said briskly, "At what time will you call?"

"Shall we say eleven o'clock?"

"I will be waiting."

"Good night, Miss Tregarth."

"Good night, Dr. St. Cleer."

Outside in the muffling darkness behind the inn, Lamorna and Dirk shared a last passionate embrace. "Come to me," he begged her. "Soon. I've waited—so long."

She nodded. "Wait for me."

Twenty

The following day Sir John announced that business affairs connected with the price of corn would take him to Falmouth for a fortnight. At these words Lamorna's face grew warm and she tried to hide her pleasure and relief. A horrible thought occurred to her—what if he wished her to accompany him? But she needn't have worried. He had another companion in mind.

"What do you say, Kitty? Will you come with me? There will be much to do and see in Falmouth, I promise you."

Kitty's gaze was bent downward. "I—I'd rather stay here, Father."

"Nonsense. 'Tis years since you visited Falmouth. We'll go to all the shops and I daresay there will be parties and a ball or two to attend. A change of scenery will do you good."

In surprise Lamorna saw that Kitty was trembling; she lifted a flushed face to her father. "B-but Millie's puppies will soon be born."

Sir John gave a derisive laugh. "The bitch will do very well without you, Kitty."

"Please, Father," she begged, her voice quavering. "I prefer to stay here."

His face darkened. "Not to see that young whelp Philip, I trust."

Kitty looked shocked. "Of course not, Father."

"Leave the girl be, John," said Denzella. "If she has no wish to go, then surely there's an end on it. There will be many other opportunities to see Falmouth—I very much doubt the place will be laid waste in the near future." There was amusement in her tone.

For an instant John's eyes flamed with fury, but Lamorna had no time to reflect on this as Denzella's next words caused her blood to run thick and slow.

"Why not take Lamorna? She has never seen Falmouth. Kitty and I will do very well on our own." Lamorna, a lump in her throat, did not see the odd exchange of glances which passed between her husband and his cousin. On his part, barely suppressed rage; on hers, cool significance.

From far away Lamorna heard John say, "Another time, perhaps. Now that I have time to reflect I believe I should go alone."

Lamorna's head spun in relief; she reached for her wine-glass, not trusting herself to speak.

Denzella's mouth tightened. But she did not dare argue; she had done her best. If Lamorna had shown a little pleasure at the notion, perhaps John would have been persuaded to take her with him. But the wretched girl had noticeably shrunk from the very idea—she was as bad as he. There would be no heir to Kilworthy if the present circumstances continued. Denzella seethed inwardly. Was it for this she had lain awake night after night, planning? Was it for this she had convinced her cousin to marry again, and to take the vicarage girl? Her anger and frustration rose, demanding a target.

She had been grossly deceived in Lamorna. With every luxury provided, she had only one duty in return—to please her husband. How dare this insignificant, dowerless chit use her energies to tend sick villagers when she refused to lift one finger to charm her husband? Lamorna was as much a failure as Constance had been. Within a few months Denzella had realized the true state of affairs, while Lamorna was still stupidly ignorant. She managed to derive a contemptuous satisfaction from the girl's prolonged innocence, yet her hands itched to take her by the shoulders and shake her until her teeth rattled.

John left for Falmouth early the next morning. Kitty, to her surprise, was up betimes and suggested a walk in the gardens. Happy to oblige, Lamorna got her straw bonnet and the two of them spent a pleasant morning speculating on how many puppies Millie would deliver. Yet Lamorna's thoughts were concentrated in quite another direction; her surroundings were little more than an inconsequential background to the intoxicating significance of the day. After luncheon Kitty retired to her room to rest and Denzella left for Landrawna to see Mistress Poldew. Watching her ride away from the window, Lamorna then changed her elegant morning gown for one of lavender sprigged muslin.

"Where 'ee be goin', my lady?" asked Maggie.

"For a ride," was the airy reply.

Maggie studied her mistress's radiant face, the newly-washed lustrous brown curls, her sparkling violet-blue eyes. Lamorna was humming to herself, barely aware of her.

"Don't go, my lady," she said.

Lamorna glanced up with a nervous laugh. "What?"

"Don't go, Miss Lamorna."

"Go where, Maggie?"

"To him. The fair-trader. I—I be afeared for 'ee."

Stiffening, Lamorna said, "There's no reason, Maggie. Why shouldn't I go out riding? I do it often enough."

"No good will come of it, my lady," said her maid. "Just now there came a fearful feelin' over me, not like I've had in a long time."

"What do you mean?" Lamorna's voice was sharp.

"I were a 'footling', Miss Lamorna. Before I were born I weren't facin' the right way; the midwife took hold o' my feet and pulled me out. Most would've died and their mothers likely, too. There be not many footlings in this world, that be a fact. Some say that they can see into the future. I can't, not like that, but once in a while a feeling'll come over me, a warning. Before I was took ill with the smallpox I had 'un. I knew summat bad were in store."

"And you sense that I am in danger now?"

Maggie nodded stubbornly.

"What about before my marriage? Had you no sense of warning then?"

Maggie had not thought her mistress's voice could sound so cold or spiteful. Wretchedly she shook her head.

"Because, Maggie, that would have been the time to warn me, before I made the worst mistake of my life. But instead you tried to make me forget Dirk just as Deborah did. And now when I'm happy, when we've been given another chance, you want me to be a prisoner at Kilworthy."

"I only want 'ee to be safe," said Maggie softly.

When Lamorna reached Dirk's townhouse, she cast a quick look up and down the street before urging her mare down the narrow alley to the mews. Despite the warm weather, the hood of her cloak was pulled low over her face. She had avoided the town's busy areas and taken a roundabout route.

She knocked at the side door, her heart thumping madly. He opened it himself and they took one long look at one another. In her eyes was a brilliance which made his heart turn over. Taking her small hand, he drew her inside.

Then her hood fell back, revealing the tumbled curls, the rosy cheeks. She gave a breathless gasp as his mouth fastened on hers, as the tremors shot through them both.

Lifting her in his arms, he carried her upstairs. Seeing her against his pillow sobered him; he realized what she was prepared to risk, that she had everything to lose while he had only to gain. But she reached for him and his momentary hesitation fled. His pulses throbbing maddeningly as he caught her to him and was lost.

On the day that Mark St. Cleer was to call, Tamara had risen early. The pain in her wrist was unrelenting but that was not the only reason for her sleeplessness. She could not stop thinking about the good-looking young doctor, the way he had stood up to Joshua on behalf of the miners, and the way he had gently held her burned wrist as he cleansed and bandaged it.

Tamara's maid helped her into her pale green bodice and overskirt which was drawn back to show the pretty printed petticoat beneath. She refused breakfast but drank three cups of tea. A little before eleven she went below to the drawing room, relieved that Isolde did not feel well and was staying in bed. She had not told her family of Dr. St. Cleer's proposed call; she had merely said that they had met accidentally in Padstow and he had tended her. By the time the rest of the Roscarrocks and Tregarths had returned to the inn, both Mark and Dirk were gone.

At half past eleven Tamara began to pace the room, glancing from time to time out the window or at the tall mirror to adjust her lace-trimmed cap. She had given up all pretense of reading and her wrist hurt too much to do needlework.

Perhaps he had decided not to come; perhaps he had decided it was unwise. Yet he had promised her that he would. Her wrist throbbed and stung, her tension and urgency mounted. She had thought of little else but this visit since Midsummer Eve and now it looked as though he had forgotten all about her.

Where on earth was he? It was now ten minutes short of the noon hour, and he had said eleven o'clock. This morning upon waking he must have had second thoughts; he assumed she had realized the inadvisability of his calling at Tregartha and would instead summon Dr. Pendarvis. He wasn't coming.

Nearly frantic with disappointment, she went out of the drawing room and began to climb the stairs. She would send for Dr. Pendarvis, and she would have a few words to say to him about his nephew's neglect.

As she reached the landing there came a sharp rapping at the front door. Pausing, she heard the footman open it and

Mark's voice announcing himself and asking to see her. Taking a deep breath, she slowly descended the staircase. Mark stood in the hall; when he saw her he bowed. "Good day, Miss Tregarth."

"Good day, Dr. St. Cleer," she answered coolly and led the way into the drawing room.

"How is your wrist?"

"It pains me dreadfully."

"I am sorry to hear that." Sitting down beside her, he took her arm and unwound the bandages.

"I had given you up, Doctor. 'Tis an hour later than you said and I assumed you were not coming." There was a rare haughtiness in her voice born of unhappiness, pain, and frustration.

Mark looked directly into her eyes. "A cottage child was taken ill in the night, Miss Tregarth." He did not add that he had just returned to his house a short while before riding to Tregartha, taking only enough time to change his clothes and eat a quick meal. He was exhausted, and there were other calls to make.

"In the night? Yet half a day has passed since then."

"Your injury was not as serious, Miss Tregarth. An hour later—several hours—would make no difference."

Her face flamed; she felt as though she had been flatly rejected. "Oh, no? If you had any idea of the pain I'm suffering! But of course that is beside the point—your other patients are far more important than I!" She flinched as he began to spread some ointment on her blistered skin. "Ow! What a foul smell! Do you expect me to use this?"

"Not if you don't want your flesh to heal, Miss Tregarth. Perhaps you'd prefer to complain about the pain," he said deliberately.

She snatched her hand away. "How dare you? I'll wager you did not treat the child so unkindly!"

He stood up, setting down the jar of ointment. "The child

is dead. Apply this ointment several times a day. Then wrap your wrist with fresh strips each time."

Stunned, she could only stare at him. For the first time she noticed the lines of strain about his eyes and mouth, his weary expression. Lifting his black bag, he turned to go.

"Dr. St. Cleer, please, I ask your pardon. I am not at all myself today . . ."

"Henceforth I suggest you send for my great-uncle, Miss Tregarth," said Mark. "He will no doubt oblige you by calling punctually. Good day to you."

Tamara heard the great door shut behind him. She burst into tears.

Millie had her puppies, five of them, while John was still in Falmouth. Mrs. Quill discovered them at the back of the buttery early one morning, tiny hairless balls, eyes tightly shut, mouths rooting for their mother's milk. Kitty was delighted with the news and spent much of the following days at their side.

In another week or so Dirk would be off to France once his ship was loaded to his satisfaction. He did not enlighten Lamorna about the cargo leaving Cornwall—ore confiscated from Wheel Charity and prepared in kettles in the cellars of Landrawna, ore that would never make a profit for the Tregarths.

"John will be returning soon," she told him one afternoon. "Denzella had a letter from him yesterday. How I dread it—not that he pays me the slightest attention. For that I am exceedingly grateful."

His fist clenched. "I could not bear it if I thought he—I'd take you away for good whether you wished it or no." He bent and kissed her.

"I'll never understand why he wished to marry me," she mused. " 'Twas Denzella's notion but he agreed to it."

"I'll never understand the gentry, nor do I wish to," said

Dirk roughly. "They be devils, most of them. They'd grind us into the earth with the heels of their boots if given half the chance."

Lamorna was shocked at his animosity. "Oh, surely not all of them. Dr. St. Cleer is a good man, and my uncle—and Tamara."

"Tamara Tregarth," he repeated, his eyes narrowing.

"What is it, Dirk?"

Shaking his head, he said, " 'Tis naught. 'Tis only that I've no cause to love the Tregarths."

"Because Joshua Tregarth is a magistrate?"

When he did not reply, she clasped his arm. "Tell me, Dirk."

And so he did.

Before Dirk sailed for France, he and Lamorna met on the moor at the dolmen Boscivey Quoit. The ancient monument of three pillars supporting a capstone was considered ominously enigmatic by the local people and generally avoided. Strange lights were seen from time to time dancing above the dolmen; they were presumed to be piskies at work and no one liked to disturb the contrary creatures. Their lights had led many a traveller astray in the darkness. Fear of the gigantic structure made it an ideal hiding place for smuggled goods, though some of the fair-traders made it their business to steer clear of it as well.

Inside the dolmen they could not be seen, and it was safer to meet there than in Padstow. After a time they headed toward the sea and came upon a tiny old chapel. It was roofless, with ivy coiled about the crumbling walls, and red flowers growing along the foundations. Dismounting, Dirk pushed aside the concealing vines and brambles and they stepped into the cool interior. The floor was of smoothly polished stone, and in it was carved a basin where water gushed and gurgled.

Lamorna knelt down and touched her fingertips to the

water. "A spring has been filling this basin for many years," she said.

"Since the days of the Old Church, before Queen Elizabeth?" Dirk asked.

"Far before that. When the first monks came here from Ireland one of them built this chapel. That was over a thousand years ago, and the spring itself must be much older."

Dirk flushed. He knew little of history; his education had been too sketchy to include it. The reminder that she knew far more than he did of many things mortified him.

She rose. " 'Tis a holy place, a holy well. Can you not feel it? 'Tis here I make my vow to love and honor you, Dirk Killigrew. For you are in truth my husband before God." Her eyes were grave, the violet-blue had deepened.

He took one of her hands in both of his, his embarrassment forgotten. "Here I take you for my wedded wife. I vow we'll never be parted, even in death." His voice shook slightly.

"Shhh. 'Tis bad luck to say such a thing," she whispered. Suddenly cold, she shivered.

"I think the rain is coming in from the sea," he said, putting his arm round her. "We ought to go."

She nodded, leaning against him, but the chill remained.

When Lamorna awoke the next morning she was in low spirits. Dirk was gone for weeks and John would be returning shortly from Falmouth. Life at Kilworthy would return to its usual pattern and the realization oppressed her.

" 'Tis for the best, my lady," said Maggie. She had matured a great deal in the past months and no longer addressed her mistress as an awe-struck village lass. " 'Ee can settle down now, stop flittin' about like a bird about to burst into song. I do hope Miss Denzella b'ain't took notice of 'ee." Ever since coming to Kilworthy, Maggie had sensed something odd in Denzella, something which surfaced once in a while when she was displeased. Maggie did not like her eyes, which seemed to have no color of their own but were gray or blue or green depending on what she was wearing; they, too, were unnatural. She might be the master's cousin, but Maggie thought she was not that different from Old Rose who used to live outside of Rowenstow. Miss Denzella was thought a wise woman but Maggie did not trust her and went out of her way to avoid her as much as possible.

"I'll look in on Kitty—perhaps she'll want to take the puppies out to the garden later." Lamorna went down the hall to Kitty's room and knocked on the door.

"Go away," came the answer, followed by a painful moan.

"What's wrong—are you ill?" asked Lamorna. Without waiting for a reply, she went inside.

The girl lay curled on one side, her face creased with pain.

"What is it, Kitty? I'm sorry to intrude but perhaps there's something I can do for you."

"No one can do anything!" cried Kitty, sitting up. " 'Tis—'tis only that my—my courses have begun. There—are you satisfied? I didn't want them—I—" She dissolved into angry tears, and Lamorna hurried over to the bed and sat down beside her.

"You are growing up, Kitty, that's all. There is nothing to be afraid of. I wondered why you had not started them before; I was barely thirteen. 'Tis natural, my dear. Do . . . do you know what to do?"

Kitty's head nodded, still pressed to the pillow.

"Well then, I'll order some chamomile tea to be brought up. Deborah always made me a pot when I needed it, and this afternoon you ought to feel better."

"I don't want any tea. Please leave me alone, Lamorna. And promise me you'll say nothing to Denzella."

In surprise Lamorna said, "Not if you don't wish it, Kitty. But 'tis nothing to be ashamed of."

Kitty made no response.

* * *

Stricken with remorse and self-loathing, Tamara had made inquiries about the dead child Mark had attended and sent baskets of food and sundries to his family. Not that worldly goods would make the slightest dent in their grief, but she had to do something to make up for the way she had acted with Mark. And she was determined to make amends there, too. Tamara had, simply and thoroughly, fallen in love with him. He had to be shown that she was not like the rest of her family, deserving of his contempt. She knew he would not call at Tregartha again, so she would have to go to him. She dismissed the stricture that unmarried young ladies did not visit the houses of gentlemen as unimportant. Thinking about the doctor had kept her awake for several nights running; the pain in her wrist gradually eased, and Lord Trevanion no longer filled her with misery. She was certain she would not marry him now.

Locating Mark's house was not difficult; she merely questioned a boy at the blacksmithy. Yet finding him at home was much harder. On two mornings she knocked at the whitewashed stone cottage trimmed in dark green, but was disappointed to realize the place was empty. On the third occasion she called at mid-afternoon, hoping she would have better luck. On the ride across Whistmoor the sky opened up, drenching her quickly. Ill-tempered, she would not consider going back but urged her horse onward along the track as the rain pelted them furiously. By the time her horse was clattering over the stone bridge beside the church, her straw bonnet was ruined, her hair dripping, her clothes sodden. A cool wind made her shiver; she longed for a cup of tea and a fire. She no longer cared that she looked a mess, but if he were not at home she would likely burst a blood vessel.

Mark was shocked to see Tamara standing on his doorstep, wet, bedraggled and woebegone, a far cry from the haughty young lady he had attended in the drawing room at Tregartha.

"Miss Tregarth!"

"I—I've come to apologize. I've tried to before, but you are seldom at home, Doctor."

"You must get out of the rain," he said. "Come in." Taking her arm, he led her into the small but pleasant parlor. On either side of the stone fireplace were rows of shelves filled with books; a red carpet covered the polished floorboards and there were red curtains at the windows. Tamara went gratefully over to the hearth and spread out her hands.

Mark left the room but was back shortly with a towel. "You had better wait out the storm here," he said. "I doubt it will last long. If you will permit me, I'll make tea."

Tamara rubbed her hair vigorously and took off her riding jacket. Beneath it her chemise and bodice were only slightly damp. She sat down on one of the carved oak armchairs and held out her stockinged feet to the warmth of the blaze.

A short while later Mark returned, carrying a tray which he set down on the tapestry runner atop the gateleg table. He poured out two mugs of tea while Tamara belatedly played to convention, saying, "I daresay you consider it most forward of me to come here like this, but I very much wanted to apologize for my behavior the other day when—when you called at Tregartha."

"There was no need, Miss Tregarth; I fear I myself was rude. The boy's death was preying on my mind."

"What was wrong with him?"

"I believe 'twas his appendix that ruptured. Yet I cannot know for certain. Poor lad, his sufferings were excessive, and I could do nothing. He could not even hold down the laudanum I tried to give him for the pain."

"And I scolded you for being late."

"His mother had sent for a charmer at first," he went on as though he had not heard her. "When her spells worked no improvement on the lad, I was summoned. And was as ineffectual as that toothless old crone had been." He shook himself. "Will you have more tea, Miss Tregarth?"

"Yes, please. But Dr. St. Cleer, you did all you could. My

friend, Lady Roscarrock, speaks very highly of you. You have done well by a number of the villagers."

He gave a fleeting smile. "I owe a great deal to Lady Roscarrock. Had she not placed her trust in me, none of the people of Landrawna would have. How is your wrist? As you are here I should look at it."

She held out her arm for his inspection. "Won't you call again—at your convenience, of course—to make certain it continues to heal properly?"

"Your brother would not welcome another visit from me, Miss Tregarth, for any reason. He has spoken to my great-uncle who suggests I give Tregartha a wide berth."

Tamara colored. "I care nothing about what my brother thinks. I—I wish you to call."

Mark rose, took a long pipe from the mantel, and began to fill it. "I have heard, Miss Tregarth, that you are to marry Lord Trevanion. May I offer my sincerest best wishes?"

There was a short silence. Then Tamara said in a low, muffled voice, "I will never marry him. I would rather starve."

Mark faced her, smiling faintly. "You would not rather starve, I am certain. You can have no idea what it is to be hungry—or poor."

"Have you, Doctor?" she asked sharply.

"Aye, Miss Tregarth. Medical school was very expensive and so were food and lodgings in London. There were times when I did not know when next I would eat."

She frowned. "But your family—your uncle . . ."

"My parents have been dead many years, and my uncle I had no intention of imposing on. Do not look so distressed, Miss Tregarth. I assure you I am far better off than most of my patients; I consider myself a most fortunate man."

She gazed into the fire. "But . . . you have no wife. Do you not get lonely?"

"I am used to a solitary state. And I have little with which to support a wife, would one have me."

Tamara could think of nothing to reply to this that would

not have been outrageous. Even her temerity had limits. "Well, as you will not come to Tregartha, I will come here," she said, flushing. "You—you saw the blisters oozing . . ."

Mark sighed. "Miss Tregarth, that would scarcely be wise. You are engaged to be wed—surely I do have to tell you that by coming here you—"

"—And I have told you that I will not marry him," she cut in heatedly. "My brother chose the bridegroom, not I." Tamara rose. "I believe the rain has stopped, Dr. St. Cleer. Thank you for the tea. I shall come again soon."

When she had gone, Mark carried the tea things into the kitchen. The widow who cooked and cleaned for him would see to them when she came to prepare his supper. She was neat and efficient and had a light hand with pastry.

In the parlor he took down one of his medical books, but he found himself reading the same paragraph over and over. The study of rickets was unable to hold his attention. The scent Tamara used—lily of the valley, he decided—was still in the air. She was not the spoiled girl he had first presumed; he suspected it was she who had sent food to the family of the dead little boy. It would be just like her—impulsive, generous . . . But she could well afford to be generous, living in luxury at Tregartha. She had no notion of another way of life, no matter her words of protestation. That she would marry Lord Trevanion he had no doubt, though he found the idea most unsettling.

On the night that John returned he was annoyed that Kitty did not come down to dinner to greet him. "Where is the girl?"

"She has not felt well these last couple of days," Lamorna said. "I looked in on her before dinner and she was sleeping." And it was one of those deep, heavy sleeps from which it was not possible to rouse her, she thought to herself.

"You're looking well, Lamorna, I must say. What has

wrought this change—my absence or my return?" he asked ironically.

"Lamorna has been riding regularly every afternoon," said Denzella smoothly. "Apparently it agrees with her. As for myself, I have never quite trusted horses. Doubtless because I was raised in a town rather than in the country. Skittish, temperamental beasts, I've always thought."

"No jewels tonight, Lamorna? Is my homecoming not sufficient reason to wear them?" asked her husband, frowning.

"I am sorry, John," she said simply. She had not worn any of the Roscarrock heirlooms since he had left; tonight she had not remembered to ask Maggie to take them out.

"Tell us about your trip, John," said Denzella. "Does the price of corn this year suit you?"

"It does. I have decided to sell a large portion abroad this year, so more will need to be grown. Tomorrow I will instruct Mr. Trennow to have the men plow the field close to the Shuddering Stone."

Denzella raised her brows. "Is that wise, cousin? You know the old tale. They may refuse."

"Then they shall receive no wages," said John. "I believe they will comply with my wishes."

"What are you talking about?" asked Lamorna.

John grimaced. "The villagers have some ridiculous notion about not plowing or building on that field. 'Tis said it was once a burial place. But 'tis my land and I will not be ruled by superstition. If the people wish to work for me, they'll do as I bid them."

"You know what they'll say," said Denzella. "That misfortune will come to Kilworthy, that disturbing the ground that has always lain fallow will bring a curse on our heads."

After dinner Denzella and Lamorna went to the drawing room. She had to admit that Lamorna was looking especially beautiful, despite her lack of jewelry. John had noticed . . . perhaps there was still hope for them.

"Kitty should be up and about tomorrow," she said, pouring tea. "The first two days are the worst."

So Denzella knew. "She was quite overwrought—I was most anxious, but she refused to allow me to help, or even to sit with her."

"A typical moodiness appropriate to the occasion. It takes some like that. 'Tis about time—I was wondering when the girl would begin to grow up. Before long I will speak to John concerning her marriage."

"Marriage!" Lamorna cried, choking on her tea. "For Kitty?"

"Oh, not this year, but in another or two, perhaps."

"But Kitty is still a child in many ways—she is not like other girls her age. I cannot believe you are considering such a thing!"

Denzella's voice was cold. "This is not your concern, Lamorna. Need I remind you that you have but one service to perform—that of a good, obedient wife. The sooner Kitty is married, the better. She is a great heiress and will be much in demand."

Lamorna regarded her in dismay. "Surely John will not wish to lose her so soon."

"All fathers must lose their daughters one day," was the airy response.

Not long after, Lamorna went upstairs. She could not stop thinking of Denzella's determination to see Kitty wed within a year or so. That diffident, awkward, withdrawn girl, with her episodes of volatile emotions . . . it was madness. It would be a number of years before the girl was ready for marriage.

Maggie was already in her room, turning down her bed.

"I forgot to wear jewels tonight," Lamorna said. "Sir John was most displeased; yet I am surprised he noticed." A sudden fear struck her—did this attention denote a rekindled interest? Was he planning to visit her bed tonight? Her blood went cold at the thought.

"My lady . . . my lady!"

"Yes, Maggie, what is it?"

"I have summat bad to tell 'ee, my lady. 'Tis about the puppies."

"The puppies?" repeated Lamorna abstractedly.

"Ais, my lady. Millie came whinin' into the kitchen; she were wantin' to feed they, but they couldn't be found."

"Oh, Maggie, do you mean they are lost? Lost about the house somewhere?" In a place the size of Kilworthy that was a calamity. "We'll have to search for them—everyone must help. You ought to have told me before. The poor things . . . though they are probably asleep somewhere."

Maggie bit her lip. "I—I already looked for they, my lady. So did some o' the others. There b'ain't no need to look any longer." She paused. The distress in her face caused Lamorna to forget all about her husband. "They—they'd been drowned, Miss Lamorna, drowned in the tub o' water Kate had brought to scour the scullery floor."

Twenty-one

Sick and appalled, Lamorna went down the corridor and round the corner to Kitty's room. She knocked softly, not wanting to wake her were she still asleep. But Kitty called, "Come in."

She was huddled in a chair by the fire, her legs drawn up, her chin resting on her knees.

"How are you feeling, Kitty?" Lamorna asked, dreading to begin.

"If you've come to tell me about the puppies, I already know." Kitty did not look up from the flames; her face was ghostly pale except for the shadows under her eyes and cheekbones.

"I'm so sorry, Kitty. I promise you I'll find out who did such a horrible thing and send him or her packing."

"They were so small and helpless," Kitty said softly.

"Shall I sit with you?"

The girl shook her head. "They couldn't protect themselves," she murmured. Lamorna touched her shoulder and then left her alone.

But she herself was not about to retire for the night. Going to the kitchen, she told Mrs. Quill to make certain that all the servants assembled out in the yard at eight o'clock the following morning.

There was no doubt that the puppies had been deliberately killed. Who could have been cruel enough to do such a thing? Millie was known to be Kitty's dog, and the girl's delight in her puppies had been evident since their birth. It was almost as though someone had wanted to hurt Kitty and had chosen this way of doing so. But why should any of the staff wish to cause her pain? What had that timid girl done to any of them?

Lamorna slept fitfully, her dreams hideous. She had no appetite for breakfast or even the pot of tea which Maggie brought. Shortly before eight o'clock she went below.

In the yard outside the stables the servants, or at least most of them, had gathered and stood waiting, talking in low voices. Standing before them, she saw on a few faces impatience and resentment, but most appeared curious, even excited.

"As you know, Millie's litter of puppies was found drowned yesterday afternoon. Miss Kitty is terribly upset. It seems clear that someone at Kilworthy is to blame; if any of you knows who is responsible, I ask that you come and tell me privately." Her eyes moved over the crowd but she was no more enlightened than before. They were waiting for her to dismiss them; two of the maids were whispering back and forth.

"Kate, have you anything to say?" she asked.

The girl went scarlet, twisting her apron round her finger. "No, my lady," she mumbled.

"Very well. You may all go." Lamorna felt defeated; she very much doubted whether any of them would come to her with the truth. Watching them disperse in different directions, she heard a voice behind her.

"Such a to-do about nothing," Denzella said. "Do you realize how often whole litters of puppies and kittens are drowned? And you ought to know the servants will not betray one another. 'Twas a foolish thing to do, Lamorna."

"It was a brutal act, Denzella, wicked," cried Lamorna. "These puppies were Kitty's, not some poor family's in the village who could not afford to keep them."

Denzella shrugged. "They were beginning to get underfoot in the buttery. As time passed they would have become a nuisance."

"But to *kill* them, Denzella! They could have been sent to the stables or elsewhere. I cannot understand how you can take this matter so lightly. Someone deliberately killed Kitty's puppies! Have you seen Millie searching and crying for them? 'Tis enough to break your heart."

"She'll get over it when her milk dries up," said Denzella, turning back to go to the house.

Lamorna stood still, outraged by Denzella's callous indifference. She was content to let the matter drop, to regard the drowning of the dogs as of no consequence. Perhaps she herself was responsible! But what on earth would have been her reason? Surely she had no desire to hurt or punish Kitty. And despite what she had said, the puppies were as yet no trouble, confined for the most part to their basket, sleeping for long periods.

How I hate it here! she thought. The most magnificent estate in north Cornwall and yet a cheerless, dismal place. A house with no heart and no soul. Oh Dirk, how can I bear it? Her shoulders bent, she made her way upstairs and down the hallway. Passing John's room, she heard sounds within. Her husband, she thought, shuddering. There was a vile taste in her mouth. She decided to see Kitty; she did not wish to be alone just now.

Kitty was sitting in bed, drinking hot chocolate. "I did not hear you knock," she said coldly.

"I'm sorry, my dear. I didn't think—I wanted some company. May I open the curtains?"

"If you like."

Lamorna twisted the casement handles and pushed open the windows to clear the stuffy air from the room. Then she sat down on the window seat.

On the small table beside Kitty's bed was a blue bottle. "What is that?" she asked, only vaguely curious.

Kitty followed her glance. "Only laudanum."

Lamorna frowned. "Why do you take laudanum? You haven't a toothache, have you?"

Kitty shrugged. "Some nights I cannot sleep; it soothes me."

So that was the reason for her sluggishness some mornings, her difficulty in waking. The girl drugged herself, and possibly often.

Lamorna tried to speak lightly. " 'Tis useful, I know, for pain once in a while. My aunt took it occasionally for the stiffening in her joints. But she said, too, that it caused odious dreams."

"Your aunt was wrong," said Kitty in a hard, cold voice. "I do not dream at all."

Lamorna rose; she had no wish to antagonize the girl. "Oh? I'm relieved to hear it. I'll leave you to finish your breakfast. Come and see me later if you've a mind."

But Lamorna was determined to speak to John; the realization that Kitty drugged herself with laudanum was troubling. She went down the corridor to his room and knocked on the door.

He wore a silk dressing gown, elaborately embroidered with flowers and butterflies. Sitting at the gateleg table, he was eating his breakfast of ham and eggs. A jar of mustard stood beside his tankard of ale. At the sight of his wife, his brows raised.

"To what do I owe this unexpected honor?" he asked, rising.

She flushed. It was the first time she had been in his room and the realization was jarring. "I wish to speak with you privately, John."

"We can scarcely be more private than this. I understand you were up betimes this morning, addressing the servants. A most useless act, I daresay."

Her mouth tightened. " 'Tis about Kitty I wish to speak, sir."

"Yes? You will permit me to go on with my breakfast while it is still warm, I trust."

She nodded impatiently, glancing about the large room with its carved walnut furniture and panelling embossed with leaves, vines, and fruit. "She takes laudanum, John. She has just told me so."

"Surely, Lamorna, you must understand if she felt a need to resort to that last evening."

"The puppies, yes . . . but I fear she has taken it on many other occasions as well. Quite a few mornings she has proven difficult to rouse—I often wondered at the cause."

"Your concern is well-meaning, I know, but I do not believe it does her any harm. She is somewhat nervous, like her mother."

Lamorna drew her brows together. "You mean you know of it? Her use of this drug?"

John was cutting himself another piece of ham. "Yes, I know and Denzella does as well. So you see, Lamorna, there is no need to worry yourself."

"It cannot be good for her. There is sometimes a languor, an almost benumbed state that until now I could not account for. And her moods are odd, unpredictable. A few times she has flown at me furiously for no reason."

"Denzella would say it is her age, Lamorna."

" 'Tis more than that, John. The laudanum, I am certain, is having an adverse effect on her. My aunt always said that if taken too frequently it could be harmful. Perhaps if Denzella were to curtail her doses . . . perhaps Dr. Pendarvis or Dr. St. Cleer should talk to her."

He set down the tankard of ale, his eyes blazing icily. "We will speak no more of this, Lamorna. Such a suggestion is highly offensive. Kitty is in no need of a doctor. Pray leave me to finish my breakfast in peace. You seem bent on upsetting the household this morning—be good enough to leave the servants to their tasks as well."

There was nothing else to say. She turned and left him.

"Come away with me," Dirk begged her on his return. "Leave him. I'll buy us a house in Brittany—no one in France will know that we are not wed."

She gave a hopeless sigh. "If only I could . . . pray do not tempt me."

"Why not? What's to stop you? If you love me and trust me to look after you . . ."

" 'Tis not that, my love. I cannot leave Cornwall. You know my uncle is not well—I cannot hurt and disgrace him so."

He felt weighed down by helplessness; he had not considered the Reverend Hall. "Yet—yet surely he wishes you happiness above all else. If he knew the true state of affairs at Kilworthy, the fact that your marriage is no marriage . . ."

She shook her head. "He does not know and I cannot tell him."

"It was he who urged you to marry Sir John," said Dirk, a hard edge creeping into his voice.

"And he sincerely believed it was for the best. I cannot blame him, he did not force me—I agreed of my own free will. If we went away, what would become of him? John holds the living at Rowenstow. Do you think he would keep my uncle on as vicar? There would be a terrible scandal and my uncle would be the one to suffer. I cannot slink away like a coward leaving him to face disgrace and dishonor on my account."

"Then we'll take him with us."

She shook her head. " 'Tis no use, Dirk. He would not come with us and I would be ashamed to ask him. No, my love, I cannot do it. Please do not press me again—'tis almost more than I can bear to refuse you."

He put his arms round her to comfort her but his heart was heavy. For he had often of late envisioned them leaving Cornwall for a place where she would be his alone. What had at first seemed a sweet dream had grown more and more plausible, taking on an urgency and an anticipation he could not disregard. Whereas holding her, kissing her, had once seemed impossible and then tantamount to bliss, it was now not enough. Their stolen hours only made him hungry for more, his pleasure overwhelming but fleeting. Afterwards he was left

ECHOES OF THE HEART

dispirited and uneasy. Every time she returned to Kilworthy was worse than the time before; there was always the fear that something would happen to prevent their next meeting, that once out of his sight she might come to some harm. Yet she refused to be moved from her resolve.

That afternoon as Lamorna rode away from Dirk's house in Padstow, she did not notice the young woman lurking in a doorway opposite. It had been a long time since she had thought of Rosina Nance, or been troubled by her.

But Rosina had not forgotten her. She had meant to call on Dirk herself when she had seen the cloaked lady ride from behind his house on her white mare. Lady Roscarrock visiting Dirk Killigrew, as bold as you please! Rosina was stunned. The fine lady embroiled with a smuggler! All that she had, and she must have him, too! Kilworthy, the jewels, the silk gowns, every splendor was at her fingertips, and none of it was enough for her! She wanted to beat Lady Roscarrock 'til she was black and blue. Then what would Dirk think of her with her pretty face ruined? But that was not the way.

Rosina went down the street and turned the corner. Passing the inn and a group of shops, she crossed over to the butcher's. Inside she made a purchase, took the wrapped parcel, and began the long walk back to Landrawna. With every step her hatred and bitterness threatened to overwhelm her.

When finally she reached her cottage, she looked about her in loathing. Though it was superior to many of the hovels in the village, it was still a far cry from Dirk's townhouse in Padstow. How she had dreamed of living there, imagining what she would do all day—and all night in Dirk's bed. He would not wed her while Lady Roscarrock lived. Oh, there were other men—the smithy in Pendreath, the cabinetmaker in Landrawna. Both could give her more than she was used to, both were better off than her father and brothers, but she had wanted neither. She had wanted only Dirk Killigrew.

The staggering defeat had swiftly become a vengeful hatred;

she would curse the two who had wronged her, who had smashed her hopes and thrown her desires back in her face.

Tying on an apron, she banked up the fire. Then she unwrapped the brown paper to disclose the large and bloody heart of a sheep. Rosina was not squeamish; her movements were steady and deliberate. Reaching for a tin on the kitchen shelf, she opened it and counted out nine pins. Then she stuck each in the sheep's heart before taking up the long fork and thrusting the heart into the flames. Soon a nauseous, pungent odor arose, and Rosina began to chant:

> 'Tis not this heart I wish to burn
> But the lady's heart I wish to turn
> Wishing her neither rest nor peace
> Til she is dead and gone.

When the heart had burned to a crisp, she shook it off the fork with a gesture of contempt and watched it fall to ashes in the fire. Then she rose and set about preparing supper.

On a fine day in September Joshua Tregarth rode to Wheel Charity. It was a pity that his mood did not match the day. He appreciated neither the brilliant blue sky nor the blooming Michaelmas daisies nodding their heads in the breeze blowing across Whistmoor. His wife was in the last stages of pregnancy and he longed for the child to be born so that he would no longer have to tolerate the sight of her swollen face, her enormous belly, and awkward gait. Joshua did not agree with the old Cornish saying about the three most beautiful sights in the world: "a woman with child, a ship in full sail, and a field of corn waving in the wind." Joshua was no sailor and no farmer, and in her present condition his wife was distasteful to him.

Joshua rode along the track skirting the field which Sir John had only two months before put to the plow. A few

Landrawna men had actually gone to Kilworthy to ask that he reconsider his decision to sow the land, reminding him of the belief that to do so would be to evoke some terrible vengeance. Sir John had given them short shrift—and well he should have, he mused. Their objections were ludicrous in these enlightened times. Joshua abhorred waste; he thought John should have planted corn in that field long before this. Now the villagers could no longer work their silly charms at the godforsaken Shuddering Stone, at least not from early summer to harvest-tide.

When Joshua reached the mine he observed the vigor of activity—the women and children working on the surface, crushing and washing the ore, the noise of the clanking chains, the furious rumblings.

"Good day to 'ee, your honor," said the grass captain.

"What's wrong with you, man?" asked Joshua irritably. "Can you not stand upright?"

The old man tried to straighten his back, wincing as he did so. "Beg your pardon, sir, but my rheumatism be actin' up."

"If it is so bad that you can scarcely stand, then perhaps you should be relieved of your post."

The grass captain blanched. "Oh no, your honor. There b'ain't no call to do that. Tes not bad." If he lost his job he and his wife would be left to the mercy of their neighbors; they might even be forced to sell what meager possessions they owned.

Joshua shrugged. "Very well. Go and tell Mr. Bodmin I want a word with him."

"Aye, sir," said the old man, hobbling as fast as he could to the engine house, sweat pouring down his face.

Reece had been expecting some sort of confrontation with his employer and took the news of his presence coolly. He put on his brown coat and went outside to where Joshua still sat on his horse.

"Good day to 'ee, Mr. Joshua," he said.

"I fear it is not a good day at all, Bodmin. I have come to

inquire as to why Wheel Charity's profits have steadily decreased these last three months."

Reece nodded. "They are down a bit, sir, I'll give 'ee that."

Joshua's lip curled. "How generous of you to agree with me. Compared with Wheel Faith, they are disappointing."

"Well, 'ee do know, sir, that there b'ain't any rhyme or reason to a bal. Last year when Wheel Faith were in a slump, before 'ee blasted that new load, the men here couldn't dig fast enough to bring up all the ore in plain sight. We'll be comin' about again, sir. These new pitches b'ain't so rich as afore—I went down in the shafts myself last week."

"Then why have you not blasted further? That is what I employ you to do—to keep the mine producing as much as possible."

"Tesn't that the shafts not be producin', just that they b'ain't so rich in tin. But still we be makin' a good profit, even if tes not so high as other times."

Joshua eyed him coldly. "See that the profits do not drop any lower, man. Blast if you have to."

"I'll do my best, your honor," said Reece. As Joshua rode off, he folded his arms across his barrel-like chest. On the next run Dirk would have to be content with less tin. They had been rather reckless this last time, the men coining too much tin in the cellars and loading it onto the *Cormorant*. Joshua Tregarth was no fool and as for Reece himself, he was determined to keep his job.

Some weeks later Tamara put on her green cloak, slipping a bag into its folds. The autumn wind was chilly and for that she was grateful; no one would wonder why she was wearing her most voluminous cape. It was three o'clock in the afternoon. Isolde was in her room taking a nap, and her father and brother were out; the servants were either in the kitchen or outside occupied with their various tasks.

Tamara went down the hallway to the staircase; she longed

to hurry but forced herself to walk casually. Were she seen, it would be assumed she was going for a walk or ride in the fresh air. The past three days it had rained without stopping and she had paced in her room, feeling she would go mad. But when this morning had dawned moisture-laden but clear, she had known it would be the day.

Passing the drawing room, she caught her breath as a petulant voice called, "Tamara, is that you?"

"Yes, Isolde. As it's a fair day I'm going to Padstow to buy some new lace. Is there anything I can get for you?" To her relief her voice sounded perfectly normal.

Isolde shook her head. "Be sure you are back by six o'clock. Lord Trevanion will be arriving at eight to dine with your brother. I shall stay in my room, of course, so you will have to be the hostess. We are pleased, Tamara, that you have come to your senses. Lord Trevanion will make you a fine husband. Perhaps before the year is out you will be with child yourself. With all of his daughters, Lord Trevanion is most anxious for a son."

Tamara licked dry lips. "I had better go if I am to return by six." This time her voice trembled slightly.

"Very well. Oh, you might get me some rose-colored embroidery thread—I'm nearly out of it." Isolde was stitching a sampler to announce the child's birth; only the name and the word "son" or "daughter" were to be filled in later. Isolde longed for the child to be born; she knew her husband disliked the sight of her and she stayed to her room as much as possible. But he would be pleased when the child came, she was certain. She hoped for a girl.

Clutching her bag beneath her cloak, Tamara hurried across to the front door. Once outside she went round to the stables where one of the grooms had saddled her horse. As she mounted the block and sat on the horse, the animal shied a bit, sensing her tension. To her horror her bag slipped from her hand and hit the mucky ground with a thud.

The groom reached over and picked it up. "Thank you,

John," she murmured, wondering whether he could hear her heart hammering in her breast.

"She be a bit frisky today, miss," he said. "Tes the nip in the air, I reckon, and bein' kept indoors these last days."

"I'll be careful," said Tamara. Her nerves tight as a drum, she trotted away from the house and took one of the lesser used tracks across Whistmoor. Once out of sight of Tregartha, she urged her horse to a reckless gallop.

The windows of the Pendreath church reflected the stately bark-spotted sycamores, now skeletal and leafless, beside the stream. The scent of woodsmoke was in the air. Tamara rode over the arched stone bridge past the cottages whose doorsteps vaulted the stream. She tied up her horse in front of the inn before taking a roundabout route to Mark's cottage.

Quaking at her own daring, she went inside the kitchen door and up the stairs. There were two bedchambers; she crept into one and drew aside the bedcurtains. Taking off her cloak, she climbed on the bed and closed the curtains about her. It was stuffy, but that was the least of her worries.

The soldiers from Launceston, requested by Joshua Tregarth to abort the local smuggling trade, were posted at Port Isaac. Their predecessors, the former excise men, had been dismissed and sent back to their garrison at Bodmin. For them this was a mixed blessing; no longer would they have to face the magistrate's censure, but neither would their low wages be supplemented by the bribes the fair traders left for them in the clefted boulder known as the Gauger's Pocket.

Joshua had come to the small inn at Port Isaac to meet with the officer-in-charge. Handing his horse over to one of the ostlers, he entered the taproom and ordered, "Two tankards of ale and a private parlor. I'm expecting Major Dickinson to join me; pray show him in here when he arrives."

When the major strode into the room in his scarlet regimentals, Joshua recognized instantly that this man was a vast improvement over the last revenuer; even his appearance was forbidding. Under his powdered wig his face was harshly angular and he wore a black patch over one eye. The other eye seemed to burn with intensity.

"Mr. Tregarth, your servant, sir," he said.

"Major Dickinson," Joshua said, bowing slightly. "Sit down; I've ordered some ale."

The landlord came in then, bearing a tray with two tankards of foaming ale. He set one down before each gentleman. "If there be anything else I can do for 'ee, your worship, 'ee have only to call."

Joshua nodded, waving the man away. "See that we are not disturbed."

"Well, major, you have been in Port Isaac some weeks now. Have you discovered anything of note concerning the local trade?"

"I have, sir. One of my men managed to learn the identity of their leader by plying an old man with drink. He is one Dirk Killigrew, formerly of Landrawna, now, I believe, of Padstow."

Joshua's grip tightened on the tankard's handle, but he gave no other sign that the name meant anything to him. After some moments he replied, "Yes? And the next run?"

"I am told that the ship will arrive in a week's time, more or less."

"And the storage places for the cargo?"

"We have heard of a farmhouse out on the moors, quite isolated. Apparently it's one of the places for the drop. Our source has a grudge against the farmer."

Joshua raised his brows. "Your men have not been wasting their time, I see."

"In another day or two I will post them along the headland to watch for the ship."

Joshua shook his head. "You have not nearly enough for that, and these scoundrels know of more secret coves and inlets than you or I could discover even in daylight. I fear little would be gained by such a maneuver. The farmhouse stands a better chance of success."

Major Dickinson was not used to being told his business by a civilian, and he resented it. But he had to acknowledge the wisdom of the magistrate's words. Stringing men along the cliffs would likely not result in the end they both sought—capturing the moonlighters. Even if the ship were spotted, what chance had a handful of soldiers against the smugglers and their associates on land? Unless they had a particular location to surround and search, they would never begin to crack the smuggling ring. More people were involved than one might imagine; much of the countryside gave aid to these men.

The major loathed Cornwall, its backward and superstitious ways, the lack of decent roads, the eerie moors with their weird stone formations that the populace either feared or revered. Nor was the local food to his taste; he had no fondness for fish, and he liked his meat and potatoes on his plate, not wrapped up in a crust with God-knew-what inside. Behind the bland, amiable faces of the villagers was a deep-rooted contempt for his uniform and its significance. The Cornish were lawless; in their inside-out world the smugglers were considered respectable and those who tried to stop them, nefarious.

But Major Dickinson never shirked his duties; he pursued them with a relentless, single-minded energy which generally served him well, though that intensity made him few friends. His own men were deeply in awe of him and did their best not to incur his displeasure.

"I will hunt down this Dirk Killigrew, Mr. Tregarth," he said. "Have no doubt on that score."

"I do have to remind you, Major, that the last revenuers posted to these parts were a disgrace to their uniforms. They were less than competent and likely paid off. If you manage to arrest Dirk Killigrew—for I believe they will disband of their own accord once their leader is caught—I will write a commendatory letter to your commanding officer."

"I cannot speak for the jury, sir. They have been known to acquit smugglers, I'm told."

"I will worry about the jury, Major. Your job is to arrest Killigrew, and, if possible, ensure that he is charged with a crime no jury could overlook."

The major's one blue eye bore into Joshua's own. "I'm not certain I understand you, Mr. Tregarth."

Joshua raised his brows. "Why, I wish only to see justice done, Major Dickinson, and for the Crown to receive its proper due. Dirk Killigrew and his crew must be stopped."

Tamara had lain in bed for hours, every nerve and muscle tense and strained. She had heard Mrs. Goss enter the cottage to prepare Mark's supper and stifled a nervous giggle, picturing the expression on the woman's face were she to see Tamara now. On her visits to the doctor's house Mrs. Goss had always treated Tamara with respect, but she would be scandalized by this outrageous behavior.

Later came the sound of footsteps and voices below. Delicious cooking smells wafted up the stairs and Tamara's mouth watered; she had eaten little that day out of anxiety. It grew dark, and there came a pounding on the door. By now her family would have sent out parties looking for her; Lord Trevanion would have come to dine and perhaps even now had realized her disappearance was no accident. Whatever course Mark chose to follow, she was ruined after this night's piece of work. Forcing his hand in this way had seemed her only hope. She was certain he cared for her, though to her frustration he had never declared himself, knowing her to be pledged to another man. There would be a fearful scandal now and her own family would surely disown her. If only Mark would not despise her for her desperate flight and concealment in his own house!

Her belly gave a sudden lurch as she wondered whether those searching for her would come here. But that was ridiculous—who at Tregartha would connect her disappearance with the young doctor from Pendreath? Perhaps the villagers themselves suspected—little went unnoticed in a place this small—but surely none of them would betray her. For once she was glad that her family was disliked and feared; it wasn't likely that the local people would lift a finger to help the Tregarths track down a wayward member. Perhaps leaving her horse at the inn had been foolish, but it was too late to fret about that now.

Eventually Tamara dozed off, lulled by the realization that the cottage was once again empty. Mark must have been summoned on a call, and Mrs. Goss left after cleaning up from the last meal. When she awoke she had no idea what time it was or how long she had slept. Was Mark home? Was he already asleep?

Sitting up, she felt a little dizzy. She pushed aside the heavy bed curtains and breathed in the fresh air from the open window before creeping stealthily to the door. There was a faint light coming from below; either Mark was still awake or a lamp had been left burning. She could not wait until morning; besides, it was likely close to that now. She was already ruined in the eyes of society so she might as well proceed with her plan.

Her heart hammering, she moved down the stairs, the floorboards creaking beneath her.

"Mrs. Goss?" came Mark's startled voice.

Tamara made the turn in the narrow stairway and reached the bottom step, a lump in her throat. She stood there, unable to move. Now that the time had come to confront him, she was terrified. Her audacity shocked her. What if he should throw her out? What if, after all, she had been very much mistaken and he did not love her? What on earth would she do if he refused to help her?

Mark appeared in the parlor doorway, a candle in his hand. He wore no coat and his muslin shirt had come untucked from his breeches. She gazed at him, her lip trembling.

"Tamara! Miss Tregarth!" Dumbfounded, he stared at her standing in the shadows.

"Shhh. Pray do not say my name. The window's open; someone may hear."

His mind reeled. " 'Tis after three o'clock! What are you doing here?"

She moved forward. "I—I had to come, Mark. They were going to force me to marry Lord Trevanion—I couldn't bear the thought!"

"Are you aware that your brother has men combing the countryside for you? I—I've been looking for you myself. They said you'd gone to Padstow, but your horse was spotted here in Pendreath!"

"And were you worried?" she asked softly.

Raking his fingers through his hair, he said irritably, "Of course I was worried. I've been in a frenzy . . . and to find you here—'tis madness!"

"I've left Tregartha forever, Mark."

He seemed not to have heard her. "You—you must return home. I'll invent a plausible story and explain to your brother."

"I will not go back!"

"But, Tamara, you are acting on impulse, you do not realize—"

"—I assure you that I have thought of little else for weeks. Don't you understand, Mark? I—I love you. And I thought—I hoped you felt the same. I've come here because in this cottage I've felt safe, and happy."

He regarded her solemnly. "I am a poor man, Tamara. I cannot give you most of the things you have taken for granted all your life. You must allow me to take you back home before it is too late and you do something you will forever regret."

She tilted her chin. "You wouldn't force me to go back—you couldn't be that cruel! Do you wish to see me married to that—that . . ."

"Tamara, have you considered how far apart are our stations? You know the way I live, my limited means of support.

Your family would never countenance a match between us. They would likely never forgive you."

"I know that, and I promise you that I do not care. I want only to be with you. But, if you do not want me, then I shall go elsewhere." With a touch of her former pride, she squared her shoulders.

His resistance fell away. Pulling her into his arms, he said, "Does this answer you? Of course I want you—how can you doubt it? I've loved you all this time, even though you were promised to another, even though I repeatedly told myself you were not for me. And I thought you were amusing yourself by coming here, using me to spite your brother."

"Oh, Mark, we've wasted so much time! I kept coming, hoping you'd speak, but you never did and I couldn't wait any longer. I hoped that once I was compromised you'd marry me to save my reputation." She smiled, half-embarrassed, half-provocative.

"Tamara, are you certain?" he asked, looking into her face.

"I have been certain of nothing else since Midsummer Eve," she said, and lifted her mouth to his.

Two days later a letter was delivered to Tregartha stating that Tamara was now the wife of Dr. St. Cleer of Pendreath.

Her family, who had realized that her flight was deliberate, was enraged. The concern for her safety they had felt in the first few hours of her disappearance had already turned to fury and shame. She had disgraced them; she had grossly jilted her fiancé; she had brought dishonor to Tregartha.

"Dr. St. Cleer?" shrieked Isolde. "How can such a thing be possible?"

"The chit's been deceiving us all," said Matthew. "Secretive, sly puss. Thank heaven her mother's not here to see this day. I won't be able to hold up my head to Lord Trevanion."

"She can rot with that doctor for all I care," declared Joshua icily. "Her name will not be mentioned in this house, nor is anyone to have further dealings with her. I told you many times, Father, that you always kept her on too loose a rein."

Matthew shook his head. "The girl was always headstrong. Not at all like her mother. Don't know where she got it from."

"That is scarcely relevant. She'll be shunned by everyone from her class, of course. If we do not acknowledge her nor will any of our friends," said Joshua.

"An elopement—the height of deceit! Yet you are forgetting her friendship with Lady Roscarrock, Joshua. I'll warrant she knew all about this disgrace!" Isolde spoke resentfully.

"I am confident that Sir John will take our part in this. The girl will no longer be a welcome guest at Kilworthy if her own family refuses to accept her."

In this Joshua was right. Tamara had abandoned her family and her home, jilting her esteemed fiancé to marry a penniless doctor, John said. Lamorna was not to invite her to Tregartha, nor would she be permitted entrance did she come of her own accord.

"Dr. St. Cleer is a very worthy man, John," said Lamorna. "And I believe Tamara loves him very much."

"Love," said Denzella witheringly, "will not last a twelvemonth in a five-room cottage when one is used to Tregartha. But she won't be able to atone for her reckless foolishness; she's made her choice. And her family has made theirs."

"I daresay she was well aware of the consequences when she went to Dr. St. Cleer," said Lamorna coldly. "And they made very little difference to her."

"I hope, Lamorna, that you knew nothing of her ill-conceived flight," said John. "I should not like the Tregarths to think that you condoned the girl's scandalous behavior."

"They may think what they like, though I can honestly say that I knew nothing except that she had a growing affection for Mark St. Cleer."

John rose, tired of the subject. He went outside to the yard to inspect the oxen his steward had just bought at market that morning.

"You are quick to defend your friend, Lamorna, but I wonder how your uncle will view her infamous behavior."

"Were he in full possession of all the facts, I believe he would approve. He did not force me to wed John as Tamara's family was forcing her to wed Lord Trevanion. I believe she looked at me and saw a reflection of her own bleak future. And she had the courage to cast it off, as I did not."

Denzella could not believe her ears. She stared at the young woman before her whose voice and manner were filled with disdain. "How—how dare you? You ungrateful, good-for-nothing chit! After my cousin plucked you from that wretched vicarage and brought you here—here where you have everything, yet you cannot do the one thing asked of you: bear your husband a son!"

Lamorna rose, white and trembling. "Ask your cousin the reason for that," she said. "Ask him why he has not come to my bed since the first days of our marriage. The fault, Denzella, does not lie with me."

"I tell 'ee the searchers be comin', man! They be headed this way—us have to hide the goods!"

"Who says so?" cried the startled farmer, Thomas Hayle.

"Don't be daft! I tell 'ee I seen 'un myself! Someone squealed, and now we mun hide the cankers and all else Zachy Sawyer stored in the barn."

"Where be Zachy now?" asked Hayle.

"Gone back to the *Cormorant*. What do that matter? We've got work to do."

There was a long moan from upstairs. The men looked uneasily at one another. "Tes a bad night for 'ee, Thomas, but it can't be helped. Nature do have a way o' strikin' when us least expect. And tes not her first," said Tim.

"No, she be safe delivered five times afore," said Hayle, nodding gravely. "Heaven grant a sixth time."

"Did 'ee send for the midwife?"

"No, Emma wants the young doctor from Pendreath."
"What, the one that just wed the lass at Tregartha?"
"Aye."
"I don't hold with doctors. He did sew up the captain's head like it were a piece o' cloth—fearful to see, it were."

Thomas scowled. "He got better, didn't he? Enough o' this talk. If we mun hide the goods, we better get on with it."

The men hurried outdoors, glancing across the dark, undulating moors for a sign of approach. Another moan, louder this time, came from the upstairs window.

"Poor Emma," said her husband.

"Her'll be a sight poorer if 'ee be locked in jail," was one of the men's sardonic response.

In the barn they began to feel for the kegs hidden beneath piles of straw.

"Where'll we put 'em?"
"In the well."
"No, not room enough. And the doctor'll likely be needin' water."
"Aye. Tes you who have the head tonight. The floorboards—we'll take 'em up."
"Not enough time for that."

Another moan carried on the night air reached them.

Tim slapped his leg. "We'll take all of it up there!"
"Up where?"
"Where do 'ee think, man? In with your wife!"
"Are 'ee mad, Tim Grandee? She be lyin' in!"
"Aye, tes a place they'd never look. Tes the only place, I tell 'ee, where all of it'll be safe. What soldier'd enter a room where a woman be about to give birth?"
"But—but the doctor!" sputtered one of the others.
"We'll have to trust 'un. Come on!" Tim reached down for a keg and lifted it to his powerful shoulders. The others, shaken but resigned, did likewise and followed him to the farmhouse.

A short while later Major Dickinson reached the farmhouse

with eight of his soldiers. Two went round to the scullery door, four others to the barn and various outbuildings, and two accompanied him to the front door.

"Open up, open up in the Queen's name!" bawled the sergeant.

A long, drawn-out groan met their ears, followed by a sharp shriek. The soldiers exchanged startled glances. Then heavy footsteps were heard descending the stairs, and a harassed-looking, tall man flung open the door.

"What do 'ee mean comin' here at a time like this? What do 'ee want?"

"Are you Thomas Hayle?" asked the sergeant.

"Aye."

"And is this your farm?"

"None'll be denyin' that. What do 'ee want?"

Major Dickinson stepped out of the shadows into the light of the door. "We've come to search your house and outbuildings. Out of the way."

"Search it? What on earth for?" cried Thomas indignantly.

"Information has been laid that a cargo of contraband was delivered here earlier this evening."

"Oh, excise men, are 'ee? Well, 'ee be fooled right and proper. There be nowt o' that here. Tes the wrong place, I tell 'ee. Someone be havin' a laugh at your expense."

"I do not think so," said the major. "Step aside, man. Go ahead," he added to his own men, "you have your orders."

"Thomas! Thomas!" came an agonized cry.

"Now 'ee've done it!" shouted the farmer, red-faced. "Tes my wife up there, and she do have enough to contend with tonight without the house bein' torn asunder!"

"Is she sick?" asked one of the soldiers uneasily.

"Do her sound sick? No! Her be havin' a babe! And I do pray 'twill be a girl for I've already five sons. None of they better enlist in the army, disturbin' respectable folk in the night and intrudin' on affairs what be private!" He turned to the stairway, calling, "I be comin', Emma! And all of 'ee can look as much as 'ee've a mind to—I've better things to do than troop about with 'ee!" He bounded up the stairs, two at a time.

The two soldiers looked sheepish but the major's face was inscrutable, his one eye blazing in its socket. "What are you waiting for?" he growled.

They searched the downstairs rooms, lifted carpets, looked up the chimney, inspected the walls for hollow sounds, examined cupboards for secret compartments. While they were still at it, the four others who had been searching the grounds came into the house.

"Well?" asked the major.

"Nothing, sir. The outbuildings be clean."

The major's face hardened. Jerking his head, he said, "Upstairs, then."

The upstairs rooms revealed nothing except cupboards and wardrobes filled with linens, and five boys of various ages who were having difficulty sleeping. The youngest, not more than two, began to wail when he saw Major Dickinson.

Thomas Hayle came out into the hall, closing the door of his bedroom behind him. "Now look what 'ee've done, upsettin' the little 'un. Tes all right, Rob. The soldiers don't mean 'ee any harm. They'll soon be gone." He glowered at the major.

Major Dickinson ignored him. He said to the sergeant, "Try the door across."

"What?" thundered Hayle. "My wife be in there! Have 'ee lost what sense 'ee were born with? I've been a patient man but I'll lodge a complain now if 'ee do disturb her further!"

The sergeant's face fell under his glare; he glanced at his commanding officer.

"Sergeant," said the major softly in a voice of steel.

Swallowing hard, the man said, "Aye, sir." Stepping to the door, he tentatively knocked on it.

" 'Ee ought to be ashamed," cried Hayle. "Tes a fine day when a poor woman can't be left to give birth in peace!"

A shriek followed closely on his words and another. The

sergeant, highly uncomfortable, knocked again. He was wishing himself anywhere but there.

The door was partially opened by a young gentleman, his shirtsleeves rolled up, wiping his hands on a clean cloth.

"You are the doctor, sir?" asked Major Dickinson.

"Aye, I'm Dr. St. Cleer," said Mark.

"I have a warrant to search this farmhouse, sir. That means every room."

Mark frowned. "You must be well aware, major, that Mrs. Hayle is inside in a very delicate state. I cannot permit anyone in here but her husband. I have the welfare of my patient to consider."

There were more piercing cries. The soldiers winced; a few had turned bright red.

Mark looked harriedly over his shoulder. "This birth is not an easy one, Major. I cannot be disturbed any longer and neither can poor Mrs. Hayle."

"Dr. St. Cleer, I was given information that this farmhouse received smuggled goods not long ago. I hope I am a reasonable man, and I have no wish to distress the lady you are attending. So I put the question to you, sir. Are there any such goods in that room?"

"Doctor, oh, Doctor! Tes comin'! I feel it!" came the harsh scream.

"Would I be delivering a baby in the midst of a cargo, sir?" cried Mark angrily. "The idea is absurd! I ask you to leave me to get on with my work or this poor woman's ordeal will be on your head."

She had begun to thrash about in the bed. "It's all right, Mrs. Hayle. It won't be long now." And he shut the door on the soldiers.

They trooped downstairs ahead of the major. "Wild goose chase, if you ask me," said one.

"Proper fools we look," muttered another.

As the major came out the farmhouse door, they stood to attention. "Get the two out back," he said coldly. "We're returning to Port Isaac." It appeared that he'd been deliberately led astray, that they'd all been made laughingstocks. He had not appreciated the reproach in the doctor's manner, nor had he wished to agitate the farmer's wife. Damn this place and its populace, he thought, mounting his horse and riding off across the moor.

Upstairs in the Hayles' bedroom the farmer's wife gave a tremendous push and her baby was born.

"Oh, Emma!" cried her husband elatedly. "Tes a girl!"

She smiled weakly as Dr. St. Cleer wiped her new daughter and handed her to her.

"Thank 'ee, Doctor, thank 'ee," said Thomas. "Emma were right to summon 'ee after all, much more than she knew."

Mark smiled. "She's a beautiful baby, Mrs. Hayle. And I'll stop by tomorrow to look at you both."

"Doctor, I'll pay 'ee well for this night's work," said Thomas.

Mark shook his head. "I ask only my fee for the birthing, Mr. Hayle. Nothing more."

"Well, if 'ee be certain, sir," said the farmer. He glanced at the pile of kegs in the corner of the room behind the bed. "Emma, my dear, 'ee had a rough time of it, I know, but 'twas 'ee who saved us, 'ee and the doctor."

"Your wife must rest, Mr. Hayle. She was not merely play-acting, you know."

"Aye, doctor. Her sister be comin' tomorrow to look after her for a few days. If 'ee won't take money, sir, I'll see 'ee gets an anker o' Cousin Jack."

Mark picked up his bag. He turned to go, then said, "Rather than brandy, I think my wife would like a bolt of cloth for new curtains, if you can manage it."

Thomas grinned. "Aye, sir, I'll see to it. Good night to 'ee. The gentlemen won't be forgettin' this, Doctor."

" 'Ee be a good man, Doctor," said Mrs. Hayle from the bed, her face pale but radiant. "Much happiness to 'ee and Mistress St. Cleer."

Later that night as they sat by the fire drinking the mulled wine that Tamara had made, Mark said ruefully, "I've eloped with a lady of impeccable lineage, I've lied to the Queen's men, and abetted criminals—all in one week."

"You are truly a reprobate," said Tamara, and kissed him.

Twenty-two

Shifting the bundle onto her hip, Lamorna rapped on the door of Mark St. Cleer's cottage. When Tamara herself opened it, the two gazed at one another for a long instant; seeing the glow on her friend's face laid to rest any doubts she had had about Tamara's future happiness. Lamorna felt a piercing inside which she knew to be envy.

"Lamorna, dearest, I've been hoping you'd come. But I did not dare send a message to Kilworthy for fear you'd be forbidden to visit here!"

"Oh, Tamara—as if I would let them stop me," Lamorna said as the two embraced.

"Come in—I'll ask Mrs. Goss to make us some tea."

Lamorna glanced about the tidy parlor. "How nicely you've arranged things."

"It was a little bare before, was it not? I'm going to make some new curtains, and pillows for the chairs."

Lamorna unknotted her bundle and Tamara stared in disbelief at the contents.

"My clothes! Lamorna, how did you come by them? I took next to nothing when I left Tregartha."

"That is what I supposed. Once in a while it is helpful to be Lady Roscarrock. We were invited to Tregartha to your new niece's christening, and while I was there I spoke with one of the maids and arranged to have some of your gowns and things packed for you. Today I picked them up."

"Does Joshua know—or Isolde?"

"No. Apparently they are pretending your room does not exist," she said with a wry smile.

"As I no longer exist for them. Oh, don't think it concerns me at all! Every day I am grateful for the courage I was able to summon to run away. Had I not come here, Mark would never have spoken his feelings—he was too honorable. But I knew how I felt about him on Midsummer Eve, or at least very soon after when he called at Tregartha. It seems so long ago now."

Lamorna nodded wistfully. Those long, warm days did seem ages ago when she had stolen time away to be with Dirk. Now the winter was fast approaching and he was gone again to France. There was a bleakness in her spirit, which echoed the dreary landscape.

"What of you, Lamorna?" asked Tamara.

"Things are very much as they were. I rarely see John; Kitty, too, avoids me. I fear I have the blue devils today," she said, tears stinging her eyes. " 'Tis been weeks since I've seen Dirk. There must have been some trouble—he was not long in Cornwall the last time."

Tamara put her arm round her shoulder. "I'm going to ask for that tea. Then we'll have a long talk."

Lamorna nodded forlornly. Annoyed with herself for her real envy of Tamara, she could not stop imagining scenes in which she shared Dirk's house in Padstow. For a few moments she succumbed to the blissful dream, allowing herself to dwell on the impossible. But Tamara had been free to go to Mark, while Lamorna was married to John. Her place was at Kilworthy, no matter how meaningless, how futile her existence there.

A knock sounded at the door. Brushing away her tears, she went out of the parlor and lifted the latch.

In the kitchen Tamara had also heard the rapping. "I'll answer it, Mrs. Goss. You bring the tea in when it's ready, and some of your delicious heavy cakes."

"Ais, mistress," said Mrs. Goss. She liked Tamara and was

pleased to see her master so happy, however amazed she had been that the lady had left a grand home and a rich titled husband-to-be to marry the young doctor. Not that she hadn't seen for herself the way the wind was blowing . . .

Tamara passed through the narrow corridor to the front of the house, and paused. Before her stood Lamorna, locked in a desperate and joyous embrace with Dirk Killigrew. Hastily Tamara moved into the parlor and knelt to bank up the fire. She heard the two come in behind her and turned about. Lamorna's face was flushed, tears sparkling on her eyelashes. Dirk held her hand tightly in his, his own cheeks tinged with color.

"How do you do, Mr. Killigrew?" said Tamara, trying to sound as though this was a perfectly natural occurrence. "We were just about to have tea. Will you join us?"

"Thank you, Mistress St. Cleer. The truth is I came to see your husband."

"He is not at home now, I'm afraid. Pray wait with us—you are most welcome here." Tamara smiled. "Surely you do not need me to tell you that. Ah, here is the tea. We shall need one more cup, Mrs. Goss. Please, both of you, sit down."

Lamorna seemed unable to speak; she had barely taken her shining eyes off Dirk.

"You have come to see Mark?" prompted Tamara, pouring tea.

"Aye. Not long ago he did some of my men a great favor. I did not have the chance to thank him before."

Tamara smiled in amusement. "You are talking about the Hayle farmhouse, no doubt. It was a close call from what I heard. Mark tells me there is a new officer in charge of the excise men, a Major Dickinson, who seems tenacious. He came at my brother's request." She made a face. "Joshua takes his duties as a magistrate very seriously."

Dirk's face had tightened. "Mr. Tregarth's no friend to the gentlemen," he acknowledged in a tone suddenly gone hard.

Lamorna touched his sleeve. "Tell her, Dirk."

He gazed at her, speechless with astonishment.

She nodded, giving him an encouraging smile. " 'Tis the right thing to do. And she is my dearest friend."

Dirk set down his teacup, embarrassed and uncertain. "Lamorna, I . . ."

"Go on, my love."

"One of you tell me, I beg of you, before I go mad with curiosity," laughed Tamara.

Dirk frowned. "Lamorna wishes you to know, Mistress St. Cleer, well, that—that you and I share the same father."

Tamara stared at him open-mouthed. Whatever she had expected, it was not this. Then a light dawned in her face. "Then you, you were that boy . . ."

"Aye," said Dirk curtly, a muscle jerking in his cheek. "The very one who came to Tregartha many years ago begging. 'Tis not a memory I cherish."

"And my—our—brother ordered you beaten."

Dirk shrugged. "I daresay he had cause after I had gone for him. 'Twas long ago, Mistress St. Cleer. And I won't offend you by claiming kin. No one knows of this but Lamorna and a close friend of mine."

"We are brother and sister, Dirk, and that makes me proud and happy. You must call me Tamara and come to see us whenever you can." She hesitated, biting her lip. "I—I was very ashamed of the way my brother treated you on that day. You were so cut and bruised. The only way I saw to make amends was to bring you a little food."

It was his turn to look dumbfounded. "You brought those things? The brandy and the blanket?"

She nodded. "It wasn't much, I fear."

" 'Twere everything—it was everything," he hastily amended, "on that day." Staring down at his hands, he added, "I always believed it had been one of the servants."

There was an uncomfortable silence; Dirk's face had taken on a forbidding look. Tamara could imagine the painful memories that had been stirred up but she was not to be put off. "Mark will be delighted with the news. You don't know how pleased I am to have gained a kinsman when the rest of my family has cast me off."

Once again his gaze met hers. "I admit, Mistress—Tamara, that when I heard you had left Tregartha I was . . . surprised."

"Perhaps you better than anyone can understand my actions," she said gravely. "When Providence offered me something better, I took it." Then she smiled broadly. "Though it was a bit of a blow to my vanity that Mark needed persuading."

When Dirk left a short while later, saying he could not wait for Mark but would call again soon, Tamara spoke seriously to her friend. "All this greatly preys on my mind, Lamorna. And now I am concerned for Dirk as well. Were Sir John to learn of your attachment . . ."

"Dirk wishes me to go to Brittany with him."

"Perhaps, after all, that would be best."

"But my uncle—he would be the one hurt by it and he does not deserve to be."

"Have you spoken to him yet about Dirk?"

She shook her head. "I cannot."

Tamara pressed lips together. "I know 'tis difficult, Lamorna, but if you and Dirk were found out, the consequences might be worse than if you merely ran away with him. I think you ought to confide in your uncle. He is a kind man and loves you deeply."

"He would be so ashamed of me," protested Lamorna. "I cannot believe he would approve of my leaving John. Oh, Tamara, everything is such a muddle!"

"But I fear things will only worsen if—if you continue like this," warned Tamara somberly.

It was a cold night in February when Rosina was awakened by her brothers coming in from their late shift at Wheel Charity. Ordinarily she slept undisturbed, but that night the wind whistled fiercely about the cottage, rattling a pane in her window. She had a sore throat and was unable to settle into a deep slumber.

The two young men were moving about below; she heard the chink of crockery and the thuds as one of them pulled off his boots and tossed them aside. She decided to get up and join them in a cup of tea; she'd add some honey she had put by last summer to soothe her aching throat. Shivering on the bare floorboards, she wrapped a shawl about her shoulders and went out into the tiny landing.

"That tin'll be halfway to the Frenchies by daylight," one of them was saying.

"Tes good to have an extra bit o' money in our pockets, eh?" said the other. "A few more runs and I'll be able to ask Dolly to wed."

"And about time, too, as 'ee didn't wait for the parson's blessing," he laughed. There came the sounds of a mock scuffle. Rosina stood at the top of the stairs, huddled in her shawl. What were they talking about?

"Aye, we hit on a good thing joinin' forces with the gentlemen, and Dirk Killigrew be better'n most."

The other grunted. "Don't 'ee let Rosina hear 'ee say that."

"It were all in her head—he never courted her. And come spring her'll be marryin' the smithy. I reckon she be through thinkin' o' Dirk Killigrew."

Rosina's face burned scarlet. She remembered the spell she had worked against Lady Roscarrock last autumn, all to no avail. So Rosina had made one last try for Dirk. Just before Christmas she had baked a saffron cake and dressed in her best gown and her mother's coral necklace, which played up the creaminess of her skin. Reddening her cheeks and lips with the mixture of tallow, lard, and berry juice, she had carefully arranged her hair in long ringlets before sticking a sprig of holly into the cake and setting out for Padstow.

She had not had to walk far; a man with a cart took her up, offering to drive her the distance as he was himself going to market in Padstow. She sat beside him and allowed his thigh to press against hers, giving him side looks from her long-lidded green eyes. He kissed her cheek once the cart had stopped, but she jumped down before he could claim more favors.

"A happy Christmas to 'ee and your wife," she said.

The man chuckled and drove on. Smoothing her hair, Rosina walked the rest of the way to Dirk's house. She had not seen him for months; perhaps the spell had worked some good and his infatuation with Lady Roscarrock was paling. There was only one way to find out.

She had knocked at his door, her heart thudding under her chemise. A middle-aged woman wearing a white cap opened it and as she recognized Rosina her expression became stiff.

"I've come to see Mr. Killigrew," said Rosina. "To bring him a Christmas present."

"The master be out just now—'ee can leave it with me."

Rosina tossed her head. "No, I thank 'ee. I'll come in and wait for him." She had not come this far to be summarily dismissed.

The woman pursed her lips; it was clear she wanted to send Rosina packing. But instead she said grudgingly, " 'Ee can wait in the kitchen."

"I'll wait in the parlor!" cried Rosina, entering the house.

"Don't touch anything, my girl," said the woman, "or 'twill be the worse for 'ee." She did not make Rosina any offer of refreshment but left her abruptly.

Rosina was furious. How dare Dirk's servant speak to her so! She longed to put the woman in her place. How sweet would be her revenge if she came to this house to live and the housekeeper was forced to do her bidding!

The parlor door opened behind her. "Rosina!" There was surprise in Dirk's voice, and dismay as well.

"Happy Christmas, Dirk," she said, her gaze resting admiringly on his belted leather coat and well-cut breeches, the fine ruffles at his sleeves, the shiny black boots. He was even more handsome than she remembered, with his chiselled face and high brow. " 'Tis been a long time," she said.

He nodded rather abstractedly. "Would you like a glass of wine?"

"Thank you," she answered, remembering to be careful in her speech. "I've brought a present for you. A—a cake."

She held it out and he hesitated before taking it. "Thank you, 'twas thoughtful of you." He poured two glasses of burgundy.

"I mind how 'ee—you—used to be fond of my saffron cake," she said, taking a sip of wine.

"Rosina . . ." he began awkwardly. Why on earth had she come? Hadn't he made his feelings clear long ago?

Setting down her wine, she moved close to him, the carnation scent heavy in the air. "I've missed you, Dirk. Won't you come to Father's cottage on Christmas Day and eat with us?"

"I don't think so, Rosina."

She tilted her chin. "Be your old friends not good enough now?"

He stifled an exclamation. "Take the cake to one of the men who are pining for you, Rosina. They are far more deserving of it than I."

"But 'tis you I want, Dirk Killigrew," she said softly, looking at him through her lashes.

Sighing, he said, "It's no use, Rosina. How can I speak plainer? I've no wish to cause you pain, but . . ."

Her eyes became as hard and cold as jade. "So 'tis still Lady Roscarrock. And what if Sir John knew his lady wife were cuckolding him with a base-born fair-trader?"

She had thought he would be enraged but he only shrugged. "Perhaps 'twould be better if he knew after all."

She glared at him for several moments. "I wish 'ee nowt but misfortune, Dirk Killigrew. Misfortune and misery to 'ee and that prettified Lady Roscarrock with her white hands and silk gowns and satin flounces. 'Ee thinks her far above I, but I be no married lady who slinks out like a cat in heat!"

His face darkened savagely. "Get out, Rosina."

In a rage she threw down the cake; it crumbled into pieces and crumbs on the carpet. Then she flounced out of the house, her humiliation complete. As was her renewed desire for vengeance.

She had at first considered going to Denzella and informing her of Lamorna's infidelity, but then it occurred to her that she might be playing into Dirk's hands—he had seemed to want their love affair to be revealed. Why? Was it because he hoped that Sir John would repudiate his wife and she would thus belong to Dirk once and for all? Rosina had no intention of helping that to come to pass, but she was determined that her deep grievance against Dirk and his paramour not go unsatisfied. The evil charm had not worked so something more would have to be done.

And her brothers had just given her the means. It sounded as though Dirk and his crew were smuggling tin out of Wheel Charity and taking it to France to sell. Joshua Tregarth would doubtless pay well for such information; the magistrate's resolve to see the smugglers arrested and imprisoned would be further fueled by the knowledge that he himself was being robbed of a portion of his profits. Rosina realized she had been going about her eagerness for revenge all wrong; she had wished somehow to come between Dirk and Lady Roscarrock but her efforts had failed. The way to harm Dirk, and therefore to hurt Lady Roscarrock as well, was to expose his dealings as a fair-trader.

It did not trouble her in the least that she would be betraying half the men in Landrawna as well.

Isolde handed her baby girl back to the nurse. "Send my maid to me."

When the woman came, she said, "I'll wear my new gown, the blue brocade. And heat the irons for my hair."

"Ais, mistress."

An hour later Isolde, peering at her reflection in the mirror, gave a final twitch to her gown. She had got her figure back and the farthingale and paniers made her waist look appealingly narrow. The puffy, haggard look was gone from her face as well. She now had a daughter and Tamara was no longer a thorn in her side, though the scandal of the girl's flight and marriage had been galling. Isolde had been relieved to be in confinement and unable to face people in the following weeks. By the time Arabella had been born, the talk had somewhat died down and Isolde had been able to greet her friends on the occasion of the christening with no apparent discomfort.

Going in search of her husband, she found him in the library. "There you are, my love. I heard you went out early this morning."

She waited for him to look at her, to give a few words of approval on her appearance, but he did not. "What is it, Joshua?"

For a few moments he did not answer; his narrow face was set in hard lines, his mouth compressed. "I've been to the mine."

"Again? 'Tis the second time this week, is it not?"

He was annoyed. "The first occasion I went to Wheel Faith. Today it was Wheel Charity."

"And what has displeased you?" She had no interest at all in mining, but all that concerned her husband concerned her.

"Something is wrong—very wrong. For a time I allowed myself to be appeased by the excuses, but no longer."

"What excuses, pray?"

"For months now Wheel Charity has been producing less ore—and thus less profit—than Wheel Faith."

"That has happened before, has it not? I thought there was no controlling or predicting these things."

He made an impatient gesture. "My father said the same,

so did Reece Bodmin. And I believed them, until this morning."

"What happened this morning?"

"I went down into the shaft myself."

Isolde clutched her throat. "Joshua! You might have been hurt. 'Tis dangerous."

He ignored her outburst. "The walls looked rich with ore; I saw no signs of decline. Our profits should be higher, not lower."

She was at a loss. "Then what . . . ?"

"Do you not see, Isolde?" he asked irritably. "The mine is not producing less. There is only one explanation."

"And what is that?"

"That a portion of the tin is not making its way to the smelting factory. Instead it is being stolen."

"Stolen!" She sat down in the carved high-back chair. "But how is that possible? I don't understand. The miners cannot be sending it to the factory themselves."

"That would scarcely be possible," he replied with scorn. "No, I am convinced that there is only one place the tin is going—across the channel to Brittany."

"You mean, it is being smuggled?" she asked in astonishment.

"That, Isolde, is precisely what I mean."

"I do not believe it. Who would dare?" When he made no comment, she went on, "Does your father know? You must put a stop to it!"

"He is, I daresay, playing cards at the Bull and Clover. If only he were a better player—he loses far too often. I am well able to deal with this myself. I shall see to it that the blackguard responsible is put behind bars."

"You sound as though you know who is responsible," she said.

"Oh, I am fairly certain of his identity. He once came begging here and got nothing, so now he steals what is mine. He has managed to elude Major Dickinson and his men thus far, but I am confident that it's only a matter of time before he is caught. And at the very least I'll see him transported to the West Indies as slave labor. He's ideally suited to the task."

When Rosina Nance called at Tregartha three days later Joshua reluctantly agreed to see her. What she told him caused him to set off immediately for Port Isaac, but not before he had shown his appreciation. On her way home from Tregartha, Rosina stopped at the millinery shop in Pendreath and purchased a green silk bonnet trimmed with dyed feathers. In the days to come she was the object of many envious glances; none of the other bal maidens possessed anything so grand.

On a cool spring evening Lamorna was in her bedchamber getting ready for a dinner party given by the Tregarths.

"What will 'ee wear, my lady?" asked Maggie.

"Oh, it does not matter. The plum silk, and John will wish me to wear the amethysts, I daresay."

Maggie scrutinized her mistress, noting her languor, her pallid complexion, the faint sheen of moisture on her upper lip despite the slight chill in the room. To her dismay Lamorna gave a sudden moan and rushed behind the screen which enclosed the chamber pot. The sounds of wretching followed. Quickly Maggie poured cold water into a basin, dipping in a fresh cloth. As Lamorna stumbled out from behind the screen, Maggie helped her over to the bed. She lay down, the violet-blue eyes dulled in her white face.

"Tes the fifth night runnin' 'ee be sick," said Maggie.

Lamorna said nothing, closing her eyes.

"My lady, 'ee do know what be the cause as well as I. The strips I tore up afore Christmas—you've had no use for them for two months or more. There be no denyin' it, my lady, much as 'ee might wish to. There be a babe growin' in your belly."

"Oh, Maggie, I've no wish to deny it but . . ."

" 'Ee mun tell him when he returns from France this time."

"And you know what he will say."

"In two more months your condition'll be known. 'Ee must tell him."

"He will entreat me to go away with him, and I fear I will no longer be able to refuse."

"And about time, too, my lady. Sir John will know tes not his, so 'ee must be gone before he and Miss Denzella learn the truth. Tes time to stop thinkin' of your uncle and *his* shame and think of your own."

She pushed up from the bed, her face frightened and defenseless. "I must dress. They'll all be waiting for me if I don't hurry."

In a short while Maggie had her mistress ready, her hair caught up in a diamond-studded comb, loose ringlets falling over her shoulders. She had dabbed a touch of rouge on Lamorna's pale cheeks and swept the powdered haresfoot over her face.

Downstairs John, clad in puce satin and a powdered wig, said coldly, "Your pock-marked maid is becoming inefficient, Lamorna. We shall be late to Tregartha."

"It wasn't Maggie's fault," said Lamorna. "She works well and hard."

" 'Tis time Kitty had a maid of her own," said Denzella, splendidly arrayed in mulberry taffeta, her hair scented and powdered. "She is a young lady now and needs a girl to attend her."

"Perhaps," said John.

"What a pretty gown, Kitty," said Lamorna. "Is it new?"

Kitty nodded; she wore pale lilac and a string of pearls round her neck, a recent gift from her father.

"Dressing for that stammering whelp, Philip Nancherrow?" asked John in a playful tone. "Now that we are all assembled it's time we were off."

As they rode Lamorna was thinking that Kitty might benefit from some male attention. In the last few months she had spent most of her time alone in her room, refusing Lamorna's suggestions to ride or shop or see Tamara in her new home. Nor would she accompany Lamorna on her visits up the coast to Rowenstow. She even ignored her dog, Millie, who had been banished to the stables.

At Tregartha they were the last to arrive. Gathered there was a large group of local gentry including Lord Trevanion, Tamara's jilted fiancé. His interest had since alighted on another young lady, who was not present due to illness. Despite the shameful treatment accorded him by one of the Tregarths, he still visited at Tregartha. The cook was excellent and Matthew kept a fine wine cellar. Lamorna was seated beside him and was grateful that he was more interested in his food than in making polite conversation. Across the table she observed Kitty's snubbing of poor Philip, whose painful stammerings grew worse before he lapsed into silence. Lamorna felt very sorry for him.

From the minstrel's gallery above floated a series of tunes, lively and serene at turns. At each end of the room the enormous fireplaces wafted their heat toward the diners. Lamorna could barely eat; the smells of the food nauseated her and she felt uncomfortably hot and weak. With an effort she looked at the gentleman seated on the other side of her.

"Some more wine, Lady Roscarrock?" asked Major Dickinson.

She shook her head. She had no wish to enter into conversation with the revenue officer—of all people, he had been seated beside her! Fortunately his attention was called elsewhere.

"Still no luck catching the moonlighters, eh, Major?" someone was asking.

The major shrugged.

"I've always thought the Crown could do with a bit of competition," said another. "Never liked the tax myself—the Queen don't need it."

"Nevertheless it is the law, sir," said the major stiffly. "The Crown is due all revenues from the sale of imported goods."

He wished he had not come tonight; most of the Cornish landlords no more approved of his job than did their poor tenants. With their own purchases of smuggled goods, the gentry did much to encourage the trade. Few sided with Joshua Tregarth in his desire to see the scoundrels apprehended. Although the major had realized that there seemed to be a personal quality to the magistrate's single-minded determination. Not surprisingly, Joshua had wanted guards posted at Wheel Charity to prevent the taking of any more tin; he had dismissed his mine captain and replaced him with a man from Fowey who would have no truck with the local fair-traders.

" 'Tis a way of life here, sir," said one woman. "The smugglers are viewed as boldly heroic."

"I am surprised at your tolerance, Mistress," said Major Dickinson, his blue eye staring into her powdered and patched countenance.

"Well, if you do catch them, you must send me word," said the woman, a wealthy widow.

"Send you word?" repeated the major, startled.

"Yes, for I have heard that the leader is a devilishly handsome man. I should like to see him, though not in so unpleasant a place as a gaol cell."

Lamorna gripped her hands together in her lap; she wondered how much longer she had to sit there. To her enormous relief Isolde rose to lead the ladies from the banqueting hall. Beside Lamorna the major stood up to pull out her chair. With a murmured "Thank you, sir," she kept her gaze downward. Major Dickinson noticed her lack of appetite, her flushed cheeks and subdued manner. He wondered whether she had a fever, and hoped it was not contagious. He had much to do, and soon.

Excusing herself from the other ladies, Lamorna went to the privy. She was ill again, and afterwards stood trembling, trying to collect herself enough to join them in the drawing room. Taking a series of deep breaths, she walked unsteadily down the corridor and took a seat as far from the fire as possible. Her head now ached, but the evening was not over by any means.

"That Major Dickinson is as stiff as a poker," observed the widow. "No sense of humor at all. A pity—he's not bad looking."

"My dear, he is positively sinister!" cried another. "That patch! Lud, I shouldn't care to meet up with him on a dark night."

"There is little chance of that unless you are out helping the fair-traders; 'tis clear his interest lies only in his duties."

"And yet they have thus far managed to elude him—he must be quite out of patience."

"The major will be successful, I assure you," said Isolde smoothly. "The smugglers obviously do not spend all their time in Cornwall, but Joshua has been given to believe that they are even now on their way to our coast. The major is quite close to making some arrests."

Lamorna blanched. Knowing her stunned alarm must be written all over her face, she regarded her hands in her lap. What did Isolde know? Was she merely speaking in defense of the major and her husband, or was there a very real and imminent threat to Dirk and his crew?

"Why, my love, how thrilling! When?"

"Possibly tonight," was the complacent answer.

Lamorna's head reeled; there was a faint ringing in her ears. She sat very still, every fiber tuned to the conversation.

"Major Dickinson has his work cut out for him," said Denzella. "From what I hear these men are very clever—they won't be taken easily, or without a fight."

"If most of the countryside were not in league with them, they would have been apprehended long ago," said Isolde severely. "But not everyone is seeking to protect them. My husband has received some useful information about a likely landing tonight. And he has learned where the smugglers organize their booty for distribution. They will be caught redhanded, you'll see."

"What did she say?" cried one elderly lady, who was hard of hearing.

"That the smugglers will be caught tonight," said her daughter in a loud voice.

"What? Caught, you say? For shame, Mistress Tregarth. Leave 'em be, I say, leave 'em be!" she called out.

Her daughter reddened and tried to quiet her. For her pains she was rapped on her wrist by her mother's fan. "Your father was always one of the gentlemen's best customers!"

Isolde ignored this outburst while a few of the other ladies tittered. Lamorna took the cup of tea she was handed; her throat felt raw and dry. Gulping the hot liquid, she tried desperately to clear her head.

The major must know about the fougou beneath the ancient fort. She had seen for herself the round stone chambers filled with boxes, kegs, barrels, and parcels wrapped in oilskin. The soldiers were going to set a trap there tonight; they would be hiding inside or behind the crumbling walls while the unsuspecting crew brought up the cargo from the cove below. They had to be warned—*he* had to be warned! She had to send word—but how, and to whom?

Rising from her seat, she stole from the room. Out in the corridor she told one of the maids she was feeling unwell but did not like to disturb her husband. Would she fetch her cloak and later inform Sir John that she had left for Kilworthy?

"Ais, my lady," said the woman, bobbing a curtsey.

Lamorna stood in agony while she waited for the woman to return. If Denzella or John were to come out into the hall now . . . if somehow they got wind of her leaving . . . why did the maid not hurry? Frantically she twisted her hands together. She had nearly decided not to wait for her cloak when the woman returned.

"Tes a raw night for spring, my lady," said the maid.

Lamorna nodded, almost wresting the cloak from her grasp. Babbling her thanks, she threw it over her shoulders, hurrying down the hall to the front door. The footman was opening it for her when a man spoke behind her.

"Lady Roscarrock."

She froze, recognizing Simon Pettinger's voice. When she turned about, Simon was troubled to see her overwrought appearance. He had glanced at her from time to time during dinner, noticing that she scarcely spoke to her companions and looked quite unlike herself. Simon did not know the extent of her involvement with the captain of the fair-traders, but he could not forget the way she had clung to him on Beltane last, and tonight her agitation was evident.

"G-good evening, Mr. Pettinger," Lamorna said breathlessly. A sudden thought occurred to her. "Do you know if Major Dickinson is still in the banqueting hall?"

He shook his head, his eyes grave. "I fear not, Lady Roscarrock. He left perhaps a quarter of an hour ago."

"Oh, God!" she cried and, whirling round, she rushed out the front door.

Mr. Pettinger hesitated only a moment, then hurried after her. Where on earth could she be going when Sir John sat comfortably in the hall drinking port?

Outside he did not see Lamorna. But she would need a horse if she were leaving Tregartha, so he ran round to the stables in time to see her mounting her white mare.

"Lady Roscarrock!" he called above the whine of the wind. "Where are you going?"

"Home, sir," she snapped.

"Alone?"

"Certainly alone."

"Wait, I will accompany you—you should not ride alone in the dark."

"No!" was the fierce reply. In the lantern-light of the stables her face was stormy, her eyes glittering wildly. She resembled some avenging angel, he thought, or one of the Furies, determined and defiant. Simon had to jump aside as she set off galloping across Whistmoor.

He stood there, aware that he should return to the house and inform Sir John. Instead he called to the groom for his own horse, and took off after her.

"We've taken three men from the headland into custody," said the sergeant. "They won't be lighting any fires to raise the alarm."

"Good work," said the major. "Without their signals the ship will likely anchor and begin unloading. We can't hold the men for long, but at least we can prevent them from warning the crew. Have you posted the men where I instructed?"

"Aye, sir, they be about the old fort and inside that tunnel-place."

"They must not make any sudden moves. Remember, Sergeant, the smugglers must be caught in the act of hauling and storing cargo, not merely climbing up the cliff or walking about."

"The men know that, sir."

"If any of them has been bribed, I'll know it and it will be very much the worse for him," said Major Dickinson coldly.

"You've no cause to worry about that, sir. They're not Cornish men, you know. They'll do their duty."

"I'm holding you responsible, Sergeant, if any do not."

"Aye, sir," was the gruff response.

"Very well, back to your own post. We may have a long night's wait ahead of us. Remember—the element of surprise is all."

The sergeant gave a brief salute and strode along the headland. The brisk wind ruffled his hair and numbed his ears; he hoped that tonight the major was correct and they would finally see some action.

* * *

Out in the channel the *Cormorant* sailed closer to the Cornish shore. Zachy and a few of the crew were on deck keeping a sharp lookout for wavering lights to guide them. The wind was raw and fierce; Dirk and the rest were working to maintain the *Cormorant*'s course in the turbulent waves. They were used to rough nights, but never took their situation lightly.

The great sails flapped and billowed as the sea spray swept over the ship. Shouts and oaths mingled with the howling wind and the waves smacking against the hull.

"Can 'ee see owt?"

"No." Zachy peered ahead, his hand shielding his eyes from the shower of stinging saltwater. He could just make out the outline of the cliffs, but no guiding lights were visible. Not that Dirk could not steer without them, but the beacons made the job much easier. Hadn't Elias Pollard got the word and sent the lads to await them? His sentries were a critical part of the night's work, especially with the soldiers keeping careful watch of late. And this was another large cargo they were carrying. The last run of tin had fetched such a good price that Dirk had been able to purchase even greater amounts of French goods, among them beautiful woven tapestries, fine china, even jewels. Their customers who could afford such luxuries would be delighted. The crew would be paid well for this run and there would be food to spare in Landrawna and Pendreath.

Sir John's decision to sell much of his corn abroad for the higher prices it would bring had resulted in a harsh winter for the two villages. Were it not for the "gentlemen," many families would have been forced to resort to parish relief. At least the Reverend Pettinger was known to be more generous in doling that out than the Reverend Poldew.

Zachy moved forward as the ship surged beneath his feet. "Only a few miles to go, Dirk, but so far there b'ain't no lights."

Dirk frowned in the darkness. " 'Tis early yet," he said. "We'll get as close as we can and then drop anchor."

"I don't like it," said Zachy uneasily. "We've loyal friends but there may be others not so loyal. I mind the time someone gave the nod to the soldiers about the Hayle farmhouse. There'll always be some who'll fill their pockets at our expense."

"It was quick thinking to store the goods in Mrs. Hayle's bedchamber."

Zachy grinned. "Her named the girl Brandy, I heard, because her was born in a room filled with casks! I wonder what the searchers made o' that." The two men laughed as another lurched up to them.

"There be lights now, Cap'n. Tes safe to land, I reckon."

Gazing at the jagged line of towering cliffs, Dirk made out the dim lights of the swaying lanterns. "Aye. You know what to do—we've plenty of work before the dawn breaks."

Zachy went off to issue orders while the *Cormorant* tossed its way into the cove below the ruined hill fort.

Lamorna urged her horse as fast as she would run. For the first time in years she was riding like a man, her skirts thrown up, her knees pressing into the mare's flanks. How much easier it was, she thought vaguely, as the wind lashed her hair and howled over the moor like the hounds after Tregeagle. She had long since lost her diamond comb—well, she hoped someone would find it and have good fortune. She had to reach the cliffs soon. Even now the *Cormorant* could have anchored, the sailors walking into a trap! If only she were not too late . . .

Gradually she realized that blending with the wailing of the wind were other sounds—shouts and the thundering of horse's hooves from behind her. Looking over her shoulder, she saw with horror that another rider was fast approaching her. Oh, God, not John! Who in the world . . . ?

"Lady Roscarrock, stop!" came a faint call, definitely not her husband's.

"Lamorna!" Simon Pettinger was shouting as loudly as he

could but the wind carried much of the sound behind him. The cold air was piercing, but he scarcely felt it in his urgency to reach her. His horse was gaining on hers, creeping up beside it until finally they were riding abreast. "Lamorna!"

She glanced across at him, her mouth open, her eyes wide with terror. "No! Leave me be, Simon!" she shouted.

Mr. Pettinger reached out and seized the reins from her hands. The mare's head jerked; she stumbled. His own horse gave a terrified neigh and he pulled tight on his own reins. Lamorna shrieked as she was nearly thrown over her mare's head. Belatedly Simon realized he could have killed them both in his mad attempt to stop her.

"How dare you—how d-dare you?" she sputtered furiously. "Let go my horse at once!"

"I wish only to help you, Lamorna. Tell me where you are going!"

"You had no right to follow me—you'll ruin everything! Let go of my mare *now!*" She was nearly hysterical.

"You must let me help! It's the fair-traders, isn't it? I heard Major Dickinson myself tonight."

"Then you must know they'll be taken, arrested—'tis a trap! I must warn them—oh, God, don't you *see?*"

"You ride back to Kilworthy. I'll go."

"You!"

"Some of them are Landrawna men; I've no wish to see them transported, their families starving. You return home—you can't be seen on the cliffs by the soldiers."

Her lip curled. "They can do nothing to me. I am Lady Roscarrock."

He winced at the terrible bitterness in her voice. Was she so unhappy at Kilworthy, was life there so intolerable? " 'Twill be better if I go, Lamorna. I promise you I will warn them; you can trust me." If it's not already too late, he added to himself.

"I can't go back to Kilworthy! I must *know!*"

"Then wait here. I will return as quickly as I am able and

tell you what has transpired. But you must not become involved—you must not ride to the cliffs!"

"Involved!" she echoed with a humorless laugh. "Then go, go! But if you are lying and mean to betray them, may God strike you down in a hideous way!"

Her words ringing in his ears, he thundered off toward the sea. Lamorna slipped down from her sweating mare and leaned against her, giving way to sobs. Could she trust Simon Pettinger? Why had she allowed him to persuade her to remain on the moor? What was happening on the headland? Was it already too late? Was Dirk being taken away by the soldiers even now?

The bile rose in her and again she vomited miserably. Then she crumpled up on the heath, huddled in her cloak, weak and dizzy. She could not have ridden to the cliffs now no matter how much she wished to. If only Simon warned them in time, if only she could put her faith in him! She was cold, and she grew colder.

Then there came a sound on the wind and she sat up, her heart in her throat. Musket shots. "Oh, no!" Stumbling to her feet, she clutched the mare's reins. Before she could mount, she heard a rider approaching her. It was Simon, his hair flying about his face, looking almost as frenzied as she.

"What has happened?" she cried. "Simon, tell me!"

"Get on your horse—ride, ride!"

"But—"

"—Now, Lamorna!"

She did as he ordered, following him across the moor. Eventually he called her to stop, convinced they had not been followed.

"In God's name, sir, tell me!" she gasped. "Did you warn them in time?"

"I fear not, my lady," he said.

"Oh, no! No!"

"Three men were taken into custody. But the ship hoisted anchor and sailed out of the cove."

"Who—who was taken?"

" 'Twas Zachy Sawyer and Charlie Potter and Joe Nansen."

"Not—not any other?" she gasped.

"No, my lady," he assured her, knowing full well her concern.

She seemed to collapse; he reached over and steadied her. She felt slight and frail in his grasp. Her hair smelt of the night air.

"You must go home, Lamorna," he said. "It's very late and it must not be suspected that you had any part in all this."

"I heard shots . . . was anyone hurt?"

"One of the three arrested was winged. He tried to run."

"You must fetch Dr. St. Cleer. The soldiers will not see to his wound."

"I will."

"You said the ship sailed away—how was that?"

"I—I gave them a signal."

"How?" she asked, gripping his coat.

He shrugged. "I had little time to think, and no tinder box with which to light a fire. So I took up a number of stones and cast them below into the cove."

"And they understood—they knew they were being warned?"

"They must have, for 'twas then the ship made ready to sail."

"Oh, Simon!" she cried gratefully. "You are truly a good man. Those men owe you their lives." She had flung her arms about him in her giddy relief.

Never before had he held her; he allowed himself a light caress on her hair, swallowing with difficulty. He realized she was softly weeping. "You must go home now, Lamorna. I will escort you and explain to Sir John . . . something."

She shook her head, disengaging herself. "No, Simon. You go to Dr. St. Cleer's in Pendreath. I can ride now, knowing—what I know. I will be all right."

He hated to leave her; tonight they had shared something

which had deeply affected him, and he would never be the same.

"You are certain, my lady?" he asked sadly.

"Yes."

"Lamorna, I fear you may do yourself great harm by—by persisting in—all of this."

"Good night, Simon," she said wearily and rode away.

Sighing deeply, he turned his horse in the direction of Pendreath.

Twenty-three

Lamorna slid off her mare in front of the stables, handing the reins to the only groom who had not yet gone to bed.

"Has the master come back?" she asked.

"No, my lady."

"And Miss Denzella?"

"Her and Miss Kitty did return nigh on an hour ago, my lady." In the dim lantern-light he observed her odd appearance—the smudges on her face, the tumbled locks and ripped gown. "Be 'ee all right, my lady?"

"Y-yes. The mare stumbled on the ride home and I fell."

Lamorna had expected to face Denzella and be subjected to a series of scorching questions, but the house was dark and silent. Relieved, she slipped down the corridor to her room where Maggie was waiting.

"Lady Lamorna!" she gasped. "Where have 'ee been?"

"Shhhh. Did Miss Denzella speak to you earlier?"

Maggie shook her head and began to help her mistress out of her gown. "What a state 'ee be in! I've been so afeared—why did 'ee not come back afore, with the others?"

Lamorna collapsed wearily on the bed. "There was a trap laid tonight for the fair-traders. I learned about it at Tregartha and knew I had to warn them."

" 'Ee left Tregartha afore the others?" Maggie was horrified.

"Oh, I doubt anyone noticed. I told one of the maids I felt

poorly." She sighed deeply. "There was a Major Dickinson seated next to me at dinner."

"Aye, I've heard of him."

"Well, he knew about the landing scheduled for tonight, and the fougou. Someone—betrayed them to the soldiers. I knew I had to do something, but it was no use. Oh, Maggie, Zachy Sawyer and two others were arrested and taken away!"

"Tes a miracle 'ee weren't arrested as well, my lady," said Maggie, horrified. " 'Ee ought never to have gone to the cliffs."

"The soldiers never saw me. 'Twas Mr. Pettinger who warned those in the cove below."

Maggie's jaw dropped. "The parson?"

Lamorna nodded. "He's a good man, Maggie. He—he saved Dirk and the rest. Were it not for him, they'd all have been taken."

"He still do love 'ee."

"Oh, no, that was long ago."

"Long ago but not forgotten. Why else would he aid the gentlemen?"

"He said . . . they were his parishioners. He'd no wish to see them gaoled."

Maggie laid the hot bricks beneath the bed covers. "Wishin' they no harm and helpin' be two very different things."

Lamorna was almost asleep. "He never asked me why I was so desperate to warn them," she murmured.

"Mayhap he knew," said Maggie.

Sir John rode back from Kilworthy in time for luncheon the next day. He and a few of the other men had stayed up until very late playing cards while Joshua waited to learn the outcome of the soldiers' ambush.

"He was most displeased when he heard that only three of the moonlighters had been taken, and only a trifling portion of the cargo. Apparently those on ship caught on that something was wrong and hoisted anchor, but the three taken into custody will be called before the Assizes in a few weeks."

"Joshua Tregarth will be hated by the villagers after this," predicted Denzella.

John shrugged. "I daresay he will not lose any sleep over that. Where is Lamorna?"

"Her maid says she is not feeling well. She left Tregartha quite abruptly last night without telling me."

"Did she?" John was uninterested. "Kitty, your new gown was vastly becoming. And I was pleased that you gave no encouragement to Philip . . . a younger son with only a portion held in trust . . . Kilworthy must seem like quite a prize." He let the words sink in while Kitty made no reply, pushing the food about her plate with her fork.

Denzella rose and excused herself. She was filled with disgust at her cousin and had nearly stormed at him. Did he not care that his wife had caused talk by leaving Tregartha early last night? Was he so lacking in family honor, even curiosity, that her peculiar behavior did not trouble him? The marriage was a complete and total failure, that was undeniable, but was John prepared to give his wife the freedom to do whatever she wished?

Denzella knew perfectly well that Lamorna had not ridden straight home after leaving Tregartha. This morning she had questioned the groom as to her return, and his explanation of a fall from her horse weighed very little. A toss had not kept the chit out at all hours; it was clear she had gone to meet someone. What Denzella found astounding was that she had not bothered to be circumspect; she had not even provided herself with a better reason for exiting the dinner party than that she was unwell! This flouting of her husband before all the gentry would not go unpunished, Denzella assured herself. She would not permit Lamorna to further disgrace John and Kilworthy. Before a scandal erupted and the entire countryside was talking about Lady Roscarrock and her lover, Denzella was determined to put an end to the degrading business. She did not have to stand helplessly by—she had been the one to choose the girl and she would find a way to deal with her dishonor.

Last night at Tregartha she had rebuked the maid for not coming to her instantly after Lamorna had gone. And the girl had protested defensively, "Her didn't ride out alone, Miss Roscarrock. Mr. Pettinger went after she. And Lady Roscarrock did say I wasn't to bother 'un."

"Mr. Pettinger, you say? Well, that's all right then—he'll see that she arrives safely back at Kilworthy." That had been her calm response, but inside she was puzzled. Yet when she and Kitty had returned to Kilworthy themselves long after Lamorna's departure and she was still not home, Denzella's disbelief turned to venomous ire. Simon Pettinger and Lamorna! Surely it wasn't possible! That unassuming, even dull, curate—he would never have the gumption to cuckold his employer! Then Denzella recalled the obvious interest he had shown Lamorna before her wedding to John—Denzella herself had done her best to keep them apart on Lamorna's second visit to Kilworthy, fearing that Simon might upset her plans. She grimaced. Those plans she had made so painstakingly had gone up in smoke and now this was the result! Lamorna betraying her husband with the curate of St. Petroc's! Since her marriage to John, the two had doubtless met often in Landrawna, especially when the girl had taken it into her head to nurse the sick. There were many days when she was gone all afternoon—out riding, she claimed. But Denzella was now aware that she did far more than ride. Her eyes were opened and she recalled a number of occasions when Lamorna had shown signs of duplicity. Why, even now, the slut might be with child and planning to produce her bastard as the heir to Kilworthy!

The *Cormorant* was moored in a hidden cove up the coast from Wheel Charity. Most of the crew had crept back to their homes a week earlier, but the cargo remained in the hold of the ship. After nightfall it would finally be unloaded and alternate storage places used. Dirk was not concerned about the cargo.

"I've got to go to Bodmin gaol," he said grimly to Ralph. "With Joshua Tregarth as magistrate we can't run the risk of their being tried and perhaps transported. I must break them out."

Ralph nodded unhappily.

"Then we'll sail back to France and they can lie low there. The soldiers won't stay in these parts forever, but we'll make no more runs for a good while."

"How do 'ee plan to break them out, Cap'n?"

"Blast a hole in the wall," said Dirk deliberately.

Ralph paled. "But—but 'twill make a powerful noise that way."

"Aye, but I've no wish to kill any of the excise men on guard there. Short of shooting them, there's no other way to rescue Zachy and the others."

"Tesn't the soldiers I hate but he what laid information against we! I'd like to see 'un swingin' in the breeze! Pearl do say all be stumped as to who done it."

"I also wonder who it was who gave the warning, the one who threw the stones into the cove from the cliff," said Dirk.

"Thank Heaven for 'un, else we'd all be sittin' pretty up Bodmin gaol. Cap'n, I'd like to help 'ee break out Zachy."

Dirk shook his head. "I can't let you, Ralph. 'Tis far more dangerous than fair-trading, and a serious crime. You must think of Pearl and the child coming."

"Aye, but I be goin' along of 'ee for all that," said Ralph. "Pearl will understand and thas a fact. I be goin' whether 'ee like it or not."

Dirk pressed the younger man's shoulder. "You're a good lad, Ralph. And our luck has held thus far—we'll get out of this mess."

If only Lamorna will come with me to France, he thought gravely. *This time she will have to agree.*

Lamorna received a letter from her uncle several mornings later, brought by a farmer riding south to the market at Padstow. She was sitting with Denzella in the drawing room when one of the footmen entered and handed it to her.

"What is it, Lamorna?" asked Denzella, her eyes narrowing.

" 'Tis my uncle—he is ill. He is asking that I visit soon. He would never ask unless he were very ill . . ." Her voice trailed off as she gazed at the shaky writing with a sharp feeling of dread.

"Do you think you ought to go? 'Tis a long ride and you have not felt well these last few days."

Lamorna stood up. "I must go. At once."

"Then you ought to take one of the grooms with you."

"There is no need," she answered briskly.

"You are looking quite pale, Lamorna, and I've noticed your appetite is poor. Are you certain you are not unwell?"

"I—I'll take Maggie with me," Lamorna answered swiftly, and hastened from the room.

Denzella went back to her needlework; she had recognized the vicar's handwriting and knew that the girl spoke the truth. This was no excuse for a clandestine meeting. Once she heard Lamorna and Maggie leave by the front door, she put aside her embroidery and went upstairs to change her gown. Stopping by Kitty's room, she said, "I'm going into Landrawna, child. I must speak with a few of the women about the upcoming Beltane festival. It's not far off now."

Kitty nodded listlessly. Denzella studied her for a few moments; she was maturing swiftly. Her breasts now swelled beneath her chemise and her face had become more defined, less child-like. Though her eyes had never been childlike, Denzella conceded. They were as old as the ages, and as hopeless.

"You are growing up, Kitty," she said. " 'Twill be your salvation, I daresay." She was gone on her words.

Kitty sat in her window seat and began to tremble. Denzella was wrong, hideously wrong. Her changing body was not her ally; it was her adversary, her cruelest betrayer. She stared, repelled, at the new roundness of her breasts. The blue bottle stood in the cupboard close to her bed. If only she had the courage to drink and drink . . .

Denzella rode into Landrawna and made straight for Simon Pettinger's cottage. His housekeeper told her that he was at St. Petroc's, so Denzella walked the short distance to the church. She found him in the anteroom, making some notation in the parish records.

"Good day, Mr. Pettinger," she said.

He looked up, startled. "Miss Roscarrock, I did not hear you come in," he said, rising. "I've just been going over some entries—I fear a few of the dates may be wrong. Is there—is there something I may do for you?"

"I was passing the church and thought to speak with you."

"Yes, Miss Roscarrock?"

" 'Tis about my cousin's wife. I am concerned about her."

Mr. Pettinger gave a slight start but quickly recollected himself. "Lady Roscarrock? I—I hope she is not unwell."

She was carefully watching his face and manner. "Perhaps you have heard, Mr. Pettinger."

When she did not go on, he swallowed with difficulty. "Heard what, Miss Roscarrock?" Could it be she knew about the frenzied ride to the cliffs? Had she learned about Lamorna's involvement with the captain of the band? He stared down at his handwriting on the page of the open book.

"Her uncle is very ill, I believe, Mr. Pettinger. She received word this morning. I thought you might already have heard."

He shook his head. He was so weak with relief that it did not occur to him to wonder why on earth Denzella should seek him out to tell him that the Reverend Hall was ill. "I did not know, and I am most sorry to learn of it."

"Should his condition worsen, she will no doubt be in need of your comfort," said Denzella.

He missed the irony in her tone. "Of course, Miss Roscarrock. Any—anything I can do . . . I will be at her disposal. Perhaps you might assure her of that."

"Oh, I will, Mr. Pettinger. No doubt she will be vastly grateful." She paused, allowing her words to sink in. "I understand that you accompanied her back to Kilworthy that night some weeks ago when we all dined at Tregartha."

Was that what Lamorna had told them? Uneasily he said, "I was glad to be of assistance."

Denzella glanced down at the record book. "You are busy, sir, and I should leave you. I hope we shall see you at the Beltane festival?"

He managed to nod and smile weakly. Satisfied, Denzella went out of the church. Mr. Pettinger was obviously hiding something which concerned her cousin's wife and he had been distinctly uncomfortable in her presence. His face was easy to read. Yet she wanted proof of Lamorna's iniquity. Why had she not thought of it before? She would search the girl's room periodically to see what turned up.

Lamorna sat at her uncle's bedside, holding his hand in hers. His grip was frail; she looked sadly at his shrunken appearance, the grayness in his face. She had not visited in a number of weeks and was shocked at the change in him. Self-reproach consumed her.

"Why did you not write to me before?" she asked. "I would have come, even to stay with you for a time."

He shook his head. "No, dearest, your place is at Kilworthy. But it gives me great pleasure to share some hours with you now. Tell me what you have been doing of late."

Scarcely knowing where to begin, she bit her lip. If only

she had the courage to tell him all! But to burden him now with her guilt and unhappiness would be very selfish—she did not want to be the cause of any further deterioration in his condition. She talked about Tamara and Mark for a while until she realized in relief that he had fallen asleep.

"Has a doctor seen my uncle?" she asked Deborah, going into the kitchen.

"I fear there be nowt a doctor can do if my nursin' won't help," was her heavy answer.

"He must see a doctor. I will ask Dr. St. Cleer to call as soon as he is able."

"Him that married Miss Tamara? 'Twas shameful the way her own family cast her off, though no more'n what you'd expect."

"There must be something he can do for Uncle Samuel," said Lamorna miserably.

"Sit down, my lady, do. 'Ee look near to droppin'. I'll make a pot of tea."

"Where is Maggie?"

"Her's gone to the village to see her family."

"We should be leaving soon. My uncle will not hear of me staying here."

"First 'ee mun have summat to eat. I won't let 'ee make the journey as pale and limp as a cloth."

"I'm not hungry."

"Mayhap not. But 'ee must eat for the babe's sake."

Lamorna gave a gasp. "How did you know? Did Maggie . . . ?"

Deborah shook her head, her homely face soft. "Her didn't tell I, Miss Lamorna. I've known 'ee since 'ee were a babe yourself—did 'ee think 'ee could hide it from me?"

"Is—is it apparent?" Lamorna asked worriedly.

Deborah frowned. "Why do 'ee ask that? Tes nowt to be ashamed of. I've often wondered why 'ee weren't breedin' afore now."

She turned to prepare the tea while Lamorna leaned on the

ECHOES OF THE HEART

table, hiding her face in the crook of her arm. She felt infinitely weary and overwhelmed by all that was happening. She had not seen Dirk since Zachy's arrest; she did not dare to seek him out lest she put him in jeopardy. For all she knew he had sailed back to France.

"Here, Miss Lamorna. Drink this," said Deborah. "And tell I what be the matter. For tes easy to see that summat be very wrong."

Lamorna lifted her head, her lips quivering, the violet-blue of her eyes dark with despair. Deborah felt a clutch in her belly.

"Sir—Sir John has not been a husband to me . . . our marriage has been no true marriage."

Deborah regarded her in stunned dismay. Then gradually the full meaning of Lamorna's words struck her. She put a hand to her throat. "Be 'ee sayin' that the babe . . . tes not your husband's?"

Lamorna nodded wretchedly, not meeting her gaze. Deborah sat down across from her at the table, something she very rarely did in all her years at the vicarage.

"Who be the father, then?" she asked quietly.

Lamorna had expected cries of horror and fierce reproaches. But none came. "I love him and he loves me," she said.

"Love do count for nowt if 'ee be wed to another," said Deborah. "Does he know?"

"No, I haven't told him yet. I haven't been able to; I haven't seen him in a while. No, Deborah, 'tis not what you're thinking. He hasn't abandoned me. He wants me to leave Cornwall, to leave John and go away with him."

There was a long silence while Lamorna gazed down into her barely-touched cup of tea. Then Deborah said, "Mayhap 'twould be for the best."

Lamorna raised her eyes in astonishment.

"Your uncle won't last much longer, Miss Lamorna. I've seen death hoverin' about 'un. And if Sir John do find out the truth he'll be knowin' the babe be not his. The disgrace will be beyond measure, unless he be willin' to pass the child off as his own."

"I would never do such a thing, Deborah!" cried Lamorna fiercely. "The child is mine and—his."

"Then 'ee must go away, Miss Lamorna."

"I will, once Dr. St. Cleer has seen my uncle. And once I've managed to inform—him—of my intentions. I'll be back soon, Deborah. To see Uncle Samuel, and to say goodbye."

Deborah nodded sadly, for once having no more to say.

On the ride back home Lamorna said to Maggie, "I must see Dirk. I cannot wait any longer. Deborah noticed my condition and I fear it will not be long before Denzella and John learn of it. I've decided to go with Dirk to France as he has been entreating me."

" 'Ee oughtn't to go to Padstow. Not with the countryside in an uproar over the fair-traders. Tes likely he's not there, and now 'ee can't be seen callin' at his house. The soldiers might even be watchin'. They must know he be the cap'n of the *Cormorant*."

"Then what shall I do? I must talk to him!"

"I'll take a letter to 'un myself," offered Maggie. "Tes better that way. I'll go first to Padstow to seek 'un out."

Lamorna reluctantly agreed. "Tomorrow morning, Maggie."

The night was moonless, and chilly for late April. Dirk and Ralph rode across Whistmoor, following the pony track to Bodmin. Securing their horses to a boulder on the heath, they made their way on foot to the town and the stone gaol. The stench from the building was foul; Dirk smelt it even before putting his face up to the barred window at the back. There were two soldiers on duty, and Dirk and Ralph had had to wait for the one posted at the rear to relieve himself some distance away.

"Zachy!" called Dirk softly. "Joe, Charlie, do you hear me?"

There came the sound of shuffling and a voice said, "Tes the cap'n. Wake up!" Zachy's face appeared at the window. "I knew 'ee'd come for us, Dirk," he said, reaching his hand through the bars.

Gripping it, Dirk said, "Ralph is here as well—we'll have you out of this filthy place soon. I saw two men on guard. Are there others?"

"No, but they patrol often. Take care they don't see 'ee, Cap'n," warned Charlie.

"There's little time. We're going to blast this wall. Get back as far as you can."

Zachy and the other two disappeared into the blackness of the gaol. "The soldier's not come back yet, Ralph. Go round to the side and keep watch. After the explosion, run for your life—no matter what happens."

"Aye, Cap'n. Good luck to 'ee."

The soldier posted at the back was taking his time, perhaps exchanging words with his companion or taking a drink on the sly. Dirk knew he had to work fast. He poured out the gunpowder, making a trail away from the wall. Then, taking out his tinderbox, he bent over, striking the flint on steel until the sparks flickered in the darkness. Lighting the trail of black powder, he hurled himself backwards. Suddenly there came the call of a bird—it had to be Ralph, warning him that one or both of the guards were approaching. Dirk swore, his heart thudding. He saw a vague shape alongside the wall.

"Get back, man!" Dirk shouted. "Get back!"

But it was too late. On his last words came a tremendous explosion which rocked the ground and shattered his ears. He was knocked off his feet as a portion of stones and timber crashed from the wall. The air was filled with sulphurous fumes; his eyes burned and watered, but he could make out three men scrambling out of a jagged gape.

"Are 'ee all right, Dirk? Hurry, they'll be on to us. Come

on, lad!" He yanked Dirk to his feet as Ralph came running toward them, the other soldier in hot pursuit. A shot rang out. "You there, stop!" But his musket had missed its mark; he heard the retreat of footsteps growing dimmer.

"Peter, where are you?" he called out. There was no answer but the smouldering of the timber. The smoke was clearing; he stumbled over the pile of stones and saw the blackened opening.

"Oh, Gawd! Peter! Peter!" But what remained of Peter was scattered over a wide area.

When Joshua Tregarth learned about the gaolbreak from Major Dickinson, a small smile formed about his narrow mouth. "So, they've played into our hands quite well."

The major frowned; his blue eye glittered. "I do not take your meaning, sir. I lost one of my men last night."

"That is regrettable, but can only work in our favor. Now the charge against the smuggling captain, Dirk Killigrew, is murder. Murder, need I remind you, Major, is a capital offense. He and his men have been stealing tin from my mine, they have smuggled cargo after cargo of contraband ashore, but now they have engineered a gaolbreak in which an excise man was killed. When he is caught—and you must see to it that he is indeed caught—no jury will be able to acquit him. He has deliberately and cold-bloodedly caused the death of one of your enlisted men, Major. And I will issue a warrant to that effect for his arrest."

Carrying her mistress's note tucked in her laced bodice, Maggie reached Padstow late that same morning. She passed the Bull and Clover, nodding at the tapster, who stood outside smoking his pipe, then turned the corner and walked swiftly in the direction of Dirk's house. But as she drew near she saw several uniformed soldiers standing on the doorstep, their muskets in hand. One was pounding on the door.

She watched from across the street, her heart in her mouth,

as the door was opened by his housekeeper who was none-too-gently pushed aside as the soldiers entered. With a quivering hand Maggie felt the outline of the letter inside her chemise, wondering in agony whether any second she should see the captain taken out, shackled and with a rifle pointed at his back. But to her immense relief, they soon trooped out, having failed to find their quarry. Captain Dirk must be lying low somewhere, she thought. Then how shall I get this note to him? she asked herself.

Clasping her shawl about her head, she quickly turned and hurried back the way she had come. Something must have happened—why else should the soldiers force their way into the captain's house? As she approached the inn again, it occurred to her to ask one of the stable boys lolling in the yard, a piece of straw in his mouth.

"You, lad, do 'ee know why there be soldiers up the street?" she asked in wide-eyed innocence.

" 'Course I know," said the boy importantly.

"Well, then?"

"There were a gaolbreak last night in Bodmin and one o' they guards were killed. The gentlemen blasted a hole in the wall with a fearful explosion. Now they do say the cap'n be wanted for murder—damned shame, I say. Still, they likely be halfway to France by now."

Just then the landlord stuck his head out the door, calling, "Take Mr. Trencoe's horse! I don't pay 'ee to yammer away!"

The boy hurried to do his bidding and Maggie rushed away from the inn, the knot in her belly tightening. This was worse and worse. The captain wanted for murder—perhaps, like the lad said, he had already fled to France. And where did this leave her poor mistress? Captain Dirk couldn't forsake her now! She could not remain at Kilworthy much longer, not with her condition beginning to show. If Dirk were on his ship anchored off the coast, how would Lady Roscarrock contact him? How would he learn that she had changed her mind and was preparing to leave with him? With a murder charge hanging over his head, he'd be a fool to come ashore. Miss Lamorna would have to go to him—but how on earth were they to discover his whereabouts?

Zachy Sawyer's sister, Bessie, lived in Landrawna. If anyone knew, she might. But a couple of hours later when Maggie climbed the steep street above the half-moon-shaped harbor, it was to find Bessie's cottage empty. They were doubtless making themselves scarce, trying to avoid interrogation by the excise officers.

Maggie stood in front of the cottage, uncertain of what to do next. There wasn't any other person she dared ask about the fair-traders, especially now that there was a Judas in the midst of the villagers, someone who had disclosed the fougou. It had been someone aware of their movements and the timing of the landing, someone who doubtless knew the moonlighters well.

Tired and defeated, Maggie crossed the fields above the village to Kilworthy. She found Lamorna in her room, pacing frantically.

"Thank Heaven! I feared all sorts of wild things. Did you see him? What did he say?"

Maggie shook her head. "I be that sorry, my lady. I fear I've bad news for 'ee."

Lamorna caught her breath. "What? What, Maggie? Pray tell me!"

"The cap'n be wanted for murder now," the girl said somberly. "Last night the three men escaped from Bodmin gaol and one o' the soldiers were killed. He weren't at his house in Padstow and 'twere a good thing else he'd be clapped up in irons now."

Slumping down in a chair, Lamorna went limp. "I should have suspected that he'd do all he could to save those men—naturally he could not let them go before Joshua Tregarth in the dock. Now he must leave Cornwall and not come back and this time I will go with him—if 'tis not too late for that. Dr. St. Cleer has promised to call on my uncle. I shall ride up to Rowenstow once more to say goodbye. Perhaps John will be able to petition Parliament for a divorce—I know I am doing wrong to leave him, have done wrong by him . . . may God in his mercy forgive me . . ."

Maggie opened her mouth and shut it again. She longed to blurt out the ugly truth about the master of Kilworthy, but again she felt compelled to hold her tongue. It was better that her poor mistress did not find out; she had enough to burden her now. And once she were aware of the vile state of affairs she would likely insist on doing something about it. No, the knowledge that Maggie possessed could not be shared with her mistress, not if Maggie wished to see her safely away from Kilworthy forever. She was certain that Miss Denzella knew the truth; if any of the servants suspected, they hid it well. No one dared allude to such a monstrous thing—they had their livelihoods to think of. And everyone was just a little afraid of Miss Denzella. Maggie had no wish to see her mistress go up against the older woman in this matter. There was too much at stake—for both of them. Miss Lamorna ought to leave Kilworthy as soon as possible, ignorant of the hideous facts. There was nothing she could do to help, and much harm that might result.

" 'Ee do have no choice but to go, Miss Lamorna," she said. "And I be certain the cap'n wouldn't leave Cornwall without lettin' 'ee know. Somehow he'll send word, don't 'ee fret."

Sighing, Lamorna nodded and took the letter from Maggie. Without thinking clearly, she stuffed it in a drawer beneath a folded pile of chemises. Hopefully there would be another chance to make certain it was delivered.

It was late when Mark arrived at Kilworthy. Kitty and Denzella had retired for the night, and John had gone out shortly after dinner. Lamorna received the doctor in the drawing room where she poured him a glass of port, knowing by his grave expression that the news was not good.

"His heart is very erratic, Lamorna. He—well, I fear there can be little time left to him."

Lamorna sat down, her eyes staring unseeingly into the blazing fire. She nodded numbly.

Mark set down his wineglass, his brow furrowed in concern. "There is something else, Lamorna. Dirk is now wanted for murder. It seems there was a gaol-break last night in Bodmin . . ."

When she did not respond, Mark wondered whether she had heard him. "Lamorna . . ." he said gently.

She turned to face him, her eyes dark with despair. "I know. Joshua Tregarth wants him arrested. If Dirk is caught, he'll—he'll hang." Her voice quavered. "His own brother."

"Tamara believes that 'tis due to that relationship more than anything else. His hatred goes back a long way."

"And Dirk bears much ill will himself. I know he has been stealing tin from Wheel Charity though he has not told me himself. I heard it spoken of at Tregartha. 'Tis because he longs to be avenged . . . for his mother's sake and his own." She rose. "You must go home, Mark. 'Tis very late and Tamara will be worried. I am grateful to you for riding up to see Uncle Samuel. Take—take my dearest love with you to Tamara; I do not know when next I will see her."

Mark nodded. He had a fair notion of what she might be contemplating. Holding out both of his hands, he said, "If there is anything either of us can do . . ."

With a faint smile she pressed each hand. "You have done much already. Good night."

"This be foolhardy," Zachy claimed yet another time. "If 'ee were caught—"

"I told you not to come with me," growled Dirk. Furtively

they moved from one sculpted yew to another and then crept round the side of the manor house to the back.

"And who's to look out for 'ee while 'ee do speak to her?" whispered Zachy with faint scorn. "Bessie could have taken her a letter."

"I must see her for myself. It may be for the last time if she does not agree to come with us."

Zachy acknowledged this with silence. Then he asked, "Do 'ee know which window be hers?"

"Aye."

"I'll stop here and watch. But 'ee must hasten, Dirk. The whole countryside be swarmin' with soldiers lookin' for 'ee. More arrived from Launceston this afternoon."

Dirk moved silently toward the dark stone wall of the house. Stepping onto a window ledge, his fingers gripped the sill above and he hoisted himself, panting slightly. Stepping out onto the projecting stone bracket which divided the two first floors, he carefully moved along it. Though the way was narrow he had no trouble keeping his footing; his years as a sailor had made him lithe and nimble, despite his size. He counted the number of windows, grateful that all were closed and curtained, and paused outside Lamorna's. Softly he rapped, hearing his heart thudding in his chest. From a distance came the bark of a dog in the night air.

And then her face, blurred and pale, appeared through the leaded panes and she was staring wide-eyed at him. As she opened the casement, he swung inside and took her into his arms.

"Thank God, thank God," she cried softly, "I was terrified lest I never see you again! Maggie went to Padstow—"

He covered her mouth with his in a long, desperate kiss. She drank him in for a few moments before pushing him away. "You mustn't stay. 'Tis too dangerous."

"I came to tell you I'm leaving Cornwall, perhaps for good. Did you hear about what happened at Bodmin gaol?"

She nodded, resting her head on his broad chest.

He raked his fingers through his loose hair. "I never meant for the soldier to be killed. I tried to warn him—"

"—Hush," she said, putting her fingers across his lips. "I'm coming with you. No, not now. My uncle is dying; tomorrow I must ride up to see him. Then I will meet you whenever and wherever you say. But it must be somewhere on the headland. It is taking too great a risk to come inland as you have done tonight."

His heart took a great leap. "I've scarcely dared to hope that 'ee—you—would agree to accompany me. The *Cormorant* is moored in a cove—you'd never find it on your own. I'll meet you and take you there."

"Where then?"

"At the old chapel—with the holy well."

"St. Isaac's oratory," she whispered. "Where we were bound in truth."

"Aye." He crushed her to him, bruising her open mouth. "I must go. Zachy is keeping watch. Go to the chapel tomorrow night. I'll be waiting."

" 'Tis tomorrow already . . . Beltane."

"Is it so? To think that I cursed this day last year."

She shivered. "Dirk, you must be careful. I—I wish it wasn't Beltane . . . 'tis perhaps bad luck, unChristian . . ."

His smile was lopsided. "Hush, my love. Indeed 'tis for the best. With all the merry-making your flight will not be noticed. Until tonight then."

It was only after he had gone that she realized she had not told him about the baby. She reproached herself again and again, wondering how all thought of their child had flown from her mind. It seemed unnatural somehow—and another ill omen.

She was unable to go back to sleep. Eventually the glimmer of dawn stole into her room, casting a pewter light which grew pale and gauze-like. When Maggie came later with her hot water, she said, " 'Tis tonight, Maggie! I'm sailing with him to Brittany."

"You've seen 'un!"

"Yes, not many hours ago. He came here—by the window. We are riding up to Rowenstow this morning, and I want you to go to your family's cottage and remain there."

"What did 'ee say?" asked Maggie sharply.

"Yes, Maggie, I've thought it all out. You must not return with me to Kilworthy this afternoon. When I am gone there will undoubtedly be a great scandal and you must not be here. I have some gold sovereigns to give you, and when I am settled in Brittany you may, if you wish, buy your passage across the channel. But I want you to think it over carefully. You mustn't decide in haste. There is no earthly reason for you yourself to leave Cornwall."

"I'll stay for a time, but then I'll come to 'ee, my lady when 'ee do send me word."

Before long they were riding along the track which followed the headland. When they left the house Denzella was already in the field with the village women, seeing to the making of the Green Lady. Just one year before she had sat watching them, unaware that she would see Dirk that night and her life would swiftly change again. She recalled the series of dizzying emotions which had struck her—the shock and overwhelming joy when they had stood facing one another . . . her fearful dismay that he would soon learn of her married state . . . the bitter shame when he discovered it . . . Rosina Nance's gloating scorn. Lamorna's whirlwind of memories halted abruptly. Rosina Nance—she had not thought of that young woman in ages. But once she had loved Dirk. Had that love turned to hate and a lust for revenge because he had not returned her feelings? Could *Rosina* have betrayed the crew of the *Cormorant*? Certainly she would have had the means, but was she cold-blooded enough to have laid information against all the men because Dirk had rejected her? It was a sobering thought, but doubtless mattered little now. The harm had been done and the identity of the betrayer was of scant importance.

She spent several hours by her uncle's bedside. In just two

days his condition had worsened; he was too weak to talk and lapsed in and out of consciousness. Smoothing his white hair, she kissed his brow, gave his hand one last squeeze, and left the room, quietly weeping. But she took comfort in the knowledge that he would never know she had dishonored him; he would not be made to suffer by her abandoning John and her home to run away with another man.

She went into the kitchen, wiping her cheeks. " 'Tis goodbye, Deborah. I am leaving Kilworthy tonight for good."

"So 'ee be goin' away with the father?"

Lamorna nodded. "I've realized my place is with him. I won't be coming back."

Deborah turned away, bending over the hearth. Her voice was muffled. "The young doctor said your uncle won't last the week. Tes as good a time as any, I reckon."

"I'll miss you, Deborah, and this dear house. Would I had never left it."

The older woman turned round to face her. "I won't judge 'ee, Miss Lamorna, but I want to know who this man be takin' 'ee from kith and kin."

Lamorna propped her chin on her hand and looked dreamily into the fire. "Do you remember that night, Deborah, that the two sailors were pulled from the sea in the cove below?"

Though there had been a number of shipwrecks and near-drowned sailors at Rowenstow, Deborah did not have to ask which one she meant. Her jaw dropped. "No, Miss Lamorna, not . . . I can't believe . . ."

"Dirk Killigrew," said Lamorna softly. "I knew it even then."

"And tes his babe 'ee be carryin'?" Deborah asked, astounded.

She nodded, smiling. " 'Tis a long tale and one I haven't time to relate. But he was always the one I loved, Deborah."

"Your uncle ought never to have taken him in," declared Deborah. "He were warned: 'Save a sailor from the sea and he'll turn your enemy.' "

"I know 'tis very difficult for you to understand, but I assure you he has not brought me misfortune. Pray do not speak of such foolishness again. And do not be angry, Deborah." Rising, she went over to the stout old woman and put her arms about her. For a few moments Deborah's arms clasped her tightly.

"I reckon I ought to say instead that there be no flyin' in the face of Providence. Things be *meant,* one way or another. Now go, Miss Lamorna, go and God bless 'ee."

Twenty-four

It was evening when Lamorna rode into the stableyard at Kilworthy. Millie ambled out to greet her and she bent to stroke the dog's soft fur. Millie gave a low sound of satisfaction and rolled over so Lamorna could pat her belly.

"I'll miss you and the mare both," she murmured.

One of the grooms came up behind her, taking hold of her horse. "I'm sorry, my lady; I didn't see 'ee ride up. I were in the back seein' to the other horses."

"Why, are you alone?"

"Aye, my lady. The rest be in the fields makin' ready for the Beltane celebration."

"Oh, yes." The women would likely be down there as well, those that weren't busy in the kitchen with the final food preparations. Denzella would be distracted by the numerous details involved in hosting several hundred people on Kilworthy grounds; she would not have time to concern herself with Lamorna's whereabouts or movements. The timing was ideal for her flight.

As she had hoped, the ground-floor rooms of the great house were dark and empty; the purple-gray twilight filtered indoors, where it deepened gloomily.

She hurried lightly up the stairs and went down the corridor to her room. Just as she reached to turn the knob, the sound of stifled sobbing met her ears. Kitty. What could be wrong, and why was she not with the other women and Denzella?

Lamorna hesitated, mindful of other occasions when she

had gone to the girl's room and angered her with her concern. But the choked sobs continued, and Lamorna's heart was too soft to ignore them. Outside Kitty's closed door the sounds were louder and unmistakable. She gently twisted the knob and opened the door.

The curtains were drawn tight against the bank of windows and no candles had been lit. "Kitty?" she called, realizing then that the crying had abruptly ceased. From the bed came a horrified gasp.

Lamorna stood on the threshold, a curious feeling of disquiet, even dread stealing into her. "Kitty?" she said again.

A log shifted in the glow of the fire, shooting sparks and making a sudden loud crackle. Her eyes growing accustomed to the dimness, she looked again toward the bed and stared blankly, her mind sluggish, uncomprehending.

There were two forms in Kitty's bed. She could now see the girl's white breasts, luminous as pearls. There had been fingers touching, stroking the pale, round flesh, petal-smooth.

Lamorna's incredulous gaze took in the man beside her. *No, she thought, 'tis impossible . . .* Blinking, she could not move.

"Get out, Lamorna," said John.

The voice, harsh with cold, sliced through the fog in her benumbed brain. Reeling, she gripped the back of a chair for support. Her belly churned violently, spewing a wave of bile into her throat.

"You . . . you . . ." she stammered at the two who lay together like lovers, at John's caressing fingers. "T-'tis an abomination!"

Kitty uttered a stifled shriek and another. The sounds were horrible, chilling. Dizziness overpowering her, Lamorna whirled about and staggered from the room, lurching down the three steps to the corridor floor which rose and fell before her outraged gaze.

Stumbling into her room, she was wretchedly ill, barely reaching the chamber pot in time. She had had little to eat that day, but her belly pumped up copious amounts of bitter fluid while her mind beheld in abhorrent detail the scene she had just witnessed. The horror surged forth, obliterating all else as though her very regard had made her a party to the loathsome shame of it all. Though from John she had discerned neither shame nor regret, merely an indifferent disdain.

Gradually the turmoil inside her slackened and she was able to stand up. The room had ceased to spin. With fingers that shook she poured water in the basin and sluiced her face and neck, rinsing out the bitter taste in her mouth. Then she tottered to the bed and lay down, her mind suddenly brisk and vigorous, the thoughts coming rapidly one after the other, as though to compensate for its recent inertia.

The early nights of her marriage when John insisted on taking her silently, in the dark, as though it were not her body he desired . . . his puzzling impotency as she began to assert herself, his conspicuous disdain for her as a woman . . .

And Kitty who had begun to come out of her shell before her father's marriage only to withdraw again into what must have been the pattern of her young life . . . her perplexing bursts of hostile anger, rebellious rifts in the long intervals of remote suffering, directed at Lamorna whom she perceived had betrayed her with her inability to hold John's interest. *She had hoped I could liberate her,* thought Lamorna. Oh God, Kitty, I'm sorry, for my blindness, for what you've had to endure . . . Now she could understand the girl's taking of laudanum, a device surely to deaden her senses so that she could blot out the reality of what was happening, what must have been happening to her for many years . . . her despair at the start of her womanly courses.

Lady Constance, retreating to her bedchamber, an invalid absorbed in the malaise of her body, a response to intolerable circumstances . . .

It was all there before my eyes, she thought lamentably, yet I could not see it.

And Lady Constance was dead.

A figure stood in her doorway. Catching her breath, she sat up.

"You knew . . . didn't you?" she whispered. "All this time . . . you knew."

Denzella's expression was contemptuous; she said nothing.

Lamorna went on, "You persuaded him to marry me after Lady Constance died. She—she took her own life, didn't she? Why could I not see any of this before?"

Denzella moved into the room, a large, formidable figure in her dark blue gown, her eyes pale and glowing. Lamorna got off the bed and faced her defiantly.

"You're white as a ghost, Lamorna. You had better sit down again."

Lamorna's knees felt wobbly but she stood her ground. "John killed the puppies on his return from Falmouth, didn't he? Because Kitty loved them."

"No, Lamorna. Kitty drowned them herself."

"*Kitty!* I don't believe you!" She was breathless, aghast.

"You have been a profound disappointment to me, Lamorna. You were young, pretty, and, I thought, docile . . . you could give John what he craved—"

"—Craved!" She spat out the word. "He's a beast!"

"You were only a few years older than Kitty; I believed you were the answer. I thought it would end."

"But it didn't. You used me, deceived me and my uncle . . . letting us believe that John cared for me when instead . . ."

"You wed him of your own accord. And you, like Constance, failed him, too."

"I—failed him!" Lamorna could not believe her ears.

"When I came to Kilworthy I did not at first realize, but I was swifter to grasp the truth than you, Lamorna, who have been married to John and living in this house for over a year," said Denzella with scorn.

"If you knew, why did you not try to stop it? How could you allow such—such vileness to continue? Surely you could have done something to help Kitty!"

"I did. I got rid of Constance and offered you in her place."

"You . . . got rid of Constance?"

Denzella's lip curled. "She hadn't the mettle to kill herself. She would have continued to live on, year after year, a useless, self-made invalid, skulking in her bedchamber, denying the truth yet submitting to it."

"You—*murdered* her?" Lamorna was awash with cold, regarding the older woman with horrified loathing.

"I merely put an end to her futile existence. Kilworthy needed an heir; she was obviously not going to provide one, for various reasons. I persuaded John to marry you—that you already know. 'Twas not too difficult; he recognized the wisdom of my careful arguments; he does not wish Kilworthy to pass from this branch—the main branch—of the family on his death. As far as you were concerned, we did not imagine a refusal."

Stung, Lamorna said nothing.

"After all," Denzella went on, "it was a tremendous honor for you, a privilege. You were nobody, and John gave you his name. You had only to please him, to bear him a son."

At this she cried, "How could I bear him a son when he shunned me as though I had leprosy, when he made no attempts to come to me after failing once?"

"Had you been clever you would have guessed; you would have done what was necessary to hold his interest, to satisfy him. But quite to the contrary, you began to reveal a side we had not suspected existed."

It was Lamorna's turn to look derisive. "To think for myself, you mean?"

Denzella's face hardened. "To challenge him rather than show your gratitude for the honor he had done you."

"*Honor!* That—that *fiend!* He's destroyed his daughter, ruined her life forever, and you—you are as sick and evil as he is himself!"

With a vicious swing Denzella slapped her. Lamorna cried out, clapping her hand to her stinging cheek, her eyes streaming.

"How dare you? You see yourself as a victim in all of this, don't you? The pathetic, betrayed wife. Well, I know you for what you truly are, you filthy whore! I know all about your obsession with that smuggler!"

Lamorna blanched while Denzella smiled mockingly. "Oh, yes, my dear, I've suspected something for weeks, though at first I believed the curate was your lover."

"Simon?" Lamorna had a wild desire to laugh.

"Oh, he no doubt carries a torch for you, but it's not him on whom you've bestowed your favors—the favors that should have rightly been your husband's. You left a most interesting letter in one of your drawers, a letter you had written but for some reason did not send. I made some inquiries, discovering that the man you wrote to is the captain of the local smuggling operation and now wanted for murder. A bastard son of some village slut, no less—and this is the man with whom you've betrayed your husband! A low sailor, a common criminal—"

"—He's a finer man than John could ever hope to be!" cried Lamorna.

Denzella's eyes narrowed. "You have failed all of us, Lamorna, and Kilworthy most of all."

"You speak of the house as though it were a living creature! 'Tis mere stone and timber, and harbors evil. I would that it were destroyed!"

"Destroyed! The finest house in Cornwall—you must be mad! And to think 'twas you I chose to provide it with an heir!" said Denzella with bitter fury.

"Thank heaven I did not succeed!"

"No, instead you are carrying the bastard's seed. Oh, yes, I know you are with child—I've noted the signs of late. And now you think to run off with this brute and disgrace our home, fling the name of Roscarrock into the mud!"

Lamorna spoke quietly and deliberately. "There is nothing I can do, Denzella, to further blemish the name. Already it lies stinking in the slime. I'm leaving this house forever, and I'll take Kitty with me."

Denzella stretched out her arm, gripping the heavy candlestick on the mantel. Lamorna's eyes widened in terror; she stepped backward with a cry. Denzella seized her arm and, raising the candlestick above her head, struck Lamorna, who dropped like a stone. For a few moments she gazed down at the crumpled form of her cousin's wife, then she bent but could feel no flutter of pulse.

Suddenly to her ears came a series of ghastly cries. It didn't sound like Kitty . . . then who? Rising, she went from the room, closing the door behind her.

John stood in the corridor, leaning against the wall. When she reached his side he turned to her, his eyes wild and staring. "She's dead, Denzella! My Kitty . . . my dearest girl . . . she's dead!" He covered his face with his hands.

Pushing past him, Denzella found Kitty lying on her bed, the bedclothes drawn up to her chin. Her face looked strangely aged, blue hollows in the pallor. Shaking Kitty roughly, she then gripped her by the shoulders and pulled her up; the girl fell heavily onto the bed. Denzella glanced about for a hand mirror and thrust it against Kitty's nose and mouth. After holding it there some moments she saw no film of breath on the surface. Her foot trod on something; picking it up, she saw it was an empty blue bottle.

John spoke in a harsh whisper behind her. "She—she was with child . . . I told her we'd go abroad. When we returned we could say the child was mine and Lamorna's . . ."

Denzella straightened and turned to face him. "It was a terrible accident, John. Certainly it was an accident. Kitty had a severe toothache and took too much laudanum. She was young and unused to opiates, of course."

He gave a groan. "I went to my room—after—after . . . I heard you and Lamorna arguing in her room. I promised Kitty I'd look after her as I always had . . . we'd go abroad."

"You will go abroad, John. After the funeral," said Denzella, her mind working swiftly. "We will tell people that Lamorna is indisposed, that she is not well enough to attend the funeral.

Then you will leave Cornwall. In a few months you will write to me, informing me of Lamorna's sad death in childbed. Then you will return to Kilworthy."

He gazed at her, uncomprehending. "Lamorna . . . dead? It's Kitty who's dead, who's gone from me—she would not trust me . . ."

"John, think—I implore you. Lamorna discovered all a short while ago. She was determined to take the girl away from you, to disgrace and dishonor you. She had to be silenced. Not only that, she was pregnant with another man's child—a common smuggler, a base-born murderer."

John stared dazedly at her. "What . . . what . . . ?"

She regarded her cousin who, in mere minutes, had been transformed from an indolent, supercilious aristocrat into a helpless, sniveling man. Yet the contempt she felt did not show on her face. She took his arm and spoke gently. "While you are away I will look after Kilworthy. When you return all of this will be long in the past. 'Tis for the best, John. This tragedy never would have occurred but for Lamorna. Had she been able to cure you of your obsession as we hoped, Kitty would be alive and 'twould be your child Lamorna was carrying."

"You are telling me that—that the fault is Lamorna's?" A gleam of eagerness came into his glazed eyes.

"I am. Go to you room now, John. Tomorrow the gentry will be calling to pay their last respects. And you will be what you are—a grieving father."

"Denzella, what would I do without you? How can I bear it . . . my dearest girl," he shuddered.

"Go to bed, John. You must rest and compose yourself for tomorrow. I will cancel the Beltane festivities and send everyone away. There is no need to concern yourself with anything more tonight."

"I would have looked after her," he moaned. "Why could she not *trust* me?" With stiff, jerky steps he moved down the corridor, not pausing to look in at the still body of his wife on the carpet.

Dirk rowed ashore in the darkness, dragged the boat onto the beach, and climbed up the side of the cliff to the headland above. It was only a few miles to the ruined chapel and he made it without incident. There was no sight nor sound of the soldiers who were supposedly combing the coast between Port Isaac and Padstow.

Once inside the roofless oratory, he stretched his legs in front of him and settled down to wait. He hoped that she would not be long and could not help wishing that she had left Kilworthy with him the night before. The thought of a future with her still filled him with disbelief and a slight but gnawing apprehension that would not be assuaged. If only they were already aboard the *Cormorant*, safe out in the channel! He was not so much afraid for himself as for her, or, the unthinkable, a life without her. To quell his vague qualms he began to envision the weeks and months to come. He had plenty of money in the Roscoff bank and connections with the town merchants. If they wished, he and Zachy and the rest could continue the trade from Brittany to the Scillies, which the revenuers left alone. He and Lamorna would have a comfortable existence in France. In his mind's eye he could picture the house they would live in, the furnishings and luxuries he would buy for her—nothing in comparison with what she was leaving, naturally, but fine just the same. And he recalled that day on the moor at Rowenstow when he had stood beside her in his patched, ill-fitting clothing and longed to blurt out his feelings, his aspiration to care and provide for her if only she deigned to come to him. Struck with the absurdity of such a notion, he had despised himself . . . and resented the emotions she evoked in him.

He strained his ears for sounds of her approach, but all he could hear was the muffled roar of the waves lashing the rocks below. It was then that he realized what was missing, and he was stung with a sudden sharp alarm. The stone basin in the floor of the chapel not three feet from where he sat was silent. There was no gurgling and bubbling of water fed by the underground spring. Frantically he scrambled across the stone floor, feeling the curved smoothness that was dry and cold. The spring—what in God's name had happened to it? It had filled this basin for uncountable years . . . and to have stopped now, to have somehow gone dry . . . His blood thickened, became sluggish. The cold from the stones at his back stole through him; he began to shiver.

Denzella had gone through the gardens to the fields beyond where the Beltane festival was already underway. She had considered several ways of getting rid of Lamorna's body, none of which satisfied her until she saw the enormous mound of furze, bracken, and twigs waiting to be lit.

It took several minutes to quiet the crowd and inform them of Kitty's sudden death, but she was pleased at how swiftly they dispersed once they heard the news. Sir John's only child—gone. The gentry weren't immune to the tragedies the rest of them periodically suffered. Soberly they trudged back to the village, claiming that this was what came of plowing the field of the Shuddering Stone which, it was said, had lain fallow since long before the first Christians set foot on Cornish soil.

Denzella had learned much that day while Lamorna was up at Rowenstow. Upon finding the girl's letter to her paramour, she had gone into Landrawna where the women had not been back long from making the Green Lady. She had called on two of the widows she had assisted in the past and casually steered the conversation to the local smuggling trade, saying what a shame it was that the soldiers seemed to be everywhere. Gradually she found out a few facts which she could only guess at from the contents of the letter. And she had discovered something else of interest—that Rosina Nance had been mad for Dirk Killigrew.

Denzella recalled Rosina's coming to her on Beltane last and asking for a love potion. Decidedly it must have been meant for the captain of the smugglers, but she had been spurned because somehow he had become involved with Lamorna. How bitter must have been her disappointment!

"Quickly!" she cried to one of the maids gathering up platters and bowls to return to Kilworthy. "Send Rosina Nance to me. Get the others to help you find her."

"Ais, miss," said the maid, too numb from the shock of Kitty's death to wonder about her mistress's request.

Unwillingly Lamorna rose from the blank depths to a glimmer of pain. She stirred, resisting the return to consciousness until the agonized throbbing in her head was felt in every part of her body. She moaned and touched her hair, which felt matted and sticky. Aunt Marya—why did she not come? Pushing up on one elbow, she watched the room spin horribly. Nausea overwhelmed her; choking and gasping, she sank down again. I'm sick, she thought. I've hurt my head and I'm so sick . . .

She awakened again a short time later, her mind clearer. This time she recognized her surroundings and did not expect her aunt to help her. Images came to her—Denzella, the raised candlestick. She tried to kill me, because . . . because of John and Kitty—*John and Kitty*—oh, God! And because of Dirk and our baby . . . Dirk was even now waiting for her. The recent horrors flooded her mind in revulsion and disbelief. Had it actually happened? Had she actually witnessed that scene in Kitty's bed?

She moaned, sweeping her hair from her face. She had to leave, to flee while they were all down at the Beltane festival. Somehow she had to get up, go down the stairs, and make her way to St. Isaac's oratory on the cliff. Denzella might return at any time; she had to get away from Kilworthy *now*, in spite of her excruciating headache and weakness.

Taking a steadying breath, she lifted her head and slowly rose to a sitting position. For an instant she kept her eyes closed and when she opened them, the room no longer tossed like a ship. Gingerly she got to her feet, fighting the blackness which surged to claim her again. Lamorna dashed water on her face and then went over to the door.

The corridor was dark and silent. What time was it? How far along were the Beltane celebrations? She crept down the hall to the stairs, her breath coming quickly. The realization that she was in deadly danger spurned her on despite her pain and lethargy. Wait for me, Dirk! she prayed silently. I'm coming as fast as I can.

Outside, she skirted the gardens and set off across the fields. She had only to reach the headland and follow the track north. She could see just barely enough to make her way. Soon the orange glow from the bonfire came into view. With a lurch of fear she began to run.

Dirk could bear it no longer. For hours—how many?—he had been waiting, listening for the sound of her approach. Something must have gone wrong; she should have come before now. Zachy and the others were waiting on the *Cormorant*; they must be as alarmed and frantic as he. Were it not for Lamorna, all of them would have sailed for France before tonight. Where was she? Had her husband prevented her from leaving Kilworthy? Was she ill, had she been hurt, or been spied and stopped by the soldiers on her way? His imagination provided one possibility after another, all of them chilling, all of them dire.

He could not remain idly waiting, his back pressed to the crumbling wall of the chapel. He would head south along the cliff and then climb the hills to Kilworthy. He was convinced that she was in grave danger.

The sea smelt strong; there was little wind. Below the surf battered the rocks, but Dirk did not heed it nor the cry of a gull not commonly heard at night. Had she lost her footing and fallen from the cliff? Had she stumbled into a bog on the moor? Wildly the terrors boiled over in his mind, filling him with savage turmoil. To come so close, to reach this night which was to be the beginning of their future, and yet not to have her . . . he ran along the headland, peering into the gloom, his boots scraping the stony track.

"You there! Stop!" came a shout, and he whirled round to glimpse the outline of a tall man close behind him. There was no chance to fumble for his pistol. Realizing the man was a soldier, he took off at an even faster pace and vaguely heard the shot ring out. He was struck in the shoulder and the force of it hurled him to the ground. Dizzily he tried to move, to get to his feet. He had to find Lamorna, to help her, but the reeling blackness overpowered him and he slumped heavily onto the heath.

Lamorna, the blood pounding in her ears, her breath coming in great gasps, did not hear the pursuing footsteps until it was too late. She was shoved roughly to the ground and her mouth stuffed with cloth. Gagging, her eyes bulging with terror, she squirmed while her hands and feet were bound.

"Hurry, girl, her flight has cost us precious time. It will soon be dawn," said Denzella. "I was so certain she was already dead."

The two women dragged their burden back across the fields to the raging bonfire. So this was what Dirk's lady-love was reduced to, thought Rosina. She was carrying his child, Denzella had told her, before they had gone to her room and found it empty. "She's gone to him—she must be stopped!" Denzella had stormed furiously, for, if Lamorna managed to escape, all her careful plans surrounding Kitty's death and John's subsequent trip abroad might go hideously awry. His secret obsession could be revealed, and the name of Roscarrock dishonored forever. Lamorna might even have discovered Kitty's body, though Denzella had doubted it; upon awakening, she would have assumed all of them to be at the bonfire and would likely not have gone to the girl's bedchamber.

Rosina had said, "If she be goin' to him, tes likely he be on the *Cormorant* or close by, so she'll be headin' to the cliffs." And Rosina had been proven correct. She had derived much pleasure in knocking Lady Roscarrock off her feet and pushing the cloth into her mouth to stifle her screams.

They half-ran, half-stumbled up the hill and across the meadow to where the bonfire raged in the darkness. As they paused before it, Lamorna began to struggle as hard as she could. From the dense flames came a blast of heat and a mighty roar. The shrieks she could not utter exploded in her mind.

"Now, Rosina!" commanded Denzella, and together they hurled their bound and gagged victim into the Beltane fire.

Tamara learned of Kitty's death from the vicar of Pendreath, whom she met in the street the following morning. Stunned and heartsick, she listened to his account of an overdose of laudanum taken for a toothache. It was the general opinion that because Kitty was slight and frail, the amount which would have resulted in only a deep slumber for some had proven to be too much for her.

Tamara had hurried home to change her gown and set out for Kilworthy. But the house was already full of other members of the gentry paying their last respects and she was refused admittance. Denzella, however, spoke to her outside and conveyed the news that Lamorna was too ill with shock and distress to see anyone; she was keeping to her room.

Later that afternoon, Mark had worse to report.

"Dirk Killigrew has been arrested."

Her hands flew to her throat. "Oh, Mark, no! No wonder

Lamorna is staying in her room, refusing to see anyone. Dirk . . . he will hang, won't he?" she added in a choked voice.

"I fear so." Mark looked pale and haggard with lines about his mouth she had not seen heretofore. He had gone to Bodmin upon learning of Dirk's capture to treat his shoulder wound, but he had been denied admittance by the guards. Aghast, he had protested, "But the wound will fester—the shot must be extracted at once!"

The sergeant had shrugged. "He isn't long for this world, and our orders are *no doctors*."

"It's inhuman, man!" Mark had cried, but to no avail.

Tamara was quietly weeping and there was nothing he could say to comfort her. Now was not the time to tell her what he had just heard from his great-uncle, Dr. Pendarvis. Sir John meant to go abroad after the funeral and take his wife with him.

A fortnight later Rosina dressed in one of her newly-made bodices and skirts, tied on the strings of her bonnet, and set out across the moor to Bodmin. Her days as a bal maiden were over and soon she would be wed to the smithy at Pendreath, bringing with her a satisfactory dowry of linens, pewter, and other assorted things provided by Denzella. No longer would she have to spend long hours hammering the ore and wear the ugly, coarse apron and sacking over her head to protect herself from the dust. Her fiancé had promised to hire a woman to do much of the heavy work about the cottage; he was pleasantly besotted with her, with no need of any potion to make him so. It was unfortunate that his hands were rarely free of blackened grime, but his trade would keep her better than her father's had.

No one suspected it had been she who had laid information against the fair-traders, not when her own brothers had been working to smuggle tin from Wheel Charity. She was promised to the smithy and no one spoke to her of Dirk Killigrew, who was imprisoned in Bodmin gaol.

When she reached the gaolhouse she sauntered over to the guard, looking the picture of pleading femininity. "I've come to see the prisoner, if you please, sir," she said.

"Which prisoner might that be?" he asked, eyeing her curvaceous figure beneath the low-cut chemise and bodice.

"The one that's to be hanged—the smuggler. Tes just for a few minutes."

"And what be that fellow to 'ee?" asked the man suspiciously.

"I'd like to tell 'un goodbye, that be all," she said.

The man grunted. "There be no harm in it, I reckon. I be the gaoler today, not them soldiers who wouldn't let in the doctor to tend to 'un. But don't be so foolish as to think 'ee can help him escape. The poor bloke be very poorly, and he'll be swingin' in the breeze afore long."

Rosina followed the man down the dark corridor. A rat slipped past her and she had to hold up her skirts to keep them from treading in the filth on the dirt floor. The stench was abominable.

"I've brung 'ee a visitor," called the gaoler. "No more'n a few minutes, mind. And I'll be just down a pace so don't think o' tryin' anythin'."

Through the long iron bars she saw a figure which looked scarcely human. He was filthy, his long hair matted and greasy, his clothes torn and soiled. His eyes seemed to burn with fever, and he had grown very gaunt. The only light came in through the tiny window near the top of the wall—the gaol had been repaired and made more secure.

At the guard's words Rosina had seen Dirk's black eyes leap with a wild hope, but as she came forward he had turned away, his shoulders slumping.

"A fine pass 'ee's come to now, Dirk Killigrew," she said. "I saw just now how 'ee hoped I were *she* come to see you. Do 'ee truly think she'd come to a place like this, *Lady*

Roscarrock? Tes a far cry from your house in Padstow, I reckon. Tes nowt but a hole, and 'ee be its rat."

He made no answer, standing with his face to the wall.

"Her won't be comin', Dirk Killigrew. Her be gone, gone with him."

At that his head shot round; his eyes blazed in his smudged face. "With who?"

"Who do 'ee think? Her husband, Sir John, of course. To Holland or some such place. Miss Kitty be dead, do 'ee know that? The shock were terrible hard on the master. After the funeral he and his lady wife went away. Mayhap her child'll be born in foreign lands."

"Her child!" The words came out in a strangled cry.

"Aye, didn't 'ee know that neither? I reckon Sir John'll be pleased to have another now that Miss Kitty be gone. Mayhap 'twill be a son to inherit Kilworthy."

Dirk's head struck the stone wall; he let out a long, harsh sound like a wild animal. Rosina winced and hurried back toward the door, the ghastly cries following her. Without a word to the startled guard, she fled the gaol.

When they led Dirk to the gibbet he did not resist.

"He were an easy 'un," said one of the guards later. "At the last I feared a struggle. Some of 'em do fight, just before, and he were a big, strong 'un."

His companion shook his head. "If you ask me, he were dead already."

The news took longer to reach those up at Rowenstow, and by the time it did, Samuel had breathed his last. Deborah was readying the house for a new vicar and Maggie had gone to help her.

"Zachy Sawyer and a few o' the band sailed for France, I reckon, for they be gone and there be no sign o' the ship. With all the soldiers surroundin' the gaol it weren't possible to rescue the cap'n. My poor, poor lady!" said Maggie.

"With him took prisoner her could do no else but go with Sir John if he wished it," said Deborah. "Mayhap they reconciled over their troubles, Miss Kitty dead and all."

"That be another thing that do fair worry me," said Maggie. "Miss Kitty chancin' to die on the very evening Miss Lamorna were goin' to flee with the cap'n, and then his capture on the same night. Summat be wrong—I fear there be much we don't know. I've a bad feelin' about Miss Lamorna . . ."

"Now don't 'ee be foolish, girl," said Deborah uneasily. "Her'll come back and tell us all one day, and 'ee'll likely be workin' at Kilworthy again."

Maggie said nothing. She had no desire to torment the old woman who, one by one, had lost each person she had cared about and looked after for many years. Dirk was gone, and Miss Kitty as well, who had died taking her monstrous secret with her. Maggie had considered going to Pendreath to see Mrs. St. Cleer, but what, after all, would such a thing accomplish? They would be no closer to learning the truth, and the two of them, a maidservant and an outcast whose own family would have nothing to do with her, would be helpless against Denzella's position and version of events. There was too much they did not know, as she had told Deborah, and any half-formed speculations of what might really have happened on that Beltane night were of no consequence.

But in her heart Maggie was certain of one thing: she would never see Lamorna again.

Part Three

1902

Twenty-five

Derek laid Laurel on the bed, and then stood back while Dr. Polgreen and the odd woman, Minerva Grey, bent over her shuddering form. Her eyes were wide and staring, like a terrified mare's, and she was struggling; she seemed to have no comprehension of her surroundings nor did she recognize the two who were working so earnestly to calm her.

Seized with an acute, primitive fear, Derek suddenly bolted from the room, plunging down the dimly-lit corridor to the wide staircase and the floor below. The rest of the house party was just entering the French doors from the terrace and watched, astonished, as he pushed past them and outside.

"What on earth—?" began Diana. "What can have happened now?"

Lyle laughed abruptly. "If you ask me, he's got the right idea. This place is cursed—I told you!"

"Now Lyle, calm yourself. You'll only hurt your leg if you move too quickly."

"Damn my leg," he hurled over his shoulder as he climbed the stairs.

Diana turned a flushed, defeated face to her guests. "It's late and you must all be exhausted. I'm certain Dr. Polgreen and Miss Grey are looking after Mrs. Tregarth and will do what is necessary. Naturally you will wish to retire now."

"Yes. Good night, Miss Cardew," said Mrs. Roslyn. "Come, dearest," she said, taking Annabel's arm. A sea voyage was just what they needed after this bizarre weekend; she would see to it that her daughter no longer pined for Lyle Cardew, whom she was now convinced was half-mad. Had he proposed to Annabel, she would have refused her consent. The sooner they departed Kilworthy, the better. A pity that good manners prevented their leaving at once.

"Good night, Diana," murmured Cynthia Lantallick.

"Di . . ." began Michael, at a loss.

"Come along, Michael," said Cynthia coolly.

Diana looked up, smiling faintly. "Yes, Michael, go along. I'm perfectly well, I assure you." They watched her sweep down the black and white tiled floor and enter the drawing room, the hem of her ivory satin gown trailing behind her.

"Damned strange—all of it," announced Michael. "I could use a drink. Ring for a maid, Cynthia."

"Do it yourself," said his wife.

Derek stumbled into the night, his mind in turmoil. He was conscious of nothing but the intense urge to flee, to put as much distance between himself and what was happening at Kilworthy as possible. The bonfire lit the sky to the north. Shuddering, he sprinted away from the fiendish orange glow to the fields which undulated to the cliffs. He had no destination in mind, nor did he examine the compulsion which had overtaken him, propelling him onward.

Soon the stair-step roofline of Landrawna rose before him, the cottages dark, the streets quiet. He hurried down one lane and turned into another, the heels of his shoes scraping the cobblestones. A dog began to bark and it was echoed by others, but Derek took no notice, running through the village to the headland path leading northward. Dry sobs shook him as he lurched along the cliff but he did not stop. The sea crashed and pounded below, the salt-laced wind was in his eyes, his nostrils, his mouth. There was just enough moonlight for him to see his way. At some point during his race along the headland it came to him where he had to go, where this headlong flight was compelling him. The image rose in his mind like a beacon and he yielded completely to the sudden awareness.

Lyle had knocked at the door to Morva's room and then abruptly gone in, not waiting for a response. Somewhat to his surprise she was still fully dressed and sitting up in bed. From across the room her gaze bore into his.

"I thought you'd come," she said.

"Only to say goodbye. I'm leaving, Aunt. I'm getting out of this rotten place, going far away. I told Diana and now I'm telling you. Tonight—now." His voice rang out in mixed defiance and trepidation, the grooves of strain prominent about his mouth.

Morva regarded him with detached pity. "You can't, Lyle. I'm very much afraid . . . I'm certain that that will not be possible. Not tonight, not ever."

"What!" he shouted.

"It's no use, Lyle. I cannot escape, and neither can you. I told you that before."

A cold wave of dread washed through him, but his air of bravado gained strength. "You're wrong, Aunt Morva. You'll see. I came up here, didn't I, to this part of the house?"

"To tell me my impressions have been all wrong? That our day of reckoning does not face us? Then why are you leaving?" she asked him sadly.

"Because I'll go mad if I stay here another night!" he cried.

"Very well, go," she said, her shoulders drooping. She sounded infinitely weary. "Go ahead, my boy. Though I doubt you'll get far. Whatever pursues you will take its recompense."

"You witch—why don't you shut up?" he said, furiously. "I'll show you!" Whirling round, he took an uncertain step, stopping at the sight of Diana in the doorway.

"Lyle, for God's sake, what is it? Aunt Morva, you should be asleep. Didn't one of the maids come to help you undress?"

"No, as you can plainly see," was the tart response. "I sent the girl away."

"Well, I'll ring for someone, shall I? You need your rest."

"No, Diana. I prefer to remain awake."

"What, all night?"

"I do not believe it will take all night."

Diana was exasperated. "What on earth are you talking about? Lyle, you look terrible. Go to bed. We'll talk in the morning once everyone is gone."

"I told you I'm leaving tonight, Di! No matter what this old hag says!"

"Lyle! What a ghastly night . . . first Derek's wife and now this. *Why* must you leave, Lyle?"

"What about Mrs. Tregarth?" Morva asked swiftly.

"Oh—I don't know. We all thought she was sleeping, but she came down to the bonfire and made a shocking display—screeching like a Bedlam inmate. Derek took her back to the house so Dr. Polgreen could attend to her, though what he can possibly do I've no notion, and then Derek tore out of the house as we were coming in . . . perhaps I should go and look for him."

Morva shook her head. "It's no use, Diana. Why can't you accept that once and for all? Derek was never meant to be yours."

Lyle guffawed bitterly. "There she goes again with that sooth-saying or whatever it is. She's a witch, I tell you, Di."

"Derek Tregarth's wife is pregnant, Diana. Did you know that?" asked Morva.

Diana stared at her. "How—how do you know this, Aunt? You've seen her—she told you?"

"Oh, yes, I saw her, no thanks to you, Diana. I tell you she is carrying a child and this time it must live."

"This time . . . what do you mean? Does Derek know? For a concerned husband he is certainly acting very strangely. Unless he has just admitted the truth to himself—that his wife

is as mad as they come. I very much doubt he will welcome the child."

"Still blind and deaf, I see, Diana," said Morva regretfully. "Would you like me to tell you what I believe?"

"Don't listen to her ravings!" Lyle cried.

"I knew about Lyle, you see," said Morva as though he had not spoken.

Diana frowned. "Knew what?"

"That he returned from South Africa a changed man—"

"—Shut up, Aunt Morva!" came Lyle's strangled voice.

"I knew that he could never sire a child, that his wound had made him impotent."

Diana stood in stunned silence.

"And I knew it was not a mere accident, not a coincidence. That he was being punished for something, as I have been punished all these years with useless legs, helpless, powerless."

With a great, outraged cry Lyle lunged past his sister. He fell with a crash to the floor and lay there, sobbing. Diana made a move to assist him but he shook her off.

"Well, n-now you know!" he sputtered. "Now you know why I never went to see Annabel, why I didn't want her here!"

"Oh, Lyle, I don't—I can't—I'm sorry . . ."

Slowly and carefully he got to his feet. "But I don't care, not any longer. That's all over. I just want to get out of here, away from Kilworthy . . ."

"Lyle, wait—"

"Goodbye, Diana. I'll send for some of my things later."

The two women watched him stumble closer to the door, his head bent, his arms slack. Then as he reached the threshold he abruptly stopped, his back going rigid, his arms rising to shield his face.

"No!" he managed to shout, and then, *"What—do—you—want?"* The words came out in hideous torment.

"Lyle, for God's sake!" cried Diana, appalled. "There's nothing there!"

Her brother spun round, his eyes wild, his face scarcely recognizable, his lips drawn back in unimaginable terror. Diana clapped her hand to her mouth, moaning, as he began to shiver uncontrollably, his shoulders quaking. His inflamed gaze torturously swept the room until it lighted on the ornate silver candelabra on Morva's bureau. While his sister and aunt looked on helplessly he lunged for it, seizing its base, the candles flaring.

The bulk of the hedgerow loomed jagged and splintery as Derek drew near. He thrust himself through the slender breach, tearing his hands and face on the bristles and thorns. And then he paused, gazing at the vague shape in the semi-darkness. The four crumbling walls, roofless, the gaping opening which they had entered less than a day before. He remembered red flowers blazing against the spread of ivy clinging to the granite, although surely there had been no hedgerow, no brambles concealing the oratory from view. Or had there? That morning he had been consumed with inexplicable fear, even revulsion, as he stood over the smoothly sculpted basin beside Laurel. But now there was an acute disappointment in him, a keen sense of loss which he understood no better.

Where is she, he thought wretchedly, and then—*Lamorna.* The name came to his mind unbidden and he drew a ragged breath.

She ought to have been there by now, he thought confusedly. It must be very late—what was keeping her? He had been waiting for hours . . . hadn't he? St. Isaac's, they had agreed. So she could not have made a mistake, gone somewhere else. Glancing down, he noticed that the basin in the stone floor was silent. Kneeling, he groped for the shallow pool of water, but his fingers met dry, cold hardness. The holy well—the spring—what had happened—how could it have gone dry?

Fear began to gnaw at him, an obscure but sickening fear. He stood up shakily and stumbled out of the oratory.

Something had gone very wrong. She could be hurt somewhere, or perhaps she had been prevented from joining him. Perhaps she was even now at Kilworthy, a prisoner.

Yet he could not wait, could not delay sailing another night. It was too dangerous, and his men who were to accompany him to France awaited him on board the *Cormorant*. He could not remain in Cornwall another day. Zachy had pleaded with him not to go ashore tonight, had offered to meet Lamorna himself and bring her to the ship. But as an escaped prisoner he was wanted as well, though the charge on his head was not murder. Still Dirk would not allow him to take the risk.

It had seemed almost effortless, uncomplicated, their arranged meeting at St. Isaac's oratory and the subsequent descent to the beach where the small boat waited. But something had gone very wrong . . . she had not come.

He set off across the heath in the direction of Kilworthy. She was in dire danger; he was convinced of it. He would risk all to find her. He would not skulk back to his ship and leave her helpless, unprotected. As he ran, the night air suddenly erupted in a loud clash. He staggered and fell to the ground.

"Lyle, what are you doing?" shrieked Diana. "Put that down!"

He turned to her, gripping the candelabra with white knuckles. His face was ghostly pale, his lips tinged with blue. "D-don't you f-feel it? How c-cold it is?"

"Cold?" she repeated. The night was a mild one, and the remnants of a fire glowed in Morva's hearth. Diana glanced at her aunt for elucidation.

Morva was singularly calm. "She can't feel it, Lyle," she said softly. "Even to me it's faint."

"*Faint—!*" he shouted, flailing one arm in the direction of the doorway. "I tell you it's in here—with us! *Faint!*" He held up the candelabra, waving it in front of him.

"Be careful!" shouted Diana.

But he was past hearing. "I'll s-stop you!" he cried. "I'll put out this c-cold once and for all!" Taking a few unsteady steps, he thrust the burning candles into the heavy draperies.

"Lyle!" screamed his sister, lunging toward him.

He gave a high-pitched laugh and swiftly set the fringed tablecloth aflame. Diana tried to wrest the candelabra from his clutch but he shoved her aside. Pulling the burning cloth to the floor, she began to stamp out the flames. To her horror the hem of her gown caught fire and she uttered a piercing scream. "Lyle, Lyle, help me!"

Her aunt sat motionless in the bed as her brother, still shaking with cold, pursued his desperate campaign. Very soon the entire room was ablaze.

Minerva Grey sat slumped beside Laurel's bed. Never in her life had she felt so completely drained of all energy, all emotion. She gazed down at the young woman who now slept peacefully, her face serene and child-like. The blisters were gone from her skin and the ugly red welts were rapidly fading. Her fever had subsided; her forehead felt cool to Minerva's touch and only slightly moist. The pulse beat slow and steady in her throat.

Minerva drew a deep breath. It was over, at least for Laurel it was over. She had relived her former life, her spirit reconciling with it, and could now resume her present existence unencumbered by the burdens of the past.

Laurel stirred in her sleep, murmuring softly. "Dirk . . ." There were tears on her cheeks. She shifted again, and this time opened her eyes. "Derek," she said. Puzzled, she looked at Minerva.

"He will come soon," said Minerva, though she had no such certainty. As Dirk Killigrew, he had died believing that she had forsaken him at the last, even indirectly caused his own capture and death by hanging. The anger and blame was strong in him, obscuring his other feelings of love and loyalty. More than that, the events of the past few days had made him feel increasingly threatened, conscious of a peril his bewildered brain associated with Laurel.

"You've been ill, Mrs. Tregarth," she said. "You had a high fever, but it has broken now and you must rest."

Dazedly, Derek got to his feet. What was the explosion he had thought he heard—like a shot of some sort? He was alone on the brackeny heath, the night vast and silent about him except for the distant sound of the sea. He had been on his way somewhere . . . Kilworthy. His mind clicked into focus; he was suddenly imbued with a fresh vigor. There was something wrong at Kilworthy, and Laurel needed him. What on earth had he been doing out here, leaving her alone? The knowledge that she was in danger propelled him across the moor to the lush fields sloping upwards. Gradually the gloom lightened and then he noticed the fierce shimmer on the horizon. Baffled, he thought, it's too early for dawn, and then, oh, of course, it's that silly bonfire Diana ordered.

But then it struck him that the bonfire could not be seen from the direction he was heading; Kilworthy stood between him and it. Stopping in his tracks, he stared, aghast, at the sickly orange light against the purple sky. God, that wasn't the bonfire, his mind flared. *It was Kilworthy that was burning!* And Laurel was inside! He began to run.

"Miss Grey! Miss Grey!" There was an urgent pounding at the door of Laurel's room.

"Who—who is it?" she asked, having fallen into a deep sleep. With a great effort she tottered across the room just as

Dr. Polgreen thrust open the door. He was still in his evening clothes and looked very rumpled.

"Miss Grey—there's smoke pouring into the corridor! We've got to get out! Take Mrs. Tregarth!" He glanced over to the bed; to his surprise and relief Laurel was sitting up and seemed quite normal.

"There's a fire somewhere, Mrs. Tregarth. Kilworthy is burning—we've all got to get out!" Hurrying over to the bed, he put his arm round her and helped her to her feet. Then he looked across at Minerva, who still stood by the door.

In Heaven's name, what was wrong with her? She looked dreadful, ill, her face gray, her lips almost bloodless. The woman was a mere shadow of herself—how on earth was he to get two sick women out of the house himself? He wasn't certain that Minerva even comprehended the danger. Fear clutched at his stomach and he began to perspire.

"Miss Grey," he began, licking dry lips, "the house is on fire! Miss Grey, do you understand? *The house is on fire!*"

Then footsteps came crashing down the hall and Derek, his face dirty and badly scratched, his elegant black suit torn, was in the doorway.

"Thank God, Derek!" cried the doctor. "Take your wife—I'll help Miss Grey!"

Derek gathered Laurel up in his arms and hurried down the corridor while Dr. Polgreen led Minerva Grey, who sagged against him. The air was thick with smoke; it burned his eyes and nostrils, and crept into his mouth, trying to choke him. They descended the stairs as the air grew clearer, then lurched out the French doors.

The servants were huddled in a group, and near them, Annabel, her mother, and the Lantallicks.

"Oh, thank Heaven!" cried Mrs. Roslyn. "We were so afraid . . . have you seen Miss Cardew or anyone else?"

Dr. Polgreen coughed and wiped his streaming eyes. "Are they not outside? Perhaps in the front?" he asked hoarsely.

"The top floor's an inferno," said Derek grimly. "I hope

they were not up there, though I'm very much afraid it's too late for their aunt."

Annabel gasped. "Mamma—Lyle was going up to see her, don't you remember?"

"How did it start?" asked Cynthia. "It seemed to spread so rapidly."

Minerva slumped down on the garden bench. Though she had been ignorant of the fire when it had begun, she now knew precisely its moment of conception. At the very same instant that Laurel had relived her own death as Lamorna—tossed, bound, and gagged, into the Beltane flames two hundred years before.

"There is nothing we can do," she managed to say. "The three of them are gone."

No, the *four* of them, she added to herself. Kitty Roscarrock's tortured soul has been set free by the conflagration, the great purifier . . . And her rage has burned itself out.

Several days later Minerva Grey sat in the compartment of the train bound for London. She had regained enough energy to undergo the journey home, but she was not alone. Derek had sent for Bridget to look after her mistress while at Tregartha and had asked her to travel with Miss Grey.

Derek had brought both Minerva and Laurel back to Tregartha and ordered them put to bed immediately. Dr. Polgreen had supervised their nursing, asserting that they were both suffering from shock and needed plenty of rest. He was relieved to observe that Derek's strange behavior at Kilworthy was quite gone; his concern and love for his wife was plain to see.

Laurel had told him about the baby, and they had talked for a time before she had fallen asleep. He stayed awake, watching her, his eyes glowing with wonder and a deep, quiet joy.

Dr. Polgreen called every day to see his patients, and only

once did he refer to what had gone on in Laurel's bedroom at Kilworthy.

"A remarkable recovery—she'll do very well now. The child, too. I won't conceal from you I was badly frightened that night. But Miss Grey begged me to trust her, and I'm glad I did. Because the next time I saw Laurel she was much improved, though I was worried for Miss Grey herself. She's an exceptional woman, Derek. You—we—owe her a great deal, perhaps even Laurel's life." Derek was indeed humbly grateful, though he could recall little of his actions that night or during the earlier part of the weekend. He knew only that his nightmares had stopped, and Laurel was his forever.

"Some tea, Miss Minerva?" asked Bridget.

Smiling, she shook her head. "Not now. I believe I'll try to sleep."

"You do that, my lamb. I wouldn't mind a wink meself."

Closing her eyes, Minerva mulled over the events of the past week. What had proven to be her most difficult ordeal was now resolved, and the two tragic victims, Lamorna and Dirk, Laurel and Derek, could begin anew. She had not explained their story to them; it would have been too much to take in, and besides, there was no need. A catharsis had come to them both, chastening and cleansing until they were free from the past's harmful taint. Minerva had bid them goodbye, confident they would face their present life and its joys and struggles together.

She could even find it in her heart to feel pity for Lyle and Diana Cardew and their bedridden aunt whom she had never seen. Their burnt remains had been found in the vast wreckage that had been Kilworthy, and people shuddered at the fate they had met. But only Minerva knew that it was justified, that the great wrongs they had each of them performed two hundred years before had reached out to claim them.

Diana had been a refined, polished version of Rosina, but the veneer of elegance had not served to diminish her single-minded pursuit of Derek Tregarth. Rosina's betrayal of the smuggling band had led to the arrest of three men and the accidental killing of the soldier during the explosion. But it was the part she had played in Lamorna's death which could not go unpunished.

As for Denzella, the score against her had been even higher. She had planned and committed two murders, three if one considered Lamorna's unborn child. She had not protected Kitty from her father's loathsome desires, and then she had concealed the truth behind the girl's death, all because of her intense devotion to a manor house and to a way of life. It was odd to compare what she recalled of Denzella with the image of the frail, crippled Morva Cardew. The accident that had left her paralyzed had only served as part of the retribution. She had been condemned to live at Kilworthy as helpless and feeble as Denzella had been forceful and autocratic. Minerva had sensed the poor old woman's fear and been convinced there was no hope for it. Perhaps Morva had realized this as well. And it was to her that Lyle had gone.

Sir John had been a rather commonplace aristocrat, except for his unnatural compulsions. Indolent, easily bored, selfish . . . Minerva wondered whether he had changed at all later in life. So was Lyle a rather commonplace young man except for the injury which had maimed him and his terror of something at Kilworthy which stalked him relentlessly, singling out him and no other.

Had Kitty always been there, her soul rooted by the rage she could not express in life? When Lyle returned from South Africa he had only then become aware of her. Minerva recognized that Kitty had lashed out at Lyle with all the ferocity she had repressed during the years when he, as John, took advantage of her youth and innocence in such a heinous way. The welter of emotions that Minerva had grasped in the six-sided room had evoked her empathy as never before. And, she hoped, never again. Some things were too intolerable, even for Minerva. She knew that she had lost forever the sprightliness of youth.

Cynthia Lantallick was little altered from her incarnation as Isolde Tregarth. Both were proud, haughty women, though she had sensed a bitterness in Cynthia which was lacking in Isolde. And Minerva could not help but notice how Cynthia had seemed to despise Laurel as Isolde had despised Lamorna.

Joshua Tregarth was the most difficult to explain. How that cold, ruthless, shrewd man had two hundred years later become the rather ridiculous figure that was Michael Lantallick was mystifying. A foolish, inept man, resentful of what he saw as Derek Tregarth's luck, always looking to blame others for his own misfortunes. Minerva had heard that he and Cynthia were shortly to leave for New Zealand; they had lost all their property due to business mismanagement and an imprudent lifestyle. Michael certainly had none of Joshua's fanaticism for upholding the law at any cost. To Joshua Tregarth financial disgrace and exile would have been far worse than death, Minerva realized, and who knew what faced Michael in the years ahead?

Curiously Derek expressed no animosity toward Michael, which would have been understandable, even expected, under the circumstances. He seemed wholly disinterested in the man who had once been his half-brother and nemesis.

And what of me? thought Minerva wryly. She had felt far removed from that ebullient young lady, Tamara Tregarth, until she recognized that both of them had broken away from the conventions of their day, refusing to conform, to be confined in a narrow, limited world.

But in this life Dr. Polgreen is not for me, she mused, though we have respect and fondness for one another. And I have none of Tamara's beauty or high-spirited charm. But isn't my gift far more significant for being so rare? I am content with my life.

Mark St. Cleer had been a faithful friend to Dirk Killigrew and Lamorna Roscarrock. Though in the end he was powerless to help them, he, as Dr. Polgreen, had proven himself a devoted friend for much of Derek's adult life, and now his deep affection extended to Laurel as well. He was to deliver her baby; Laurel would not consider another doctor. Minerva found herself amused by his fascination with Cornwall's old folklore and superstitions which Mark, as a physician in the new Age of Enlightenment, had scorned. So did time and distance provide new perspectives.

While at Tregartha, Minerva had been visited by Martha, Derek's old nurse. She had come into her room, stooped but with great dignity, to express her appreciation for the miracle Minerva had performed in uniting Derek and Laurel. Minerva, who had not known of Martha's existence until then, supposed that she was Deborah. Deborah, who had looked after Lamorna and mistrusted Dirk, then later in this life taken care of Derek. Both widowed young in life, both loyal to their very bones.

She saw no echo of Maggie, but acknowledged that she might not yet have entered Laurel's life. Nor was there a progression of Matthew Tregarth or Simon Pettinger. Not all souls crossed in every incarnation; there were other lives.

Derek had been given his rightful surname in the present. On the surface he had appeared self-possessed, not plagued by doubts or insecurities such as the ones which had tormented Dirk. Although a good businessman, he had not had to labor and struggle as had Dirk, nor was he filled with shame at his origins. Yet Derek had suffered, too. Minerva learned from Martha of the nightmares which had afflicted him, the black moods which descended all too frequently. As Dirk he had had no way of learning the truth about Lamorna, that she had met her death weeks before he would go to his.

Minerva opened her eyes. "I think I'll have that tea after all, Bridget; my mind is too lively for sleep."

And Bridget was quick to oblige.

One day that summer Laurel and Derek rode up the coast in the carriage with Henry Polgreen. His research had uncovered a former vicar of a parish in the uppermost nook of Cornwall, a wild, remote place of pitiless purple-slate cliffs, deep gorges, and gorse-strewn headlands.

The carriage stopped just outside the small stone church and they climbed out. "This is the original Rowenstow church," said Dr. Polgreen. "The vicarage was torn down years ago, apparently, after the parish was combined with another and the church rarely used. The building is still looked after, though."

The place had an air of desolation, the wind a mournful quality. Dr. Polgreen went down the straggly path to the church and Derek followed, his arm about Laurel.

Inside, they looked at the carved bench-ends, the Norman arches, the granite pillars and stained-glass windows.

"I understand there was once a mural on that wall of 'Christ Blessing the Trades'. I daresay it was ruined by dampness or perhaps painted over deliberately in the last century. A shame."

"Look, a mermaid," said Laurel, pausing before one of the bench-ends.

The doctor smiled. "Such things were quite common, I assure you. The Cornish often decorated their churches with secular images."

"I used to come here as a boy," said Derek. "The church fascinated me for some reason. I can't think why—it seems rather ordinary."

"The church, perhaps, but its vicar was not," said the doctor. "Here is the plaque to him: 'Simon Pettinger, Beloved Vicar of Rowenstow from 1710 til his death in 1751.' It's said he assisted his parishioners in their smuggling endeavors by holding the lantern on moonless nights. When the excise men came, he'd see that the goods were well hidden in the tower stairs. He was also diligent in burying sailors that washed up on shore, and kept a book in which he noted the emblem or letters tattooed on each body. People from far away would write to him, trying to locate a loved one who might have perished off the coast of Rowenstow. Sailors had the marks enscribed in their flesh so that they might be identified after death, and the vicar jotted down every one he saw. If the tattoos described by a parent or wife matched one of those in his book, he would assure them their loved one had received a reverent burial. His name was known as far away as Denmark by grieving, but grateful, families. Later in life he became quite an eccentric recluse, and the vicarage swarmed with dogs. When he died, it's said there were seventeen dogs living there."

"Perhaps that's the reason they tore down the vicarage," said Derek dryly.

"Look, over here," called Laurel. "Here is another plaque from about the same time—well, earlier, really: 'In memory of Lamorna Hall Roscarrock, 1688-1710?' "

"Hmmm, that's odd," said Henry Polgreen, coming to stand beside her. "The Roscarrocks were the original owners of Kilworthy, but somehow the estate went out of the their hands. I wonder who put this up? It's doubtful her husband would have. This was not the Roscarrocks' parish church."

"Simon must have done it," said Laurel. "He must have known her. Perhaps she came from Rowenstow."

"The question mark after the date is rather peculiar, if he knew her well enough to put up a plaque in her memory," said Derek.

"If he did indeed order it made, I should very much like to know why," said the doctor, a puzzled frown on his face. "It would reveal something more about the Reverend Pettinger himself. As far as I can gather, he never married and died of pneumonia. All the dampness, I suppose. These places built on the cliffs wreaked havoc on the lungs. As for Lamorna, it would be fascinating to learn who she was and how she came to marry a Roscarrock from a bleak, remote location such as this. In their day they were a proud and powerful family, now gone forever, like Kilworthy."

He sighed and took one last look around the austere little

church. Outside the wind had picked up, its forlorn whine reaching their ears. All three of them were silent for a few moments until Henry Polgreen added, "One more thing I've recalled about Simon Pettinger. Apparently he taught many of the Rowenstow children, and some adults, to read—a highly unusual undertaking at that time." He smiled. "Well, shall we go? I thought we'd stop at the inn at Port Isaac for tea."